On Blue Island, a curse causes men to turn into monsters—part wolf and part man. Once a wolf-man, they become part of The Pack.

For generations, the people of Blue Island have protected The Pack. Now, their new leader seeks to end the curse once and for all. All she needs is a child…

The Ashley family, going through hard times, has moved to a new home in Grantham. Little do they know, but the hard times have only just begun. Blue Island is only a short distance away.

The youngest, Elliot, seeks to reconnect with his former best friend. His older sister hopes to connect with this new boy from school. Their mom is a teacher trying to end the school year on a good note with her most troublesome students. Their dad desperately seeks a new job. He is originally from Blue Island but moved away when very young. The island wants him back… or at least his blood.

Elliot's former best friend, Tucker, is still adjusting to being homeschooled. Tucker does not know if he wants to see Elliot again, but when a chance comes… he takes it.

The fifth-grade troublemaking boys do not believe in their teacher. She claims to care about them like a parent.

A dark plan is set in motion to lure a child to the island where The Pack is waiting. When tragedy strikes, terror is unleashed, and all their problems become one: survival. A group of children and teachers fight for their lives as they find themselves surrounded by horror. Some members of The Pack have no intention of becoming human again. They just want to drink their blood!

Drink the Blood is a thrilling adventure about loyalty, friendship, and family… being hunted by monstrous wolf-men. Blood will be spilled. *Who will drink it?*

DRINK THE BLOOD

GREGORY SAUR

Other Novels by Gregory Saur

Stuck in the Past (with Jack Irish)
Otherworld: Orcish Delight
The Royal Pains & Angels in the Outhouse
Panterror! The Epic Babysitting Adventures of Rachel Pugsley
The Pond Scum Gang
Soccer Star
Diving Catch
Best Shot Forward
Safe at Home
Making Waves
Visitors From New Earth City
Drowning Hate

<u>*Finding Innocence* Trilogy</u>
Finding Innocence, Book One: Strange Old World
Strange New People: Book Two of Finding Innocence
*Book the Third: Strange Happenings, the Conclusion of
        Finding Innocence*

DRINK THE BLOOD

GREGORY SAUR

Saur
&
Saur

A Saur & Saur Publishing Project

Drink the Blood

Printed in the United States of America.

ISBN (hc): 978-1-949317-24-4
ISBN (pb): 978-1-949317-25-1
ISBN (eBook): 978-1-949317-26-8

For more about this book and other books visit Gregory Saur Books on Facebook

*To all teachers everywhere,
a friendly thank you for your service.*

Chapter 1

Pain. It was everywhere. Burton Raycroft couldn't move. It hurt so much! It felt like a fist was punching against his stomach from the inside. Sharp, piercing pain stabbed through his nose and mouth. Bolts of burning pain also shot through his arms and legs. Through it all, his muscles were starting to spasm. It was like a horrible fire had been lit internally and had spread up and down his body.

"Help," he managed to gasp. "Help… me…"

A tremendous invisible weight suddenly pressed against his chest, squeezing out his breath. From his belly, a volcano of agony erupted as the internal fist turned into a battering ram. Pain radiated up and down his limbs, exploding into his head.

He wanted to scream but couldn't. He could barely draw a breath.

"Hurts…" he managed to hiss. "Hurts so bad!"

"Shh, my child." Somewhere above the fuzz and agony, his mom leaned over him. "It is but a natural process."

"Ughhh…" Burton felt his fingers clench. His nails started burning like matches suddenly lit. Through the anguish, he felt the urge to reach up his hands, grab his mother's head, and squee—a cry of fear and pain ripped through his throat.

He remembered lying down on his bed after dinner. He'd just had another argument with his mother, and his body had felt so tight it was ready to snap. He had hated his mom then. Now, he just wanted her comforting arms around him and telling him it would be okay. He wanted her to take away this terrible pain!

"Lie still and let it happen," his mother's soothing voice said above him. "Don't you worry. It will be okay. Drink the blood, Burton. Here..."

That was when his nose and mouth exploded, shooting a geyser of blood. He let out an agonized roar, drowning out his mother's shrieks.

"Come on, Woody," Sticks said crossly. "Stop dawdling!"

"I'm not dwad-dwadoling," Woody said, out of breath. "I'm just going slow!"

Salisbury started to giggle, but Sticks grabbed her arm and tugged her forward. A flash of lightning lit up the sky as the three children scurried across the street. Their parents had no idea where they were.

"Are you sure about this?" Woody said, sounding scared.

"Hey," Sticks growled. "This is for you. You're the one with the dumb wart."

"Maybe it'll fall off on its own," he said hopefully.

"Nah," Salisbury said, shaking her head. "You need the witch. When my mom got a wart, she went there and got it taken care of in, like, a whisker."

Salisbury didn't always make sense, but she knew about witches. Woody leaned against the back of Sticks, fighting back a moan.

"We're nearly there already," Sticks said, stepping lightly away. "It's too late to go back anyway."

Sticks led the way. At eight years old, she was the biggest and tallest. And she lived the closest to the witch's house. Holding an old flashlight nearly as big as her torso, she crouched low and scampered past the silent houses of the northern section of the neighborhood. This is where all the prominent families lived, where the witch lived.

"Why did we have to go in a lightning storm," Woody complained, struggling to keep up.

"Because that's what gives the witch power," Salisbury explained. A half-year younger than Sticks, she was an expert on the old ways. Her mom served as the librarian and knew much of the folklore. Her stories of witches and monsters had kept Salisbury up many a night.

"Let's just get it over with!" Sticks said. "Come on, it's only two houses down!"

Woody whimpered but obediently trotted after the two girls. Only six, he was Sticks's cousin and did everything she said.

A warm, sharp wind blew from the north, brushing back their hair from their faces. It felt like a giant was breathing on them. A jagged bolt sizzled from the water beyond the trees, and a heavy rumble followed.

"See!" Salisbury cried gleefully. "The power is here!"

"I just want to go home!" Woody said, feeling tears leak from his eyes.

"First, we get rid of your wart!" yelled Sticks, clearly enjoying herself. She cut across a wild, unkempt lawn where the grass reached her hip. She tucked the flashlight under her arm. "Watch out for snakes!" she called back.

The other children had no time to be afraid. Sticks carried the only light. If they didn't follow close behind her, they would be left in the dark. They all wore pajamas and sneakers.

Nobody else knew about their foray into the night. If their parents found out, the storm would be the least of their worries.

Out of breath, the children reached a worn stone walkway. It led to the dark door of the witch's house.

Sticks stepped in that direction. Suddenly the porch light snapped on and the door creaked open. Freezing, the small girl clicked off the flashlight and stared.

A dark shape appeared in the doorway. The children turned into melting popsicles as they watched with quivering fear.

"Come inside, quick!" commanded an old woman's voice. "Hurry! A storm is about to hit!"

"How—How did she know we were there?" Woody asked as the children ran for the door.

"She's a witch," Salisbury said in triumph.

"Or I saw your light bobbing around my front yard like a headless chicken," the old woman said wryly.

"How did she hear us?" Woody gasped as he entered the house.

"She's a witch, stupid," Sticks said, cuffing his shoulder as she followed behind him. She had her cumbersome flashlight tucked under an arm and trailed the other two.

"Or you children whisper too loud," the old woman said, rolling her eyes, making way for the children.

Once the children were past her, she shut the door and turned to stare down over them. "Now tell me why you three are here and not asleep in your beds."

In the small foyer, Salisbury and Woody both looked at Sticks.

Wearing a gray nightie and busted sneakers, Sticks stuck up her chin and hugged her flashlight like a security blanket. "Woody has a wart, and we heard you cured those things."

"So you came at midnight in the middle of a storm?" the old woman said in disbelief.

"That's, that's when you have your strongest powers," Salisbury said. She bit her lower lip. "That's what my mom says."

The old woman snorted, fighting to keep down a smile. "Right. Of course. Tell you what. It's good for you that an old lady like me needs a potty break at night. You three wait here, and I'll get something for this wart."

"She's going to do it!" Salisbury said excitedly as the woman disappeared into the darkened house. "She's making a spell."

Woody squeezed his eyes shut tight. "Will it hurt?"

"No," Sticks said emphatically. Standing up to the witch made her feel brave. "Nobody is going to hurt you with me here."

The three waited in the cramped foyer. Only the porch light provided light, leaking from the windows on either side of the door. The old lady returned a minute later, holding a tube and a Band-Aid.

"I'll put some of this stuff on." She eyed the little boy severely. "And then you keep it covered. We'll see if that helps your wart."

"Toothpaste?" Woody said, his eyes cracked open.

"It's medicine," the old woman said with a grunt.

"It's a spell," Salisbury said in a hushed tone.

"Just show me the wart," the old woman growled.

The little boy in his pajamas and sneakers obediently held up his hand where a small wart had formed on the bottom of his right thumb. He watched in awe as the old lady squirted pale paste on it and then handed the Band-Aid to Sticks.

"Put that on it," she said gruffly. "I'm calling your ma and tell her to pick you three up."

Sticks nodded and started to comply. She just pressed down the Band-Aid when bright lights from the street shot into view. A vehicle zoomed towards the house.

Built on a dead end, the old woman's house had to be the destination.

"Wow," Salisbury said, amazed. "That was fast!"

The old woman stood with a start. "Whoever that is, it's not any of your parents," she said, sounding worried. She reached by the door and snapped off the porch light, plunging them into darkness. "You three, go hide in my living room. Whatever you do, don't make a sound!"

Sticks gave no argument. When a witch tells you to hide, you listen. Tucking the flashlight under her armpit, she snatched Woody's arm and Salisbury's hand and led them into the dark room. Feeling her way with her feet, she found a long couch. Crouching, the three children hid behind it and waited in the darkness.

Chapter 2

It was past midnight on a warm, cloudy night when a jeep rolled to a stop in front of the house.

Thunder rumbled overhead, and lightning lit up the sky in the distance. In the brief flash, a dark silhouette of a hulking beast lit up against the garage. Then, it was gone in darkness.

Climbing from the jeep, a tall woman snorted and adjusted her heavy fur coat. Even in the heat, she wore it like a badge of honor. What once had belonged to a mother bear now belonged to her. Everything she wanted, she got. That was how her world worked. Only now, she didn't just want something but *needed* it. And only one person could give it to her. And she'd better do it. Or Morgan meant to take it.

Morgan Raycroft was not a woman to be trifled with. Smoothing down her skirt below her coat, she marched from the road toward the silent house. Another bolt sizzled overhead, revealing her raven black hair, pulled tightly from her cold, sharp face. In the brief flash, her skin appeared to glow the color of ivory.

Tall heels clicked on the dark concrete as she went up the driveway, accompanied by a thick roll of thunder. She never flinched when more lightning lit up the garage door in front of her. The garage door now appeared blank, the color of cream. A faint growl rumbled from the roof above it.

"Quit your bellyaching," Morgan said with disdain, not looking up or slowing. "Go join the others. You know why I'm here."

The growl turned into a whimper that got lost in the booming thunder.

The house was a simple two-story structure built when Morgan was a little girl. She remembered being so excited about moving into it. Now, she saw it as nothing more than a worn-down tomb, just waiting to hold the dead.

Raindrops started to splatter around her. Following the stone walkway leading from the driveway, she eyed the door before her. In the night, it appeared black, but a sizzling bolt of lightning revealed it to be blood red. The rain intensified, striking against the pale siding of the house like claws scraping on pavement.

Morgan grimaced. This would not be easy. But it had to be done. The Pack was counting on her.

Not bothering to knock, she threw her shoulder into the door and barged in. Thunder crackled from the sky behind her.

"So you're here," said a voice from the darkened kitchen.

Startled, Morgan quickly stood straight and clawed at the wall to the right of the door. Finding a light switch, she snapped on the lights in the foyer. She'd meant to give the old woman a scare, not the other way around. Her eyes searched for the voice. Past the stairs, in the back left, she saw a shadow standing in the kitchen.

Snorting, she made her way there, stopping only to turn on the lamp in the family room separating the foyer and kitchen. She found the term "family room" ironic since her family had no room in this house and hadn't for many years.

"Yes, I'm here," she said, stopping at the edge of the kitchen. "You knew I was coming, did you?" Many thought the old woman was a witch, but Morgan had never believed it. For the first time, she had her doubts.

The old lady, a broad, rotund figure, stood at the head of the table watching her.

Morgan swallowed a glare and nodded curtly at the woman. She tried to get the upper hand back. "Sylvia, I thought you would be sleeping."

Sylvia Raycroft, Morgan's mother, head of the Raycroft family, leader of the Blue Island Community, and Protector of The Pack, gave Morgan a cool look. "As usual, Morgan, you thought wrong. What brings you to my home at this time of night?"

Morgan twisted her mouth into a thin smile. "It was my home too."

"Yes, it was. But no more. Why are you here?"

"You're right to the point."

"I'm too old for games. Tell me your business."

"I want to see the family book."

"At this time of night?"

"Yes, at this time of night."

The two women stared at one another, neither willing to back down.

Morgan stood nearly a foot taller than her mother. Her smooth, ivory skin seemed to glow in the muted lamp light. Framed by dark hair, restrained tightly back, a sharp, pointed nose, and a wide mouth with full lips, her lean face radiated a fierce beauty. Morgan never backed down from a challenge. Her narrow green eyes flared with unfiltered hatred at her mother.

Sylvia Raycroft did not seem to notice. Wrinkles creased her forehead, but her own pale green eyes radiated warmth, tinged with sadness. Her dark gray hair was parted in the middle and secured in a tight braid. Wearing a shapeless gray nightgown, she appeared simple yet strong like a rock. Finally, she blinked. Stepping forward, she swept around the table toward her grown daughter. Despite her round, elderly appearance, she moved like a younger, nimble woman.

"Tell me, what happened? You are here because something happened."

Morgan seethed. How could such a homely nobody woman wield so much power? And how did she know something happened? It was like she could read her mind.

"It's Burton," she finally said. "He turned… he's joined… He's now part of The Pack."

Sylvia blinked. She noticed the dark spots marking Morgan's forehead—traces of dried blood.

"No… How could you… how could…"

"It happened in an instant!" Morgan said. "I had no time to do anything! I could only watch it happen." She took a breath. "I was powerless to stop it. But you. You have power to fix it. I want to see the book. I want to see how to change him back."

"You can't change him back," Sylvia said sadly. "How could you let him turn?"

"I told you! It happened too fast. I could do nothing!"

"You know it can be fought! My husband lived all his life with it and never turned."

"That was years ago!" Morgan shouted. "Open your eyes, Mother. Things are different now. The Turning is coming fast and sudden now. Burton already has his teeth and claws! Your grandson is baying at the moon and running on all fours!"

Sylvia groaned and leaned back to support herself on the table. All at once, she looked twice her age of seventy-four. "Oh, Burton…"

"We can change him back," Morgan pressed, her voice sounding hungry. "You know how. That's why I came."

"No. There is no way. It is impossible."

"In your book, *Mother*. There is a way. This is your grandson! My boy!"

Sylvia stood up straight and stared at her daughter. "As long as I'm head of the family and Protector of The Pack, we will never use that book."

"Not even for Burton? You have the power to reverse the curse, you fool!"

"It's not a curse, Morgan," Sylvia said, sounding tired. "It can even be a blessing if you allow it to be."

"What sort of rot is that? A blessing?" Morgan barked out a caustic laugh. "The others are right. You have lost your way. Our people are fractured, Mother. They need to be united. They need a new leader."

"Say what you want, Morgan," Sylvia said coolly. "With me in charge, that book will not be touched. You know that."

Morgan twisted her face into a snarl. "Yes, Mother. I do know that. I was hoping I was wrong, but that rarely is the case, is it?" She reached into her fur coat and pulled out a thick folded cloth. "This was my baby blanket, Mother. I think it's fitting if it's the last thing you see on this earth."

"Morgan!" Sylvia said, her face growing alarmed. "What are you doing?"

"Taking over the family business."

Sylvia stumbled back, her back hitting the table. Suddenly, her mouth dropped open, and she started to choke. Her right hand clasped at her chest.

"Mother!" Morgan screamed, dropping the blanket. "I didn't mean it! I only meant to scare you! Mother!"

Sylvia collapsed to her knees. "The-the power…" she gasped. "It's coming for you… be warned…"

Morgan's eyes went wide. Under her mother's nightgown, she saw a red pendant glowing from a silver chain. Slowly, her tongue ran out of her mouth. She licked her lips hungrily.

"You don't… know…" Sylvia said between deep breaths.

The light from the pendant bathed Morgan's face in red, like blood. As if in a trance, she bent and picked up the blanket. "This is for my son. This is for The Pack." She then moved toward her mother. Her eyes glinted in the red light.

Sylvia let out a weak scream as darkness approached.

Outside, the rain beat against the window, and thunder bellowed the sound of doom. Only three small children heard the panicked cries of an old woman and the murderous howls of an enraged daughter.

When Morgan stood from the body, she dropped the blanket and looked down at her hand. In the struggle, she'd ripped the pendant from her mother's neck. Now she backed away from her deed, shocked at what just happened. Then she heard a noise behind her. Turning, she saw three children creeping toward the door. They'd just reached it when it burst open. A monstrous shape barged in, looming over the children.

Screeching in fright, the children huddled together.

Sticks felt the heavy flashlight slip from her armpit and crash to the floor. It could've been her heart. All bravery fled out the open door. Only terror remained. She grabbed Woody's shoulders and squeezed tight as Salisbury pressed against her side.

"What happened?" demanded Morgan's brother. "What's this?"

"Our mother is dead," Morgan said calmly. "And these children are about to see what happens to those who bother

The Pack." Lightning flashed from outside the window. "I'm in charge now."

Woody swooned in his cousin's arms as Salisbury slumped to the floor. The girl covered her face, sobbing. Sticks just held up her cousin and tried desperately to keep from wetting herself. She forced herself to look up and not show fear. It was not easy.

Morgan's brother leered down at her. His waist was covered in a loin cloth, and all seven feet of him was covered in thick brown mangy fur. A snarl uttered from his pointed snout, and a thick red tongue ran over his sharp teeth. Saliva dripped from his black lips. Sharp claws extended from his massive hands.

"I believe, I obey, I fight, all for The Pack," he said, his voice deep and guttural. His eyes remained fixed on Sticks. "The Pack has a new leader now. Let it be done!" Then he roared.

Sticks couldn't take it. Dropping Woody, she covered her ears and felt wetness run down her legs. Her cousin slid down and slumped against Salisbury, not stirring as the screams of two little girls split the night.

Chapter 3

Days later…

Sunlight streamed through his windows as Elliot lay on his back in bed. On top of his sheets, with his hands clasped behind his head, he still wore his gray tank top and pajama pants. He ignored the bustle below him as he stared up at the white ceiling in disbelief. This had to be the worst life ever.

"Hurry up, sport!" his mom's voice called from down in the kitchen. "You need to be dressed and ready to go in five minutes!"

Elliot only tightened his mouth and wiggled his bare toes in frustration.

It was the first Saturday in May, and he was going to a funeral. And then he would be off to baseball practice—the first practice since the "second incident." With his mom as the coach. All this just a few months after he'd lost his best friend because of the "first incident."

Shortly after, he'd been uprooted from his old school to be dragged to this dump of a house where nobody knew him or cared to know him.

This late in the school year, with only a few weeks left, kids were more interested in summer plans than in making friends with the new kid. Elliot really missed Tucker.

"Yo, Elliot!" his older sister Skylar yelled from down the hall. "The bathroom is free! Just don't pee all over the floor! Wait! Hold on, I need to fix my lipstick. Sorry, dipstick!"

Elliot sighed. How did so many bad things happen to him all in a row? Was his life cursed? Or was this world telling him he was a bad kid? It was tough being a ten-year-old.

It all started last fall with his best friend Tucker… and "the first incident." Shortly after that, his dad was laid off from his project manager job—the day of Elliot's championship baseball game for the fall season. The game of "the second incident."

Elliot still felt the burn in his heart when thinking about it.

His dad was supposed to have helped coach that game but had never showed up. Elliot had worked with his dad all season on his baseball skills, mainly fielding and throwing. He was supposed to start at second base. Without his dad's support, Elliot had ended up in his usual position—right field. Nobody had ever come close to hitting the ball near him all season. He spent games hunting four-leaf clovers while barely watching the game. Then, in the final inning of the championship game, his team was up by two runs when the opposing batter hit a weak fly to right field. There were two outs and two runners on base. Elliot remembered this clearly. At the clang of the ball smacking against the metal bat, his head had snapped up to see the ball rising straight toward him.

He remembered his eyes going wide and lifting his glove in anticipation.

"Get it, Elliot!" his head coach had screamed as he'd charged from the dugout. "Grab it!"

Distracted by the screaming, Elliot had taken his eyes off the ball just for a moment. It'd smacked off the heel of his glove and then bounced past him.

The coach's howls still haunted him. By the time he'd retrieved the ball, the first run was about to score. Burning with shame, he'd thrown the ball toward second base wildly and missed the cut-off man. The tying run had rounded third by then. Luckily for Elliot's team, the pitcher had retrieved the wild throw and then had thrown a strike to the catcher just in time to tag the sliding runner.

Elliot's team had won the championship, but when given his trophy, the head coach had leaned close to Elliot's ear and whispered, "You don't deserve this, but take it. And tell your dad not to bother offering to help next time."

Just thinking about it made Elliot's stomach hurt all over. He recalled ducking his head down and trudging over to his waiting mom and sister.

"It's okay, kiddo," his mom had said, distracted, barely glancing up from her phone. "We can't catch them all. Let's go home and find your father. I have a mountain of work to grade."

Mrs. Ashley was a fifth-grade teacher and spent more time with her students and school than with her family.

Only Skylar had noticed the trophy exchange. That night, after finding out Mr. Ashley was jobless, she'd crept into Elliot's room, finding him wide awake.

"What did he say to you?" she'd asked. "Your coach. I saw him say something when giving you the trophy."

Tangled in his sheets, Elliot had rolled to his side and stared at the wall, blinking away tears. Below them, their parents' raised voices were muffled but clearly full of anger. "Nothing," he muttered.

"Come on, Elliot," she'd said, moving to sit on the edge of his bed. "I know I call you names, but I'm your older sister. Only I'm allowed to do that. Tell me what that jerk said."

Elliot had turned to look up with a furrowed brow. Seeing her earnest gaze, he'd grimaced and told her.

Skylar had then called the coach a name that made Elliot raise his eyebrows alarmingly.

"Don't worry, kid," Skylar had said, patting his back. "It was just a game, and Dad will get a new job. One day, you'll throw a baseball in that jerk's face. And I hope I'm there to see it!"

That had been back in early November. Their dad had yet to get a job, and over the winter break, he'd announced they were moving to a new house.

"It's where I grew up," he'd explained. "It's older and smaller, but you'll each get your own room."

"We already have our own rooms," Skylar had exploded. "And our own friends. And our own lives!"

"It's cheaper," their dad said glumly. "As in, it's free. My grandmother owns it and is letting us have it."

"Don't worry," their mom told them. "Once your dad gets a new job, we'll see about moving back..."

It had been a gloomy Christmas and a miserable winter. In early March, the Ashley family made the move during a rainstorm.

The "new" old house was over a forty-minute drive from Whitney County, Virginia, over the York River to the next county of Grantham. Their mom stayed at her old job with a longer commute, but the kids had new schools and no friends.

And then two months later, their great-grandmother passed away suddenly—a woman the kids never even knew. This is what led to the funeral Elliot was supposed to be dressed for. His dad never mentioned his family, but Elliot's great-grandmother was the one who let them have the house, so they had to attend her funeral. His dad's mom had died years before Skylar and Elliot had been born. She and the rest of his family were never talked about.

Swishing his lips back and forth, he looked around his room with glum disinterest.

It had been his dad's room when he'd been Elliot's age. Small and tight—just like Elliot, his dad joked—it still had some of his dad's baseball posters from the nineties. Hanging on the wall above his bed, players with bulging muscles crushed baseballs with mighty swings.

Mr. Ashley had been a star ballplayer in high school and would've played in college if he hadn't hurt his knee. He'd been a homerun king and expected Elliot to follow in his footsteps. Too bad Elliot had yet to grow past four and a half feet and still was among the smallest in his class. And he stank at baseball.

"Elliot, the bathroom is yours!" Skylar yelled. "Don't stink it up!"

With great effort, Elliot rolled out of bed, getting to his feet. Stretching out his arms and feet, he resisted the urge to run to the bathroom. He didn't want to go to the funeral and definitely didn't want to go to baseball practice. He could pretend he didn't have to go as long as he stayed put.

In his cramped room, he stood to face the bookshelf holding his favorite graphic novels, painted monster figures, and the shameful baseball trophy. Next to the trophy was a framed picture of Tucker and him. Taken last summer when their dads took them fishing, the two stood together holding up their catches. Tucker held up an eighteen-inch croaker while Elliot proudly displayed a clump of seaweed strewn over a deflated bike tire. The boys had their arms around each other and smiled into the camera. It was a picture of BFFs...

Who knew then that they would no longer be friends or talk in just a few months? And it was all Elliot's fault.

Chapter 4

Elliot tore his gaze from the picture and stared out the window to the right of the bookcase. It faced his neighbor's yard with a sprawling two-acre lot with bright green grass dotted with trees before rising into a fancy three-story brick house. In it lived a childless couple who hated kids. They'd already complained to Elliot's parents about him making too much noise playing in the backyard and leaving his bike out on the driveway too long. Elliot felt a pang in his chest. His new neighborhood had no kids his age. Not that it would've mattered. No kid could replace Tucker.

Elliot's room had a small closet in the corner, just to the right of the window. It held all his toys and nice shirts and pants. A dresser sat next to the closet for the rest of his clothes. A second window peered into his backyard next to the head of his bed. Under this was a small desk holding his laptop and books for school. His phone sat next to his unfinished math homework.

Turning from the window, he moved to the desk and snatched up his phone. Biting his lower lip, he checked for messages or missed calls. Like every day since October, there was nothing from Tucker.

Lowering the phone in disappointment, Elliot glanced over the desk through the second window. He saw his dad standing out in the trees far from their house. His phone clunked back onto his desk. He felt his stomach tighten.

His dad wore his navy blue suit and seemed oblivious to branches and leaves poking his hair and shoulders. Staring up, his thick blond hair hanging above his collar, arms stretched out from his side, he appeared to be unleashing a silent howl toward the sky.

Elliot wrinkled his nose and scratched the back of his pants as he watched. Since the move, his dad seemed to be growing farther away from his family. His job search seemed to be wilting him. No longer exuberant in the mornings, he now spent hours in the garage pumping iron, with equipment left over from his high school days, and listening to old CDs of rock music from his childhood. Maybe losing his grandmother hurt him, but Elliot thought it could be his fault. Ever since the "first incident," he couldn't help but feel his dad no longer looked at him the same, and perhaps it was his fault for his dad being laid off.

"Elliot!"

Elliot visibly jumped, and he whirled in surprise. Skylar had cracked his door open and stared at him in horror.

"What are you doing?" his sister cried.

"Nothing," Elliot said hastily. He brushed hair from his eyes and glared defiantly back at his older sister. "What are you doing in here?"

She glared back. "Trying to find out why you're not dressed and downstairs, nincompoop!"

Skylar was fifteen and a high school sophomore. She couldn't drive a car yet, so instead drove everyone crazy, especially Elliot. A star field hockey player in her old school, she usually played softball in the spring but sat out that season because of the move. She wanted to help out the family until their dad got a job. This mostly meant she bossed Elliot around more than usual.

"I was just getting ready," Elliot said. He wiped his hands on the side of his pants. "You were, like, hogging the bathroom."

"I told you it was free! Besides, you could've gotten your clothes while waiting!"

"I was… but I was watching Dad."

Skylar's dark hazel brown eyes softened. Slightly slanted and gleaming with intelligence, they gave her an air of confidence and inner strength that rarely backed down. She wore a simple black dress that showed off her trim, athletic figure. With a heart-shaped face and long dark blond hair down past her shoulders, she had a long, slender nose and full mouth, now covered in dark red lipstick. Unsurprisingly, she already had a gaggle of friends in high school. Everything seemed to come easy for her.

"You're worried about him, huh?"

Elliot shrugged. "I just wish we never moved."

"I know, but we had to. Besides, Grantham isn't so bad."

Elliot gave her a mischievous smile. "That's only because you met Teddy Malone."

Skylar's cheeks turned the shade of her lips. She swiftly moved into the room and shut the door. "How do you know about him?" she demanded.

Crossing his arms, Elliot smirked. "Like, I hear you talking to him on your phone. And who dropped you off from school yesterday?" His naturally high voice went an octave up as he batted his eyes and puckered his lips. "'Bye, Teddy!" he sang, mimicking his sister. "I want to kiss you, but I'm, like, afraid my mom might see!"

"Elliot, shut up!" Skylar hissed, moving into the room with clenched fists. "Don't you dare tell Mom or Dad, got it?"

"Or what?" Elliot teased.

"Or I'll spank your puny butt," Skylar snarled. "Mom and Dad don't need anything new to worry about right now. You know that. Now get dressed. Mom will totally have a cow if she finds you like this."

Elliot frowned but did not comment. He hunched his shoulders and brushed past his sister to the door.

Neither sibling voiced it, but they both worried more about their mom than their dad. The trip from Grantham back to Whitney was taxing, causing their mom to leave just after they woke up on weekdays and often returning well past dinnertime. Her students were a real handful, and she usually went straight to grading or planning when she came home. This left their dad to bring them to any afterschool activities. Their mom slept in on weekends and made supper for the entire week. She bore it all with a smile, but the kids could see her sunken eyes and lines of stress creasing her forehead. Skylar had inherited her looks from her mom. Before the move, they'd often been mistaken as sisters. That was no longer the case.

Skylar raised a hand and mussed up Elliot's hair as he passed. "Want any help getting ready? I can totally put your hair in a ponytail."

Elliot turned and stuck out his tongue at her. "You're, like, not even kind of funny."

"And you're, like, not even kind of dressed," she retorted. She gave a swift kick to his backside. "Get moving!"

Elliot turned to fight back, but their Mom's calling interrupted his actions. "Okay, kids! We're in the car! Let's go!"

Elliot quickly raced for the door.

"Hey, what about your suit?" Skylar called.

"I need to pee!" Elliot said over his shoulder.

"Fine," Skylar huffed. She stared for his closet. "I'll get it for you. Just remember to lift the seat and don't make a mess on the floor!"

"I will if you stop being so annoying, dirt brain!" Elliot slammed the bathroom door before his sister could respond.

Chapter 5

Back in Whitney, Virginia, Tucker Romero also happened to be in the bathroom. He stood in front of the mirror, sucking in his breath as he flexed his arms. Feet apart, elbows up, he struck his best bodybuilder's pose.

"Oh, yeah, Tucker," he whispered. "You the man." He imagined his legs thick with muscle, his stomach shredded with abs, and his arms ripped with bulging tendons.

"Tucker!" cried the shrill voice of his younger sister Maria. "I have your underpants out here, and your friend is at the door!"

"Wh-What?" Tucker spluttered, nearly losing his balance. His arms dropped to his belly as he whirled to the closed door in terror, making sure he'd remembered to lock it. "Elliot is here?"

"No, doofus. Your weirdo friend Philly-o-cheesesteak."

Tucker relaxed and blew out his breath. Of course. Elliot had moved to another county and Tucker had been taken out of middle school to be homeschooled. His only friends were light-starved kids still walked by their parents, some even wearing leashes.

"It's Phileo, dirt brain," he said.

Phileo Benedict was in his homeschool cohort and lived three houses away. Tucker had never known he existed before and still didn't know what to make of him. Before meeting Tucker, Phileo must've lived in a box. He had the social graces of a pampered chicken, and Tucker wasn't sure if maybe he was an alien dropped off from another planet to study humans.

Just his luck, Phileo had decided Tucker would be the subject of his fascination.

"Whatever," Maria said, annoyed. She was not a fan of Phileo. "What do you want me to do with your underpants? Give them to Phileo Dirt Brain to sniff?"

"No!" Tucker nearly shouted. "Sheesh! Can't a guy have any privacy here? Just drop it and go to your room. Read some of your anime books!"

"It's Manga, stinky head. Let me know if you need any toilet paper! I'll send your dirt-brain friend to bring you some!"

"Wait, tell Phileo that I'm busy—no, I mean, I'll be down in a second! Okay?"

"Sure, Tucker," Maria said sweetly. Eight years of being cute and the youngest in the family had twisted her brain. She was a mixture of pure evil and bright-eyed innocence, letting her get away with anything. Tucker needed her on his side to survive childhood.

"Maria, I mean it," he warned.

She was already gone.

Tucker blew out his breath and glanced again in the mirror. Wearing only his boxer shorts, he saw nothing like the muscular bodybuilder he'd envisioned. Instead, he saw a stocky boy of average height with a slightly round belly and flabby arms. Sucking in his stomach, he saw the outline of muscle just starting to timidly emerge.

As a little kid, he'd been short and round like a beach ball. In the last year, he'd grown over three inches and had started thinning out. His mop of curly dark brown hair framed his round face and hung just past his neck. Bouncy and unruly, his hair was his favorite feature, and he refused to get it cut shorter. Matching his dark brown eyes, it softened his large nose and wide mouth.

He gritted his teeth in the mirror and clenched his fists just above his belly button. "One day, I'll be Mr. Universe!"

Staring at his image, he felt a pang of sadness. For a brief moment, he missed Elliot, his old best friend. The two of them used to posture in the mirror during sleepovers, each trying to outdo the other with goofy bodybuilder stances.

From down below, he heard the doorbell ring. Phileo, not Elliot, was still waiting. Lucky him.

"Coming!" he called, quickly grabbing up his shorts and T-shirt.

From below, the doorbell rang again.

Tugging on his shirt, he fought to find the arm holes. "Maria!" he called. "Are you at the door?"

He only heard the doorbell in response.

Once dressed, he opened the door to find a pile of clothes strewn on the floor. His underpants were scattered on top of his crumpled shirts and socks.

"Maria!" he shouted. "What did you do to my clothes?"

"What you told me to do, munch-breath!" yelled his sister. "I dropped them!" Maria was safely in her room with her door closed and surely locked. "Let me know when you and your Philly cheesesteak friend leave!"

Tucker knelt and quickly gathered his clothes. Hearing the doorbell call impatiently, he panicked. He tossed the clothes in the bathroom and shut the door. Then rising to his feet, he raced down the stairs.

"So there you are," Phileo said, staring down his nose at Tucker. Only a few inches taller, Phileo stood as if he loomed several feet above Tucker. He wore pressed khaki pants and a neon blue polo shirt tucked in tightly. Both clung to his bony frame of gleaming pale skin. Short blond hair was parted in the middle and slicked down with an abundance of hairspray. He reeked of fruity cologne.

"Phileo!" Tucker said, out of breath. "You walked all the way here? Dressed like that?"

"No, of course not. My mom dropped me off."

A tan Range Rover SUV idled on the road by Tucker's driveway. The side windows were tinted, but Tucker could feel Phileo's mom staring at him from behind the wheel.

"Oh, right. Of course. So, um, what are you doing here? I mean, um, want to come in?"

Phileo stared above Tucker, his long, pointed nose aiming at the doorframe. "Is your sister home?"

Tucker's mouth nearly dropped open. "You mean, Anita?" Anita was in college on the other side of the state. Phileo had seen her once over winter break and remarked that Tucker had a "very striking" elder sister.

"No," Phileo said, annoyed. His blue eyes were spread far apart on his face, and his mouth appeared too small between them. It gave him a fish-eyed look that sometimes gave Tucker the creeps. Phileo cleared his throat and seemed to examine Tucker with distaste. "Your sister, Maria. I—my mom would like to invite her to a tea party."

"Huh?" Tucker blinked rapidly as he fought to process what was happening. Was Phileo asking his little sister out on a date? Or was it his mom asking her on a date for Phileo?

Phileo stuck a hand in his right pocket.

Okay, this is it, Tucker thought, squeezing his lips tight. *Phileo is totally going to pull out a laser blaster and demand that I take him to my leader—my eight-year-old sister.*

Instead, the taller boy pulled out a gold envelope, sealed and sprinkled with glitter. "Here. Give this to Maria." He pushed the envelope into Tucker's hand and quickly spun away. "She can call my mother to tell her when she's coming," he said over his shoulder. "The number is in the card. Okay?"

Tucker could only stare dumbly as he took the card. Now, he really missed Elliot.

Chapter 6

In Grantham, Elliot finished flushing and was washing his hands when his sister barged through the door carrying Elliot's blue suit jacket and gray pants on a hanger. She held his bright white dress shirt in her other hand.

"Can't you, like, knock?" Elliot said, wrinkling his brow at her. "I could be taking a shower."

"Shut up and get this on. Wear the shirt over your tank top."

"Okay, okay, I got it!" Elliot dried his hands on his pajama pants. "Get lost!"

"Just hurry up." Skylar laid the clothes on the counter by the sink. "Be down in one minute."

"I will, like, as soon as you leave," Elliot growled.

"On my way out," Skylar replied sweetly. "Love you, jerk-face."

"Love you too, barf-brain."

The door slammed, and Elliot took a deep breath as he faced the mirror. Eyeing his thin arms and lean frame, he tightened his lips. So far, he'd yet to start developing his dad's muscular build. His hair, dark blond like his sister's, hung just above his neck. Brushed to the right, loose strands drooped over his pale blue eyes, some tickling the top of his nose. Sharing the same facial features as his mom and sister, he had a sharp chin and big ears hidden by his long hair. He just wished he carried Skylar's confidence and his mom's strength. He used to think he did… until the "first incident."

The "first incident" that ruined Elliot's life was entirely his fault. It was when he lost his best friend Tucker, which led to the terrible baseball game and "second incident."

Tucker had one dream in life. He wanted to be a famous kid chef, an idea born from watching TV with his parents. At first, he could barely cook anything more than toast and scrambled eggs. Under his mom's guidance and his dad's encouragement, he started developing serious chef skills. His favorite shows were the chef competitions and he and Elliot would often watch them together. Tucker always cheered on his favorite contestants while Elliot made fun of the various food dishes, saying stuff like they tasted like poo or were made out of worms and snot. That was the first problem. Elliot never took Tucker's dream seriously.

The boys had been in the same class since kindergarten. They were looking forward to their fifth-grade year, the final one at Leewood Elementary before middle school. Then, their school announced a junior chef competition to kick off the year.

The school wanted students to create healthy courses to serve the teachers for Open House night. Winners of each category would have their meals prepared for the teachers and receive special plaques.

Of course, Tucker entered, and Elliot, being a good friend, did as well. They meant to go in together, but the contest rules said only one chef could prepare a dish, no partners. It never said anything about destroying friendships, but that is precisely what happened.

On the big night, contestants returned to school carrying their meals. They were to set up in the cafeteria and were separated by grades. Fourth and fifth graders were sent to the back and would be judged last.

Tucker and Elliot were the only fifth-grade boys competing, and they chose the back corner table.

"We'll save the best for last," Tucker told Elliot as they entered the cafeteria. "Our food will be on the judge's taste buds when they make their final decisions."

"Okay, yeah," Elliot said. "Whatever you say, Tucker."

A group of girls from their class were setting up at the next table from the corner. Walking by, Tucker noticed Kelsey Jimmers, the prettiest girl in the grade, making eyes at them. He paid her no attention. He knew she liked Elliot and didn't care. At that moment, he just cared about his food creations.

"Okay, this is it," he said. "My first stop to being a top chef!"

Elliot laughed. "Or your first failure!"

"Shut up," Tucker told him. His parents were still at work, so he'd come with Elliot's mom.

He carefully carried his wrapped containers stacked on top of each other, separated by a cooling rack. A bag over his shoulder held serving spoons, sampling spoons, and a stack of paper bowls. He hoped other contestants would want to try his food once he'd been declared the winner. Elliot only had a single tray that he wielded like a football. He hadn't even brought something to serve it with.

"How long do you think this is going to take?" Elliot asked as they reached the table.

"Not sure," Tucker said with a grunt. He lowered his burden and got busy setting it up. "We just need to be ready before the judges come."

"Yeah, okay, but they'd better hurry. I'm getting hungry."

Tucker chuckled. "Well, don't touch any of mine before the judges come. I worked hard on the presentation."

Elliot barely heard him as he surveyed the busy cafeteria. "I don't, like, know anybody here."

"You know Kelsey and her friends," Tucker said, placing his bag on the floor under the table. He separated the two bowls and glanced over at the table of girls. Kelsey flashed him a smile, and he instantly ducked his head down.

"Yeah, well," Elliot said, "I meant anybody I could, like, play pass with. You know, while we're waiting." He pretended to throw his pan like a football.

"Oh, no, you don't," Tucker glared at Elliot. "No playing around until the judging is done, man. Come on and set up your food. We're going to be the best!"

Tucker had made broccoli slaw with a dressing featuring homemade mayonnaise, lemon juice, and vinegar. Packed with crunchy almonds and dried cranberries, he knew it would be a winner. For dessert, he had whipped up a pumpkin pudding garnished with mint leaves and sprinkled with graham cracker crumbs.

The contest emphasized health, and Tucker ensured everything was fresh, low in calories, but big on taste. Amazingly, he did everything himself, and his mom only helped by providing the bowls to put everything in. He couldn't wait to see what the judges thought.

Standing over a seat at the long table, he set up the giant bowl of broccoli slaw next to his dish of pumpkin pudding. He wiped his hands on his gleaming white apron, which matched the paper chef hat he wore for the occasion. Under his apron, he wore tan slacks and a red collared shirt. He usually only dressed up for church, but this was a special occasion.

Next to him, Elliot knelt on a seat and slapped down the pan of "his" creation.

Tucker looked at it with mild alarm. He recognized Elliot's mom's recipe for Marshmallow Munchies—only "accessorized" by Elliot. Popcorn and rice cereal were mixed together and coated with melted butter and marshmallows. Elliot's addition was crushed-up chocolate candies.

"Hey, Elliot," Tucker said, wrinkling his nose, "the contest is, like, supposed to be healthy."

"Relax," Elliot said, tilting his head toward his friend and smiling sideways. "Everything is totally organic. My mom said so."

He wore simple blue jeans and a black T-shirt with the Orioles baseball logo. Tucker sometimes felt like an idiot next to him. Elliot always looked cool, no matter how he dressed. Why couldn't he at least wear the chef hat Tucker had brought for him? He saw it crushed and folded, abandoned on the seat on the other side of Elliot.

"Besides," Elliot continued, "like, I don't even care about winning, right? I just want something good to eat when we're done."

"Right," Tucker said, grinning tightly. "Want to check out my pudding?"

"Yeah, sure." Elliot turned to Tucker's dish and leaned over the table to sniff. "That smells amazing." Then he cracked up. "But it looks like poo with green toilet paper."

"What? No, it doesn't!"

"Okay, yeah, but it does! Look at that!"

Tucker felt his cheeks burn. "Well, don't put your finger in it!"

Elliot smiled playfully. "Why not? It'll look like I picked my butt!"

"Stop it, Elliot!" Tucker said. "I worked hard on that."

"Okay, okay, yeesh, Tucker." Elliot leaned away from the pudding. "Relax. Like, have a Marshmallow Munchie or something." Elliot straightened and sat abruptly on his seat. "I'm sure the judges will love it." He started bouncing on his seat like a pogo stick.

"Yeah, I don't know," Tucker said nervously. Between the din in the cafeteria and Elliot's bouncing, he was starting to feel sick. He licked the sweat off his upper lip and glanced around the cafeteria.

Over twenty kids were competing, but most were little kids with their parents. The judges—the principal and two bored-looking teachers—were now at the third-grade table sampling oatmeal bars. He saw one of the teachers gag and turn his head away to choke down a swallow.

"No sugar," he heard the mom say, standing over the little girl. "All natural ingredients."

"Right," their principal, Dr. Chocker, replied with a smile. Turning his head toward the boys, he made a disgusted face.

"Oh, man, this could be bad," Tucker whispered. He held a deep fear of principals, especially Dr. Chocker.

"Uh, hello, Tucker," Elliot said, pausing his bouncing. "You're, like, the best here. All you need to do is, like, hide that green toilet paper stuff."

"It's mint."

"Mint? In pumpkin pudding? Is that, like, even legal?"

"Oh, gosh. Dr. Chocker just looked at me!"

Elliot stared over at the principal and immediately ducked his head. "See? I told you mint was bad. Dr. Chocker has, like, radar for finding bad things in school."

"He probably saw you bouncing on your butt," Tucker hissed back.

Dr. Chocker choked down his bite and turned away from the boys, moving to the next student's healthy fare. He did not look enthused. The two teachers, Mr. Harris, a special education teacher, and Ms. Lurtz, who taught third grade, obediently followed him like chastened puppies.

Dr. Chocker threw one final look back towards the corner. He then put on a wide smile and turned to shake hands with a parent.

Elliot let out a sigh of relief. "Man, if I get in trouble here, my mom will kill me."

Tucker groaned. "I'm going to be sick…" He wished his mom had come. She would know how to deal with the stern principal. Hands gripping the table's edge, he kept his eyes on Dr. Chocker, trying to read his mind. Would he like the broccoli slaw and pudding?

Dr. Chocker was a tall, thin-chested man with a bulging belly. Balding in the front, he tried combing wisps of light brown hair over his gleaming forehead. Keeping his thicker hair on the sides trimmed short, he created a box canyon of baldness.

He always wore a gray suit and blue tie. The kids of Leewood Elementary guessed he had five of the identical suits. There were many dares for somebody to spill grape juice on his jacket to see if the stain remained the next day. So far, nobody had taken the dare. Something about him made kids wary. A glance from his calm gray eyes, evenly placed over his hooked nose, made kids suddenly snap to obedience. He rarely strayed from his office, but when he did, kids were on high alert. Nobody wanted to attract his ire.

Tucker swallowed a lump in his throat. What if the principal didn't like his food…? Suddenly, he stood from the table and stumbled to the back entrance of the cafeteria.

"Hey, where are you going?" Elliot asked.

"The bathroom! I need to go bad. Look after my stuff, Elliot!"

Chapter 7

When Tucker returned from the bathroom, he saw a scene straight from a horror movie made just for him. Kelsey Jimmers stood in front of the table with her phone poised in front of her, fighting down giggles. On the other side of the table, Elliot knelt on a seat over Tucker's pumpkin pudding.

"So," Elliot was saying, "um, this is straight from Dr. Chocker's toilet… oh, yeah, that green stuff? He totally blew his nose after picking it. Yeah." In his hand, he held Tucker's mom's serving spoon and was scooping up the pudding, destroying Tucker's careful presentation.

"Elliot!" Tucker exploded, not hiding his anger. "What the heck? What are you doing? Get away!"

Elliot's hand froze, and he stared at the phone, making a wide-eyed expression with his mouth open. Kelsey giggled louder as she kept her phone trained on him.

"Oops, I'm so busted," Elliot whispered. Then he turned to Tucker, forcing a smile. "Relax, I'm helping you. I'm hiding all the green mint stuff. I mean, like, the judges will totally hate it."

"Leave it alone!" Tucker cried, moving swiftly to him. "Drop the spoon! Just let it go!"

"Okay, okay, yeesh!"

Tucker grabbed Elliot by the armpits and physically yanked him away from the table. He pushed him away, nearly knocking him down. "You're ruining it!"

"No, I was helping you," Elliot protested. "Ouch, did you just grab me? I mean, like, I was trying to help."

"Calm down, Tucker," Kelsey said. "Chill. He was just being funny for my video."

Tucker glared at her until she stopped filming and beat a hasty retreat back to her table.

Elliot moved back to Tucker's side. "Sorry, man, but I really thought the green stuff needed to go."

"No, you need to go," Tucker growled. Still, he didn't say anything when Elliot stood at his shoulder. Tucker took the spoon and smoothed out the disturbed pudding. The graham cracker crumbs and mint leaves were a complete soggy mess. Biting his lower lip, Tucker did the only thing he could think of. He buried the leaves and crumbs and smoothed down the surface of the pudding.

The judges had reached the table with the girls. They would be next.

The next several moments were the worst in Tucker's life. The judges came to their table with wilted smiles and expressions of relief.

"Last one," Dr. Chocker nearly moaned, licking crumbs off his upper lip. Usually clean-shaven, he currently wore a faint mustache of various crumbs. His lean face appeared slightly green.

"Ooh," said Mr. Harris on his right, eyeing Elliot's Marshmallow Munchies with unmasked desire. "Now those look amazing."

"Totally organic," Elliot said, brushing hair back from his eyes. "Yeah, even the chocolate is, um, organic."

"As long as it's real sugar, kid, I need one," Mr. Harris said, licking his lips. A younger teacher with a stocky build, he worked with kids with disabilities. Still, most students knew him. He always managed to find ways to join them at recess. He was easily the most popular teacher in school, with a good football arm and excelling at soccer against third graders. Students loved him, but some teachers treated him as an overgrown student. He enjoyed his job, but at the moment, he looked miserable and starved for sugar.

Tucker fought hard not to scream. This couldn't be happening to him. For a terrible moment, he thought the judges would skip him entirely.

Ms. Lurtz, a petite first-year teacher, grabbed Mr. Harris's sleeve and pulled him to face Tucker. Her hair was tied severely in a bun, and she wore an intense look that brooked no nonsense. Though small, she seemed to tower over the male teacher. "First, we have to go through this one," she said. Then she gave Tucker a smile. "Who are you, young sir?"

"Um, I'm Tucker… I've gone here since kindergarten."

"Right," the teacher said as she stared at the slaw. "What is this green stuff with the cherries?"

"Ew, I mean, are those wood chips in there?" Mr. Harris asked, not disguising his disgust.

"That's my broccoli slaw with cranberries and almonds," Tucker said through clenched teeth.

"It looks great," Dr. Chocker said, faintly smiling. He then turned to Elliot. "It's great to see the boy of one of my favorite teachers here. Where's your mom?"

"Um, she's meeting with the other fifth-grade teachers, I think," Elliot said. "They're, like, busy planning the next test or something."

"She's always working, isn't she?" Dr. Chocker said, grinning. "You have a great mother, young man."

"Yeah, thank you. Um, are you going to try Tucker's food?"

Tucker swallowed his anger and nodded his thanks at Elliot. "I have paper bowls here if you each want a sample—"

"Oh, we'll just take a quick spoonful," Mr. Harris said, eyeing the marshmallow dessert by Elliot. "Let's get it over with."

Suddenly, Tucker's broccoli slaw looked wilted and plain. He watched as the judges took hasty bites with their plastic spoons. They didn't even wait to taste it before making obligatory remarks about its taste.

"Yum," said Dr. Chocker.

"Good," added Ms. Lurtz.

"Not too bad," Mr. Harris said, swallowing. "What's next?"

Tucker only bit the inside of his cheek and pointed at the pumpkin pudding. He blinked away his disappointment. He still had one more shot at impressing the judges.

"It does smell good," Dr. Chocker said, sniffing.

"It looks... interesting," Mr. Harris commented. "What is it exactly?"

"My homemade pumpkin pudding," Tucker said hastily. "It's, um, really good." He eyed Elliot. "Um, it's all organic and has lots of flavor."

Mr. Harris was already inching toward Elliot's Marshmallow Munchies.

"Hmmph," Ms. Lurtz said, cleaning her teeth with her tongue. "Who's the first victim?"

That was when disaster struck.

Of course, it had to be Dr. Chocker. And, of course, he had to scoop up a massive spoonful of pudding... that, of course, had to include one soggy, slippery mint leaf. Taking a bite, he started to swallow and then immediately choked.

"Dr. Chocker, are you okay?" the male teacher asked, alarmed.

"What did you put in this, kid?" Ms. Lurtz demanded, staring at Tucker.

Stricken, the boy could only stare in horror.

The principal's face turned a shade red. Then, all at once, he unleashed a mega cough, spraying pumpkin goop all over the table. Glops of brown sludge landed on and in the pudding bowl. More splattered across Tucker's apron and his shocked face. The slimy mint leaf stuck fast to his apron, like a wad of snot fired like a spitball. It was right over his heart. Of course, nothing touched Elliot's side.

Tucker did not win a prize that night. Elliot ended up winning the category for Best Dessert.

That was only the start of the "first incident." That night, Elliot was at Tucker's house for a sleepover. The boys were fooling around on Tucker's bed. Elliot was doing his best to cheer up his friend… by swinging his first place medal around and singing "We are the Champions" while Tucker sat glumly at his feet, bouncing on the mattress.

Then, in a fit of anger, Tucker reached up and yanked the front of Elliot's waistband. Caught by surprise, Elliot fell to his bottom. While doing so, he swung the medal and nailed Tucker in the eye.

Crying out in pain, Tucker rolled to his side and tumbled from the bed. As he fell, he managed to catch his right ankle between the mattress and the footboard. Landing with a solid thump, a sharp pain shot up his knee. Screaming out, he clutched at his leg.

Sitting on the mattress, stunned, Elliot looked toward his friend. "What just happened?" he asked.

Tucker ended up with a sprained ankle and a black eye. Elliot was sent home while Tucker went to the emergency room. Waiting with his parents for the doctor, Tucker's phone pinged. A classmate had sent him a link...

Kelsey Jimmers had posted the video from the cafeteria of Elliot ruining his pudding. It ended with Tucker pulling Elliot away in anger. There were already hundreds of views and a list of comments, growing by the minute. Surprisingly, nearly all supported Tucker.

That poor kid has a jerk friend!

I totally agree. Roly-poly needs better friends.

Cute kid ruining a hardworking kid's project. Real cute. Hope he gets the pudding dumped on his rotten head.

Hey, both kids go to my school. One's a real jerk. I bet you can't tell which one! LOL!

Tucker only read a few comments before his parents yanked his phone away. They'd watched the video with him and were less than amused.

When Elliot called a few minutes later to check on Tucker, Tucker's mom answered. She told him never to call again and that Tucker would no longer be allowed to his house.

Just like that, the friendship was over. The two friends had not spoken since.

That Monday, Tucker switched classes. By the end of the week, his parents had removed him from Leewood Elementary to be homeschooled "in order to stimulate his mind in a safer environment."

Elliot had been grounded from video games and his phone for a month. His parents— especially his mom—were just as upset at him for making fun of Dr. Chocker in the video as for messing up Tucker's pudding. As part of his punishment, he had to write a letter of apology to the principal and personally ask for forgiveness in his office before returning to school. He ended up missing recess for the week.

That had been the week before the championship baseball game and Elliot's dad being laid off.

Just like that, Elliot's whole life had come crashing down. While grounded, he did write an apology letter to Tucker. Sending it in the mail, it arrived back in his mailbox the next week, unopened. Of all the punishments, losing Tucker, by far, had to be the worst.

Chapter 8

As Elliot hastily changed for the funeral, Tucker collapsed onto his couch and picked up the controller for his Xbox. Video games helped him relax and think. After Phileo's visit, that was just what he needed to do. The unopened golden invitation lay on the couch next to him.

Maria walked in from the stairs just as he loaded Minecraft. "What's with all the blinds being closed?" she asked, eying the darkened room with distaste. "Are you trying to be a depressed Goth or something?"

"No, I, you know, didn't want Phileo to see me through the window," Tucker mumbled. "In case he came back."

Maria wrinkled her nose and then nodded. "Good call, big brother. Now I feel bad about throwing all your clothes in the toilet."

"Ha, ha, very funny," Tucker muttered.

"What did he want?"

Tucker kept his eyes on the screen, loading his creative world. "You don't want to know."

"Then why did I ask?"

Tucker shrugged. "I don't know. Because you're stupid, I guess."

"Oh, yeah?" She ran in front of their flat screen that hung just below the mantle of their family room. "Tell me, or I'm pulling the plug! And then I'm telling Mom that you called me names!"

"Okay, okay!" Tucker dropped his controller to his lap in surrender. As the middle child, he knew he had no chance. His younger sister only needed to cry for a second, and Tucker would instantly be grounded for the rest of the day without video games. "He wanted to invite you… he wanted to invite you to a tea party. Okay?"

Maria stared at Tucker for a long moment. She was a small, skinny girl with brown frizzy hair hanging past her shoulders. Wise beyond her years, she could see right through her older sibling. Her dark brown eyes never wavered.

Tucker felt his cheeks burn and mouth grow tight. "I'm serious."

"You have strange friends," Maria finally said.

"Uh, yeah, whatever!" Tucker snatched up the controller in a huff. "Now get out of the way!"

"Why don't you start cooking again?" Maria said as she reluctantly sidled away from the TV. "You know, your stuff is better than Mom's. You don't cook all healthy like she does."

Tucker ducked his head. "Because," he muttered. "That's why." In truth, he hadn't made anything for the family since the horrible contest. Creative baking and cooking just brought up bad memories. "Now, leave me alone."

"Sure, big brother." Maria calmly smoothed down her unicorn T-shirt and slapped the sides of her white shorts. "I'll be upstairs barfing if your Phileo weirdeo friend comes back."

"Yeah, yeah, okay. I'll be sure to tell him that. Now get lost."

Maria heaved a sigh at the stairs. "You know, Tucker? I miss Elliot." She then marched up without looking back.

"Yeah, me too," Tucker mumbled when she'd gone up. "Me too."

Alone in the darkened room, he shifted up in his seat and focused on his game. Back in the summer, Elliot and he had started an amusement park village where almost every ride proved fatal in a most creative way. He meant to finally finish it.

He would later trash the invitation.

Donnie Brasco and Jake Brasco were free.

"We ready to party?" whooped Jake from the back. "Let's go!"

Behind the wheel of his pride and joy, a maroon 1997 Ford pickup, Donnie pressed on the gas and the truck zoomed forward. They'd just left the main road and were on the narrow route to Blue Island. No cops patrolled this area, and there was no traffic in either direction. The road was theirs.

The boys were on a mission. Cousins and seniors at Grantham High, the only high school in the county, the boys had only five weeks left until graduation. And then it was straight to the workforce. Both were slated for jobs with their dads and uncles in a seafood packing plant. That left only five weekends of freedom before being buried in fish guts. They meant to spend each one wisely. For this weekend they planned to spend the days hunting at Blue Island.

Of course, the boys heard the tales of the island—how no visitors were welcome and all sorts of strange things happened there. People vanished regularly, monsters roamed the woods, and witches lived there… right. Ghosts, monsters, goblins, the boys heard it all. It was a load of fish guts. The boys knew Teddy Malone, a kid one grade below them in school. Teddy had grown up on Blue Island, and he was just an average pretty boy. The Brasco cousins had nothing to fear.

After a mile of cutting through fields of high grass, the road entered thick woods. High, twisty branches, bright with spring leaves, waved above them, providing welcome shade. It was only the first weekend in May and already the temperature hovered near ninety. The shade was most welcome.

In the back with Jake, the cousins had everything they needed. A cooler full of drinks, a backpack of canned food, and Donnie's dad's tent were all jammed against the cab. Jake sat atop the cooler and pulled off his T-shirt. Waving it in the air above his head, he howled with joy. "I wish the girls could see me now!"

"They would puke!' Donnie yelled back. "Your flabby whale belly would blind them!"

"Ah, there's just more of me to love, and you're jealous!" Jake crowed back. Still waving his shirt, his left hand slapped his plump belly and jiggled it. "Come on, girls, where you at?"

"Avoiding you, fatty!" Donnie hit the brakes and laughed when Jake nearly tumbled over the cab. He then sped back up.

"Not funny, bro," Jake said, wiping sweat from his brow. He leaned heavily against the back window.

Both boys had their blond hair buzzed short and were cursed with pasty complexions. Jake's face was already turning beet red from the sun. Pulling his shirt back on, he sat back on the cooler and stared down at the most important items they'd packed. Two long bolt-action rifles were secured in a single tan gun case with a box of ammunition next to it.

"Watch your driving, man. You don't want to damage our guns."

"You mean my guns," Donnie yelled back. "Don't worry. If they break I got two more in the car!"

"Really?"

"Yeah, one on my right and one on my left!" Donnie took both hands from the wheel to flex his arms, showing off bulging biceps.

"You're stupid," Jake muttered.

While Jake carried a rotund figure, Donnie was all muscle. He had already worked in the packing plant the previous summer and then starred on the school's football team as a linebacker and starting right guard. With money, a truck, hunting rifles, and good looks, he had everything Jake lacked. Still, Donnie was cool. He always let Jake tag along with him and his teasing was all in fun. They were family and family stuck together.

"Yo, Jake!" Donnie shouted. "Check your phone. Mine has no bars, man."

Jake slid his phone from his hip pocket, frowning as he checked it. "Nope. No signal here, dude."

"Guess that means we arrived at freedom!" Donnie cried. "Nobody can bother us!"

Jake jammed his phone back into his pocket and sat against the cab to keep from falling. "Slow down, dude!"

He knew nobody could bother them, but if they ever got in an accident… they also couldn't call for help.

Donnie only laughed and pressed the gas harder.

The Ford surged forward, racing over the cracked pavement. Soon, the road exited the woods, and the pickup came to a narrow bridge crossing a strip of the York River. This is when Donnie slowed the truck to a crawl.

Their destination rose before them. Blue Island had gotten its name from the blue tinge it radiated in the early mornings when it was frequently covered in thick fog. However, at midday on this Saturday, the bright sun glinted off the greenery of the dense forest in front of them. The island was nearly fifteen miles long and around three miles across at its widest point. Mainly flat, a hilly area rose near the center, somewhere lost in the trees. Somewhere past the hills was where the Blue Community sat, a backward town where most of the population lived. Apparently, the same families had lived there for generations. Visitors and outsiders were not tolerated. Even if Teddy was from there, there were enough stories about the town to make the Brasco boys wary. They planned to steer far from that area. The woods would be safer.

Crossing the bridge, the boys eyed the thick forest with excitement. Since so few ever visited and the locals seemed to keep to themselves, they figured the woods should be teeming with deer, wild turkey, and who knew what else, maybe even bear! An abundance of prey waited for the boys. They couldn't wait to get on the hunt.

As they neared the start of the forest, Donnie steered the truck off the road, sending it bumping along through tall grass.

"Yo, Donnie, you hear that?" Jake asked, rising hesitantly from the cooler. He stared into the trees in puzzlement. Thick bushes and sharp thorns blocked much of the way, but there were plenty of gaps marking trails to slip through.

"I don't hear nothing," Donnie said. Turning his truck, he parked it behind a thick oak towering from a clump of green shrubbery. They should be hidden from the road. Switching off the engine, he rested his hands on the wheel. "Not a sound."

"Yeah," Jake said uneasily. "That's weird, dude. Not even a bird, man. It's quieter than a dead skunk."

Donnie slapped the side of his neck. "Well, there're enough insects. Plenty of those. Come on, let's get moving."

Jake grabbed up the gun case with the two rifles. He surveyed the thick line of trees uneasily. "You know, maybe we should scout around before we set up camp."

"You mean start hunting now?" Donnie climbed from the truck and stretched out his arms. "I'm down with that!" Suddenly, he frowned. "Hey, did you just fart? That smells like death!"

Jake didn't smile. He jumped from the truck and sniffed the air. "Oh, yeah, I smell it. It's getting stronger. Dude, it reeks!"

Donnie suddenly went on alert. Through the silence, the sound of buzzing insects cut through like a chainsaw. Looking for the source, he spotted a swarm of black flies by the edge of the trees… where the horrid stench was coming from.

Donnie made sure to keep his voice level. "Uh, Jake, let's break out those rifles and take a look-see."

The boys were both dressed in black T-shirts and camouflage pants. Despite the heat, Donnie went to the truck's cab to grab a jacket matching his pants, which he pulled on. While he did this, Jake knelt with the gun case before him. Unzipping it, he pulled out the two bolt-action rifles.

"Should I load them?" he asked.

"Uh, yeah, duh. That would be smart." Donnie kept a lookout, watching the silent woods as his cousin loaded the weapons. Sweat beaded his forehead, and he felt his heart start to race. He had the sense that something watched him back.

Soon, the boys had the guns loaded and in hand.

"Okay, buddy," Donnie said coolly. "I'll take the lead. Follow behind, and whatever you do, don't point your rifle at my back!"

"Yeah, you got it." Jake's red face dripped with sweat. He'd left his hat in the back of the truck. He now regretted it.

The sun beat down from overhead, baking the boys as they slowly approached the buzzing swarm. The stench of death, blood, and rotting meat grew more potent in a grim greeting.

"What do you think it is?" Jake asked nervously.

"Probably a deer," Donnie answered. "Coyotes or something got it."

"Or maybe a bear?"

"Yeah, maybe a bear."

"Whatever it was, it sure spooked the animals, man. I don't even see or hear a squirrel!"

"Well, shut up then. Maybe we're the ones spooking them. Remember, not many people come around here."

Donnie snaked through the tall grass, nearing the tree line. Jake remained right behind him. The boys moved in a crouch, their rifles at the ready. The buzz of insects grew intense, and they saw a black swarm ten feet from them.

"Stop," Jake hissed. "I think there's something in there, man."

"Yeah, flies and a carcass. Dude, it's dead."

"No." The bigger boy put his hand on Donnie's shoulder. It trembled. "Don't you feel it? It's like something is watching us."

"You watch too many horror movies, dude." Donnie took a step forward and then froze. He felt it, too.

A faint rustle came from the bushes to their left. He could've sworn he heard a growl.

Snapping his rifle to his shoulder, he aimed at the bushes.

"What is it?" Jake hissed.

Donnie relaxed. A warm breeze ruffled his short hair. "The wind, man. Come on, let's stop being wimps."

Rising to his full height, he stomped toward the swarm. Three feet away, he saw a clearing of matted, torn grass… in a pond of blood.

Raising a hand to his nose, he gagged. Staggering back, he waited to bump into Jake. He never did. Instead, he stumbled to a knee, catching his fall with the stock of his rifle.

"Jake, did you see that? Jake, it… it was a cow, man… mangled…" Donnie all at once turned his head and vomited. He only knew the species of the animal by the head lying amid the gore.

Coughing up more vomit, he turned his head to look for his cousin. He only saw tall grass. "Jake?" he called. "Jake, where are you?"

Donnie swallowed down panic. That was when he heard it. A low growl of a very large animal came from the bushes. Deep and gravelly, it sounded pure evil.

"J-Jake, are-are you there?"

"D-Donnie," Jake whimpered from behind him. "I-I saw some-something…"

Donnie felt his breath return. Jake hadn't vanished. He'd ducked down to hide in the tall grass only a few feet from him. "Yeah, I know. It's in the bushes. Let's head back to the truck."

"N-No…" Jake's voice quivered with terror. "I saw it at the truck."

Donnie felt his blood run cold. Still on a knee, he chambered a round in his rifle. "Jake," he said, trying to sound calm. "We're being hunted."

"Oh, sh—"

A savage roar unleashed from the bushes.

Donnie went to lift his rifle when a dark shape charged from the cow carcass. Eyes bulging, he tried to shift his aim when he froze. There were two of them!

His mouth fell open in a silent scream as the shape leaped on him, claws extended and mouth open. It was a monstrous fiend from the world of nightmares. Donnie barely got a look before it crashed into him. Pain exploded and everything went black. Just before it did, he was sure he spotted Jake's hat on the beast's head.

Chapter 9

Jake shot to his feet at the roar. Dropping his rifle, he took off in the tall grass in a panic. Behind him, he heard Donnie go down in a heap of grunts and thumps. *Please go after him*, he said, tears streaming down his face. *Let me be!*

At first, he thought his selfish prayer had been answered. He made it fifty yards when he heard heavy panting to his left.

Then, the grass rustled on his right, and a beast growled. Two of them now ran with him. There was one on either side of him, mocking him.

Jake couldn't take it any longer. He collapsed to his knees, blubbering. It was impossible! He was going to die. He could feel the hot breath on his neck, sharp teeth just above his head.

Grabbing grass stalks, he buried his face in the earth and tried not to scream. Warm wetness soaked the front of his pants, but he didn't even notice. What he had just seen had turned his brain into a quivering mush.

When looking back at the truck moments before, he'd spotted a man-wolf wearing coveralls standing in the back of the pickup. The thing had been massive, nearly seven feet tall.

Its upper body bulged with furry muscle, and its wolfish head carried a mouthful of sharpened teeth. The beast's pointed ears were pinned back, and its gleaming eyes had stared straight at Jake. It had run a long, black, pointed tongue over its black nose and had looked to be grinning.

That was when Jake had sunk to a shocked sitting position, abandoning Donnie. His cousin was now surely dead, and he would be next.

"Oh, please—"

Thunderous roars from all sides of him drowned out his prayer.

His screams soon joined them until they instantly cut off. The roars died. Silence descended once more. The cousins would not return that weekend.

In other news, a family in the Blue Island community received a new, used pickup truck that day, along with two brand-new bolt-action hunting rifles. They would not be driving the truck off the island any time soon—it wasn't quite registered in their name. The cell phones had been crushed and buried.

It was the island's way—defend The Pack, take what is useful, and destroy the rest. By nightfall, practically all evidence of the Brasco cousins ever being on the island was gone.

Skylar and Elliot had never met their great-grandmother or any member of their dad's family. Their dad had been born on Blue Island, but his mom took him to Grantham when he was just a baby, right after his father had died in a hunting accident.

"Did you ever want to go there to visit?" Skylar asked from the backseat of their minivan. They were on the way to the funeral.

Mr. Ashley grunted from the driver's seat. "Nope. My mom hated the island and made sure I never set foot near it.

Besides, I knew the island killed my dad. I didn't want any part of it. Just in case, though, my mom used to tell me all sorts of scary stories about the place. Then, one day, she stopped and never spoke about it again." He blew out his breath. "All I know is that my grandmother helped my mom leave that place. She bought the house for us to live in and would send my mom money every month. I owe her for that."

"Of course, dear," Mrs. Ashley said from the front seat. She'd put down the stack of papers she'd been trying to grade to listen. "You know, I'm like the kids. I never met a single member of your family. Not one showed up for the wedding."

"Yeah, well," Mr. Ashley said, tapping the steering wheel in agitation, "I didn't invite any."

"Not even great-grandma?" Skylar asked. "I bet she would've come."

"No, not even her," Mr. Ashley said curtly. He gripped the wheel tightly. Since being laid off, he'd grown a full beard and mustache. Both were neatly trimmed for the funeral, and his sandy blond hair sported a fresh haircut. Standing, he was just below six feet but had developed a soft middle while working as a project manager at an insurance company. That had since flattened out. Spending more time exercising and eating less between looking for a job, he put on lean muscle and carried his weight well. A lot of moms would give him looks when he dropped Elliot off at school.

Mrs. Ashley turned in her seat to look back at Skylar. "Your dad's mom passed away during his first year at college. Nobody from the island went to her funeral."

"But you did, Sweetie," Mr. Ashley said, managing a grin. "Meeting you my freshmen year is what got me through it all. I couldn't have done it without you."

"Nobody in her family went to the funeral?" Skylar asked in disbelief. "Sorry, Dad, but your mom's family sounds pretty rotten."

"You have to remember. She left the island and left her name behind by marrying my dad. She was a Raycroft. The Raycrofts were one of the original families that settled on the island." Mr. Ashley shrugged his broad shoulders. "It was like when she left, she was dead to them."

"But we're still going to your great-grandma's funeral," Skylar said. "That's cool. Do you think anybody will recognize you, Dad?"

"Not a chance," he muttered.

Mrs. Ashley, an older version of her daughter in looks, smiled and reached out to touch his arm. "We'll just pay our respects and be on our way."

Behind his mom's seat, Elliot listened with mild disinterest. Head against the window, he stared out at the flat land slowly turning into woods. The gas stations and shopping centers petered out, turning into farmland with shabby barns and decrepit houses. Then, the road entered thick woods. They hadn't seen a car on the road for miles. The funeral was being held at the Church of Grantham Saints, the closest church to the island. The nearer the minivan approached the church, the farther away it got from civilization. It was like going into a time machine, a trip to the past.

For some reason, Elliot's heart started beating faster. He didn't know if it was nerves about attending his first funeral or about the baseball practice afterward.

The Ashley family never attended Sylvia Raycroft's funeral.

Chapter 10

When Mr. Ashley pulled the minivan into the graveled parking lot, he slammed the brakes, and the van jolted to a sudden stop.

"Um," Elliot said, his first words since the van left their driveway, "guys, did I really have to wear a suit?" He stared with raised eyebrows at the crowd gathering in front of the church.

"Yes, kiddo, I—" Mrs. Ashley looked up from a paper she'd been hastily trying to finish grading and gave a start. "You know, maybe we are a tad bit overdressed."

"You think?" Skylar said, looking in horrified wonder. "Are we at a funeral or a slumber party for the middle-aged midlife crisis convention?"

Mr. Ashley just ran a tongue across his mustache and had no words.

"You better move, Doug," his wife said, slightly nervous. "They're looking this way."

The church was a white clapboard structure with a peaked roof. A bell tower rose from the center, but it curiously lacked a cross and resembled more of an old-fashioned schoolhouse than a place of worship. Of course, this could be an image created by the people assembling at the steps and making their way through the parking lot.

The Ashley family—the males wearing suits and females dressed in conservative black dresses—definitely seemed overdressed.

Three brick steps led to the church's front doors, which were currently being taken over by a trio of beefy men looking like wrestlers on their day off.

Built like a snowman, the man on the top step crossed his thick arms over his massive chest. His back propped the door open, but his round torso threatened to block the entrance. He wore super baggy gray sweatpants and a black leather vest with no shirt. Tufts of dark hair sprouted from the top of the vest, nearly blending in with his beard. All his hair was below his bald dome.

A step below stood another man, tall and thin, like a scarecrow. With a greasy blond mullet, his long, lean face appeared wolfish. Even from the van, the family could see a sneer spread across his unshaven face. He wore ripped blue jeans and a jean jacket opened in the front to show off his bare chest. On the bottom step, the shortest of the three was picking his nose. Plump and grizzled, with wispy gray hair hanging from his egg-shaped head, he at least had an undershirt. He just didn't wear anything over it. Under his dirty T-shirt, he wore faded flannel pajama pants.

"Those must be the bouncers," Skylar joked, prompting her mom to give her a stern look.

"Skylar, just what do you know about bouncers?"

"Movies, Mom. Calm down."

The other attendees of the funeral were dressed no better. Men and women had the same dress code. Sweatpants were popular, and many sported bandanas in their hair. These were not farmers or country folk. They walked like predators as if they owned the place. Many gave the van sneers of disdain.

Elliot shifted in his seat to face his sister. "Sky," he hissed. "Isn't that Teddy?"

Skylar gasped and stared at where her brother pointed.

"Who's Teddy?" Mrs. Ashley asked.

"Nobody," Skylar said quickly. She kicked Elliot in the ankle and mouthed for him to shut his mouth.

"Ouch!" Elliot yelped. He glared at his sister but said no more.

Skylar ignored him. Her mouth was in her throat. It was indeed Teddy Malone. Looking out of place in a blue dress shirt and tie, he stood talking with a hulking teen wearing jean overalls. His light brown skin and dark curly hair made him easily recognizable. *What was he doing there?*

"You two settle," Mr. Ashley said. "Coming here may have been a mistake."

A hulking man with curly iron-gray hair down past his shoulders started approaching the van. He wore black leather pants and a matching vest over a dirty T-shirt. He also wore a snarl of hatred, which he directed at the driver-side window.

"You don't think somebody recognizes you, do you?" Mrs. Ashley said uneasily.

"I doubt it," Mr. Ashley grunted. "Okay, gang, that's enough. Maybe we don't need to attend the funeral after all."

"Doug, just step on it and get us out of here."

Mr. Ashley nodded but had a hard time following the advice. The small parking lot was packed with pickups and hunting ATVs. People were streaming toward the church, not giving way to the van. Slowly, he backed from the approaching man. As the back tires reached the pavement, he swung the wheel hard, turning the van back toward home. Then he hit the gas.

"Let's say we stop for lunch and remember great-grandmother over some burgers," he said lightly. "Sound like a plan?"

Nobody had objections.

The lone waitress of Ma's Diner watched the well-dressed family enter the tiny restaurant in fascination. She nearly swallowed her thick wad of bubble gum as she hastily stood from the back table. After smoothing down her stained apron, she brushed back her once red hair, now mostly white.

"Well, I'll be," she said. "Y'all have to be 'bout the cutest family this place has ever seen!"

Mr. Ashley smiled tightly as he stood before his family, surveying the mostly empty diner.

Located on the corner of Raycroft Road, the only access to Blue Island, where it met Route 18, the main road leading to Grantham, the diner was the first respectable restaurant they came across. Painted white with red trim, it appeared welcoming. More importantly, it didn't have any strangely dressed people leering in the parking lot. They were about the only customers. Besides their van, a few pickups dotted the small parking lot.

Inside, small square tables were in the middle, with booths on the right side and back wall. To the left was a counter separating the eating area from the kitchen. A few men dressed as farmers—flannel shirts and faded blue jeans—sat over plates of eggs and grits. Covered plates of cookies, pies, and donuts lined the counter in front of them. Country music wafted from the kitchen. Everything looked clean and normal. He let out his breath.

"Come on, kids," he said, reaching up to loosen his tie. "Go find us a seat."

"Go pick out a booth," Mrs. Ashley said from behind Skylar and Elliot. She smoothed back Elliot's hair. He'd left his suit jacket in the van but still stood out with his black tie and white dress shirt tucked in his gray slacks. "She is right, you do look cute. But we need to eat fast to make it on time for baseball this afternoon."

Skylar gave her brother a sympathetic look. She knew he dreaded baseball practice. Smoothing down her black dress, she bumped his backside with her knee. "Maybe you'll get food poisoning here and can't go," she whispered.

Elliot paid her no mind; he was lost in a game on his phone and never looked up.

"Y'all do know it's a day early for Sunday's brunch," the waitress said, moving to greet them.

Mr. Ashley chuckled awkwardly. "Yeah, well, we'll do with Saturday lunch. You must be Ma."

The waitress lifted her eyebrows and she stopped midstride. "I'm not your ma, honey. This place here is owned by Frank Dickens. I just take your orders."

Mr. Ashley turned red, and he loosened his tie more. "Oh, er, sorry."

The waitress grinned wide to reveal surprisingly white teeth. An older woman north of sixty, she wore a plain blue dress with a rumpled collar under her smudged apron. Wrinkles lined her eyes and mouth, but her deep blue eyes sparked with life. With a straight spine, her body looked as fit as an athlete. She brushed back strands of her white hair coming loose from a pulled-back bun.

"Don't be," she said in a friendly way. "You're welcome here! You have some cute kids, you do. Dressed up real nice. My name is Erma Jenkins, but call me Erma. Y'all wait right there, and I'll grab some menus." She moved toward the counter with a spry step.

Skylar nudged her brother's shoulder toward the closest booth. She couldn't get her mind off seeing Teddy Malone at the church.

Elliot was still engrossed in his game as he slid into a seat. Skylar followed, bumping his hip.

"Why do you think Teddy was there?" she whispered close to his ear.

"He's your boyfriend. Ask him," Elliot muttered back, intent on his game.

"He's not really," Skylar admitted. "Yet." Then she elbowed Elliot in the arm. "Whatever you do, don't tell Mom or Dad about him. Got it?"

Elliot winced and gave her a dirty look. "You totally messed me up."

"Good. I'll do worse if you tell."

Elliot rolled his eyes as he went back to his game.

Mrs. Ashley gave her children an odd glance as she slid into the seat across from them. She still had a small pile of papers to grade that she'd carried with her. "You two look a little secretive," she said.

"We're just glad to be away from that church," Elliot said, putting down his phone and glancing at Skylar.

"Yeah, real glad," Skylar added quickly.

Mr. Ashley took the menus from Erma and sat across from Skylar. "We're actually coming from a funeral," he explained as the waitress raised her eyebrows.

Erma's cheeks went ashen, and her country accent faltered. "Hold on. You-you don't mean the witch's funeral, the Raycroft woman?"

Mr. Ashley stared up at her in surprise. "Excuse me?"

Mrs. Ashley put a hand on her husband's shoulder. "As a matter of fact, yes," she said. "Only we never really got past the parking lot."

Erma crouched low over the table. She spoke in a hushed tone. "You did good taking your children away from that place. Those people are no good. They live out on Blue Island and have their own way of life. A spooky way of life. You know why they had to gather at that church so far from the island? Because the last church on the island closed near sixty years ago."

"They did dress… interestingly for the funeral," Mrs. Ashley said carefully. "Like they hadn't been to church in some time."

Erma nodded gravely. "That they have not. There are some real spooky stories about them people. You keep away from that island."

Skylar spoke up. "Are—are all people from there… bad?"

"No, not all, but most. And those gathered at the church today would be the worst."

"What about the, uh, Raycroft woman?" Mr. Ashley asked. "You don't seem to think much of her."

Erma rose to her full height. "I'll never speak ill about a soul, especially one now dead. But Sylvia Raycroft was the leader of them. Some said she had powers and stuff. She was the matriarch of Blue Island. That's what today's church gathering is mostly about. It's more of a meeting to see who takes her place than a funeral. All decent folk on the island will steer far away from that."

Mr. Ashley grunted. "Well, you certainly seem to know a lot about that place."

"So I should," Erma said, now chewing her gum furiously. "When you're the waitress at the best place to eat in town, you hear everything." She took a breath, and her country accent returned. "Now, what can I get y'all to eat?"

On their way out, Erma stopped the family and asked if she could take a picture of them with her phone. "We never had such a nice-looking family come here and visit," she explained sweetly.

Thinking nothing of it, full of delicious burgers and fries, the family agreed.

As soon as the van left the diner, Erma made a phone call.

Back on the steps of the Church of Grantham Saints, Morgan Raycroft waited impatiently for her brother to finish the call.

She'd just finished giving an emotional speech about uniting the Blue Island community and finding ways to advance the island to a better future. The thunderous applause when she'd finished let her know she would indeed take the place of Sylvia Raycroft. She would lead The Pack and control Blue Island. A surge of hope swelled in her chest. Her plans and dreams would come true just in time to save her son.

"That was Erma from the diner," her brother Kenton said, lowering his phone. "You were right. That lost minivan earlier? That was our sister's family, all right. Doug Ashley is his name, and he lives back in Grantham."

Morgan felt a smile spread across her face. "Well, well, well," she muttered. "My nephew never stopped to say hello. Perhaps I should make a visit to him." She glanced at her massive brother, who looked positively stupid in his sweatpants and leather vest. "What did Erma learn about him? Tell me everything."

"Well, he's got two kids, a girl and a boy. His wife is a schoolteacher."

"And?"

"She says they're all nice-looking... cute kids, attractive wife, like Minnie. She'll be sending a picture of them any minute."

Morgan bit back her exasperation. Morgan was the youngest of the Raycroft siblings. Kenton was the middle child, with their brother Razor between him and Morgan. Razor had left the family to live with The Pack and was the only sibling not at the church—his wolf form would not allow it. Their elder brother Ryan was busy serving as the funeral director. The fool had actually loved their mother. She wished he was out here now. Working with Kenton was like working with unfinished clay—fat, lumpy, and never did quite what she wanted. There should be a fifth sibling, an eldest sister, but she'd run off after abandoning her family. And now… her son had returned. How interesting.

"And what else? Come on, Erma is the queen of gossip. I know she gleaned more than that!"

"Well, uh, she said they had to leave in a rush because the boy has baseball practice this afternoon."

"Now that's more like it." Morgan rubbed her hands together in glee. "Go get Moe and Stan out here. And when you get that picture, send it to me."

"Wh-what are you going to do?" Kenton asked, confused. He was only partially turned but still had the brains of a simple animal. He was all muscle, but he was at least loyal.

"Moe and Stan are going to take me to a baseball practice to see my long-lost family. You, brother, will stay here and make sure everything goes smoothly. The last of the putrid speeches honoring my poor mother should be finishing soon. You and Ryan make sure the dead witch gets buried!"

Chapter 11

Behind Lincoln Elementary, the Little League Rangers gathered for their first practice, led by Mrs. Ashley. It had been her husband's idea.

Skylar had constantly complained about how their mom spent more time with her classroom students than her own kids. Of course, she didn't need her mom hovering over her, but Elliot was different. After he lost his friend Tucker, he'd withdrawn into a shell of himself. Since the move to Grantham, he'd yet to make new friends. His tenth birthday in April went by without a big party. He spent most of his time playing video games or painting figurines of monsters—a hobby that started when he got a set from his dad on his tenth birthday. That was when Skylar'd had enough. He, Skylar said, needed his mom. Their mom entirely agreed, but her schedule at school and the extra travel gave her so little time…

When Mr. Ashley signed Elliot up for summer baseball, he was told he couldn't play unless they found a coach. Being new to the area, none of the other teams picked Elliot. A new team could only be formed if a parent stepped up as coach. Mr.

Ashley would be too busy hunting for a job, but he knew the perfect candidate. Surprisingly, his wife enthusiastically agreed when told the news at dinner that night. Elliot had looked stricken.

Now, at practice, the same stricken look returned. Shoulders hunched, he stood last in line as his mom stood between home and the pitcher's mound. Wearing white baseball pants and a blue T-shirt, he had his Rangers cap jammed tightly over his head. Its bill hid his eyes. His mom had never coached any sport before and didn't know much about baseball. On the way home from the diner, she'd peppered Mr. Ashley for any and all baseball advice. He'd answered the best he could but only confused her more. "What's a bunt again?" she'd asked when they'd pulled into their driveway. To make matters worse, Elliot was convinced he was the worst player on the team.

Surprisingly, practice started well. After introducing herself, Mrs. Ashley acknowledged she was Elliot's mom but already knew a few other players on the team.

"That's right, you do!" cried a tall boy, two players to Elliot's right. "Mrs. A is, like, the best teacher in our school!"

"Bobby," Mrs. Ashley said coolly. "It's rude to interrupt. But I am glad you made the long drive to join our team."

Elliot jerked his head up. He lifted the brim of his hat to glance at the boy. His eyes flickered in recognition.

Grinning, Bobby doffed his hat at Mrs. Ashley, giving a slight bow. With light brown skin, he had a square face with short dark brown hair, and an easy smile. With the lean build of an athlete, his shoulders were already broadening. He wore black sweatpants and a plain white T-shirt and looked good, like a real ballplayer. Seeing Elliot's gaze, he gave him a wink.

Elliot quickly ducked his head back down. Of course! Now it made sense why his mom agreed to coach his team. It was just another way for her to help her precious students. He recognized Bobby from his old school but never knew him. Bobby had moved to Whitney that fall. Being in his mom's class, Elliot had almost no contact with him. A new fear gripped Elliot's heart. Did Bobby know about his past baseball experience, or worse, would he tell his teammates about the embarrassing video? He knew it had been taken down from the internet the same day it'd gone up, and by the end of the month, everyone had forgotten about it. But still… he was sure some kids had downloaded it. Elliot felt like he'd been gut-punched. How could his mom do this to him?

Soon after, Mrs. Ashley had each kid introduce themselves and say what position they wanted to play. Elliot barely listened. When his turn came, he said his name and muttered he usually played right field. He was relieved when Bobby and the others gave no reaction.

Then, the kids were told to pair up and start warmup tosses. Elliot partnered with the kid next to him in line, Branson or something. Slightly chubby, the kid looked lost. He wore faded jeans and a green T-shirt much too large for him. His glove looked to have been given to him back in kindergarten. Small and stiff, it barely fit over his hand and was more like an oven mitt.

"I'm new at this," he confessed to Elliot as the two went to grab a ball from a bucket by home. It sounded like an apology, and he kept removing his hat and putting it back on.

Elliot soon saw why. His name was Brandon, and he was one kid more nervous than Elliot. He looked miserable as the boys set up in the outfield with the others. The team formed two lines facing each other. Brandon started with the ball, and his first throw sailed four feet to Elliot's right.

"Watch it!" Bobby yelled, dodging the toss while fielding a hard throw from his partner. "I can only catch one at a time!" He sounded more amused than angry.

"Sorry!" Brandon said, ducking his head. "It slipped!"

Elliot trotted to retrieve the ball. Returning to the line, he threw a light toss to Brandon, who dodged it and missed it by two feet.

"Man, sorry," Brandon muttered. Taking off his hat, he dashed for the ball.

"Hey, it's okay," Elliot told him when he returned. "Just, like, relax and look at where you throw."

Brandon nodded and threw the next one in the grass. It bounced three feet in front of Elliot, and he stopped it from going farther by putting his right foot out. It nailed him in the shin.

"Ouch!" he yipped.

"Oh, man, I'm so sorry!" Brandon said, covering his face with his glove.

"It's okay, really," Elliot told him. "Hey, come closer. Open your glove up and let the ball hit it before closing."

Brandon listened and surprised himself by catching Elliot's next toss.

"Great!" Elliot told him. "Okay, so when you throw it back, aim with your glove and, like, keep your eyes on the target. Throw at my glove, but not too hard."

Brandon nodded and managed to get the ball close enough for Elliot to snatch it with his glove.

"Thanks, Elliot," Brandon cried, sounding excited for the first time.

Looking around, Elliot was shocked that they were not the only pair having trouble throwing. Other kids were playing fetch, too. He realized that while he wasn't the best on the team, he certainly wasn't the worst.

After a few more throws, his mom had the pairs switch, and Elliot found himself across from Bobby. Bobby was the opposite of Brandon. He moved lightly and wasted little motion. With smooth throws and slick-fielding, he had Elliot sweating as the two developed a rhythm of catch and throw.

"Hey, man, you got good aim," Bobby told him after catching a hard toss. "Let's step back some and keep it going!"

Soon, the two were trading darts, and Elliot couldn't help but feel good. If Bobby recognized him from Leewood Elementary, he never admitted it. Elliot's fears melted as he focused on the game of catch.

"Okay, team!" his mom called from where she was watching the throwing from the pitcher's mound. "Let's gather around and start a scrimmage. No pressure, of course, but let's see how well you guys know this game. Everybody hits. Let's go!"

Elliot immediately felt his stomach clench up. Throwing was one thing, but batting was not his strength. His dad said he just lacked confidence. Elliot just thought he didn't want to get nailed by the ball, something that had happened to him more than once.

"Bobby's dad, Coach Garcia, will pitch," his mom announced as the players trotted to the infield. "Line up, and I'll give you your positions!"

Soon, Elliot sat in the dugout, watching Brandon go up to bat. The team had sixteen boys, so they played eight on eight, with Coach Garcia being the pitcher for both sides. Bobby's dad had features similar to his son's but with a compact build. His biceps were huge under his gray shirt. Grinning widely, he offered encouragement as Brandon settled at the plate.

"Not too close to the plate, son," he said. "I'll pitch some slow ones to warm up, so be ready."

Nodding furiously, Brandon took his stance standing straight up with the bat resting on his shoulder. He swung wildly and missed the first pitch. After some coaching from Coach Garcia, he widened his stance, bent his knees, and choked up on the bat. The next pitch went right down the middle. Brandon swung wildly but managed to send the ball skittering toward third base.

"Yes!" Brandon cried, amazed. "I did it!"

"Yes, you did!!" Mrs. Ashley yelled from where she coached first base. "Now run! Get to first!"

The third baseman missed fielding the slow roller on the first attempt, and by the time he grabbed the ball, Brandon was proudly standing on first.

"Just throw it to the pitcher," Bobby called from where he played first base. "Eat it."

Elliot felt his heart sink. He'd secretly hoped Brandon would've struck out. Then he wouldn't feel so dumb when he did the same.

The next hitter went to bat, leaving Elliot waiting to hit. Getting a batting helmet and bat, he strode to the on-deck area next to the dugout behind the fence.

Instead of watching the pitcher, he watched Bobby playing first. He and his mom seemed to have a good relationship. Both were telling Brandon how to lead off of first without going too far.

Elliot rested the bat on his shoulder and never did a practice swing as he watched. His mom suddenly seemed a baseball expert… but what did she know about her own son? She seemed closer to her student than him.

The sharp ping of the metal bat striking the ball snapped him back to the game. The batter hit a sharp grounder that reached the outfield. By the time Elliot went to bat, there were runners on second and third. Brandon gave him two thumbs-up. "Hit me home, Elliot!" he called.

Elliot just took deep breaths and fought to keep the grip on his bat. He could feel his heart pounding.

"Easy out," he heard the catcher say.

"Quiet back there," Coach Garcia said. He gave Elliot a friendly grin. "Relax, buddy. Loosen your grip. You're a small kid. Bend low and make me throw a strike."

Nodding, Elliot crouched and tried to remember what his dad told him. *Watch the ball before its release and wait for the pitch to come to you. Don't go hunting for the bad ones. Keep your head down at contact.* Hearing his dad's voice calmed him.

The first pitch seemed a little outside, and he held his swing.

"Good eye," Coach Garcia called. "A little outside."

"Strike," muttered the catcher.

Elliot gave him no mind. He crouched again and poised his bat at his shoulder.

"Come on, Elliot!" his mom called. "You got this!"

The next pitch went right down the middle. Swinging a tad late, he managed to make contact and sent a grounder bouncing toward second base.

"Great hit!" his mom yelled. "Yes!"

Dropping the bat, Elliot raced for first. The second baseman grabbed the ball and froze. With Brandon running home and the runner on second going for third, he wasn't sure where to throw.

"Just throw it here!" Bobby yelled.

It was too late. The boy finally fired the ball to Bobby, and Elliot beat the throw by a step. He was safe with an RBI single.

"I knew you could do it!" his mom said when he stood on the bag. "I knew it!" She reached her arms around his shoulders and hugged his chest, pulling him close to her. "Way to make the coach look like she knows what she's doing," she said.

"Okay, okay, Mom," he said, embarrassed but proud at the same time. "I, like, got it."

She released him and pushed him off first. "Of course you do. Your dad and I are proud of you, Elliot." She smacked the rear of his pants. "You're my boy. Now, take your lead. Just don't go too far."

Elliot wiped his batting gloves on the sides of his pants, feeling his face go warm. He realized Bobby stood right next to him, listening to everything his mom said.

Bobby nudged his arm with his glove. "Hey, man, your mom, she's all right. But next time you're out."

"Uh, yeah," Elliot said, cracking a smile. It was amazing. His team didn't hate him, and he actually knew what he was doing. The dreaded baseball practice was becoming fun.

Taking his lead, he widened his stance and bent low, watching the pitcher. As he did, he suddenly straightened.

Beyond Coach Garcia, he spotted two roughly dressed figures. They stood outside the fence between home and third and were joined by a woman. She wore a black leather jacket and tight black jeans. All three were watching him.

Elliot felt his legs start to buckle. The burger and fries from Ma's Diner gurgled in his stomach and threatened to upchuck. He recognized the two men from the funeral—the tall scarecrow guy with a mullet and his shorter egghead companion with wispy hair. Both still wore their rough outfits. The woman between the men stared back at Elliot, meeting his eyes. She appeared older than Elliot's mom but still youthful. Dark eyeshadow gave her a menacing gaze made worse by a leering smile.

Smiling at Elliot, she gave a slow nod.

Elliot felt his heart skip a beat. Chills race down his spine. He broke his gaze away just in time to see the ball slap into Bobby's glove. So engrossed by the three strangers, he'd stopped paying attention to the pitcher. Seeing Elliot distracted, Coach Garcia had calmly thrown to his son for an easy pick-off.

"Guess what?" Bobby said, smiling. He slapped his glove against Elliot's rump. "You're out."

"Got to pay attention, buddy," Coach Garcia said, sounding disappointed.

"Oh, no. Ellie, that's my bad," his mom said, her voice covering a groan. "I should've warned you!"

"Ellie?" Bobby said, lifting his eyebrows as he tossed the ball back to his dad. "Nice nickname, dude."

Elliot barely heard them. As he walked off first, he took off his batting helmet and brushed back his sweaty hair. Doing so, he snuck a glance toward third. The fence was now empty of spectators. The strange trio had vanished. Shortly after, he heard the roar of motorcycles from the parking lot. They sounded like booming thunder on a bright, sunny day.

Chapter 12

"Eight… nine… ten!" Tucker gasped with relief and lowered the ten-pound weights off his shoulders. He'd been working on his biceps and felt the burn. "Arrghh!" he cried out in triumph.

"You okay in there?" his mom asked from the other side of his door. She'd just returned from her job working as a bank teller. "Sounds like you're in pain."

"I'm fine, Mom!" he shouted. "I'm just doing my exercises."

"Sounds like you're on the toilet," Maria's voice said in disdain.

"Not funny, Maria," Tucker said, sucking in air. His curls were damp with sweat, and some dripped on his nose. "Don't you have a tea party to get ready for?" It was a cheap shot, but it had its desired effect. He heard his sister's small feet stomping away.

His door opened, and his mom poked in her head. She was short and a little stout but had a youthful, attractive face.

At the moment, it looked confused. "What's this about a tea party?" she asked.

"Oh, nothing," Tucker said hastily. "I was just, like, messing with her. Just a joke."

"Well, instead of being mean to your sister, have you considered inviting her to exercise with you?"

Tucker pressed his lips tightly and gave his mom a mournful look. "Mom, really? I'd rather ask Phileo than her!" He instantly regretted his words as soon as they left his mouth.

"Oh, that's a great idea! Maybe I can call his mother—"

"Mom, no!" he cried. "I was kidding. Maria would be a great partner! Besides, Phileo is, um, allergic. Yeah, he can't be around… metal. The weights will give him hives."

"Okay, okay, I understand." His mom sighed. "I just want to see you with friends, Tucker. I know you've been through some pain."

"Mom, I'm fine, really! I just… I just need some time alone. Really."

"Okay, then I'll leave you to it. Just don't drop anything on your foot."

"Yes, Mom," Tucker said, rolling his eyes.

The ten-pound weights were his heaviest equipment, and they were from his older sister. She had stopped using them when she left for college. At his age, he couldn't use any heavy weights. He learned all this from Elliot. The two had started exercising together back in the third grade after some kids at recess teased Tucker for being a fat roly-poly and Elliot for being a puny twig. The boys started with push-ups, sit-ups, and squats and gradually added stretching, planking, and light weights. At first, their goal had been to do the same number of reps as their age for each set, but they had since increased the number of reps.

Then came the terrible cooking contest, and Elliot was no longer welcome in his house. Tucker had stopped doing the exercises, and this was his first time since. It actually felt good, really good. He did miss joking around with Elliot and competing to see who could plank the longest, which involved positioning your body over the floor while balancing on your toes and forearms. Elliot had always won, but Tucker had been getting close. It wasn't the same exercising alone.

With his mom gone, Tucker put down the weights and wiped the sweat from his brow. He wore black shorts and a matching tank top decorated with his favorite YouTuber's logo, a gift from Elliot on his tenth birthday. Thinking about it, he felt a ping of hurt, remembering Elliot's birthday had been just a couple of weeks before. The two had always celebrated their birthdays together.

Moving to his bed, he picked up his phone and, for the first time in months, activated the SafeFam App. Last summer, he and Elliot had added the app to their phones and had their parents set it so each phone tracked the other phone. The app was supposed to be for parents to keep track of their kids secretly, but the friends had used it to always know they had a best friend nearby. He was relieved to see the app still working and tracking Elliot's phone, even if in another county.

"Okay, big brother," Maria announced at the door. "I heard you tell Mom I can exercise with you."

Dropping his phone as if it burned, he whirled to the door. "Huh, what? No way, I did not!"

Maria stood with his hands on her hips, dressed in her swimsuit with running shorts and wearing sweatbands on her wrists and ankles.

"You did, too," she cried. "You said you wanted me instead of your weirdo Philly friend! I heard you."

Tucker made to argue but knew it was useless. Besides, he could use some company. "Fine," he huffed. "Let's start with some push-ups."

"You do the push-ups," his sister said. "I'll keep count. You better do at least twenty, or I'm telling Mom you're going to a tea party."

Tucker glared at her and then let out a laugh. "Okay, fine. But if you do, I'll tell her who he really invited."

"Tea party with Phileo," Maria said, pretending to swoon. "What more can a girl want?"

Tucker laughed harder. "Yeah, okay, okay, count my push-ups, but don't lose count."

"You know, Tucker, you need some music first."

Tucker shrugged. "I always let Elliot pick the song."

"Well, today, you're letting your super smart, super cool little sister pick."

"Yeah, fine," Tucker grumbled. "I'll let my super humble little sister pick the song."

"Yes!" Maria danced over to Tucker's bed to get his phone and activate the speaker on his nightstand.

And that was how Tucker found himself doing push-ups to a Taylor Swift song while being berated by his sister, who'd turned into a mini drill sergeant.

"That wasn't all the way down, Tucker!" Maria yelled. "That's only three!"

"That was five!" Tucker complained. He strained to do another push-up without smashing his nose into his carpet.

"Three!"

"But I just did another!"

"You need to go all the way down. Three!"

Tucker collapsed on the floor with a groan. "Elliot… phone home," he murmured.

Elliot returned home from baseball sweaty and exhausted. The running drills at the end nearly caused him to barf.

As his mom parked the van in the driveway, she couldn't stop talking about how well practice had gone.

"I really think I can do this," she gushed. "I even know what situational play is! You always go for the easy out unless you're trying to hold the lead, and then... Well, I'm getting closer to knowing what it is."

Elliot wearily scooted from the backseat and opened the side door. Before exiting, he paused and looked over at his mom. "Mom, you signed up Bobby on our team, right?"

"Yes, kiddo, I did. And a few other kids, but they didn't show. Maybe next time." She turned in her seat to face him. "I hope you don't mind. You're always my son, but those boys need something to enjoy and somebody to believe in them."

"No, I don't mind. Bobby is cool. I just... do you ever check on Tucker?"

Mrs. Ashley sucked in her breath and paused a moment. "Honey, you know he's being homeschooled. I don't see him in school."

"Yeah, yeah, I know... I was just, like, wondering how he was doing."

"Yes, I know... You and he were so close. I'm so sorry about what happened. Just remember. You didn't do anything on purpose, it's just sometimes things don't go our way. Okay, kiddo?"

"Yeah, okay, Mom."

"Now get in there and go straight to the shower. Boy, do you smell! And don't forget. You and Sky are fending for yourselves tonight! Your dad and I are going on a date." She winked at him. "So I can learn more baseball strategies over a nice dinner."

Elliot trudged into the house and dropped his baseball bag with his gear just inside the front door. He then dragged himself up the stairs. He'd never mentioned the strangers at practice to his mom. He didn't want to worry her and wondered if he'd just made it all up. Maybe they were three parents watching a baseball practice? But that woman had stared straight at him and the men… they were definitely from the funeral.

"How did it go?" Skylar asked him in a greeting at the top of the stairs.

"Great. I got a hit and made no errors."

"I mean with Mom coaching, dog-breath."

"Oh, yeah. She did, like, pretty good."

"Well, that's some good news. Hey, speaking of dog-breath, have you ever considered using deodorant? You stink."

"You're so funny, snothead," Elliot mumbled, stumbling past her and into the bathroom.

"Hey, I was being serious!"

He shut the door in her face.

Staring in the mirror, Elliot brushed his hair from his eyes and heaved a deep sigh of relief. His mom had done a pretty good job of coaching. And he played decent. The only thing missing was Tucker. On a day like this, he would immediately text his best friend, no matter how tired he felt. Better yet, his best friend would've been on the team with him. Instead, he tiredly got undressed for a hot shower to soothe his sore body and sore feelings.

As he tugged off his shirt, he heard his dad call from below that he was out the door with their mom. "We'll be back late!"

Elliot didn't mind. That meant frozen pizza and a movie. He soon stood in the tub just outside the range of the showerhead, waiting for the water to warm up. The day had been hot, but after sweating during practice and sitting in the air-conditioned van for the ride home, he felt chilled.

Finally, the water warmed, and he stepped under, letting it hit his face and pour down his shoulders. After a long, stressful day, the shower felt like a blast of heaven. He stayed in that position for a good minute before he heard a loud rustling move past the door. It almost sounded like a dog panting, and he wondered what his sister could be doing to be so loud. Then he found out. Suddenly, the hot water switched to icy, and he screeched, jumping back. His right foot slipped from under him. He slammed his back into the tile wall, sliding to a painful sitting position. The freezing water poured over his lap, causing him to gasp in surprise and pain.

"Sky!" he yelled. "Turn the hot water back on!"

The first week after moving into the house, his father showed Skylar and him where the knob was for the hot water for the shower—in a small cabinet just on the other side of the wall of the tub. More to Skylar, he threatened to turn off the hot water for any long showers. Elliot had only been in for, like, two minutes!

"Come on, Skylar!" He got painfully to his feet and yanked back the shower curtain. "I'll tell Mom and Dad!"

A low growl came from the other side of the door, and he heard the loud panting again. Then something sharp clicked against the door, tapping and scraping like claws against the wood.

Elliot sucked in his breath and dared not breathe out. His knees trembled. "Skylar?" he asked, nearly choking. "Is that you?"

The clicking on the door stopped, and the panting went away. The icy water remained.

"It's just Skylar," Elliot told himself, taking deep breaths. "She's just, like, trying to scare me." And she did a good job of it.

Squeezing his eyes shut, he ducked under the icy water. At least it felt good against his bruised body...

Using the freezing water as little as possible, he completed a quick shower, screaming when doing the final rinse. Minutes later, he slipped out the bathroom door with his hair dripping and water droplets still on his arms. Wearing his boxers, he'd tugged on a T-shirt and now struggled to step into his pajama pants, fighting to pull them over his wet skin.

"Skylar," he whispered. "You are, like, in so much trouble."

His sister's door was closed but unlocked. Barging in, Elliot found his sister lying on her bed with her back to him. Wearing earbuds, she was jamming to a love song Elliot could still hear from the doorway while checking her phone.

"Hey, Skylar!" he yelled. "Why'd you shut off the hot water?"

Whirling with a start, Skylar saw him and sat up quickly, hiding her phone behind her. "Elliot!" she snapped. "You can't barge in my room! Knock! Now go get dry. You're still soaking, and you have soap on your ear!"

"That's because you turned off the hot water!" Elliot accused. "I, like, froze my butt off! And fell in the shower!"

"I did not!" Skylar said, looking surprised. "I was here the whole time."

"You're totally lying! I heard you!"

Skylar shot from her bed and glared down at her brother. "You barge into my room and now call me a liar? Listen, barf-face. I was in my room the whole time… I was texting Teddy. So I couldn't have turned off the hot water."

Elliot did not look convinced. He put his hands on his hips and instantly grimaced. "Then what caused this?" he asked. Turning his back to his sister, he pulled up his shirt and lowered the waistband of his pants, showing a dark bruise forming just above his tailbone. "That's where I fell."

"Ouch, Elliot," Skylar said, wincing. "But it wasn't me. The hot water probably just broke or something."

Elliot shook his head as he straightened. "But I heard you. You, like, sounded like a giant dog or something. You were, like, even scraping the door with your nails!"

Skylar's eyes widened. "What?"

"It was—"

A loud thump came from Elliot's room, just down the hall to Elliot's left. It sounded like something heavy had fallen.

The siblings instantly went still and eyed each other in shock. Then Elliot rushed to Skylar's side. Without thinking, she threw her arms around his back and pulled him tight.

"Wh-what exactly did you hear?" she asked.

"Okay, it, um, sounded like a really, really big dog... I heard it, like, panting. I thought it was you."

Skylar looked down at him in disbelief. "You thought that was me? Really?" She then grew serious. "Come on. Let's check this out."

"Okay... but what is it? I mean, what do you think it could be?"

Skylar released her brother. "That is what we're going to find out. But let's make sure we're prepared for the worst."

Moments later, Skylar exited her room first, holding a metal softball bat in front of her like a sword. Elliot followed right behind her. He clutched a field hockey stick in front of him with both hands.

"Is, is our house, like, haunted?" he whispered.

"Maybe it was just something in your room falling. Let's check the hot water first. To see if it was really turned off."

She didn't admit it, but she didn't want to go to Elliot's room. Whatever made that thump had sounded huge. Could there be an intruder in the house? She had her phone in her hip pocket and debated whether to call the police. Not until she had proof. This was her house, and she was in charge. She headed for the cabinet by the bathroom and saw the door cracked open.

"Oh, no," she groaned. Kneeling and putting down the bat, her worst fears came true. Elliot had been telling the truth.

The hot water was totally turned off. Somebody was, or had been, in the house with them.

Elliot kept his eye on the hall toward his room as his sister turned the knob back on. The hockey stick in his hands started to shake.

"What if it's still here?" he hissed.

"It could be Dad playing a prank on us," Skylar reasoned. "Maybe he only pretended to leave, turned off the hot water, and then really left." Not even she believed herself.

"Yeah, should we call him?"

"Not yet. Come on."

Taking deep breaths, she picked up her bat and slowly crept to Elliot's room. Elliot followed a step behind.

The house's second floor was shaped like a horseshoe with the stairs in the middle. The bathroom was near the stairs in the front of the house. Their parents slept in the room to the left of the house, while Skylar's room was on the right. Two short halls ran toward the back of the house from these rooms. The hall closest to their parents' room led to their dad's office and exercise room. Elliot slept in the back corner room at the end of the hall by Skylar's room.

Skylar stopped at the corner of the hall, where it turned toward Elliot's room. "You sure you have nothing that could fall in your room?"

"Yeah, no way," Elliot said. "Not unless something knocked stuff off a shelf."

"One way to find out." All at once, she unleashed a yell and charged the room, throwing the door open.

Nothing was there.

Elliot crashed into her back and peered around her. "Do you see anything?" he asked.

"There's nothing, Elliot," she said, relieved. Switching on the light, she walked over to his unmade bed and checked under it. "Looks like our imagination got carried away."

Elliot hadn't moved from the doorway. A faint breeze ruffled his drying hair.

"Um, Skylar? Did you, like, ever open my window today? Because, um, I know I didn't."

Tingles ran down Skylar's back. "Maybe Dad did?"

"Did he take the screen out, too?"

The window over the backyard was gaping open and missing the screen. Darkness had spread outside of it, and they heard a lone howl. It sounded awfully close.

With her bat in hand, Skylar marched to the window and slammed it shut with one hand. "Enough of that," she said. Then, she smiled at her younger brother, looking pitiful in his wet pajama pants and T-shirt. "You know, Elliot, if you want to sleep in my room tonight, I'm okay with it. We can make a bed on the floor."

"Okay, yeah… I think that's a good idea."

Lowering her bat, Skylar crossed the room to him. She flicked hair from his eyes with her free hand. "You know what? I bet it was one of Teddy's friends trying to scare me. I texted him earlier, and he said he went to the funeral with his mom. He was born on Blue Island, you know. But he doesn't really know anyone there and only went because he had to. Anyway, his friends are kind of crazy and like to do stupid stunts like scaring friends."

Hugging his stomach as if sick, Elliot just looked up at her. "We need to tell Mom and Dad."

"Not a chance, Elliot," Skylar said. She moved her arm around his shoulders and squeezed him tight. "I mean it. Mom and Dad have enough to worry about. Remember, with Dad having no job and Mom working so far away, we can't cause any trouble right now. Until we find proof of anything wrong, they wouldn't believe us anyway. It'll just make them more worried. Got it?"

Elliot nodded miserably.

"Good. You go down and get a pizza from the freezer. I'll take your sheets and make up a bed."

"Um, I kind of, like, would rather wait for you."

"Yeah, okay. You grab your pillow. Tell you what, though. I'll text Teddy and ask him if he knows anything about this."

Five minutes later, Skylar squealed from where she lay on her bed.

Sitting on a hastily made bed of blankets and his sheets by the door, Elliot looked up at her. "So, um, does he, like, know anything about it?"

"Nope, sorry, little brother." She twisted her legs and moved to sit on the edge of her mattress, bouncing in giddiness. "But he's coming over in a few minutes to check it out." Her eyes narrowed, and she looked down at her brother. "And you're not going to say a word to Mom or Dad about it."

Elliot nodded. He actually didn't mind somebody coming to check on them. Even if it was his sister's cruddy boyfriend.

"And he's not my boyfriend," Skylar told him, reading his mind.

"What am I supposed to do when he's here?"

"Stay out of our way. Go paint your monsters or something. And after dinner, you can watch a movie. *After* you brush your teeth. I don't want any stinky boy breath in my room tonight."

Elliot stared up at her innocently. "Does that include Teddy?"

She threw her pillow at him, nailing him in the face.

Chapter 13

The siblings had their pizza, and Skylar was finishing cleaning up in the kitchen, ensuring everything looked perfect. She hadn't had time to change and wore a fitted green shirt over plain black pants. Every few minutes, she rushed to check her hair in the mirror hanging behind the table.

Not used to seeing his sister in a panic, Elliot had retreated to the family room next to the kitchen. He lay on his stomach with his set of paints in front of him. Resting on his elbows, he held up a metal werewolf figure, examining it closely. He had yet to touch his paintbrush.

Then the doorbell rang.

"Remember," Skylar hissed, rushing from the kitchen to lean over her brother. "Don't tell Mom or Dad anything. I mean it."

"Got it," Elliot mumbled. "But you owe me."

"Yeah, right, I do." Skylar mussed up his hair. She then ran to the door. "Coming!" she called sweetly.

"Yo, are you okay?" Teddy asked as soon as the door opened. He looked at Skylar with concern. "I mean, really. You good?"

"Oh, yeah. Sorry about that." Skylar let out a short laugh. "It was just my little brother. His imagination… You know how it goes."

Leaning an arm on the doorframe, Teddy grinned, showing white teeth with a dazzling smile. Smelling faintly of cologne, he wore jeans with an unbuttoned flannel shirt over a dark blue turtleneck. Even on the warm night, he looked cool.

"Yeah, I guess," he said. "I have three little brothers and two younger sisters. They're always getting scared of something. Still, maybe I should check it out."

"Uh, yeah, of course. He, um, well, heard something upstairs. But whatever it was, it must've come through his window. It was wide open."

"Then let's go outside and look around. Come on."

Skylar was touched by his concern. She also felt a thrill that they would be outside alone in the dark. "Okay, let me get my shoes. Elliot," she called. "We'll be around back. Don't do anything stupid!"

Elliot glanced up at her with his brow furrowed. "You don't either," he mumbled.

His sister pretended not to hear as she shut the door.

Outside was warm and humid. Still, Skylar leaned into Teddy. A faint fog had rolled in, reflecting moonlight to create an eerie glow across the front yard.

"Okay, that looks kind of creepy," she said.

"Relax," Teddy teased. "You have me here. A big, strong guy. With a flashlight!" He snapped on a light, lighting up the walkway from the front door to the driveway.

"Ooh," said Skylar, pretending to be impressed. "That's okay then. I feel better already."

"So you should." Teddy's voice grew serious. "So, where's your brother's room?" he asked.

"Oh, yeah. It's around the back. Come on, follow me. I'm sure it was nothing…"

"You never know. Let me go first, though. Just in case."

Taken aback and a little touched at how serious Teddy was about protecting her, Skylar gave way. The two teens moved stealthily around the house, Teddy sweeping the light from the house siding to the ground before them. "So far nothing," he said with a grunt.

The backyard was a grassy clearing with two magnolia trees on either side. The yard ended in a thin line of woods that moved down a slope leading to a small stream.

Skylar and Elliot had explored the entire area when they'd first moved. Thinking about it, there were plenty of hiding places for a creep. As if on cue, a branch snapped in the woods.

Startled, Skylar let out a shriek and grabbed Teddy's arm. She felt him tense and knew he'd been scared, too.

"Just a deer," Teddy said, relaxing. His light had shot toward the noise, and the teens watched a young doe crash into the darkness. Another deer took off after.

"Oh, my," Skylar said, breathing out in relief. "Looks like we interrupted a deer date."

"Oh, yeah?" Teddy asked, shining the light in his face. "Is that what we did? Or are we going to be victims of some ax attack?"

"Okay, that's not funny," Skylar said.

"Oh, er, yeah. Sorry." The light dropped back to the ground. "Why don't you wait here and let me scout around under the window."

"Not a chance. I'm coming too."

"Okay, but stay back a few feet. I don't want to be distracted."

"Wait, you think I distract you?"

Teddy put the light back up to his face and made a funny face. "What do you think? You know, I don't make it a habit of spending Saturday nights visiting houses to make sure no monsters are hiding under windows. I only do it on special occasions… for people I like."

Skylar ducked her head. "Oh, um, right. Go, uh, do your thing, and I'll be right behind you."

Teddy started ahead of her. He noisily kicked leaves and dirt with his feet as he did. "This is to scare anything away that might be waiting," he joked.

"Wait," Skylar called. "Do you know which window?"

"Oh, er, it's the first one back here, right? I'm guessing it's this one."

Skylar laughed. "You got it."

She watched as Teddy paced back and forth under Elliot's window, making a real show of squatting on the ground and rubbing the grass and dirt.

"What is it?" she asked.

"Nothing," Teddy answered. "I'm just making sure of it."

He finally returned and stopped just in front of her.

"Skylar Ashley," he said solemnly, "I am happy to report that there are no monsters or signs of monsters at your brother's window."

"Well, there's you," Skylar teased.

"Hey!" Teddy said, sounding hurt. He rubbed his stomach with his free hand as the other shone the light on the ground between them. "I'm no monster!"

"Then what are you?"

"What am I?" his voice turned husky.

Suddenly, Skylar was aware of how close his face was to her lips. She felt her own mouth start to open and—

"Do you guys see anything?" Elliot's voice called from above.

"Oh!" Skylar gave a start. She saw Teddy clutch his stomach and nearly lose hold of the flashlight.

"Elliot!" she hissed loudly. "What are you doing?"

"I saw the light. What are you two doing?"

"Nothing!" Skylar said quickly. "Go back in and close the window." She hadn't even heard the creep open it. "Brush your teeth and then start a movie. We'll join you in just a few minutes."

"Okay, I'll be waiting."

"Nice little brother," Teddy said with a nervous laugh. "He knows when to make an entrance."

Skylar giggled. "He certainly scared you. You nearly jumped into my arms."

"What? Not a chance! I was just getting ready to catch you in my arms!"

Skylar laughed. "Whatever. Hey, you want something to eat?"

"Huh? No, I already ate."

"Well, you keep holding your belly like you're starving."

Teddy coughed and shook his head. "Really? I, uh, never noticed. Come on. Let's go take a walk away from your little brother."

"Yeah, um, sure. But it's pretty foggy out. How, um, far do you want to go?"

"As far as it goes," Teddy said mysteriously.

The two walked back to the driveway side by side. As they reached the pavement, Skylar felt Teddy's hand slip into her hand, clasping it gently. She didn't pull away. They stopped at the end of the driveway, two figures under the foggy moonlight.

"It's beautiful," Skylar said, breathing in the night air.

"Yes," Teddy agreed. His hand moved from her hand and went up to her shoulder. His voice grew husky. "You are, you know. Beautiful."

Skylar's heart skipped a beat. She felt his chest press against her shoulder.

Suddenly, realizing her parents could soon return home, she pulled away abruptly. "Come on," she said. "Let's go check on Elliot. He's going to be worried if we don't go in soon."

"Uh, yeah, of course." Teddy relaxed and ran a hand over his short curls. "I should be going soon anyway. We'll check on the little guy, and then I'll be off."

"Teddy," Skylar said as they approached the door. "Thank you. Thank you for coming."

"Of course, no trouble at all." Even in the dark, Skylar knew he was smiling. "Like I said before, I do things like this for girls I like."

"You never really said that."

"I didn't? Well, I did now!" He ran ahead to open the door for her. "And you are beautiful, you know. I meant that."

Skylar blushed as she entered the house. "Just be quiet about that. Elliot will hear."

That was not the case.

The two teens entered to find Elliot fast asleep on the couch in front of the TV. A superhero movie had barely begun. Elliot lay on his side, his arms curled by his chin, and the TV remote lay in one of his hands.

Skylar groaned as she slipped off her shoes and entered the family room. "Oh, Elliot," she muttered. "He's out cold."

"At least he looks peaceful," Teddy said, leaning in from the foyer. "No nightmares, right?"

"Yeah, but you don't understand." Skylar bent over her brother and took the remote from his limp hand. Twisting, she shut off the TV and placed the controller on the low coffee table in front of the couch. "When this boy sleeps, he's totally zonked out." Shifting back to her brother, she gave him a light slap on his side. "See?"

"Well, I can carry him up to bed," Teddy said. He flexed his muscles and smiled wide. "Wouldn't be a problem, and I can show off my muscles."

Skylar was tempted, but remembered Elliot was sleeping in her room. There was no way she was going to let Teddy in there. She'd already broken her parents' number one rule by having a boy over without them knowing. If they came home to find Teddy in her room… it was not going to happen.

"Here, just get him to the stairs, and I'll take him the rest of the way. He's small for his age but heavier than he looks."

"Not for me, he isn't," Teddy boasted. He crossed the room to the couch, and Skylar moved to the side. "You got a nice-looking brother," he said, squatting down. "He takes after his sister."

"Just hurry up," Skylar told him, blushing. "My parents could be coming home any minute."

Elliot mumbled in his sleep but remained zonked out as the teen slid his arms under his legs and back before hefting up in his arms.

"Okay, you're right. The little guy is a little heavy. Let's go." Hefting up the sleeping boy, he carried Elliot to the stairs with Skylar behind him. At the stairs, he carefully slid the sleeping boy into Skylar's arms. "You sure you got him?" Teddy asked. "I can get him up the stairs if you like."

"Oof! I got him." Skylar boosted Elliot up to her shoulder, clutching his back and thighs as his arms dangled down her back. "I've been carrying Elliot's little behind around since he was born." She gasped. "But he is getting heavy." She finally squatted low and pushed him up to slump over her shoulder. "There."

"Okay…" Teddy reached up and brushed a strand of hair from her face. "I'll leave you here then. Hey, I'll text you later, but some of my friends are coming to my house tomorrow night. We're having a study session for Chemistry. You can come if you want. It'll be at my house after six."

"Oh, uh, sure," Skylar said. Laden with Elliot, she started up the steps. "I mean, I'll try."

"Great! I'll let myself out! Hope to see you tomorrow, Skylar!"

Skylar rested on the fourth step and took a deep breath. "Thanks again, Teddy!"

"My pleasure," he called as he left, closing the door behind him.

"Okay, Elliot, he's gone," Skylar said. She slapped the back of his leg. "You can wake up now."

Muttering, Elliot opened his eyes and pushed himself up. His arms rested on her shoulder as she used both hands to support his backside her arms. "It's 'bout time," he croaked. "Now carry me."

"No way, barf-breath. Your butt is walking the rest of the way."

"Yeah, okay," Elliot said, blinking away sleep. "Then I'll tell Mom you kissed Teddy."

"Hey!" Skylar dumped Elliot back over her shoulder, giving him a sharp spank. "You'll do no such thing! Besides, we never did kiss!"

"You wanted to," Elliot retorted. He made a kissing sound.

"Okay, okay! I'm carrying your butt." She gave the back of his pants another smack. "But if you tell Mom or Dad anything, I'm going to kick it out the window!"

"Just don't drop me," Elliot mumbled. "Show-off."

Skylar kept a hand on the railing as the other held on to her brother tightly. She slowly made her way to her room. As she reached the top, she heard a mournful howl from the backyard. It was answered by another. Her blood ran cold.

"Elliot?" she whispered. "Did you hear that?"

There was no answer. Safe in his sister's arms, her brother had fallen asleep again.

Skylar hurried to her room, shutting the door with her foot. Kneeling, she gently put Elliot down. Doing so, she kept an ear out for any more howling. After laying Elliot on the makeshift bed, she turned him on his side and brushed stray hair from his face.

"I don't know what's going on, kid," she muttered. "But nobody is going to hurt us."

Her little brother snuggled against his pillow but never woke. After covering him with a blanket, Skylar jumped onto her mattress. She snatched up her phone lying on her pillow. During all the time with Teddy, she never asked if he knew if any of his friends had snuck into her house for a prank. She texted him now, but she stopped just before sending it.

"It was probably coyotes," she muttered. Deleting the text, she quickly typed another one. It thanked Teddy for coming and said she would be there the next night. As she sent it, she realized she wasn't even in his Chemistry class.

Chapter 14

After midnight, Mrs. Ashley crept from her room in a bathrobe. Mr. Ashley was in the shower, and she'd noticed Skylar's light on when they'd returned from their late dinner. It was now after midnight, and the light was still on.

Walking across the hall, she knocked lightly before entering her daughter's room.

"Darling, are you okay? Oh, what's this?"

Entering the room, she nearly stepped on Elliot's left ankle. Her son lay sleeping in a tangle of sheets and blankets, his feet sticking out the bottom. Lying on his side, his arms were bent, so his hands rested by his face, almost in a fetal position. He breathed evenly and didn't stir as Mrs. Ashley moved around him, shutting the door.

"Did something happen tonight?" she asked, worried.

"Oh, it's nothing," Skylar said, turning from the front of the window where she'd been peeking out. She was relieved to see her mom. "I thought I heard something outside, but it was just wind." She'd been checking the window all night and listening for more howls. There'd been nothing. "Elliot had a bad dream… I think he misses Tucker, you know."

Mrs. Ashley sighed and nodded. Kneeling by her son, she brushed a strand of hair from his cheek and stroked his forehead. "I know I've been busy this year, more than normal. Your dad had to stop working, and then we moved here... But my students… it isn't easy for a lot of them."

"We know, Mom. Really."

"Yes, but that doesn't make it any easier for Elliot. Or you. Are you really doing okay, Sky?"

Skylar knelt next to her mom and gave her a hug. "Well, changing schools hasn't been easy, but I'm doing fine. I promise."

"If your dad can find a new job in the area, I promise we'll move back to Whitney and your old school. I know you miss your friends. I feel terrible about putting you two in new schools so close to the end of the year."

Skylar released her mom and abruptly stood. She twisted a finger around a strand of hair by her right ear. "Well, now that you mention it… I could make some new friends here. I mean, like, tomorrow night?"

Mrs. Ashley dropped her hand to Elliot's shoulder and looked up at her daughter, instantly suspicious. "You do know tomorrow is Sunday, Skylar. A school night."

"Yeah, but some kids are having, you know, a study party. We have the state tests coming up."

"I know all about the state tests, kiddo. I also know what 'study party' means in high school. Is there going to be a boy there?"

"Mom!" Skylar turned and walked back toward the window, furiously twisting her hair. It was something she did unconsciously when she wanted to avoid speaking the full truth.

Mrs. Ashley smiled as her suspicions were confirmed. "So you did meet a boy."

"Mom! You're going to wake Elliot."

Mother and daughter glanced down at the sleeping boy.

"I doubt much can wake that kiddo," Mrs. Ashley said dryly. "He always sleeps like a rock, and he's been through a lot lately."

"Yeah, well, so have I," Skylar said, trying to sound more pitiful than whining. Then she threw up her hands. "Ugg! Okay, okay. So a guy asked me to study with his friends. All right? It'll be at his house, and both parents will be there. So will other kids from the school. We're really going to just study."

Mrs. Ashley frowned. "Okay, but 'study what' is the question I have. How well do you know this boy?"

"He's nice, Mom. He's a junior and the captain of the debate team. And he runs track."

Mrs. Ashley lifted her eyebrows. "Well, if he asked you to study with him, he must be smart and have good taste." She sighed and pinched the bridge of her nose. "I trust you, Skylar, but please do be careful."

"You mean it?" Skylar rushed back to her mother and dropped next to her again. "I can go?"

"Yes, you can go. Just look out for red flags. If anything is off about this boy, like if he smokes or asks you to drink any alcho—"

"Thanks, Mom!" Skylar threw her arms around Mrs. Ashley tightly. "I'll be careful. I promise! You're the best!"

"I try to be," her mom said, smiling. "Now go be like your brother and get some sleep. We're probably skipping church tomorrow, but I imagine you're going to have a busy day."

The next day, Sunday, Tucker returned from church with his family and went straight to his room. On the way home, his parents had started discussing his summer plans. They'd also mentioned a homeschool outing that would happen in a couple of weeks. His mom had explained how Phileo's mom had called the night before and said she was searching for a good place to take the cohort for a field trip. Since both of Tucker's parents worked, she volunteered to drive Tucker to wherever they decided to go. She even offered to take Maria too, who, fortunately for her, was in public school. She was safe.

"I wouldn't go if they paid me a million dollars," she'd announced when hearing the news.

"I don't think I get a choice," Tucker had groaned.

Now in his room, Tucker leaped face-first on his bed, splaying his arms and legs out. "I am so dead," he muttered.

"Hey, Tucker!" Maria called. "Mom wants you down to set the table."

"Tell her I'm too busy being dead," Tucker yelled back.

"Okay, but she's making chicken and dumplings!"

The Romero family always had a huge early dinner after church on Sundays. It was the one day a week the family made sure to be together, something not easy to do on the other days with their busy schedules. His mom constantly tried to outdo herself by cooking a feast. His dad helped and usually supplied the dessert. Tucker used to help out... before the pumpkin pudding incident. His stomach growled. Chicken and dumplings were his favorite, and he knew his dad would make banana pudding, his other favorite.

"Hey, well, our church believes in the resurrection! I'll be, like, totally alive when dinner is being served!"

"Better get down here before I lick your fork and knife!"

Tucker groaned into his sheets and rolled onto his back. Elliot used to come over on Sundays to join the meal, sometimes with his family. The boys had needed each other against their sisters. Without Elliot, he was hopelessly outnumbered by his single, fifty-pound, eight-year-old sister.

Staring up at the ceiling, he patted his stomach. Pressing down, he was pleased to feel hardening muscle. After dinner, he meant to get to his exercises… without Maria.

"Tucker!" his sister yelled. "Your fork is this close to my mouth!"

"I'm coming! I'm coming! Okay, sheesh!" Tucker struggled to sit up and hopped off his mattress. He started tugging at his blue dress shirt. Before Elliot's stupid video at the cooking contest, he would help in the kitchen, imagining he was a great chef. Now, he had to rush just to set the table. "Let me get changed first."

"You have, like, twenty seconds!"

Tucker rolled his eyes and glanced back at his phone. "Elliot, why do you have to be such a bonehead?"

The Ashley family usually attended Whitney Baptist Church on Sundays, but since the move, they'd stopped going regularly. It was a longer drive, and the family had yet to find a closer church. In all honesty, sleeping in on Sunday mornings was too tempting.

By early afternoon, after a late brunch, Mr. Ashley was in the garage lifting weights. Mrs. Ashley and Skylar had gone shopping, searching for the perfect outfit for that evening. Elliot had spent the morning playing video games before going off to explore the backyard. This meant Mr. Ashley had a moment to himself—something he found happening much more since being laid off.

Fighting off self-pity and anger, he turned to hard rock and heavy weights. Now lying on his back on his SuperMaxed bench, he easily pressed up a pair of fifty-pound weights. He had a smaller gym set up in the house, but he kept his heavier weights in the garage. The band Nine Inch Nails blasted from the radio behind him, singing about hurt and pain. It was a song he knew all too well.

He'd just finished his set of fifteen lifts when he realized he wasn't alone. Putting the heavy bar on the rack above his head, he sat up with a start.

"Excuse me!" hollered a rail-thin elderly lady. Her white hair was cut close to her scalp, and she wore an orange dress with white polka dots.

Mr. Ashley hid a groan. Mrs. Goodall, who did not live up to her name, was the next-door neighbor who seemed to have no other hobby than complaining about his family.

"Sorry!" Mr. Ashley called, getting up from the bench. His sleeveless gray T-shirt was soaked with sweat around the collar. He brushed down his athletic shorts, moving quickly to the old stereo leftover from his teenage years. Amazingly, it still worked. Switching off the CD player, he turned to hear the latest complaint. "Was my music too loud?" he asked.

"My ears are still ringing," Mrs. Goodall said, her nose pointed in the air. "I just came back from church, you know." Her tone held the accusing question of *why didn't you go to church?*

Mr. Ashley chose to ignore it. "Right. Sorry, I'll keep it down."

"That's not why I'm here. Did you know I heard things from your yard last night?"

Mr. Ashley made no move to welcome Mrs. Goodall into the garage. He remained standing by the stereo. "Is that right?"

"I, at first, thought it was just some wild animal. It gave my two cats such a fright!"

"Sorry to hear that," mumbled Mr. Ashley.

His neighbor paid him no mind. "Then I saw lights coming from your yard. I don't know what your kids were doing, but they'd better stay off my property! Whatever they did, they sent Maxie and Fluffy under my bed in a tizzy. Those poor dears are still afraid to step outside!"

"I'm sure it was just an animal out there," Mr. Ashley said. "Elliot mentioned something about it this morning. He's out back checking for any footprints."

Mrs. Goodall's eyes went wide. "Whatever it was, it was not friendly! If you really think it was an animal, you better keep your son close. I'm telling you, even I felt it. Something bad was out there. I hope your kids had nothing to do with it!"

Mr. Ashley nodded meekly. "Right. Sure thing, Mrs. Goodall. Now, you have a nice Sunday afternoon."

Mrs. Goodall widened her eyes at her dismissal. "I'll do my best," she finally said, spinning on her heel. "It's hard to do with you lot living here."

Mr. Ashley pretended not to hear as he turned the stereo back on, lowering the volume by only a few clicks. He'd just started adding more weight to the bar when Elliot appeared in the garage.

It was another hot, humid day. The morning fog had long since burned off, and the sun shone down without filters. Elliot had removed his shirt and wore dark blue shorts and flip-flops. His bare, scrawny chest rose and fell with anxiety. Sweat darkened his hair as he stood with his hands in front of him, obviously afraid.

"What's wrong, bud?" Mr. Ashley asked him. "Don't worry about our nosy neighbor. She was more upset about my music."

"It's not that, Dad. I was, like, wondering if you could maybe go exploring with me."

"Ah, not right now. I'm kind of busy." Mr. Ashley eyed his son's lean build. "You could join me if you'd like. Just use small weights and start building up some muscle."

"Um, that's okay. No thanks. Dad, I, um, think something, like, hit my window. My screen got knocked out… and torn."

"No kidding?" Mr. Ashley moved from the weights and wiped his sweaty hands on the side of his shorts. "Did this happen last night? Mrs. Goodall said something was out there."

"Yeah, I think so. I've got the screen out here. I put it by the wall."

"Did you find any animal tracks or anything around it?"

Elliot shook his head. He knew Teddy had checked the area last night but had wanted to be sure. He'd found the ruined screen propped against the house and assumed the teen must've placed it there.

"Well," his dad said, "go ahead and grab it. Let's see your screen."

Elliot pursed his lips and swung his body from the garage, obviously disappointed his dad wasn't following. He returned seconds later carrying the torn screen. The mesh was cut in two jagged lines in a rough X-shape.

"Ooh, wow," Mr. Ashley said, taking it from Elliot. "Looks like a large bird flew into it. Probably knocked itself silly. Well, I'll call a guy and see if we can get it replaced tomorrow. Okay?"

Elliot nodded. He scratched his ribs in disappointment. He'd wanted his dad to come out and find some sign of a break-in.

"Hey, bud. Don't look so glum." Mr. Ashley tossed the ripped screen aside and moved to stand behind his son. He crossed his arms around Elliot's shoulders, pulling him back in a tight hug. "Things aren't going the greatest right now, I know that. But I'll get a job soon, you'll see. And when I do, we'll go exploring at the river park. Okay?"

"Yeah, okay."

"Cool. Now, let your old man get a few more reps in, okay?" He gave Elliot a final squeeze and then released him. "And let's play catch later." He mussed up Elliot's hair and slapped his back. "Your mom tells me you're turning into quite the ballplayer. You'll be like your old man yet!"

Elliot left the garage feeling even more down. He wanted to tell his dad about last night so badly, but Skylar was right. His dad didn't need an extra worry and probably wouldn't believe him in any case. He wished he had Tucker with him. Reaching into his shorts pocket, he pulled out his phone and saw he had no messages or texts. For the hundredth time in the past week, he typed a text to Tucker. Then, like all the others, he deleted it without sending.

Chapter 15

Skylar's study session did not go well that night. A group of four teens, plus Teddy, had already gathered at Teddy's house when her mom dropped her off. They were all in Teddy's grade, a year above Skylar. She barely recognized any of them.

There was only one other girl. She eyed Skylar's white top and jean shorts with undisguised disgust. The teens were in no mood to study. Apparently, two students from their school, a pair of cousins, had vanished the day before. The rumors were they ran away and were driving for Texas or had joined the military. There'd been no notes or messages to friends saying goodbye, so they were just rumors. Skylar had no idea who they were, but Teddy seemed pretty shaken by it. She spent the two hours on his couch listening to the others speak in hushed tones about the missing seniors and how much their lives must've stunk.

"They had no future here," lamented the girl, giving Skylar the stink eye. "There was nothing here for them. I don't blame them for leaving."

Teddy just scratched his stomach and stared morosely at the carpet. He barely spoke the entire time and never acknowledged Skylar.

Finally, shortly after eight, Skylar texted her mom to pick her up. When she left, Teddy barely noticed. The girl, however, watched her go with a sly smile.

Monday morning at 8:30 on the dot found Mrs. Ashley right where she always stood on a school day—outside her classroom, greeting each of her students by name. Wearing a white buttoned shirt with tan stretchy pants, she smiled brightly and made eye contact. It was something she'd started the first day of school, and it had become a good way to gauge how the day would go and, on a Monday, how the week would play out.

Seeing her students arrive let her see the ones who were ready to learn, the ones who stayed up too late on their phones or playing games, and the poor few who had rough mornings for a variety of reasons and may need a hug or small pep talk. It also let her students know she cared for each of them and was there if they needed her. Many bad mornings for her students were turned around before they walked through her door, often with a simple smile and heartfelt welcome.

As usual, Bobby Garcia was the first to come up the hall.

"Bobby!" she greeted. "It was great to see you at practice on Saturday. You were great!"

"Hi, Mrs. A," Bobby said, giving her a tired smile. "Yeah, it was fun."

"You look half-asleep, kiddo. Stay up late?" She lifted her hand for a high five.

Slapping her hand, Bobby paused at the door. "Maybe a little," he said sheepishly. "I was up late watching basketball playoffs with my dad."

"Well, as long as you stay up for my math lesson, then I'm okay with it."

"Sure, Mrs. A." He started walking past her but stopped. "Wait. Should I call you Mrs. Ashley, or Coach? I'm confused."

Mrs. Ashley crossed her arms thoughtfully. "Let me think about that... I guess you call me Coach Ashley at baseball and Mrs. Ashley at school. Sound good?"

"Yup." He smiled at her, suddenly shy. "I did have fun there. Thanks for putting me on the team."

"Yes, it was a good time. I wish Marcus could've made it."

Bobby yawned and shrugged his shoulders. "Yeah. I texted him yesterday about playing games online, but he never answered."

"I'm sure he was busy." She reached up and patted his shoulder. "You go in and unpack. Then start your morning work. Remember, there's the state math test this week."

"Oh, wonderful," Bobby groaned.

"What's wonderful?" Cynthia called as she approached from down the hall. As always, her best friend Kim followed right behind.

"Your face," Bobby said snidely.

"Oh, wow," Cynthia responded. "For the first time all year, you're right. Great job, Bobby."

"Enough of that," Mrs. Ashley said, rolling her eyes. She'd been teaching at Leewood Elementary for twelve years and never ceased trying to build a strong classroom community free of insults and nastiness. So far, with her current class, she'd managed to get them to insult each other using kind words. She guessed it was progress.

"You all go in and get unpacked. It's great to see you, Cynthia, and Kim. I hope you had a great weekend."

"Too short," Kim mumbled as she went by.

"But fun!" Cynthia said, ducking her chin and giving a glittering smile.

Mrs. Ashley watched the girls enter with a grin. Kim, a solid, attractive girl with pale skin, just lacked confidence. Cynthia, lean and limber with cute outfits and strong brown skin, had too much confidence. Somehow, their friendship worked. Mrs. Ashley liked seeing the girls together.

Then trouble arrived.

"Hey, fat face," said a nasty voice. "Get your big butt out of my way."

Every classroom had its challenges, and for that year, Mrs. Ashley's challenge had a name. Marcus Mettis was a short, stocky boy who'd arrived in Leewood from a city school west of Whitney back in October. With short black hair, light brown skin, and big hazel eyes, he was a strikingly good-looking boy but had one problem. He carried a chip on his small shoulders the size of a mountain. With his sullen attitude and disregard for rules and teachers, he was well behind his classmates in learning and didn't seem to care. He was an ongoing project Mrs. Ashley had yet to figure out. She'd hoped he would show up for baseball but knew the long drive would be hard. Swallowing his attitude to play on her team would be even harder.

"Well, at least most of my students insult with kind words," Mrs. Ashley muttered to herself. "Others are just old fashioned." She sighed and stepped away from her door. Crossing her arms, she put on a stern look and waited.

Mrs. Ashley's room was at the end of the fifth-grade hall, past the bathrooms, making it the farthest classroom to reach. This allowed her students to straggle to class a few at a time. She watched her two most troublesome students coming toward her.

Impeccably dressed in tan shorts and a tucked-in red polo, his short brown hair slicked on the sides, tall Gary Mitchell strode in front of the smaller, louder Marcus Mettis.

This, Mrs. Ashley knew, was trouble.

The boys were total opposites but had one thing in common. They never failed to drive Mrs. Ashley crazy.

"The hallway is big enough for you to go around," Gary said, not speeding up. "At least most of you. Your mouth is probably too big."

"Not as big as your ugly butt."

"You would know what one looks like, all right. You stare at yours every time you look in the mirror."

"Man, what are you talking 'bout? I'm just trying to get to class, pig-head."

"Aren't we all," Gary said.

If Marcus was a challenge, then Gary proved to be a nightmare. Never an academic problem, Gary was a straight-A student in the gifted program. Yet, he received special education services due to his behavior. He enjoyed making other students mad with snide insults that often turned physical. He also had the habit of not doing his work since he knew it all and dared teachers to give him a bad grade. This rarely happened because he always aced the tests and projects. With a superior demeanor, he tended to look down on teachers but at least obeyed Mrs. Ashley enough not to cause too many problems in her classroom. He usually kept to himself and played on his computer.

Outside the class, however, was a different story. Gary currently rode the special education bus after being kicked off his regular bus for fighting, and ate lunch in the main office for starting food fights on two separate occasions.

Marcus caused trouble everywhere he went. Foul-mouthed, brash, and sneaky, he cared little about school and seemed to have no remorse when he got in trouble. Mrs. Ashley could never prove it, but she was sure he was stealing from her classroom. Over the year, the candy stash she used for rewards frequently disappeared, and many other items vanished, usually with Marcus in the area.

To make things worse, all the boys in her class flocked to him for some reason, and he managed to get them all riled up. Back in February, he missed a week of school with the flu, and amazingly, nothing mysteriously vanished in her room, and the classroom behavior improved dramatically. Then he returned, and it instantly deteriorated.

It was the end of the year, and Mrs. Ashley only wanted the two boys to make it to the summer without further trouble. It would not be easy.

"Boys, I hope you know I can hear you quite well from here," Mrs. Ashley said. "Now knock off the name-calling and hurry up to class!"

"We're not late," Gary said. "We're actually early."

"I'm going to be late if you don't get your big b—"

"Marcus!" Mrs. Ashley said, raising her voice. "I said knock it off!"

"He's not wrong," Gary said, giving a faint smile. "It is quite big."

"Just get in class and start your morning work, Gary," Mrs. Ashley said, fighting hard not to grit her teeth.

"I already did it. Last week."

"Then read a book!"

"I did that, too," Gary said smugly.

"Then go to your desk and put your head down!" Mrs. Ashley said, exasperated.

Gary grinned back as he brushed by her. "Guess what?" he announced loudly. "Mrs. Ashley told me to take a nap!"

"Quiet in there!" Mrs. Ashley called after him. "Level zero with the noise! Everyone should be working."

"Except me," Gary said just loud enough for her to hear.

Ignoring him, she put a hand to block the doorway.

"Not you, Marcus. You stay out here. I want a word with you."

"OhmyGOSH!" Marcus complained, throwing his head back. "Bruh, come on!" He slouched moodily against the wall before Mrs. Ashley, staring at the ceiling. "I didn't do anything! Gary was going slow on purpose!"

"I never said you were in trouble," Mrs. Ashley said evenly. "And I'm not your 'bruh.' I'm your teacher." Wearing her hair in a ponytail, she brushed a stray strand from her eyes. Her class hadn't started, and she was already becoming undone. It was definitely going to be a rough day and a long week. "I just wanted to talk."

"Fine," Marcus said. "What is it?" He eyed her suspiciously.

"Well, how was your weekend?"

Marcus shrugged and made no answer.

"Did you see your mom?" She knew his parents were divorced. He lived with his dad and stepmom but would rather stay with his mom and two younger sisters. They lived on the other side of Whitney, where his sisters were going to a different school.

"She worked all weekend," Marcus muttered, still not making eye contact.

"That's too bad. I wish you were there at baseball practice. We missed you on Saturday. Bobby made it. It was a good time."

Marcus's eyes flickered with interest, and he glanced up at her. "Did you seriously sign me up for the team and pay for it?"

"I told you I did. I signed up you and Bobby. Only I got scholarships from the league to help cover the cost." She winked at him. "That was the price for me becoming a coach."

Marcus grunted but still perked up a little. "Yeah, that's, uh, cool." Then he shrugged his shoulders. "But I don't like baseball. I play basketball."

"Well, if you change your mind, you're always welcome on the team. I want you to do something outside school besides video games."

Marcus immediately dropped his gaze, and he turned sullen again. "Why do you care?" he muttered.

"Because I care about all my students. Especially you, Marcus. I see a lot of good in you and want you to be your best."

Snorting, Marcus crossed his arms and stepped back from her. "Yeah, right. You don't even know what you're talking about."

Mrs. Ashley's eyes hardened. "Excuse me? Is that how you speak to your mom?"

"You're not my mom," Marcus said, glaring at her. "You're nothing like her."

"Right," Mrs. Ashley snapped, knowing she was losing her cool. "I'm not your mom. But I have a son your age, and I certainly don't let him talk to adults like that."

"Whatever," Marcus mumbled, dropping his gaze.

"Hey, I don't demand you look at me, but I do demand you respect me when I talk to you. I do a lot for you and your classmates. I only ask that you try your best in return."

"Yes, Mrs. Ashley," Marcus muttered.

Mrs. Ashley crossed her arms. She wanted to reach the kid, not push him away. "Look, Marcus," she said. "I know things aren't always easy for you. But remember what I always say. Everyone has challenges, but challenges turn into change."

It was a saying she'd heard back in high school that stuck with her. She used it in her classroom and hoped it stuck with her students. When faced with challenges, people can change for the better or the worse. She wanted her kids to rise up and change for the best. Ultimately, it was their choice.

"Whatever is going on in your life, you can turn it around. Never feel hopeless. Just remember, you may need help, and I'm here for that. Got it?"

The boy looked up at her, his eyes defiant. "Can I go now and start my work?"

Sighing, Mrs. Ashley took a step back. "Yes, go ahead. Stay off your computer, and don't talk to anyone."

Returning to the doorway, she saw more of her students coming up the hall. What a great way to start the day, she told herself darkly, putting on a bright smile. "Candace, it's great to see you!"

Chapter 16

At Grantham High, Skylar stopped by her locker to exchange some books before heading to her next class.

She'd just popped the lock and started opening the door when she felt a tap on her shoulder. Looking over her shoulder, she saw Teddy standing there uncomfortably.

"Uh, Skylar?" he said hesitantly. "Got a minute?"

She debated if she should ignore him, but slowly turned to face him. "Oh, hi, Teddy," she said neutrally. Still, her eyes were drawn to him.

She hadn't seen him all morning but had to admit the wait was worth it. Wearing a beige collar shirt and white shorts showing off his long, muscular legs, he looked amazing. His chiseled features relaxed when they made eye contact, and he forced a smile.

"I hope you're not mad at me," he said. "I want to apologize for last night."

"Mad at you? Why would I be mad at you?" Skylar flicked back her hair and tried to look confused.

"Well, for totally ignoring you after inviting you to my place to study. Does that work?"

Skylar nodded. "Okay, yes. I can see why I could be mad at you." Her voice grew serious. "But you do have a reason. I heard those guys still haven't come back or been heard from. Were you close to them?"

Teddy shook his head and looked down at the floor. "Nah, not really. Donnie and Jake were seniors and were supposed to be graduating in a few weeks. It just shook me that they could, you know, take off like that. I don't like the thought of kids in the school disappearing, you know?"

Skylar nodded slowly. "Yeah, I can get that. Well, thanks for the apology." She reached into her locker for her new books and felt Teddy's hand on her shoulder. Immediately, her skin tingled, and she stopped. "Is there something else?"

"Yeah, I'm hoping I could make it up to you."

Skylar grinned and slowly rotated back to face Teddy. She leaned back against the locker next to hers. "Oh, and how do you suppose to do that?"

"Well, you know Blue Island? They have a farm there, and they're opening it up to the public, mainly for school kids."

Skylar raised her eyebrows. "Is that how you want to make it up to me?"

"Yeah, they want some volunteers to work there that day, and, well, I'm from there, so they asked me. I was kind of hoping you could come, too."

"You want me to work on a farm? What kind of farm is it?"

"Oh, you know. Mostly animals… cute little pigs, chickens, and cows."

"Cute pigs, chickens, and cows." Skylar lifted her eyebrows. "Really?"

"Well," Teddy said, grinning. "It is missing some cute girls… So I kind of hoped you could take care of that. Really,

Skylar. It'll be fun. And the best news is I already spoke to our principal. He's letting any volunteers from our school get credit for the day. What do you say that?"

"I guess I'll say I'll think about it." Then Skylar laughed, seeing Teddy's face crumple in disappointment. "I'm kidding! Of course I'll be there! You're driving, right?"

"Don't you worry, I'm a safe driver," Teddy assured her, smiling again. Clapping his hands, he backed away from Skylar, heading toward his next class. "It'll be the time of your life," he called to her. "You'll see!"

Skylar couldn't help but return the smile. She was pretty sure she had a date.

There were four classes of fifth graders at Leewood Elementary and Mrs. Ashley had a class of twenty-two students, fourteen of them boys. With Marcus alone, it felt like she had thirty-two sometimes. Add Gary, and it felt as if she had to teach three classes at once.

After lunch, she needed a break, so she had the class working on their individual laptops and practicing for the big state math test that Thursday. She had arranged their desks in clusters of four in hopes of splitting up some of the troublemakers. With so many boys, especially with Marcus, that proved rather impossible.

"Yo, Bobby," Marcus whispered. "You really go to baseball on Saturday?"

At the desk across from him, Bobby didn't look up from his computer. "Yeah, man. It was all right. Pretty cool."

"Quiet out there," Mrs. Ashley called from her table in the back corner.

She sat with Scotty Morris, a small blond kid with thick glasses and a terrible attention problem. He was the only other student in the classroom who received special education services besides Gary. Unlike Gary, he needed every support he got. Trying to teach him how to add and subtract fractions was like trying to teach a kangaroo to walk. As soon as he got the first step, his attention bounced away, and she had to start all over again.

Marcus ducked back down at his computer and then looked up at Bobby again. "You see Mrs. A's son?"

"Yeah," Bobby whispered back. "I saw her golden child." He shrugged. "He's cool."

"Yeah, maybe I'll be there next—"

"I said quiet," Mrs. Ashley called out louder. "During Thursday's test, there will be no talking! You all should be at level zero. Marcus, I'm looking at you."

Marcus clicked his tongue and blew out his breath. "Man, why you looking just at me? Cynthia and Kim have been talking the whole time!"

"Have not!" Cynthia said immediately.

"She was asking for a pencil," Kim said.

The two girls were at the desk cluster closest to the door, across the room from Marcus. Both girls glared at him.

"For five minutes?" Marcus said. "To work on her computer? A pencil?"

Cynthia stuck out her tongue. "To show my work, dummy. You know, something you never do."

"Enough!" Mrs. Ashley said, banging her hand on the table. "Cynthia, no more of that!" Then she stood up. "Marcus, bring your computer to me."

Marcus rolled his head and got noisily to his feet. He, of course, was at the desk cluster closest to the teacher's table with his back to Mrs. Ashley. This allowed her to see his screen. As he got up, he quickly clicked out of the wrestling video he'd been watching instead of doing his math work.

"Why do you want to see my computer?" he asked loudly.

"To check on your work," Mrs. Ashley said levelly. "How far have you gotten?"

"It's too hard. Besides, why do you even care? I'm going to fail, and I already told you. You're not my mom." As soon as he said it, Marcus knew he'd gone too far.

It had been a long year, and the stress level was extra high due to state testing starting.

"Okay, that's it." Mrs. Ashley moved from her table and marched to the front of the room.

The entire class collectively sucked in their breaths to watch. Marcus slumped back down to his seat. He kicked at the floor.

"Great job, Marcus," Cynthia muttered.

"Quiet!" barked Mrs. Ashley. She rarely lost control, but when she did, she had a hard time reining in her anger. She grabbed a marker at the front of the room and turned to the whiteboard. "Just so you all know, I am actually like your parent, just as long as you're here in my classroom." She wrote in big letters *Loco Parentis.* "Do any of you know what this means?"

"Crazy parent?" Bobby said, leaning back in his chair.

Most of the boys chuckled but immediately stopped when Mrs. Ashley slammed her hand against the board.

"No! This is a law that gives all teachers and administrators the right to take care of their students like a parent would. Got it? When you're in my class, you are my child. That is what this means. I am acting as your parent as soon as you walk through my door. Do you understand me? I have the same rights as your parents and the same expectations. I expect you to be respectful and to at least try your best. Always. Am I clear? It's nearly summer, and we're having the same problems we had in the fall!"

"Yeah," Marcus spoke up. "That was when your son got kicked out of school. Great parenting, there."

That did it. Mrs. Ashley slammed the marker in the tray under the board and put a hand on her hip. "You!" she shouted at Marcus. "Get out! Go to the office. Now!"

"Oh, man," Bobby whispered as Marcus got to his feet. "That was a low blow, man."

Marcus ignored him as he strode across the classroom to the propped-open door.

"Kelsey was the one who posted that video," Cynthia said as he went by her. "Besides, Elliot didn't get kicked out. He moved, dummy."

"Silence!" Mrs. Ashley commanded. "Everyone! Marcus, go see Dr. Chocker, and don't you dare stop on your way. I'll be giving him a call in one minute."

Marcus didn't say anything as he stalked out.

Mrs. Ashley took two deep breaths to calm down. She tried hard with Marcus, but sometimes he wound her up like an alarm clock with no off button.

"The rest of you," she said. "Finish your math and then read quietly." She glared at Gary, who wisely kept his head down. "I don't want to hear a word from anybody. I'm going to give Dr. Chocker a call and tell him he has company coming. Does anybody else want to join Marcus? Just say a single word. And I will remind you that the fifth-grade team is planning a fun field trip after the state tests are done. If you can't cooperate in my class, I'm certainly not bringing you to a public place. Remember that!"

"But I thought the pool trip was canceled," one of her boys said from near Bobby.

Mrs. Ashley gave him a stern look. "I'll let that one go, Tommy. But no more talking."

"Sorry," he muttered.

At the end of each school year, the fifth grade class traditionally spent a day celebrating their completion of elementary school. For the last five years, they'd gone to a neighborhood pool down the street for a pool party. A week ago, a parent called to complain that his daughter couldn't swim and deeply feared water. It wasn't fair to use a school day to torture his daughter, the parent said. Besides, the parent wanted to know how a pool party was even educational.

If Mrs. Ashley had taken the call, she would've calmly explained that a day at the pool could be used to *teach* the girl how to swim or at least overcome her fear of water. Instead, it was Dr. Chocker who fielded the call. The principal had one policy when dealing with parents... Parents were always right. So the pool party was canceled and the fifth-grade team had to plan a new educational trip. And they had two weeks to do it, right during the state testing period.

Mrs. Ashley loved working for Dr. Chocker, but sometimes.... he deserved having to take care of Marcus.

Chapter 17

Tucker sat slumped on the couch with his workbook on his lap and pencil behind his ear. He felt a headache start to creep from the back of his skull. He was in Phileo's house with his homeschool cohort, working on historical problems in the country and how he would fix them if he had the chance.

At the moment, the only problem he worried about was surviving the next two hours. The kids had finished listening to a lecture by Phileo's mom and were now supposedly working on their individual work. Instead, two boys were arguing on the floor in the corner about Pokémon cards. A girl was drawing on the wall with colored pencils. Two other boys, twins, were playing tag in the next room. Phileo was in the easy chair across from him, trying to get his attention by clearing his throat loudly every few seconds. His mom, supposedly the teacher that day, had hidden herself in the kitchen, supposedly to make tea. She'd been gone over ten minutes.

"So, Tucker," Phileo asked finally. "What do you think about our field trip? Cool, right?"

"Huh, what?" Tucker pretended to wake up from a daze. Reaching up, he brushed curls from his forehead. "We have a field trip?"

Phileo eyed him with disappointment. "Didn't you hear my Mom?"

"Oh, yeah, of course. She said some stuff. A lot of stuff. But the field trip. Sounds really cool. Where are we going again?"

"We're going to a farm. A new one is opening up, and we're going on the grand opening!"

"Oh, wow," Tucker said dully. "That's amazing. A farm."

"I once visited a farm but was too little to ride the horses. Do you think this one has horses?"

Tucker dropped his head back against the cushion. "Um, I need to finish my work."

"I know. My mom says all our work has to be done if we want to go. It's all the way in Grantham, on an island!"

Tucker's head snapped up. "Wait, where is this place? Did you say Grantham?"

Phileo eyed him critically. "That is what I said. It's on Blue Island, and my mom said nobody has been on it for years."

"Um, wait. Where did the farm come from if nobody has been on it?" Tucker asked. In his brain, he rapidly started thinking. Elliot lived in Grantham… where was this Blue Island?

"No *outsiders* have been on the island. The farm is supposed to be a petting farm, but they might have horses." He cleared his throat loudly. "Do you think your sister Maria could come with us?"

Tucker gave him a look. "Bruh, my sister is eight. And she's the most annoying person on the planet."

Phileo just looked at him. "Did she get the tea party invitation?"

Two minutes later, Tucker was out the door and walking back to his house. He told Phileo he wasn't feeling well, which was true, and would finish his work at his house. That was the one benefit of homeschooling—you got to go home whenever you wanted.

When he entered his house, he found his mom sitting at the kitchen table, still in her bathrobe, with a cup of coffee. It was one of her rare weekdays off from work.

"Tucker!" she said in surprise at seeing him. "You're home early."

"Um, yeah, I'm going to finish my work in my room this afternoon. I was getting a headache." He dumped his books on the back of the couch as he walked to the kitchen.

"Do you want to cook something for lunch?" his mom asked hopefully. "I can help you."

"That's okay, I'm not that hungry." He slid into a chair beside his mom and leaned against her shoulder.

"Sweetheart, what's wrong?"

"Nothing… I miss, you know, how things used to be."

His mom nodded and put down her mug. Lifting her hand, she ruffled his curls. "I do, too. I liked how you used to love cooking."

"You mean burning your pans and causing the fire in the oven?"

His mom chuckled. "Well, not those times. But you were doing a fine job, Tucker. I wish you didn't stop." She sighed and rested her head against his curls. "Perhaps your father and I overreacted with Elliot… We didn't like seeing you get hurt. When your school didn't seem to support you…"

"Mom, really, it's fine." Tucker grimaced. "I like being homeschooled. In fact, we're going on a field trip to a farm. I mean, if you'd let me go."

"Of course! Phileo's mom mentioned something about that on the phone last night. I think it's a new farm just opening up for children." She lifted her head and looked at her son as if seeing him for the first time. "You never were interested in animals before. Are you sure you want to go?"

"You bet," Tucker said, raising his head and nodding. "It'll be great."

Later, he lay on his bed with his schoolbooks. His phone sat next to him, and he kept looking at it, wondering if he should text Elliot.

He must've fallen asleep because the next thing he knew, Maria was barging into his room.

"Tucker, I have a science project that I need you to do!" she announced.

"Huh, what?" he asked, blinking his eyes and finding his mattress damp with drool. "Maria, get out of here!"

"I need to make a map of all the oceans in the world."

"The only map I'm going to make you is a map of how to get out of my room."

"That's easy," Maria told him, dropping her backpack and sitting down. "I don't need a map for that."

"Maria," Tucker groaned. "I have a headache. Why are you always bothering me?"

"Because," she said reasonably, "ever since Elliot left, you don't have any friends. You need to find some, or you're stuck with me."

Tucker pushed his stomach off his mattress and stared at his little sister. "Okay, well, where are your friends?" he demanded.

"I have plenty of friends at school, at church, and in the neighborhood. I can bring some over if you want."

"No, no, forget I asked." Tucker dropped his face into his bed. "Just bring me the instructions for your stupid map."

As the buses pulled out that afternoon, carrying home the students, Mrs. Ashley got called to Dr. Chocker's office.

She entered a tad nervously, thinking it was about Marcus. She had always had a good relationship with the principal and he'd been very forgiving with Elliot and the video back in the fall, maybe even too forgiving. She still felt terrible about Tucker leaving to be homeschooled, but that had been his parents' choice. She'd tried to reach out to them multiple times but had been rebuffed each time. And now, after months, with the incident largely forgotten, Marcus had to bring it up again. It was frustrating. Elliot had acted as a typical boy—immature and careless. He hadn't meant any harm and definitely didn't mean to hurt Tucker. Sometimes, things like that happen. People needed to move on... and stop taking videos of everything.

It turned out all her fears were for nothing.

Dr. Chocker was all smiles as she sat in the padded chair in front of his desk.

"I have great news," he told her.

"What? I got a raise?" Mrs. Ashley said, surveying the spacious office with the fancy mahogany desk and matching bookshelves.

The principal chuckled in his new cushy chair and idly tapped the bottom of the keyboard on his double-monitor desktop computer. He seemed happy but a tad nervous.

"Don't be silly. I found the new fifth-grade field trip." He beamed up at Mrs. Ashley. "You all are going to Sunnybrook Farm."

Mrs. Ashley's went wide and then narrowed. "What was that? A farm? For the fifth-grade celebration?"

"Yes, why not?" Dr. Chocker frowned. "I thought you would be ecstatic. What's wrong with a farm?"

Mrs. Ashley sat back in her chair. "It's not quite the same as a pool party, Frank," she said.

While she had a good relationship with the principal, she didn't quite know what to think of him. He never seemed comfortable around kids but was great at letting teachers do their jobs with as little bother as possible. Having him choose the fifth-grade field trip was very out of character.

"Why did you pick it?" she asked.

"It's Dr. Frank to you," grumbled the principal. He reached up and wiped the bald spot above his forehead. "You and the other teachers complained that you had no time to plan a field trip, so I did it for you. You should be happy."

"I just want something that my students will enjoy. Staring at smelly animals on a hot day... I don't know."

"They'll enjoy it, I promise." Dr. Chocker put his hands on his desk and leaned forward like he was trying to sell her something. "Look, Karen, our kids need to see more of the outside world. They're too involved in their technology. The farm is going to be a terrific experience for them. It's full of animals to pet, and they even have acres of woods to walk through."

"So my students like Marcus can get lost?" Mrs. Ashley asked dubiously. Usually, farm visits were for kindergarten classes, not fifth graders. "Why are you telling me anyway? Jim, Mr. Charles, is the fifth-grade lead. Shouldn't he be the one here?"

Dr. Chocker dropped his gaze. "That's the strange part. The woman who runs the farm came here this morning to visit me. She asked for your class specifically."

Mrs. Ashley sat up straight. "Excuse me? Who was she?"

"She's from your neck of the woods. Do you know a Morgan Raycroft?"

Mrs. Ashley gave a start. "Just where is this farm located?" she asked carefully.

"Blue Island," Dr. Chocker said with a shrug. "I never heard of it, but it's just off Grantham, where you live.

Supposedly, the island has not had visitors in years. Morgan wants to open it up to the public. They have a petting farm there, and she's inviting all the schools in the area to visit for a day. It sounds like a fun time."

"Wait, so we're going with *all* the schools in the area?"

"That's just it," her principal said. "It's so late in the school year that other schools are too busy for a field trip. We're the first and only school that accepted. There'll be some homeschooled kids there too, but our fifth graders will pretty much have the place to themselves."

"So you already accepted?" Mrs. Ashley looked at Dr. Chocker in disbelief. "You didn't even ask the fifth-grade team first?"

Dr. Chocker had the grace to squirm in his chair. "Well, Morgan did mention a hefty donation to our school… she's looking to set up a partnership. This, um, field trip is sort of a test run. If it works out, all the grades will visit next year."

"Let me get this straight. This Morgan woman comes here and is *paying* our school to send our fifth graders to visit her farm? And she asked for me?"

"Ah, yes, I guess it's something like that." Dr. Chocker managed a grin. "She mentioned something about your husband's side of the family. She says she never met you but heard a lot about you and hoped you would feel honored, seeing where your husband came from. Did sound a bit silly."

"You think?" Mrs. Ashley rubbed her temples. She really didn't know what to think.

"If it makes you feel any better, I'll be going with you. I want to check the farm out. And I promise to only partner with the farm if the fifth-grade team approves."

"What about Marcus?" Mrs. Ashley said. "I can't watch him and my other twenty-one students."

"I'll have Mr. Harris come too."

She rolled her eyes. "And who will keep an eye on Mr. Harris?" She quickly raised her hand. "No. Sorry. That was uncalled for. It's been a long day."

"Go home and get some rest, Karen. Don't worry. I'm sure the field trip will go smoothly."

Most administrators, in Mrs. Ashley's opinion, fell into two categories. They were either educators working for teachers and students or politicians working for their personal careers and big salaries. The politicians couldn't be trusted farther than you could throw a school bus, but they were typically the ones who rose to the top in the education field. She really hoped Dr. Chocker chose the field trip for the benefit of the students and not for the hefty donation… she hated to find out he was just a politician.

She shook her head slowly. "You're replacing a pool party with a day with chickens and pigs. What could go wrong?"

Chapter 18

That night, Mrs. Ashley told her family about the field trip over dinner. She left out the part about Morgan Raycroft asking about her personally. Her husband had spent another fruitless day searching for a job. He was growing more and more frustrated. Worse, he seemed defeated. Mrs. Ashley hoped this Morgan woman could maybe help him. Having looked her up on the internet, she found that Morgan Raycroft owned a big chunk of the island and had a lot of businesses. Mrs. Ashley knew that if she told her husband about her intentions, he would likely get upset. He wanted nothing to do with the island. Besides, she didn't want to get his hopes up.

Surprisingly, he thought the farm trip would be fine. "You can tell me how rotten that island is when you get back," he said bitterly, wiping his mouth with his napkin. Stuck at home and probably tired of his wife's weekend leftovers, he'd made an uninspired dinner of baked chicken with baked potatoes and boiled string beans. "Elliot, eat your dinner if you want ice cream for dessert."

Elliot pushed his food around his plate, barely eating. His bones were starting to poke through his skin. He gave no reaction to the field trip news and only took a bite of potato.

Skylar at least reacted to the news with excitement. "Oh-my-gosh," she said, clasping her hands to her mouth. "Are you going to Sunnybrook Farm? I'll be volunteering there with T—with some kids from my school! Mom, I'll see you there!"

Mrs. Ashley glanced at her daughter in surprise. "No kidding, is that right?"

"Yes! Some kids are from Blue Island and are working there that day. I was invited to go with them."

"By a boy, I presume," Mrs. Ashley said, looking down to cut her chicken.

"Mom!" Skylar fingered her hair. "You'll be there, and so will, like, ten other kids and all the real farm workers. It's not like a date."

Mrs. Ashley only smiled. "I guess my fifth-grade field trip might be fun after all. I get to meet this boy."

"Mom!"

Later, while Mr. and Mrs. Ashley finished cleaning the kitchen, Elliot lay back on the couch in front of the TV. A baseball game played on mute, but he barely watched it. His head on a cushion, his knees up in front of him, he rested his phone on his thighs. After another miserable day at school, he slowly typed out a text.

I'm calling at 9 Answer

This time, he hit send. It was his first text to Tucker in months.

Elliot didn't expect a reply, so he was surprised when one came seconds later.

OK

Elliot's heartbeat quickened. He furrowed his brow and saw the time was a little past seven. He wondered if he should just call now.

"Elliot," his mom called from the sink. "I hope your homework is done!"

"Yeah, almost," he answered.

"Young man, I know I let you watch sports on the weekdays, but only if all your schoolwork is finished. You should be studying for your math on Thursday."

"Yes, Mom…" Elliot didn't grumble as he rolled to a sitting position with his feet on the floor. Switching off the TV, he headed up the stairs to his room. He knew he would be studying until nine that night.

Right at nine o'clock, Elliot hit the call button for Tucker's number. Rising from his seat on the bed, he stood on his mattress, staring down at his phone.

As he waited, he started bouncing out some of his nerves. He'd never been nervous calling Tucker before, but his hands were clammy, and his empty stomach was tight with anxiety.

He heard ringing on the other end.

"Okay, Tucker," he muttered. "Like pick up already."

After six rings, he was about to give up when he heard Tucker's voice.

"Hello?"

"Tucker, it's about time you answered!"

"Yeah," Tucker said. His voice sounded deeper and not friendly. "What do you want?"

"Oh, um, I don't know… just to see how you were, uh, doing?"

Tucker sighed on the phone. "I'm homeschooled now."

"Oh. I mean, I know that."

"That's how I'm doing." Tucker sounded tired. "Look, Elliot. My parents don't want me talking to you."

"Oh, yeah… I'm, like, sorry about before. I mean, I was, like, a real idiot."

"Well, yeah, but it's too late now. You moved away, Elliot. I couldn't see you if I wanted."

"Um, well, do you want to?"

Tucker sighed again. "Look, man. I have to get up tomorrow… for homeschool."

"You get up *early* for homeschool?"

"It's not like you think. I go to all these strangers' houses with other kids. We even have field trips. It's pretty cool." Tucker's voice grew slightly more animated, like a dam starting to break.

"Oh, yeah? Like, where do you guys go?"

"Well, maybe it's not all that great. We're going to some dumb farm… it is near where you live, but you'll be in school, of course."

Elliot could hear the disappointment in Tucker's voice. "Wait. Really? What farm are you going to? My mom is going to one with her class."

"Sunnybrook Farm?"

"Sunnybrook Farm?" Elliot nearly screamed. "Are you serious? Dude! That's where my mom's going! I'm totally going, too. I'll ask my mom to go with her class."

"You can do that?" Tucker asked. Then he cleared his throat and coughed. "I mean, I guess that would be cool. But I'll be with my friends. I probably won't see much of you."

"So what? We'll be together again!"

"Elliot, dude. I don't think we'll ever be friends again. Look, I got to go."

The call ended abruptly.

Elliot stopped his bouncing and fell back on his bed, landing hard on his backside. Flopping to his back, he stared up at the ceiling. His heartbeat quickened. Tucker would be at Sunnybrook Farm. So would he. Anything could happen.

Abandoning his phone, he rolled off the bed and ran for the door.

"Mom!" he yelled. "Mom, can I go to the farm with you?"

As Elliot worked out the details about attending the field trip to Sunnybrook Farm with their surprised mom, Skylar stepped out for fresh air. She wandered to the end of the driveway, basking in the quiet darkness. It was a warm, muggy night with a slight breeze. After several steamy days in a row, rain was moving in. Standing by the street, she watched tendrils of fog drift toward her. It rolled in like an ethereal carpet, covering the street with a ghostly blanket.

She'd left the house to gather her thoughts and text Teddy about her mom's field trip. She wanted to tell him she would definitely be going. Seeing the fog mesmerized her, and she took time to watch it drift past her ankles.

A full moon hid behind thick clouds high above her. The moon's muted light mixed with the street lamp at the end of the Goodall driveway, creating an eerie sight. It was spooky, thrilling, and beautiful all at once. It captured Skylar's feelings perfectly. She would be spending a day with Teddy on Blue Island.

Skylar had just sent her text when the trees rustled behind her house. A branch snapped, sounding like something large trying to move quietly. She started to glance that way when she heard another sound. This one came from the road down past the Goodall house.

Click. Click. Click.

Skylar frowned. Something hard was scraping against the pavement in measured movements… like footsteps.

The noise drew closer.

Click. Click. Click.

She watched in fascination as a huge shadowy shape slowly emerged in the fog. Her fascination turned into alarm. The shape headed straight for her. Skylar heard something like a low growl.

Gasping, she slowly backed away. She hoped she was hidden by the shadows and couldn't be seen.

The trees behind her rustled again. She heard what sounded like heavy panting, like from a dog.

A cold sweat broke on her forehead, and her knees buckled slightly.

Click. Click. Click.

"Run," said a woman's voice, sounding just by her ear. "Now."

It had to have been her imagination because there was no one there. At the same time, it was great advice. Skylar squeezed her phone tight and raced for the house. She didn't dare look behind her or toward the trees, afraid of what she might see.

She did hear—she was sure of it—deep, hoarse laughter. Then she was in the house and slammed the door tight.

"Just my imagination," she told herself. "The fog messed with my mind…"

She ran up the stairs to take a shower and prayed the hot water would not mysteriously go off.

Tucker sat back on his bed, staring at his phone in disbelief. He'd been shocked when getting Elliot's text and even more surprised when he answered the call. His former friend had sounded the same as always, only a little sad. He wondered if he sounded the same to Elliot.

He probably had just sounded rude. That is what shocked Tucker the most.

Tucker had wanted to talk to Elliot so badly for weeks. When he got the chance, he pretty much blew him off. He guessed he wasn't quite over the whole dumb video incident after all.

"Oh, man, what have I done?" Covering his eyes, he kicked his heel into the mattress. "Elliot will never go on the field trip now. I'll be, like, stuck with Phileo for the rest of my life."

"Hey," Maria called from behind his closed door. He'd remembered to lock it this time, so she was stuck out there. "Who are you talking to?"

"Just my imaginary friend," Tucker said to her, still rubbing his eyes with his hands. "I found a new friend, so you can leave me alone now. Only I can see him. Now go to bed. It's past your bedtime."

"You're starting to sound like Phileo," Maria told him after a moment. "You're so weird."

"Tell me about it," Tucker muttered. He reached over to grab his phone. He saw no new texts and wondered if he should send one to Elliot. He thought better of it. After all, Tucker had been right. Elliot had moved and was too far away to be real friends. His parents would never drive him to Grantham. That just left the field trip to Sunnybrook Farm. Maybe he'll see Elliot, maybe he won't. It didn't matter. Their friendship was history.

The next morning, a sickening sight lay on the street in front of the Ashley house. An unfortunate raccoon had met its demise and turned into roadkill. The only recognizable part of the poor creature was its tail. The rest was a gory mess.

When Skylar stepped out of the house for school, she saw a pair of large black vultures standing over the dead meat. She nearly lost her breakfast.

Whatever hit it had to have been traveling fast—its body looked to have been torn to shreds as it lay in a huge dark stain on the gray pavement. The two cats in the Goodall house had spent most of the night quivering under the bed.

Chapter 19

The next few weeks passed by quickly.

At Leewood Elementary, Mrs. Ashley's class got through the state testing relatively unscathed. Nearly all her class passed the reading, and most sailed through the math. Marcus and Scotty were the only ones to fail both. Marcus had finished both tests in a combined time of less than fifteen minutes. Gary, no surprise, aced his tests with no problem. Bobby managed to squeak by in reading but fell apart in math. Mrs. Ashley never told him he'd failed, but the boy knew and felt terrible about it. After heavy rain wiped out the next two baseball practices, he was a no-show for the third. When asked about it in school the next day, he said he was considering quitting without providing a reason. Mrs. Ashley was stunned. She needed his dad as an assistant coach and could only hope Bobby would change his mind. Marcus, of course, didn't make the practice either. It was probably her fault.

With state testing completed, the class fell into chaos. The students were pretty much done with learning for the year. Mrs. Ashley was left scrambling for ideas on how to control her class, mainly the boys. The field trip became her only weapon. She routinely threatened to keep students back if they misbehaved.

One day, catching Bobby and Marcus throwing paper at each other, she'd lost it and sent both to the office.

"Both of you can stay there during our field trip," she'd yelled. That had been the day of the baseball practice Bobby had skipped.

The next day, she had both boys write letters of apology to earn back field trip privileges. Surprisingly, both boys did so without complaint. Marcus even managed two paragraphs.

During this time, Mrs. Ashley barely saw her real family. School winding down meant she spent extra hours cleaning up her classroom and finishing up student files for middle school. When she did make it home, it was always after dinner and she was exhausted. And she still had final papers to grade for the last report cards.

Mr. Ashley pretty much took over the household. Looking haggard, he kept up his job search while making sure Skylar and Elliot had breakfast, got to school on time, and had their supper at night. He did the grocery shopping and all the household chores, with Skylar and Elliot pitching in.

While Mrs. Ashley greatly appreciated this, she knew her husband was beyond frustrated and wanted to work. He had two online interviews in one week, but neither went anywhere. All the job openings were beneath his salary, or he was told he wasn't the right fit at that time. She certainly hoped Morgan Raycroft could help…

It was the field trip to Sunnybrook that kept the family united. It was all they talked about when they did have a few moments together. Skylar spent hours with her new friends after school, discussing and planning the day at the farm. She refused to give away any secrets, mainly because she hadn't been there yet. She did promise it would be epic. Elliot tried to find online pictures of the farm but found very few photos of Blue Island itself. There was nothing on the farm. Google Maps, apparently, never made it out to the island. This just made him more excited. It felt like they were going to some new unexplored land. If only he and Tucker could get away and explore. He hadn't told his mom Tucker would be there but did mention it to Skylar. His sister promised to make sure the two boys found time to meet.

In the days leading up to the field trip, Elliot started working out with his dad and playing catch with him after school on the days it didn't rain. He had a lot of nervous energy to burn off. His dad appreciated the company. Mr. Ashley even got Elliot to start liking nineties rock music.

Soon, the day before the field trip arrived.

Mrs. Ashley had already arranged for Elliot to miss his school the next day, and she'd gotten Dr. Chocker's permission for him to ride with her... on one condition. They had to ride the special education bus with Gary. Mr. Harris would also be on the bus, along with a few other students Dr. Chocker promised Mrs. Ashley could handpick, but one of them had to be Marcus. She didn't mind. Spending time with her students and own kids would be a blast. She even told Dr. Chocker he was right to pick the farm as the field trip destination. All that was left was to get through the day.

The morning started rough. The students' excitement level was through the roof. With summer starting in just a few days and the field trip being on the next day, the kids couldn't sit still, stop talking, or listen to directions for more than ten seconds at a time.

During her planning period, with her students safely at the library, Mrs. Ashley stopped by for advice from Mr. Charles.

Supposedly, all teachers were equal in school, but that was not the case. At Leewood, whatever Mr. Charles said and wanted, he nearly always got. No questions. Almost finished with his twentieth year at the school, Mr. Charles held the most experience on staff and had won teacher of the year three separate years. In his mid-forties, he looked much younger. With a shaved head, dark brown skin, and a quick smile, he easily became the favorite fifth-grade teacher for boys. A former football player at junior college, he kept himself fit and never seemed to lose his temper.

Mrs. Ashley used to be intimidated around him. He seemed to keep his class in line with magic. Using a calm voice and strict discipline, he never seemed to have behavior problems with his class.

Then, one day, she walked into his class to borrow a math manual and saw him standing over a special education student, yelling at him for not finishing his work. She realized he was just like all the other teachers. Everyone had their limits. He was just better at hiding his.

Seeing Mrs. Ashley enter his room, Mr. Charles grunted at his desk and looked up from behind his computer.

"Hey, Karen," he said in greeting. "Are you all set for tomorrow?" He was not excited about the farm trip and was still angry Dr. Chocker had never consulted him about it.

"Actually, I'm excited about it," Mrs. Ashley said. "I think the kids might really have a good time."

"Yeah, yeah, I hope so." Mr. Charles sighed. "I had everything planned for the pool party… Maybe next year. What's up?"

"I was hoping you had some advice. My boys… They're still driving me crazy."

"Relationships," Mr. Charles said solemnly. "It's all about building relationships. That's what I do."

Mrs. Ashley grimaced. She did the same. "Right. It's just they're so full of energy."

"Yes, you do have a handful," Mr. Charles said, nodding. He reached up his long arms and stretched them over his head.

"I know it's hard, but you must keep firm discipline. Be consistent."

Before Mrs. Ashley could reply, Mr. Harris interrupted them by barging into the room.

The stocky special education teacher currently sported a short, spiky haircut and goatee. Both were dark with sweat, and his green polo shirt was soaked under his arms.

"Sorry to interrupt," he said. "But can I borrow a soccer ball? One of the third graders kicked mine over the fence. I'll have to find it later."

Mr. Charles raised an eyebrow at Mrs. Ashley as if making his point. He then gave the younger teacher a curt look.

"Shouldn't you be, I don't know, in class working with your students right now?"

"Yeah, I am," Mr. Harris said, grinning. "I'm working on their soccer skills. They certainly need it."

Mr. Charles didn't crack a smile. He pursed his lips as he stared at the special education teacher. "The school year isn't over, you know."

Mr. Harris frowned at the teacher, keeping eye contact. "I'm guessing that's a no on the soccer ball, huh?"

Mrs. Ashley stepped back, feeling the animosity between the two teachers. "Well, I need to be going," she said. "I still have to divide my class into groups for tomorrow's trip."

"I'll be there," Mr. Harris said, turning away from Mr. Charles. "Make sure I get an easy group, no troublemakers!"

Mrs. Ashley just rolled her eyes. The only reason Mr. Harris was going on the trip was to watch over Gary and Marcus, the two biggest troublemakers in the school.

That was the biggest disappointment she had when becoming a teacher. She always thought teachers were perfect role models and there for the students. Instead, they were just like other people, far from perfect. They had petty squabbles even worse than the kids that they were supposed to be teaching.

She left the two men in the awkward showdown to return to her room. She decided to use a combination of Mr. Charles's and Mr. Harris's methods. She would do a quick reading lesson and, if her class got through it, then have recess for the rest of the day.

The following day, Elliot woke up to find Skylar looming over him with a crazed grin. His sister smelled of sunscreen and was already in jeans and a bright turquoise shirt.

"Aaah!" he cried, twisting in his blanket. "What are you doing here?"

"Making sure you're awake, butt-breath. You have to get up early for the field trip."

On his side, Elliot pushed his head against his pillow and scrunched up his nose. Raising a knee, he scratched his thigh. "What time is it?" The muted light from the window told him it was way earlier than he usually woke up.

"Just after six." She slapped his raised knee. "Go get dressed. Teddy is picking me up in a few minutes, so I probably won't see you until you're at the farm."

Even though tired, Elliot gave her a goofy grin. "I just hope I don't see you kissing."

Skylar shoved down his knee, grabbing the back of his shirt with her other hand. "If you do, you'll be spying, and I'll make sure you regret it!" Gripping his thigh, she pinned him down.

"Hey!" Elliot protested.

Skylar just laughed. She let go of his shirt but held his skinny thigh. "You deserve this, kiddo!" She slapped the back of his pajama pants three times as he struggled to break free.

"You'll get worse if you tell Mom or Dad anything about me kissing," she warned, releasing him.

"Wait," Elliot said, rolling to his back. He shook stray hair from his eyes. "Does that mean you did kiss him?"

Already leaving, Skylar blew him a kiss at the door. "Get dressed, barf-head. Don't forget, I'm going to make sure you and Tucker meet, so be ready!"

"Tucker!" Elliot threw off his sheets and jumped out of bed to quickly change.

When he left his room for the bathroom, he wore pale green athletic pants and a black T-shirt with skeleton bones on the front, one of his dad's birthday presents. As he walked, he texted Tucker, letting him know he would be leaving for the farm soon.

"Yo, Elliot," Skylar said as she brushed by him in the hall. "Don't drop that thing in the toilet."

"Ha, you're so hilarious," Elliot said, not looking up.

Skylar stopped and turned on her brother. "Is that Tucker you're texting?"

"Yeah." Elliot lowered his phone and eyed his sister over his shoulder. "Are you sure you can let us meet?"

"Trust me, sewage breath. I got you. Just make sure you apologize and don't start a fight."

Seeing Elliot's face fall, Skylar raised her hand and rubbed the top of his head, smoothing his hair back from his face. "Don't worry, Elliot," she said. "Tucker was a good friend. He'll come around." Patting his head, she hefted her backpack, filled with lunch, snacks, and water, higher on her shoulder.

"Yeah, okay." Elliot slipped the phone in the back pocket of his pants. He managed a smile. "Thanks, booger-brain."

"Anytime, butthead."

A car honked from the driveway.

"Okay, that's me! Tell Mom goodbye. I'll see you both there. Be careful."

"You too," Elliot told her, meaning it.

Back in Whitney, Tucker shuffled to the bathroom in his boxers and T-shirt. He carried his phone, black jeans, socks, and favorite T-shirt. The shirt was dark gray with the words "TOP CHEF" in black type across the middle. It had been a gift from Elliot on his last birthday.

Inside, he dropped the clothes on the floor and set his phone on the counter. Yawning, he faced the mirror, brushing back his curls.

Phileo's mom would pick him up in twenty minutes for the field trip to Sunnybrook Farm. Thinking about the farm, his heartbeat quickened. Would Elliot really be there?

Eyeing his phone, he looked in the mirror. "Oh, what the heck," he said. Snatching the phone, he sent Elliot a single-word text.

Coming?

He then let out a deep breath. He'd been refusing to text Elliot for a long time, and just that single word felt like a mountain falling off his back.

Feeling good, he pulled off his shirt and started flexing in the mirror.

"Looking good, my man," he said, nodding to the mirror. He saw the faint lines of muscle emerging and grinned. "Oh, yeah."

"Tucker!" Maria hollered from the other side of the door. "If you're talking to your imaginary friend in there, I'm going to barf all over your bed!"

"Maria!" Tucker yelled. "Can't I get any privacy?"

"I bet you're showing off in the mirror again!"

"Am not!"

"Well, hurry up! I need the toilet!"

Tucker huffed and quickly finished his business. As he washed his hands, his phone pinged, announcing a message.

He nearly fell as he lunged to grab it, not bothering to dry his hands. Elliot had responded he should be at the farm by ten o'clock… and he had a plan for them to meet.

Tucker thought of thousands of responses but settled on one word.

Cool

Then Maria was banging on the door and calling for their mom to get Tucker out of there.

Tucker quickly got dressed. As he pulled on his shirt, he felt a surge of happiness. The night before, he'd baked cookies to bring on the trip. It was the first time he'd made something in the kitchen since the pumpkin pudding.

"Okay, I'm out!" he hollered, snatching up his phone.

Opening the door, he nearly bumped into his little sister.

"It's about time," Maria said, jutting up her chin. "For that, you owe me three of your cookies."

"I'll leave you four," Tucker told her. "But I'm giving some to Elli—" He stopped and widened his eyes. "I mean…"

"Elliot?" Maria said, her face lighting up with a smile. "You're seeing him?"

"At the farm," Tucker said, lowering his voice. "Don't tell Mom."

"My lips are sealed." Maria made a show of zipping her lips. Then, biting her lower lip, she danced past Tucker into the bathroom, slamming the door. "You better have a good day!" she yelled back at him.

Tucker certainly hoped it would be a good day. He rushed down to grab some breakfast before Phileo and his mom arrived.

Chapter 20

The forecast called for lots of sun and a high of just over eighty degrees. The weather did not disappoint. It was a crystal blue sky brushed with wisps of cirrus clouds when Mrs. Ashley pulled into the school parking lot, with Elliot half-asleep in the back. She drove her 2006 Corolla, leaving her husband with the minivan.

"Are you ready, kiddo?" she asked Elliot.

Elliot yawned and jammed his baseball cap over his thick head of hair. "Are we really riding the short bus?" he asked.

"Watch it, young man," Mrs. Ashley warned. "I don't want to hear anything like that on this trip, got it? Never make fun of anybody for being different. Remember, everyone has challenges."

"Yeah, and everyone can change," Elliot said, finishing her motto. "Change for the better."

"Okay, kiddo. Let's go. Looks like they're waiting for us."

She had purposely left the house late. Perhaps she was being overcautious, but she didn't want Elliot to have to wait in her classroom with her students for the field trip. She feared

Marcus would say something about the video in front of everyone. It was bad enough that Elliot had to ride the same bus as Marcus. She meant to keep the boys far apart. It was a good thing, she decided, that Marcus had never shown up for baseball practice.

She pulled into an open parking spot and switched off the engine. Glancing in the rearview mirror, she saw Elliot brush a strand of hair from the front of his cap. He looked nervous and not sure of himself. Her heart ached a little.

This was his first time back to his old school after the move. Since the incident with Tucker, she had to admit, he was a shell of his former self. She wondered what his old classmates would think when they saw him. He'd been in Mrs. Wayne's class, a hunched-over, ancient teacher retiring at the end of the year. When Tucker had left her class, she'd stopped interacting with Mrs. Ashley outside of teacher meetings. One good thing about moving schools was that Elliot got to switch teachers.

Elliot climbed out of the car only after Mrs. Ashley exited. He shrugged on his backpack with his lunch and water and followed timidly behind his mom.

As mother and son crossed the parking lot, two long school buses were parked at the curb in front of the school. The shorter special education bus sat in the back.

Mrs. Ashley saw Mr. Charles start directing the long line of noisy fifth graders onto the long buses, dividing them by classes. They were streaming out of the secondary entrance to the left of the main office. Veering from the main group, Mr. Harris led a surly Marcus and bored Gary to the small bus. She wasn't surprised to see Bobby following.

When given the opportunity to select students to ride on her bus with them, she let it be voluntary. She didn't want to force anyone to ride with Marcus and Gary, not on a fun trip. She was surprised to see Cynthia and Kim trailing after Bobby.

"There you are!" Dr. Chocker called, trotting out of the main door by the front office. He met them in the parking lot by the buses. "I was getting worried."

Mrs. Ashley grinned. "I'm here. You remember Elliot."

Dr. Chocker managed a tight smile. "How can I forget? Uh, good to see you, Elliot."

Peering up from under his ball cap, Elliot squinted from the sun. "Hi, Dr. Chocker," he said warily.

"Well, you two hop on your bus." The principal tugged his tie and smoothed down his gray suit. "I'll be driving separately in case I need to leave in an emergency."

"Sounds good. We'll meet you there!" Mrs. Ashley eyed the suit but made no comment. She wore shorts and a blue collared shirt. Carrying a sunhat and a small bag with her lunch and water, she was ready for the farm. She doubted Dr. Chocker would be.

She guided Elliot up the curb and to their bus. She greeted the driver at the top of the stairs with a big smile. "Thank you for driving us!"

A grizzled man with greasy black hair slumped behind the wheel. He nodded in return. "You the last one?" he asked, letting off a belch.

"No, I have my son here, too."

"Get him up here. We are about to depart, young lady."

Mrs. Ashley smiled and motioned for Elliot to climb aboard.

"Mrs. Ashley!" Cynthia called excitedly from the back of the bus. "You're here!"

"Oh, great, there goes the fun," Marcus muttered loudly from his seat in the middle.

Gary chuckled from his seat near Marcus. He wore his usual outfit of tan shorts and a red polo shirt, along with his mischievous smirk.

"Hey, none of that," Mr. Harris said, sitting across from Marcus and behind Gary. He didn't sound like he meant it as he stared longingly out the window at the other buses.

"So, who's the loco parent today?" Bobby joked, sitting behind Marcus. "You guys going to be 'Mom' and 'Dad'?"

"Okay, that's enough," Mrs. Ashley said, setting down her pack in the first seat. "Let's settle down and have a good trip. You can talk quietly but no trouble, boys."

Behind her, Elliot stepped timidly onto the bus. Keeping his gaze down, he quickly took the seat directly across from her, behind the driver. Setting down his backpack, he scooched to the window with his phone in hand.

"Is that your son?" Cynthia asked. "He's back at Leewood! I forgot what he looks like. He's cute!"

"Shut up," Kim said from beside her, grabbing her friend's arm. "You're embarrassing us."

"Hey, I saw him with a phone," Marcus said. "Does that mean we can have our phones out?"

"Absolutely not," Mrs. Ashley said. "You know the rule, Marcus." She stared pointedly at Elliot. "Sorry, kiddo. But when you're on the bus, you become a student. Phone goes away."

Elliot blew out his breath but obediently slid his phone into his backpack. Taking off his cap, he leaned his head against the window and stared listlessly out into the parking lot. He wished Tucker could be with him right now.

As the bus rumbled to life, he closed his eyes and tried to get as comfortable as possible. It would be a long trip. He would know. He'd just come from Grantham.

Tucker took a deep breath as Phileo's tan SUV pulled up in front of his driveway. He was waiting outside so Maria wouldn't have to see Phileo. If she did, he feared she might deck him.

"Here I go," he muttered, hefting his backpack full of cookies and lunch on his shoulder. "Into an alien spacecraft. Boldly, I go where no kid should go."

At least he wouldn't starve.

He carried headphones for his phone in his pocket and planned to pretend to sleep while listening to music the entire trip. Anything to avoid listening to Phileo and his mom ask about Maria and tea parties.

Trudging to the side door, he pulled it open and got the shock of his life.

"G-Good morning!" squealed a young girl about Maria's age. "Y-you must be T-Tucker! I'm L-Lily!"

Each word seemed a struggle for the girl, but the pure joy and smile she directed at Tucker came as natural as sunshine on a cloudless day.

Tucker could only stare. Lily sat strapped in a special car seat in the middle row of the SUV. Her neck and back leaned at a slight angle to the side. Super thin limbs stuck out from her white dress decorated with colorful flowers. A pink bow decorated her long brown hair, pulled back in a ponytail. She giggled at his expression. "S-Surprise!"

She was the last thing Tucker expected in the SUV. Alien technology and ray guns, yes. This? Absolutely not.

"Oh, er, hi," he finally managed to say. "I'm Tucker."

"I kn-know that," Lily said, giggling harder. "And y-you have a sister, r-right?"

Tucker felt like the biggest dope on the planet and like somebody just smeared pumpkin pudding from Dr. Chocker's toilet all over his face. So that's what the tea party invitation was about! Phileo and his mom were looking for a friend for Lily.

"Come on in," Phileo's mom said from behind the wheel. If she noticed Tucker's shock, she never let on. "We're trying to hit the road and avoid traffic."

"Sit back here," Phileo said from the backseat. "Lily bites."

"I-I do n-not!" Lily said, laughing. Drool slid down her chin, and she wiped it with a napkin clutched in a tight fist. Tucker noticed that her left hand was also squeezed tightly but held nothing.

"I know," Phileo said, smiling. "I was just joking."

"Lily has cerebral palsy," Mrs. Benedict explained. "But she's the sweetest girl on the planet."

"That's right!" Lily said proudly.

"Yeah, I'm sure," Tucker said awkwardly as he climbed past Lily to sit beside Phileo. "Um, how old are you?" he asked Lily.

"Eight!"

Tucker smothered a groan. "Okay," he said brightly. "Well, my sister is going to, um, visit you real soon," he said. "She's, well, been busy but wants to go to a tea party."

"Yes!" Lily clapped her two tightly clenched hands together.

"That would be wonderful," Mrs. Benedict said with feeling. "We've been trying to find a playmate for Lily for a while now. I was going to take her to the farm today, but they're just opening and don't have handicap access yet."

"So I-I get to g-go to the pet shop!" Lily said happily.

Her mom smiled back at her. "That's right, Lily! We'll find one as soon as we drop the boys off."

Taking his seat and dropping his backpack by his feet, Tucker elbowed Phileo in the shoulder. "Yo, dude," he hissed. "How come you never told me about your sister?"

Phileo, his hair plastered down and parted in the middle, was wearing pressed khakis and a white polo shirt. Looking at Tucker in mild confusion, he shrugged. "You never asked."

Tucker yanked on his seat belt and grimaced. "Well, I've never seen her at your house before."

"She goes to a special school during the day." He eyed Tucker. "Do you mean it about the tea party?"

"Uh, yeah." Tucker looked Phileo in the eye. "I'll definitely make sure Maria goes. She totally owes me."

"Cool. You should come too. I can show you my room, and we can play some games on my computer." His eyes got an evil glint. "I happen to be pretty good at making mods."

Tucker eyed Phileo with new respect. "Dude, are you serious?"

"My br-brother is the b-best!" Lily said, overhearing. "He m-made m-me a pr-princess Minecr-craft village!"

Tucker could only shake his head. "Bruh, man, I'm totally there." He amazed himself by meaning it. He settled back in his seat, forgetting about his headphones. Just maybe he didn't need Elliot as much as he thought he did after all.

On the bus, Marcus leaned his head against the window, staring down the line of empty seats to where Mrs. Ashley's son sat in the front. All he could see was long, dark blond hair slumped against the window.

He bit down a pang of jealousy. His dad loved him but worked as a long-haul truck driver and was often gone for weeks at a time. This sometimes made Marcus feel like an orphan. He had no real mom. His mom had abandoned him when he'd been just a toddler, leaving him and his dad and taking his two sisters. He rarely saw her, and she never acted overjoyed at seeing him. Since then, his dad had remarried, but his stepmom had never had much time for him. Soon after they first met, she'd bought a brand-new PlayStation for his room and told him if he didn't bother her, she wouldn't bother him. That had been four years ago, and that remained the extent of their relationship.

He glanced across the bus aisle at Mr. Harris and then in the seat in front of the teacher. Gary looked back at him and held up his phone.

"Play you in a game," he whispered.

Marcus grunted and glanced at Mr. Harris.

The teacher sat sideways in his seat, facing him, but his eyes were closed. "Just don't let Mrs. Ashley catch you," Mr. Harris muttered, never cracking his eyelids.

Bobby was asleep and the girls were discussing what they were doing over the summer.

Marcus grinned and slipped his phone from his pocket. "What game?" he asked.

He never meant to get in trouble, but Marcus also knew nobody really cared about him. He had to take care of himself.

Even with morning traffic, the trip to Grantham went smoothly. Once across the river, the traffic thinned even more, and the buses soon neared the road to Blue Island.

Elliot opened his eyes and blinked away sleep. He'd drifted off shortly after leaving the school and was surprised to see how far they'd gotten. He recognized the shopping center they were passing from going to the disastrous funeral. As the bus made a right turn, he stood up and looked out the window past his mom. Sure enough, they were passing Ma's Diner.

"Elliot!" Mrs. Ashley said sharply. "Keep your seat!"

Elliot quickly sat back down. "We're almost there, aren't we?" he asked.

His mom nodded. "Yes, we're close… The Church of Grantham Saints should be coming up soon. Then we should take a right on Blue Road and that goes straight to the island."

"Mom, can I, um, like, check my phone real quick?"

"No way, kiddo. You're one of my students now."

From the middle of the bus, Marcus hissed a sharp yes. "Got you!"

Elliot pursed his lips and slumped back against the window.

If anybody had glanced out the back window towards the diner, they would have spotted Erma. The waitress staggered from the diner, looking in horror as she watched the three buses rumble past.

"N-no," she stammered. "This can't be true! Morgan, what have you done?"

She then raced to her pickup, still wearing her apron. The customers at Ma's Diner would just have to wait on themselves.

Chapter 21

Several minutes later, the buses entered the stretch of road lined with thick forest.

Marcus and Gary both let out cries of dismay when the signal for their phones abruptly died. They quickly put them away before Mrs. Ashley noticed.

When the buses emerged from the trees, the island came into view. Vast, wild, and not so welcoming, it stretched before them like something lost from time. A thick forest waited on the other side of a narrow bridge with a single lane running in each direction.

"Whoa," Elliot said, kneeling on his seat to look over the driver's shoulder. "That's, like, much bigger than I expected."

Mrs. Ashley also stared in fascination and never noticed her son not sitting correctly. "So that's Blue Island," she said softly. "Looks pretty lonely, doesn't it?"

"I think it looks amazing," Elliot said. "I can't, like, see any houses or anything! It's like a wooded kingdom."

"They're built farther inland," Mrs. Ashley said. "From what I hear, there're gas stations and grocery stores, even a post office. And, of course, a farm. I think it's just before the main community. So we should get there pretty quick." Glancing over, she saw Elliot's knees on the seat.

"Elliot!" she said. "Sit down on your bottom!"

"Are we there yet?" Bobby called, sounding bored.

"Almost!" Mrs. Ashley called back. "We should be arriving in a few minutes."

"Where's this farm?" Marcus asked suspiciously. "This looks like a whole lot of nothing!"

"Reminds me of a horror movie," Gary said. "I heard that monsters live in those woods."

"If they do, they won't bother you," Cynthia called. "They'll just welcome you into the family."

"That's enough, Cynthia," Mrs. Ashley said.

"What?" the girl said innocently. "That was a compliment. Everyone likes Gary, especially monsters."

Mrs. Ashley stood up from her seat and glared toward the back. Then she sighed in exasperation. "Bobby, will you wake up Mr. Harris? Please tell him that we're almost there."

"Sure thing, Mrs. A." Bobby slid close to the aisle and smacked the seat behind the teacher. "Yo, Dad! Wake up! The mom wants you ready to go!"

Mr. Harris snorted and sat up with a start.

Mrs. Ashley was not amused. "Bobby!" she said harshly. "That was uncalled for! Apologize to Mr. Harris right now, or you can stay on the bus all day."

"Sorry, Mrs. A," Bobby muttered.

Mrs. Ashley continued to glare. "I said apologize to Mr. Harris. Now."

"Huh?" Mr. Harris looked around, confused. He yawned and blinked away sleep. "What happened now?"

"Sorry, Mr. Harris," Bobby mumbled. He slumped back in his seat.

"Thank you," Mrs. Ashley said, looking sternly across the bus. "I will not tolerate disrespect on this bus and certainly not on the farm. You represent the school, me, and yourselves. Do I make myself clear?"

"Uh, yeah," Mr. Harris said. He stroked his goatee nervously. "I mean, you, um, guys, and, uh, girls got it, right?"

"Mom," Elliot hissed. "You're standing up."

"Shut it, kiddo," Mrs. Ashley said, sitting back down. She winked at him. "That goes for you too."

Then they were at the bridge. The bridge did not look the sturdiest, with low concrete barriers on the side. If it ever collapsed, there would be no other roads to and from the mainland.

"What if this bridge gets washed away?" Cynthia said as the bus rumbled over. "We'll be stuck on the island forever!"

"It's an island, moron," Gary said. "Have you ever heard of boats?"

Mrs. Ashley glared back at Mr. Harris to say something, but the younger teacher stared out the window at the blue water under the bus. He looked a little pale.

Just like that, they were on the island. Heading into the thick forest, the road ran straight through the center. Eventually, the buses turned off at a side road, carefully maneuvering around the tight corner. The woods thinned out before opening into grassy fields. The farm was near.

Located near the island's southeast coast, Sunnybrook Farm was fifty acres of green fields lined with thick clumps of trees. While advertised as brand new to the public, it was certainly an old farm. The parking area was an unpaved grassy lot with spray-painted lines marking spaces for cars. Four cars were parked in the mostly empty lot as the three Whitney County buses pulled up at the entrance to the farm. A sturdy chain-link fence, gray and flecked with rust, lined the front of the farm to greet them. It was topped with barbwire.

"What do you think they keep in there?" Bobby asked, looking at the sharp metal thorns lining the top of the fence. "King Kong?"

"Looks like a prison, man," Marcus said.

The two boys stared out at the farm from their seats on the bus. Neither looked too excited to climb out.

"You guys are stupid," Gary said from behind them. "The barbwire is facing out, not inward. It's to keep something outside, not inside."

"Get your mind off the fence and take a look at the farm," Cynthia said critically. "It doesn't look all that great… it looks, I don't know, sick."

Behind the fence, they saw a giant barn with a sagging roof and peeling dull red paint. Gray animal pens were set up next to it. Beyond the large barn and the pens, and just behind a field full of sad-looking cows, was a smaller barn. It looked in worse shape than the first, and its second-story loft door hung crooked on its hinges. Long rickety sheds, looking as if they'd been constructed a hundred years before, were a long walk to the right of the giant barn and marked other areas for animals. Like the barns, the sheds were filthy and needed a paint job. Near it, the kids could see a chicken coop. Besides the cows, sheep could be seen in a fenced-in area beyond the sheds. No other animals were in sight.

"Lame," Marcus said after taking it all in. "This is something even my little sisters would hate. I mean, even if they were really, really bored."

"I'm sure it will be more fun than it looks from a bus," Mrs. Ashley said as she gathered her bag and stood up. She moved across the aisle to Elliot's seat and knelt behind him to peer over his shoulder. "At least, I hope so." She put her hand on Elliot's back. "Do you see your sister?"

Elliot wrinkled his brow. "Not yet. She's probably kiss—I mean, she's, um, probably visiting the pigs." He was actually busily searching for Tucker. He noticed a few kids already inside the fence, but they were with a group of teenagers and moving too much for him to get a good look.

The teenage volunteers did not have much to work with but tried their best to make the place welcoming. Inside the chain-link barbwire, the fences for the cows were wood post-and-rail. These fences were lined with colorful balloons. A large homemade poster welcoming Leewood Elementary and homeschoolers hung from the top loft window of the giant barn. Country music blared from a speaker in the main barn, and teens were running around with bright smiles. Upon seeing the buses, a group of them headed to meet them.

Mrs. Ashley watched as the bus in front of them opened its doors, and Mr. Charles climbed out. Putting his hands on his hips, he did not look happy.

Mrs. Ashley took a deep breath and patted Elliot on the back of the pants. "Remember. Be respectful out there and stay out of trouble. This could be a long day..." Then she stood and faced the back of the bus. "Leave your stuff on the bus, especially your phones."

"The internet doesn't work here anyway," Marcus said sourly.

"Actually, it does, in spots," Gary told him. "There must be a signal near here that's getting blocked by the trees."

Mrs. Ashley glared at Mr. Harris. "I said no phones, boys! I mean it!"

"Uh, yeah," Mr. Harris said, running a hand over his goatee. He hastily put his phone in his hip pocket. "No phones, kids."

Just to the right of the gated entrance, an old brick house stood with a pitched roof and a sagging porch. Built two stories, it looked as if it once was a beautiful home... back in the Civil War. Now it looked in need of major renovations. As she climbed off the bus, Mrs. Ashley spotted Dr. Chocker with a tall black-haired woman. The two were talking in front of the porch of the house. She raised her eyebrows when her principal reached out and hugged the woman. She did notice the woman slightly cringe in return. Mrs. Ashley guessed it had to be the mysterious Morgan Raycroft and wondered what the two could be discussing.

Next to her, she heard Elliot gasp, and he pressed close to her side.

"What is it?" she asked, instinctively putting an arm around his shoulder.

Elliot nodded toward the house. "I, like, saw that woman before. She, um, was at baseball practice."

"Are you sure?" Mrs. Ashley said doubtfully.

"Um, yeah. She was, like, with two other guys from that funeral."

Mrs. Ashley absently rubbed the top of Elliot's ball cap. "Well, I'm sure if you did, she had a good reason to be there. Maybe one of our kiddos on the team is from Blue Island."

"Mrs. Ashley!" yelled Mr. Charles from the front of the entrance. "Come on, I need you! We need to organize our classes into groups and get this thing over with, I mean started."

"Coming!" She gave Elliot a final pat on the back and hurried toward the line of students coming off the two large buses. "Mr. Harris, you keep an eye on Marcus and Gary! Make sure they find their group! Elliot, stay close!"

Mr. Harris scratched the top of his head and looked around in confusion. Gary stood next to him, staring down at his phone. Marcus and Bobby had vanished.

"Cynthia, where's Marcus?" he asked.

"I don't know, you're the teacher," the girl told him. She and Kim were heading toward their assigned group.

"I think he said he's going to the bathroom," Kim told him. "But he usually says that when he wanders."

"Yeah," Cynthia said over her shoulder. "Good luck!"

Mr. Harris just groaned. "Come on, Gary," he muttered. "Let's go find that… those kids."

Elliot scratched his ribs nervously as he wandered through the confusion of fifth-grade classes being organized by grumpy teachers who wished they were at a pool instead of a rundown farm. The teachers were not the only ones unhappy. Being the end-of-year field trip celebrating fifth grade, many parents made the trip. Standing outside the barbwire fence, a group of parents surveyed the farm with disapproval.

"We traded a swimming pool for a cesspool," a dad mumbled.

Mr. Charles stood a few feet away and heard him. Stiffening, he turned to glower at where Dr. Chocker was going off toward the animal pens. The principal walked shoulder to shoulder with a tall, dark-haired woman wearing black pants and a black leather jacket. Neither one looked back or acknowledged the schoolchildren.

"All right!" Mr. Charles bellowed. "Once the groups are formed and everyone is accounted for, let's move into the farm!" He was like a general going into battle, determined to find victory, even if he didn't know what exactly that meant.

Inside the fence, teenage volunteers waited to meet the groups and serve as guides.

Before entering, Mrs. Ashley got her class into one large group just to the side of the entrance. Having counted her students, she was missing three. She surveyed the faces, already knowing what she would find. Marcus... He was nowhere to be found. Bobby and Gary were also missing.

"Oh, great," she said. Then she spotted Mr. Harris talking to Marcus and Bobby in the parking lot behind the buses. Gary stood by them, checking his phone. "Marcus! Bobby! Gary!" she yelled. "Over here, now!"

As she glared at them, she saw a pickup lurch into the lot and slam on its brakes. It stopped well short of the boys, but Mrs. Ashley still felt her heart skip a beat.

"Get out of the parking lot!" she shouted louder. "Now!"

The boys and Mr. Harris took off at a trot toward her. She was ready to yell at them again for running when the pickup opened, and a familiar figure staggered out.

Erma, the waitress from Ma's Diner, kicked off her heels and raced barefoot over the rocky lot toward the farm. Wearing an apron as if she'd just come from her job, her face looked panicked, like she'd seen a ghost.

Afraid there'd been an accident, Mrs. Ashley moved to meet the frightened waitress. She reached her just in front of the first bus. "What's wrong? Erma, do you remember me?"

The waitress saw her, and her eyes went even wider with fright. "You!" she screeched. "What are you doing here? Why are these buses here?"

"Oh, we're on a field trip, Erma. Remember, I'm—"

"I know who you are." Erma grasped Mrs. Ashley's hand. "Y'all need to leave. This place—" She gasped. "Oh, you brought your son? Oh, this is bad. So bad."

"What's wrong?" Mrs. Ashley asked, growing alarmed. She glanced at where Elliot stood with his back to them. On his tiptoes, he was trying to look through the fence, over Mrs. Wayne's class, and toward the barn.

"Everything," Erma said. Her eyes shut, and then they opened.

"Erma Jenkins!" cried a loud woman's voice. "I thought I heard your voice."

Immediately, Erma relaxed, and she put on a fake smile. "Sorry," she muttered to Mrs. Ashley. "Go with your son. Get out of here." She pushed away from Mrs. Ashley and marched toward the farm's entrance.

"I'll, I'll stop by for coffee sometime," Mrs. Ashley called after her, not knowing what else to say.

The waitress never replied. Her back was ramrod straight, and her arms were straight down at her sides. "Morgan Raycroft. Just the person I came to see."

"Come walk with us, and we'll discuss your catering," Morgan said, smiling extra wide. "You came at a perfect time. I need to talk to you about lunch today."

Erma shuddered briefly but kept walking. She soon joined Morgan inside the fence.

"What was that all about?" Cynthia asked as Mrs. Ashley returned to the class.

"When you got to go, you got to," Scotty replied. "That woman looks like she was too late and just messed herself."

"You kids stay put," Mrs. Ashley muttered.

She walked quickly past them to the entrance where one of the staff stood. He'd rushed from the brick house shortly after Erma had pulled up. The burly man wearing jeans and a plain white T-shirt eyed her worriedly.

"Does Erma Jenkins come here often?" she asked. "I mean, I know her, and she seemed… spooked."

"Oh, don't worry about Erma," the man said, forcing a grin. "She's all panicked because of, you know, you all. Not everyone around here is excited about us opening our island to, er, outsiders, pardon my expression."

Mrs. Ashley pursed her lips and shook her head. "She seemed more frightened than upset."

"Heh, she's an odd bird. Old folks like her are just scared of change. You, uh, know her, you said?"

"I, well, ate at Ma's Diner once."

"Best meatloaf you'll ever find in a hundred miles," the man said, relaxing. "I bet you noticed Erma's southern accent.

She lays it on thick for outsiders." He smiled and offered his hand. "I'm Ryan Raycroft. You're Karen Ashley, aren't you?"

Surprised, Mrs. Ashley nodded and met his hand with her own, giving it a slight shake. "Yes. How did you know?"

The man shrugged and wiped his hand on his pants. He had thin black hair sprinkled with gray, trimmed short over his crinkled face. "My older sister, she, uh, was your husband's mother. I guess I'm your uncle." Just then, the radio in the man's pocket squawked. "Excuse me," he said, stepping back. "I'm a bit busy today. We'll have to catch up later. It was good seeing you."

Mrs. Ashley stared in wonder as her husband's uncle walked hurriedly back to the brick house. For what it was worth, this field trip was certainly not boring.

While she was speaking to Ryan Raycroft, Dr. Chocker, Erma Jenkins, and Morgan Raycroft had moved well up a path and were headed to the far barn behind the cows. Mrs. Ashley would love to know what spooked the waitress and where the three were going. She meant to find Dr. Chocker as soon as possible and find out.

"Can we go in now?" Dave, one of her more unruly boys, asked. "I'm getting attacked by bugs standing here."

"Yes, let's go, kiddos." Mrs. Ashley couldn't shake the sense of doom as she led her class into the farm.

After the commotion with Marcus and Bobby, Mrs. Ashley nixed the idea of splitting her class. Not so surprisingly, her class had no parent volunteers. Originally, Mr. Harris was to lead half of her class in a group, and she would have the other half, but she couldn't trust the special education teacher.

"We're all staying together!" she announced. "End of story."

Elliot didn't mind. Being in a large group would make it easier for him to get lost. He had yet to spot Tucker or Skylar, and he looked for an opportunity to slip away.

"Where's the playground?" Cynthia asked. "Don't farms like this have playgrounds?"

"Uh, not yet," the pimply faced teen serving as one of their guides said. He brushed a single long lock of black hair from his face. His head was otherwise shaven down to stubble. "It'll, uh, be built over the summer, yeah."

His partner, a thin girl with straight black hair chopped short in a bowl cut, clapped her hands. "My name is Fiona, and my partner is Bo. We're going to have lots of fun!"

The entire class stood in a huddled group with dubious looks. Large flies buzzed around their faces.

"Want to bet?" Gary muttered.

Fiona paid him no attention. "Let's go to the duck pond first. Everyone is going to the barns and pens, so we'll have it to ourselves."

"I don't see any pond," Scotty said.

"Just follow Fiona, and she'll show us," Mrs. Ashley said tiredly.

Fiona nodded. "Stay on the path, and don't wander!"

"And watch out for animal... stuff," Bo added. "It's everywhere."

Mrs. Ashley led the way with the guides in front. Her class followed in a loose clump, with Mr. Harris bringing up the rear, supposedly watching Marcus.

"We have a nice pond over past the cows," Fiona said over her shoulder. "It's quite a hike. We have to go around the field and past those trees over there. Keep close, and don't get left behind."

"What will we see there?" Scotty asked.

"Uh, ducks?" Gary guessed sarcastically.

"Oh, there are different ducks," Fiona promised. "Right, Bo?"

"Uh, yeah. Ducks," Bo agreed.

"I don't actually know what kinds they are," Fiona admitted. "But you'll see."

"Is there a goose?" Bobby asked from near the back. "Get it? Duck, duck, goose!"

Cynthia shoved his shoulder. "Bobby, you are so funny."

"I know I am, but what am I?" he asked.

"An idiot," Marcus said. He kicked Bobby in the back of the shorts. "And slow. Speed up, man."

Bobby laughed and moved to a group of boys in the middle of the pack.

Unnoticed, Elliot left the group and started wandering toward the main barn. His eyes scanned for Tucker.

Chapter 22

Over by the long sheds on the other side of the farm, Tucker eyed his phone with a wrinkled brow. He stood off to himself, trying to track Elliot's phone. The signal was spotty at best. He'd lost it just as Elliot neared the island and got it back at the farm, only to lose it again. He knew Elliot had to be somewhere close, and his nerves started to jangle. He wondered if he should wait and see if Elliot found him. A part of him hoped it never happened.

He and his homeschool group were at the pigpens. All the teen volunteers had run to the buses, leaving them with an actual farmworker. Tucker didn't know who to feel sorrier for, the farmworker or the homeschooled kids. He, at least, found it entertaining.

"Look, kids, my job is to take care of the animals, not babysit," the man whined. "Now get off the fence."

In front of Tucker, Phileo stood a few feet from the fence, eyeing the pigs with horrified fascination. In front of him, the twins, identical with blue eyes and brown hair, hopped down from the wire fence. Just past seven years old, they'd been trying to race each other to the top.

The two other boys had Pokémon cards and were squatting at the base of the fence, trying to start a game.

The lone girl of the cohort leaned against the wire fence and reached her hand in. "Come on, piggy," she cooed. "I won't bite."

"But they will!" the worker said savagely, losing his temper. "Get your hand out of there! You wanna lose a finger?" A big man with a massive chest, he sat on his thick haunches by the pen while cleaning his nails with a pocketknife. Unshaven, he wore a dirty ball cap, grimy jeans, and a worn T-shirt marred with dirt and food stains. He clearly didn't want to be near children and seemed confused as to why any would want to be around him. He threw a dark glare at the lone parent, the mom of the twins. She stood several yards away, holding up her cell phone, trying to find reception.

"What's their names?" asked the girl. A year younger than Tucker, she had dark brunette hair in a braided ponytail and wore blue shorts and green top. Her eyes dared anyone to challenge her. Tucker had learned to stay out of her way.

The man spat in the hay at her feet. "This is a farm. You don't name animals on a farm."

Tucker moved to stand beside Phileo and slid his phone back into his hip pocket. "I, um, need to use the bathroom. I'll, uh, be right back."

"Look at all that mud," Phileo said as if not hearing him. "Those poor pigs."

Eight pigs, most as tall as the twins, lounged around in thick brown sludge. They were covered in it and stared blankly at their surroundings, ignoring their audience.

"Why don't you name your animals?" the girl asked. "I could help you if you want. I'm good with names."

One of the Pokémon boys looked up. "They don't name them because they eat them, genius," he said.

"That's right, little darling," the man said to the girl, grinning wickedly to show off crooked brown teeth. "You don't name your hamburger, do you?"

He did not know his audience if he meant to scare or gross out the group of homeschoolers.

"Well, sometimes I do," the girl said earnestly. "I mean, if I'm really bored. I know I'm not supposed to play with my food, but I do."

Meanwhile, the twins climbed back on the fence.

"Cool!" said one.

"I want to ride one," said his brother.

"Get off the fence!" barked the worker, gripping his pen knife extra hard.

"So, if you eat the animals, do you have butchers on the island?" Phileo asked, stepping closer to the pigs.

The man reached back and scratched the seat of his jeans. "As a matter of fact, we do. We have a whole pack of them."

"Wow! Do you butcher your own meat right on the farm?" the other Pokémon boy asked, looking up with interest. "Can you butcher a pig now? I want to watch."

"Yeah!" said his partner. "We can help!"

They were both older than Tucker by two years but had yet to develop social skills.

Exasperated, the man rose to his feet. "Look, kids. The pigs need a nap right now. Why don't you all go look at the baby chicks, okay? They're right around the corner."

"Yes!" said the girl. "I love baby chicks!"

"You mean the chicken nuggets," the first Pokémon boy said, causing his friend to snicker.

Tucker slowly hung back as the others finally left the worker alone to find the baby chicks. The worker paid him no attention as he kicked the earth with his boot, muttering under his breath.

Turning, Tucker slowly headed toward the giant barn. He figured if he were going to meet Elliot, he'd better get it over with.

He had just started up the path that cut behind the brick house and led to the barn when he heard a familiar voice.

"Kids, get back in line this instant! Don't make me tell you again!"

Mrs. Wayne, his old teacher, spoke like an air horn. Even though she was old and stooped, her voice had never diminished and could be heard in his sleep. If she was here, that meant his class would be, too, including Kelsey Jimmers.

Panicked, Tucker moved off the path and hurried to an enclosed pen holding rabbits. Bending low, he stared at the cute furry creatures and tried to blend in with the uncut grass lining the cage.

He heard his loud former classmates pass by him and was about to breathe a sigh of relief.

"Hey!" yelled a voice he recognized as Brian Saunders. Brian was a big, brawny kid who liked to throw his weight around. He used to bully Elliot for his small size and had called Tucker meatball. "I know you!"

"You don't know him," a boy muttered. "Stop being stupid."

"Yeah, I do," Brian sneered. "Look! It's Tucker!"

"Ohmygosh, it *is* Tucker," Kelsey said. She sounded shocked.

Brian barked out a laugh. "Yeah, I knew it! It's the projectile pudding boy!"

"Class!" bellowed Mrs. Wayne. "No more talking! This is a field trip!"

Tucker's face burned as he stood and faced his class. "What's up, guys," he muttered, keeping his eyes down. He felt like one of the rabbits in the cage. He had nowhere to run.

"He's gotten taller," he heard a girl whisper.

"And cuter," another said. "What's he doing here?"

"He's part of the exhibit," Brian said meanly.

Finally, his class left him for the pigpen. Sighing in relief, he turned back to the rabbits. Around twenty of them were cramped in a tiny space no bigger than his closet. "Sorry, little guys," he muttered. "I know how you feel. I hope you guys have names."

"Tucker?" asked a girl's voice timidly.

He whirled around to see Kelsey standing there. She looked more amazing than ever, wearing lime green shorts and a pink top. Her silky blond hair was tied back in a ponytail.

"Oh, um, er, what are you doing, Kelsey?" he asked. He was shocked to see tears in her eyes. "What's wrong?"

"I only have a minute, but I had to sneak away. I-I just want to say... I'm so sorry about the video I made. I mean, I was, you know, trying to be funny, I guess." She took a deep breath. "Look, I didn't mean to hurt you. I wanted a video of your food, and then Elliot started messing around. I didn't stop him."

Tucker stared at her, slack-jawed. He never in a million years expected Kelsey to even notice him, much less apologize to him. "But you still posted the video," he heard himself say.

"I know, I know, I'm such an idiot! I didn't think it would hurt you... I thought it would make Elliot look stupid."

"Huh? I thought you liked him."

"No, you doofus. I liked you! You're always nice and... well, I'm just going to say it. You're really cute, Tucker. I just wanted you to know that. Okay? I need to get back before Mrs. Wayne has a heart attack yelling my name. I just had to talk to you."

"Oh, yeah. Okay… Kelsey, thanks. I'm, er, you're super… too."

Kelsey grinned as she raced back to her class.

Tucker was left wearing a stupid grin on his face.

Skylar wiped her brow with the back of her forearm. She didn't dare touch her face with her filthy gloves.

Since arriving early that morning, she'd been cleaning out the main barn. That meant scooping animal droppings with a pitchfork and dumping them into a wheelbarrow for another teen to bring to a disgusting compost pile. And then finding fresh hay to put down… just about everywhere. With no breeze in the barn, the air hung hot and heavy and smelled putrid.

She'd never been on a farm before, but she was sure most barns had pens for animals and pathways for people. This barn was a wide-open giant bathroom for animals. And it appeared it hadn't been cleaned for years.

"You quitting?" demanded the girl on her right. Paige was the same girl from the study session at Teddy's house who seemed to dislike Skylar at first sight. Shorter with black curly hair cropped close to her skull, she had tanned skin and a continuous sneer on an otherwise pretty face. Wearing jeans and a flannel shirt rolled to her elbows, she looked and smelled like a farmer.

"Are we done yet?" Skylar asked, surprised.

"Not even close. That big busload of kids just got here. We don't want any of those poor babies to step in anything gross."

Skylar smiled. "Hey, my mom and brother are with those buses. Mind if I go meet them?"

"Sure," Paige said bitterly. "Leave me with the rest of the mess. People like you don't belong here anyway."

Skylar carefully leaned her pitchfork on a wooden pillar and turned to face Paige. "What's that supposed to mean? Teddy asked me to volunteer, and I'm only doing this as a favor."

"Right, you are. You're only here because you think Teddy likes you. Well, if that was true, then where is he?"

"He wasn't feeling well," Skylar said, her face burning. "His stomach hurt."

Paige barked out a laugh. "Is that what he said? Listen, Sky, or whatever your name is. Blue Island kids only date Blue Island kids. It's the way it is. If Teddy is interested in you, it's because he's interested in something else. Now go find your mommy before you start to cry."

Paige turned her back on Skylar and stabbed the putrid ground with her pitchfork.

Skylar nearly stepped toward her with a raised fist but stopped herself. It was stifling in the barn and full of animal fumes. She needed fresh air. Her head held high, she marched past Paige without looking back. She did notice the boy with the wheelbarrow giving her a sympathetic look.

Outside, she breathed in the fresh air, taking several gulps. She'd exited the back of the barn, away from the school kids. She didn't want her mom to see her like this. Where *did* Teddy go? Shortly after they'd arrived, he complained of stomach cramps and vanished somewhere. Was Paige telling the truth?

"No," she muttered, seeing the herd of cows standing in the field in front of her. "She's just a jealous cow trying to get me mad," she growled. And she did a good job of it.

The smaller barn beyond the cow fence caught her eye. She saw a figure standing against the wall, looking in her direction. The figure suddenly ran around the corner, vanishing around the side.

"Teddy?" Squinting from the sun, Skylar couldn't tell, but it may have been. She started following a gravel path heading through the cow field toward the small barn.

"Don't go that way," a voice said behind her.

Whirling, she saw nobody behind her. "H-Hello?" she asked hesitantly. It had sounded like a woman's voice, just like the voice on the night she'd gotten spooked by the fog. "Anybody there?"

She only heard the sounds of little kids from behind her. A warm breeze blew from the direction of the small barn. *Stay away,* it seemed to say.

Scared, Skylar made a sharp U-turn and headed back. Tingles crept down her back. She now understood why her dad had never wanted to come to this island. Something about it wasn't right.

As Skylar neared the back of the giant barn, she heard voices. Not young voices of teens, but deep voices of men, neither very pleasant. She slowed her walking and moved off the path. Bending down, she pretended to tie her shoe.

"I don't like this," growled one of the men. His voice sounded deep and hoarse.

"Neither do I," said the other. His voice was smooth and almost pleasant, but it still rang with bitterness. "Morgan has lost her mind."

"What's her plan?"

"She's trying to break the curse. For good."

The deep voice laughed. "That's impossible. She's lost it, Stan."

"Maybe. But this is Morgan we're talking about. She believes she has a way. We're supposed to keep an eye out for a kid."

"Yeah? And what are we looking for? There're kids crawling all over this place, and every one is a thorn in my—"

"Quiet! I heard something."

Heart pounding, Skylar rose and hurried several feet backward on the grass. She then turned and started walking, acting as if she'd just arrived at the path. She kept her gaze low and tried to look lost in thought.

"You!" barked the deep voice.

She looked up to see a short, balding man in dirty clothes coming out of the barn. She swallowed a gasp as she recognized the man from the steps of the church when trying to go to her great-grandmother's funeral. It was the egghead guy. Behind him, she recognized the tall scarecrow man. Both were staring hard at her and wearing the same dress as when she first saw them at the church. Closer up, they were even more unpleasant.

Fighting the urge to scream and run, she smiled. "Sorry?" she asked. "I was just taking a break from shoveling in the barn. Is there a water fountain near here?"

"Not back here, there isn't," the taller man said suspiciously. "You were supposed to bring your own water."

Skylar nodded. "Oh, I know. I did. It's just by the parking lot, and I hoped to find some closer."

The shorter man squinted, peering at her closely. "You're not from Blue Island, are you? You're the girl Teddy brought from the mainland."

"She's Minnie's grandchild," the other man muttered, trying to keep Skylar from hearing. "So she's all right."

The shorter man all at once brightened and grinned crookedly at her. "Sorry if we startled you. Nobody is supposed to go back past the barn here, and we thought you were one of the school kids. I'm Moe, and this ugly guy here is Stan. What's your name?"

Skylar ignored the question. "Oh, yeah. Sorry. I was actually looking for Teddy," she confessed. She desperately wanted to find him now. She wanted to ask some questions and hoped he had answers.

"Look over at the farmhouse," the scarecrow man said, crossing his arms over his skinny chest. "He's probably there." He grinned wickedly. "Eating lunch, I bet."

"Okay, um, thanks!" Skylar wiped her sweaty hands on her jeans and started walking rapidly around the barn toward the house. Her heart pounded against her chest like a pogo stick. She didn't breathe normally until she was on the other side of the barn where school groups were taking over the farm.

Scanning the crowded area, she didn't see her mom. Then she spied her brother.

Elliot stood with his back to her, hands in his pocket. He was easily recognizable by the dark blond locks sticking from his ball cap. Across from the barn near a paddock holding goats, he was staring up toward the trees beyond the parking area.

Skylar briskly moved through the groups of schoolchildren, slowing only when she neared her brother. He seemed intently focused on something and never noticed.

Skylar grabbed his shoulders and put a knee into his backside. "Got you, dirt-brain!" she cried.

"Hey!" Elliot yelped, giving a start. "Sky! You poop-eater, you scared me!"

"That was my goal, dog-breath." She put her arms around his chest and pulled him tight. "Where's Mom? There's something strange going on around here."

"She's off to the duck pond or something." Elliot rested the back of his head against her stomach. "I thought I saw something in those trees… like a man or something. Only it had fur."

"You mean, like, Bigfoot?" Skylar teased.

Elliot only wiggled to a more comfortable position against his sister. "I don't know… it's, like, I feel something watching me."

Skylar grimaced. "I know the feeling. I heard some talking... I don't know what this farm is about, but it isn't about kids petting animals."

Elliot shivered. "Yeah... it's like it's evil or something."

Chapter 23

Around the brother and sister, the tours were not going well. There were no horses or ponies, and pretty much nothing for the kids to do but look at sad-looking animals in decrepit living conditions. Petting was not even allowed since most of the animals were not friendly to humans. Kids were starting to complain, and parents were grumbling.

"Mom!" a girl wailed by the pen with turkeys. "They said they eat all these animals! We need to save them!"

"I'm sure, I'm sure he was just joking, dear," her mom answered, not sounding sincere.

Elliot pursed his lips. "If I had my way, like, we'll let all these animals free."

Skylar smiled. "Yeah, me too. Guess I was wrong about how great this place would be."

"Hey!" yelled Mr. Charles, spotting the siblings. He left his class and stomped toward them, his face a mask of tempered fury. "What are you two doing?"

"Um, this is my brother," Skylar said, turning to face him. She kept Elliot close to her, keeping her arms around his chest. "We're just enjoying the farm."

"Oh," Mr. Charles stumbled to a stop. "You're Karen's kids." Then his eyes tightened. "Elliot, right? You're supposed to be with your mom. That's your group. Why are you here?"

Elliot just looked up with his mouth open.

Skylar smoothly stepped away from him and stood between her brother and the teacher. "Actually, I'm volunteering here. I asked my brother to help me, you know, watch the goats."

"Right." Mr. Charles took a deep breath. "Did you tell your mom this? Because if she does a headcount and finds you missing, it can set off a panic."

Skylar coughed. "Well…"

Just then, their mom's voice called in a panic, coming from near the fence of the cow field. "Mr. Charles!" she cried. "Quick! I'm missing students and can't find them anywhere!"

Mr. Charles's eyes blazed with triumph, and his mouth curved in a grim smile. "See?" he said. "Your kids are over here!" he cried. "I got them."

"No, not my own kids!" Mrs. Ashley arrived at the barn area out of breath and dripping sweat. "It's Marcus and Bobby… They vanished!"

Mr. Charles clenched his entire body. His eyes bulged, and his lips curled in a snarl. "That's it!" he screamed. "Everyone on the buses! Now! This trip is over! Teachers, gather your students and do a headcount. Then get them out of here! Same bus you came on." He turned to Mrs. Ashley. "Where are the rest of your students?" he demanded.

Mrs. Ashley pulled off her hat and scrunched it with her hands. "I left them with Mr. Harris. They should be following me."

"Great," muttered the male teacher. "We're probably missing three more kids now. Where did you last see Marcus and Bobby?"

"I don't know. We were at the duck pond…" Her eyes widened when she saw the expression on the face of Mr. Charles. "But I'm sure they didn't fall in," she said quickly. "It's only a few feet deep. They must've snuck off and could be anywhere. I think Marcus wanted the bathroom."

"We'll find them," Mr. Charles said grimly. "Once the buses are loaded, we'll search every square inch of this stinking place. Go rescue your class from Harris. I'll get my class loaded and start the search."

Worried, Mrs. Ashley nodded. She smiled nervously at Skylar and Elliot before turning to run back to her students. Her class had just appeared at the corner of the cow fence.

Elliot looked up at Skylar, and the two exchanged worried glances.

"What about Tucker?" Elliot whispered.

Skylar put a hand on her shoulder and squeezed it tightly. "I'm more worried about those two kids, Elliot. This place gives me the creeps. I heard some strange talking earlier."

"Then Tucker could be in danger, too," Elliot said. His eyes went big, and his bottom lip jutted out. "Please, Sky."

Skylar sighed. "Fine, butt-munch. I'll give you five minutes. Then your little tush better be on that bus, or I will kick it there."

"Thanks, Sky!" Elliot gave her a quick hug.

"Don't thank me yet," his sister muttered. "First, we need to get you to Tucker without getting caught by a teacher. Come on. Follow me."

With Elliot in tow, she navigated through the bellowing teachers and suddenly frightened students. Most didn't know why they were leaving early, but they knew something wasn't right.

The siblings eventually emerged from the crowd to an opening between the giant barn and rundown sheds.

Skylar knelt and slid her arm around the back of Elliot's shirt. "Listen, butt-munch, I'm serious. If you're not on the bus in five minutes, I'm telling Mom you're lost too. You'll be grounded for life."

Elliot nodded. "Right. But you'll be in just as much trouble after I tell about you and Teddy."

Teddy. Skylar had forgotten about him. She slapped the back of his pants, sending him stumbling toward the sheds. "The homeschooled kids should be over there. I'll wait here while you find Tucker. Remember. Five minutes."

Elliot had already broken into a run.

Several minutes before Mrs. Ashley ran for Mr. Charles, Bobby crouched outside the rickety barn and eyed the path back to the duck pond.

Marcus had found it and had pulled Bobby along with him.

"Come on, man," Marcus said to him, pulling his shirt. "This is boring. Let's explore a little."

Bobby never knew why he listened and followed Marcus, but as usual, he did so without question.

The boys were both wearing shorts and shirts. Bobby sported athletic wear—a solid blue T-shirt and black athletic shorts. Marcus had brown cargo shorts and a green tank top. Neither one had dressed for exploring, and they immediately fought off a wave of bugs, making sure to stay on the trampled path. It was odd. There were miserable caged animals and tons of bugs on the farm, but that was it. There were no birds or even squirrels in sight.

Weaving around tall grass and cutting through a clump of brambles, the boys followed the path, which led uphill to the small barn in the back of the cow field. Bobby was content with going straight back, but Marcus wanted to keep exploring. Besides, he said he needed the bathroom so badly.

"Just use the bushes or go in the grass," Bobby told him.

"It's the other way, man," Marcus said. "I need toilet paper. Besides, what do you think this barn is used for? Don't you want to go inside and check it out?"

"Nope. I seriously doubt they'd put any treasure in a trashy barn and leave it for us to find."

"Well, maybe it has a bathroom in it," Marcus said, grinning. "Then I could leave a treasure for somebody else to find."

Bobby rolled his eyes. "Suit yourself. Just watch out for axe murderers."

The two boys examined the old barn, and Marcus found a gap in the siding where boards had rotted away by the ground. He managed to squeeze through and promised to be right back.

That had been over five minutes ago.

Now resting on his haunches, Bobby leaned against the barn wall.

"Hurry up, Marcus," he muttered. He moved to his knees and ducked his head near the gap, peering into the darkness. Through it, he heard muffled voices. He immediately stopped breathing. Marcus was not alone in there.

Inside the barn, Marcus had crawled into an unused stall that smelled of old decaying meat. He stood and brushed dirt from his hands and knees. He'd figured some poor critter must've died there, like a rat or something.

Sunlight filtering through the gaps and cracks of the battered barn provided the only light. In the dimness, he saw the small earthen enclosure was entirely empty. The earth was surprisingly moist and had large swathes of dark patches, which seemed to carry most of the stink. The stall door was open, and Marcus cautiously slipped through.

He walked into a wide lane running through the center of the barn. There were stalls on either side of the lane, eight in total. The rotting meat smell permeated from each one, and Marcus struggled not to gag. He covered his nose with the front of his shirt. It was like being buried by road kill. Flies were thick and buzzed in his eyes and around his nose. Just as he was about to retreat back to Bobby, he heard voices. Looking to the front of the barn, he made out a small doorway leading to an office of some sort. A man's and a woman's voices were going back and forth. It sounded like they were arguing.

"Dr. Chocker?" Marcus said, puzzled. He'd been in the principal's office plenty of times and knew the man's voice anywhere. Curious, he crept to the doorway. Leaning against the wall next to the doorway, he slowly peeked in.

The principal stood facing the tall, dark-haired woman. Between them, the crazy old lady from the pickup stood with her hands clasped as if in prayer. She looked to be crying.

His eyes went wide, and Marcus knew he should leave then. But his feet wouldn't budge, and his curiosity kept his eyes glued to the scene. He had a nose for trouble, and what he saw set off alarm bells.

"I'm telling you, I know what you're up to," the old woman said.

"We're not up to anything underhanded," Dr. Chocker said impatiently, crossing his arms. He still wore his suit coat, and even in the faint light, Marcus could see sweat dripping off the slope of his balding head. "This is a business deal, nothing more."

The old lady looked at him and snorted. "A business deal, eh? Making a deal with evil is never good business, young man."

Dr. Chocker stiffened and tried to glare at the old woman. "I'll have you know, I'm actually a doctor, thank you. It's Dr. Chocker to you."

"You're a nincompoop," the old lady said, not backing down. "You don't know what you're doing."

"I'm sure an uneducated waitress can enlighten me," Dr. Chocker said dryly. "You sound superstitious and hysterical."

"And you sound like an idiot," the old lady spat.

"Enough!" the tall woman finally said. "Erma, you're being ridiculous. You're full of rot."

"Am I?" Erma said, turning to her. "Morgan, I know what you're planning."

"Is that right?" the tall woman, Morgan, said icily. Her fingers moved to her throat and clutched at something hanging around her neck. "And what am I planning?"

"Sylvia used to confide in me. She told me about the family book, the one with the secrets of The Pack."

Morgan went still. "Just what did you tell that Ashley woman back in the parking lot?"

"The truth, Morgan," Erma said defiantly. "That she needs to leave with the children."

"Okay, okay," Dr. Chocker said, clapping his hands as if trying to get two students to pay attention. "What is going on here?"

Erma glared at him. "Morgan Raycroft is here for one of your boys, you nincompoop. She has your children here so that she can pick him out!"

"Huh?" Dr. Chocker said, tilting his head in confusion. "She wants to adopt one of the students?"

"No. She has a lot more evil intentions than adoption," Erma told him. "Believe me."

Dr. Chocker stared at Morgan, desperate for her to explain and refute the old woman. The tall woman only fingered her necklace and looked ready to lash at Erma.

"Is this woman, this waitress, telling the truth?" Dr. Chocker asked. "What is she talking about?"

"Shut up and take your money," Morgan snapped. She kept her glare on Erma. "You have a big mouth, Erma Jenkins. You've been useful for The Pack for a long time. But like your meatloaf, everything has an expiration date."

Erma wrinkled up her nose in disgust. "You won't succeed, Morgan. Just end this now."

Morgan gave a small smile that never went past her lips. "I intend to do that, Erma. It's time to settle your bill."

From where he watched, Marcus felt an evil tension rising. He started breathing heavily. The front of his tank top had slipped from his nose, and the pungent smell of decaying meat intensified. Then he realized something. The heavy breathing wasn't from him. There was another person in the room… hiding in the shadows.

Chapter 24

Dr. Frank Chocker had been having a great day. The weather was perfect, and he'd spent the entire drive to the farm with the windows down and radio off, letting the breeze and blissful silence relax his weary bones. Being a principal was not an easy job. You dealt with teachers, students, parents, and the school board, all with their own expectations and agendas. And they usually only wanted to see you when they were mad or complaining about something. Then, you were expected to fix everything. He rarely got visitors or calls praising him.

Then, weeks before, Morgan Raycroft had walked into his office, changing his life.

Dr. Chocker had been an educator for nearly twenty years and principal at Leewood Elementary for six of them. He'd started as a special education teacher, but quickly realized that only fools and martyrs lasted in that field. He started taking classes in administration and wound up with a doctorate. He worked first as an assistant principal and then finally as a head principal. On paper, he was a respected success story of hard work paying off.

In reality, he had a major problem. It had started small but now threatened his livelihood and even his life. Dr. Chocker had become a gambler. Bored and stressed in his office, he'd started placing small bets just for fun. He made a little and lost a little but had caught the excitement bug badly.

In the halls of Leewood, he was just a boring, drab principal who was expected always to be perfect and never allowed to make mistakes. His best skill was letting his teachers do their jobs without bothering them unless they asked for help.

With gambling, however, he became somebody very different. All at once, he could be cool, calculating, and daring. Mistakes were allowed, even expected. But it was the excitement of trying to beat the odds that got him going. Soon, he started putting more money into his newfound hobby. Suddenly, he had to hide losses from his wife. She never knew about his gambling. Nobody did. That was the best part of gambling online... He could do it secretly.

Then, one day, desperate for money, he diverted funds for his school into his gambling account. It was just fifty bucks, but it was only the start. Under the guise of buying books and supplies for teachers, he secretly wrote checks to himself and used the money for his gambling. He figured as long as he broke even, he could always put the money back. He never broke even. He just became broke. In the course of three years, he now owed the school nearly a hundred grand.

On the last Friday of April, he'd received an email from the Whitney County School Board. That June, the board would conduct a routine audit of his school's finances.

Then, very soon after, Morgan Raycroft came to the rescue. She offered his school a great opportunity and gave him a lifeline that could solve all his problems.

He still remembered her sitting across his desk from him and pulling a red pendant from beneath her collar. It started to sparkle between her fingers as she held it tight. A smile spread across her face as her eyes narrowed.

"I sense you need my help, Dr. Chocker. You have trouble, don't you?"

It was like the woman could peer right into his soul. Her dark beauty captivated him, but his eyes kept falling on the red pendant. Two inches long, it was in the shape of a ruby teardrop. He could've sworn it had been dull red at first, but now it appeared like a jewel.

"I, erm, why are you here, exactly, um, Ms. Raycroft?"

"It's Mrs. Raycroft." The woman smiled at him. "I kept my mother's name but still keep my husband around, too. I originally came to talk to you about one of your teachers. You have a Mrs. Ashley here, correct? Her husband is from Blue Island, where I'm from. But now… I think I came to save you from your trouble. Tell me, Dr. Chocker. What do you need?"

Dr. Chocker's eyes widened, but for some reason, he didn't throw her out. Instead, without going into specifics, he ended up telling her about his money trouble. "I need some money fast," he heard himself say.

The woman listened sympathetically and then breathed out deeply. "How odd. And I need children, fast. Perhaps we can help each other out?" She proceeded to tell him about her idea of opening Blue Island to the public. "What better way than to have children visit and then tell their parents how beautiful the island is and how safe it is, hmm?"

That was how the field trip came to be. Morgan Raycroft promised money for the school if Mrs. Ashley's class visited the farm on Blue Island. She claimed she wanted to connect with Mrs. Ashley in hopes of meeting her husband. But really, she just wanted the children to visit.

Dr. Chocker could only lick his upper lip nervously. Then Morgan Raycroft offered the first payment to be off the books in cash… delivered on the day of the field trip.

How could Dr. Chocker refuse?

This was how he came to be standing in the rundown, smelly barn with a crazy old lady and Morgan Raycroft.

He eyed the suitcase sitting on the ground right by Morgan Raycroft's feet. Sweat ran down his armpits. It had been such a great start to the day, and the money was so close… so why did he feel like the whole world was about to fall on his head at any second?

"Maybe we should," he said, wiping sweat from his cheek with the back of his coat sleeve, "step outside and get some air. We're all, heh, starting to sound a little crazy."

The two women ignored him. He felt dizzy and flushed. Sweat ran down his pants, soaking his underwear. His great day was quickly melting into pure horror.

"Sylvia was good for The Pack," Erma said quietly. "You? You're nothing like her! You're a cancer."

Morgan drew up to her full height, staring down at the older woman. "My mother was afraid," she sneered. "She was selfish and stupid. She had the means to help The Pack but lacked the courage to do it! I plan to fix that. And if you stand in my way, I'll fix you, too."

Erma recoiled and suddenly looked afraid. "You can't," she stammered. "You just can't hurt the children!"

Morgan smiled a toothy grin. "Don't worry about the children. Worry about yourself. It's lunchtime, Erma."

A shadow moved from the corner.

Dr. Chocker's eyes went wide as he stepped back. His lips started to tremble, but he made no noise.

Erma, facing him, never saw the dark shape looming behind her.

Looking in from the doorway, Marcus stopped breathing.

The tall shadow stealthily crept from the corner and passed just a few feet by him, sneaking behind the old woman. In the muted light, Marcus saw a thick, giant man covered in hair. Wearing nothing but a small breechcloth, his hairy legs, torso, and arms bulged with muscle. Only his thick neck and round head lacked the hair. Thin wisps of stringy hair clung to his skull like worms. This revealed his huge pointy ears. It was like seeing the boogeyman.

Marcus felt his knees start to buckle. It was a good thing he didn't really need the bathroom. If he did, his pants would now be full.

He watched as Erma, oblivious to the danger, went to cross her arms in a show of courage. It would be her last move on earth.

The hairy giant rammed a fist into her back. The woman gasped in pain and fought for a breath. Her arms dropped to her sides and started to shake.

Dr. Chocker cried out and stumbled back.

Erma's mouth opened, silently screaming. Then blood gushed out, running down her lips and chin. The man behind her didn't move and kept his fist digging into her back.

"Wh-What is this?" Dr. Chocker cried fearfully. "What's happening to her?"

Morgan watched it all with glee. "Shut up," she said. "You're a part of this now, *Dr. Chocker.*"

The principal could only stare in horror.

Erma's body started to spasm, and the man stepped back, yanking his arm from her back. He held no knife. Instead, long claws extended from his knuckles, dripping blood.

The waitress immediately collapsed to her knees. Her eyes wide with shock and pain, she fell forward on her face and went still.

"D-Did you… Wh-what… please don't hurt me," Dr. Chocker said, falling to his knees.

The giant man ignored him. He turned and stared right at Marcus. Deep sunken eyes flared red in the filtered light. His nose appeared smashed and small, like a bulldog's. His teeth were long and sharp. "We have a visitor," he said in a guttural growl.

"Daahh!!" Marcus yelled, falling back. He landed on his backside and quickly rolled to his hands and knees. Stumbling to his feet, he raced down the center of the barn.

"Oh, no," he heard Dr. Chocker groan behind him. "Marcus! Marcus, come back!"

Marcus only ran faster. Reaching the stall he'd entered from, he crashed through the rotting door, falling to his knees. Landing on the moist, dark earth, he cried out again. His mind all at once connected the foul odor with the stained dirt.

The stalls weren't for the living. Blood and guts of dead animals had seeped into the dirt. Not just any animals, but big animals.

Crying out again, he lunged for the gap in the wall. Vomit already began surging up this throat.

From behind him, he heard heavy breathing and a low growl.

The evil wolverine man was after him! He had to get out of there!

Desperate, he threw his body through the opening, ignoring the pain as his right shoulder and left side scraped against the rotting wall.

"Man, what's wrong?" Bobby yelled from the other side. He grabbed Marcus by the right arm and pulled.

Wiggling loose, Marcus found himself lying on his belly before Bobby.

"Marcus, what happened?" Bobby asked, alarmed. "What's going on?"

Marcus pushed himself to his knees. He then opened his mouth and barfed up his breakfast of eggs and cereal. Green and brown sludge splattered on the ground in front of the shocked Bobby.

"Dude!" Bobby cried, jumping back. "Watch my kicks! What happened in there? Are you all right?"

His stomach emptied, Marcus looked up at him with bloodshot eyes. His body shook. "Run," he gasped. "Run."

Something in the barn crashed against the wall over the gap, causing the entire wall to shake.

Bobby needed no more encouragement. Reaching over the pile of vomit, he pulled Marcus to his feet. The boys broke into a panicked run. Ignoring the trail back to the pond, they took the path of least resistance. They raced for the cow field.

The boys grabbed the top rail at the fence and jumped over, barely slowing. The cows watched, unimpressed, as the boys continued their flight past them. On the other side, the boys reached the fence with the balloons. All festive thoughts had long fled. They were in pure panic mode.

They scrambled over and then crouched down, both out of breath.

"Where are we going?" Bobby finally asked. He put an arm on a raised knee and leaned the other against the fence behind him. He needed something to hold himself up. He'd never seen Marcus so scared before. "What happened back there?"

Marcus made no answer. Sitting against the fence, his eyes darted behind them, searching for pursuit. Nobody and nothing followed. He still didn't relax.

"I need to get out of here," he finally said. "Now."

He pushed himself up and started walking hurriedly toward the gate in the barbwire fence.

Bobby had to rush to keep up. "Come on, man. What did you see?"

"They're going to kill me, man," Marcus muttered. "Don't worry about it. Just don't look back."

"Okay, but where are we going?"

"Just out of here. I don't want to die."

Bobby felt a shiver run down his spine. He knew Marcus was not playing. Totally spooked, he followed his terrified friend.

They ended up on the small bus. Finding the door open, the boys rushed up the stairs and found their seats. There, they grabbed their water bottles and crouched on the floor. Sipping liquid, they said nothing and waited. Sweat and fear poured down their faces and bodies.

The monstrous man returned to the barn's office and filled the doorway. "The child is gone," he muttered. "There was another boy, but outside. He did not see me, but I will remember his smell."

"Who-Who is th-that?" Dr. Chocker asked. He now stood cowering behind Morgan's shoulder. Having snatched up the suitcase, he held it in front of him with both hands like a shield.

"Didn't I mention to you I had a husband?" Morgan said innocently. "Here he is in the flesh. This is Banor, *Dr.* Chocker."

There was nothing innocent about what had just happened.

Erma's corpse now lay face down in the dirt in a pool of blood.

The man scowled at Dr. Chocker. "Do what my wife says, and I won't touch you." He ran a thick black tongue over his lips. "Understand?"

Dr. Chocker looked ready to faint. He managed to nod. "Of, of course." He took a breath. "Who... Who are you people?"

Morgan sighed but seemed much more cheerful than she had a right to be. She looked down at her chest, where the red pendant hung from its silver chain. It seemed to sparkle like a giant drop of blood. "You have bigger problems to worry about than us. Who was that boy, this Marcus?"

"I, I, well, he's a student... Oh, my g-g-g—"

Morgan's voice went hard. "Hold it together! Focus! That boy just saw you take part in a murder, Dr. Chocker. We need to find him and do something about that. Don't we?"

Dr. Chocker felt tears trickle from his eyes. "Ah... yes, I suppose so... He's, he's actually a troublemaker and a known liar." He managed a sick smile. "Nobody will believe him."

"They will once we don't produce Erma Jenkins." Morgan reached up and touched the pendant. "Besides, Erma was correct about me searching for a boy. He could be the one. I *feel* that he is the one. Tell me about his family."

Dr. Chocker licked his upper lip and tasted blood. He'd bitten it without knowing. Eyeing the body near his feet, he swallowed the salty taste. "To tell you the truth, he wouldn't, ah, be missed. His parents aren't really in the picture... nobody really cares about him." He said it as if trying to convince himself. "If, if something were to happen to him... it would be tragic, but not the end of the world... I mean, you won't actually hurt him, right?"

Morgan Raycroft nodded. "That's good to hear. Go back to your teachers and find this Marcus."

"What about... you know..." Dr. Chocker nodded at Erma's body.

"Why," said Morgan, "didn't you hear what I said? She's providing lunch. My husband has friends waiting outside. They're always hungry at this time of day."

Banor growled a rumbling laugh.

Dr. Chocker couldn't leave the barn fast enough. He needed fresh air.

Chapter 25

After seeing Kelsey, Tucker staggered in a daze back to his group. He completely forgot about finding Elliot... Kelsey actually liked him. He couldn't believe it.

Kelsey gave him a wave and a smile as he walked by his old class at the pigpens.

No longer embarrassed, Tucker returned both.

Reaching the enclosed chicken coop, he found a zoo on the farm. Phileo had a lady worker cornered by the coop, trying to get her to tell him where the horses were being kept. Behind them, the twins begged their mom to take all the baby chicks home with them so they wouldn't turn into chicken nuggets. The Pokémon boys were busy tossing handfuls of raisins they'd gotten from their pockets into the enclosure, causing a ruckus as all the birds converged in that one spot. Meanwhile, the girl lay on her belly, sticking her arm through the wire, trying to get a baby chick to come to her.

Tucker rubbed the top of his head in disbelief. That was when he remembered Elliot. Elliot would never understand his new friends. Tucker stood with his hands in his pockets, taking in the craziness, and felt a smile form. These kids weren't that bad… they were just kids.

Still, a headache was starting to form. At the pigpen, he heard Mrs. Wayne yell for all the kids to return to the buses immediately and not dawdle. They were leaving.

Tucker wrinkled his brow. If the school kids were leaving, that meant Elliot, too. He was surprised to find that he didn't mind that much. Still, he wanted to see Kelsey one last time and maybe, just maybe, exchange phone numbers.

Turning on his heel, he got a new surprise as his old best friend ran full speed right at him.

"Tucker!" Elliot yelped. "I found you!"

"Yo, yo, man!" Tucker said, backing up. "Slow down!"

It was no use. Elliot shoved him in the chest and then threw his arms around his shoulders, hugging him tight. "I was, like, searching all over for you!"

Tucker couldn't help the grin spreading across his face. "Yeah, well, I'm here. You found me. Now get off!"

Elliot released him and stepped back. "Hey! You're, like, tall now!"

"Yeah, and you're, like, shorter," Tucker said, brushing back the curls over his eyes. It was amazing. Elliot looked exactly the same. In seconds, it was like the two had never been separated. "How, um, do you like the farm?"

"Totally busted. My mom lost two kids, and we're all leaving. I had to see you first."

Tucker's face fell. Then he grinned goofily. "Hey, I saw Kelsey earlier. Guess what? She never liked you."

"Duh, I know. She liked you."

"What?" Tucker howled. "And you never told me? No wonder we stopped being friends!"

"Uh, hello. I thought you knew. Everyone else did," Elliot said. "So, um, are those your new friends?" He nodded at where the twins had their heads pressed against their mom's legs, and the girl was still trying to reach into the cage to grab a baby chick.

Tucker shrugged. "Yeah, I guess. They're actually pretty cool."

"Seriously?"

And just like that, Tucker remembered that he and Elliot were no longer friends. They lived too far apart, and Elliot wouldn't understand. He wanted everything to be like always. But things had changed. Tucker had always thought he needed Elliot, but no longer. Now he knew he could make other friends and be just as happy, or even happier.

"Yeah, they're cool."

"Okay, like, I guess."

"Ahem." Phileo coughed from the other side of Tucker. "Who is this?"

"Oh, er, this is my old, former friend, Elliot," Tucker said.

"Wait. Former friend?" Elliot stared at Tucker with raised eyebrows. "Really?"

Tucker felt his face burn. "Well, you kind of moved, Elliot. After you nearly broke my ankle."

"Yeah, and don't forget I ruined your pumpkin pudding," Elliot said. "And gave you a black eye. Don't forget that!"

"Yeah, that too." Tucker didn't make eye contact.

Elliot had tears in his eyes. "I said I was sorry!"

"And I forgive you, okay? It's just… we don't live near each other and, besides, I don't think my parents will let me be friends anyway. Okay? Still, it was cool seeing you."

"Yeah, I guess. You know what? I got to go. Bye, Tucker." Elliot turned on his heel and started marching away. He paused and looked over his shoulder. "Oh, and just so you know, this farm is super creepy, and you and your friends better leave soon." He then broke into a run.

"Seems like a strange kid," Phileo said as Tucker followed Elliot's progress toward the farm's entrance.

"Yeah, he can be," Tucker said. He reached up and wiped away a tear. *This is for the best*, he told himself. It was time to move on to new friendships. "Come on. Let's get back to the others."

Cynthia was the first to spot the missing boys.

As the two long buses were nearly loaded, the bus driver for the small bus was waddling back from the brick house on the farm. Cynthia and Kim stood by the open door of the bus, waiting impatiently for Mrs. Ashley.

"Go ahead on the bus, girls," the bus driver yelled at her through the fence. "We need to be going."

Cynthia needed no further invitation. She wanted to get away from the stupid farm as fast as possible. "Stupid boys ruin everything," she said with a huff. "We didn't see any cool animals."

"I doubt there were any cool animals," Kim said behind her. "That farm felt sad."

Cynthia made to reply when she stopped short on top of the steps. "Um, hello? Is that you, Bobby?"

Bobby stood up in the middle of the bus with his hair soaked with sweat. He looked miserable and scared. "Are we leaving?" he asked hopefully.

"Yes!" Cynthia exploded. "Because of you! Where were you? You and Marcus are in so much trouble!"

Marcus popped his head from around a seat in front of Bobby. He looked at her with wild eyes. "Hey!" he hissed. "Don't tell anybody I'm here!"

Cynthia stuck out her tongue at him. "Right," she said. "Kim, go tell Mrs. Ashley we found the stupid boys. They were hiding on the bus."

Kim rushed from the bus, pushing past Gary as he walked with Mr. Harris. The teacher had the boy by the collar, intent on not losing another student.

"No running! Where are you going?" Mr. Harris demanded. "Get back here!"

"We found the boys," Kim said with a gasp. "They're on the bus!"

Mr. Harris threw back his head in a huge sigh of relief. "In that case, run faster! Tell Mrs. Ashley the good news!"

"Mrs. Ashley, I need a word with you, pronto," Dr. Chocker commanded as he marched from behind the large barn.

Mrs. Ashley whirled to face him. She'd just ushered the last of her class toward the farm's entrance and had been scanning for any sign of Marcus and Bobby.

"It'll have to wait, Frank. I'm missing two of my boys."

"That's what I want to speak to you about," her principal said. "They left the farm and headed for the buses."

"How do you know that?" Mrs. Ashley asked, narrowing her eyes. "Where have you been?"

The principal looked like a wreck, as if he'd just returned from a time machine that had aged him ten years. His gray suit drooped on him, weighed down with sweat and dirt. A smudge marked his bald spot, and dark bags hung beneath his eyes.

"The staff here, they have a nose for things like that," he said, cracking into a wild chuckle. "But seriously, I've been informed that Marcus has been, uh, getting into trouble."

Mrs. Ashley grimaced. "I know that. He's missing!"

"That's because he's hiding," Dr. Chocker said. "He, he was trespassing and, well, we, er, the farm staff need to see him."

"Forget the farm staff. I want to see him right now!"

"When you do, bring him to me."

"That will be my call, Frank." As Mrs. Ashley stared down Dr. Chocker, she heard Kim yelling her name from the entrance. Then she heard Mr. Charles bark at her.

"Excuse me, Dr. Chocker. I think I'm needed." She then broke into a run.

Kim was yelling that the boys had been found and were on the bus already.

Dr. Chocker had been right.

Mr. Charles looked like a pot ready to boil over when Mrs. Ashley reached him. He'd already sent Kim scurrying back to the bus.

"Your boys were on the bus the entire time they were missing," he said in an accusing tone. "They completely ruined the fifth-grade trip."

Relieved and exhausted, Mrs. Ashley managed a sick smile. "In my opinion, the trip was already ruined."

"Right," Mr. Charles said. Then he looked past her at where Dr. Chocker walked briskly toward them, his face a mask of worry and determination. Clearing his throat, he said loudly, "Our buses will be stopping at a burger place of my choice for lunch. The school will pay for it. And, no. The fifth grade will not partner with Sunnybrook Farm for any trips in the future. Do I make myself clear?"

Reaching the gate, Dr. Chocker's face turned red, but he nodded. "Yes, yes, of course. This trip did not go so well. But I need to speak to Mrs. Ashley. In private."

"Right," Mr. Charles said. "In that case, we're leaving." He looked at Mrs. Ashley. "I don't think the boys on your bus deserve to stop for burgers. Besides, it wouldn't be safe. They could wander off again. Send the girls to my bus, and I'll see you back at school."

Mrs. Ashley felt like she'd been slapped in the face. She was being denied the chance to celebrate the year's end with her class. At the same time, she understood. Marcus and Bobby had been her responsibility, and she let them down. Their choices had consequences for themselves and for her.

"Agreed," she said. "I'll keep Gary with me. He's gotten in enough trouble over this year to also deserve missing the fifth-grade lunch."

"That would be for the best," Mr. Charles said, nodding with undisguised glee. "That way, you can keep Mr. Harris with you, too."

Mrs. Ashley nodded and started walking to the small bus with slumped shoulders. At least she had the boys back.

Dr. Chocker quickly fell in step with her. "I can't believe you let those boys wander off," he hissed. "You really got me in hot water!"

"Look, Frank. Mr. Harris was supposed to keep an eye on Marcus. I have twenty-one other students to watch out for! At least I didn't lose any of them."

"Oh, really?" Dr. Chocker nudged her arm and pointed inside the fence.

Mrs. Ashley turned to look and groaned. Her son, Elliot, was running toward them. Skylar waved from where she stood by the large barn. "Sorry, Mom!" she yelled.

Mrs. Ashley just shook her head and waited. Black clouds seemed to form over her head.

By the time he exited the gate, Elliot had his head down and hat pulled low. As he arrived where she and Dr. Chocker waited, he slowed to a walk.

"Where were you?" Mrs. Ashley demanded, grabbing his arm. "Do you realize we had an emergency? You were supposed to be on the bus!" All the frustration and anger was boiling over. In truth, she'd forgotten about Elliot. "You know what? Don't tell me. Just get on the bus, young man. Let's go!"

Keeping a firm grip on his arm, she marched him to the bus.

"But, Mom—"

"Don't 'but, Mom' me, mister. You get up there and sit down. I don't want to hear a word." She released his arm and put her hand on his back, pushing him up the first step.

On the second step, he stopped and looked back. "Mom—"

"I'm serious, Elliot!" She put a hand on the back of his pants and firmly shoved him up the bus, following him to the top. "Sit and start eating your lunch."

Blowing out air, Elliot stomped to his seat and threw himself next to his backpack. Not going for his food, he leaned against the window with a tight frown.

Mrs. Ashley ignored him. "Marcus! Bobby! Stand up so I can see you. Now!"

The boys slowly stood and stared at the floor. Marcus seemed to be shaking.

"Thank goodness," Mrs. Ashley said, closing her eyes briefly. Then they snapped open. "Cynthia and Kim. Thank you for your help today. You girls gather your stuff and head for the first bus."

The girls knew when she was angry and didn't dare question her. They quickly started gathering their packs of lunch and water bottles.

Mrs. Ashley glared at the boys, still standing. "The other buses are going to stop at a place to eat. A burger place. And the school is paying for it! I'm sure they'll have ice cream too. But our bus is going straight to school. Do you know why? Because the students on the other buses know how to behave and respect their teachers! You boys obviously have not learned that this year. Now sit!"

"Whoa," Gary spoke up, standing. "What about me? I never wandered off!"

"Gary, you have to ride this bus because of your behavior during this year. Do you think that means you deserve a reward? Think about it. Now you sit, too. I need to go talk to Dr. Chocker." She glared at Mr. Harris, who avoided her eye contact as he slunk into his seat behind Gary. "Nobody, and I mean nobody, is to leave this bus."

"Um, us too?" Cynthia asked timidly.

Mrs. Ashley sighed. "You girls go. But nobody else!" Before climbing down, she glanced at her son.

Elliot remained glaring out the window, looking more cute than angry. She would have to talk to him later after she'd calmed down.

The bus driver eyed her with a mixture of admiration and loathing as she exited the bus. He looked like he would've liked to stop for a burger.

Climbing down from the bus, Mrs. Ashley waited for the girls to exit and hurry to the front bus with Mr. Charles. She then turned and walked to Dr. Chocker, who waited impatiently by the fence.

"Okay, Frank," she said wearily. "What is it?"

"Look, I really need to see Marcus," Dr. Chocker said. "Just him."

"No can do, Frank. You heard me. Nobody is leaving that bus until we get back to school. You can talk to him then."

"You don't understand. The workers here need to talk to him. It's serious, Karen."

"Not a chance," Mrs. Ashley shook her head firmly. "I don't trust the staff at this place. If Marcus did something wrong, then we can take care of it at school. He's my responsibility, and he's not getting out of my sight again."

Dr. Chocker suddenly brightened. "Hey, well, what if I drive him and Bobby in my car? I mean, then you can go with the other buses to have lunch. Karen, you deserve it. It's been a tough year, and you need to end it on the right note. Your other students will miss you, you know."

Mrs. Ashley smiled. "I know you're not serious. You know you can't drive students in your car. Besides, the only students I care about at the moment are Marcus and Bobby. They went on that bus for a reason, and I think it's because they were scared. It sounds like they were hiding. I know my kids. Marcus and Bobby don't hide from getting in trouble. Something spooked them."

"Right." Dr. Chocker paled. "Look, then. I, uh, understand it's been a long day, and you're stressed." He reached into his pocket and pulled out a handful of wrapped mints. "Here, take one. It'll help you relax."

"Really?" Mrs. Ashley glanced at her principal in disbelief.

"I insist. You seriously need to relax, and mint settles the nerves." Dr. Chocker grinned. "After all, I'm a doctor. You can get on that bus and head back as soon as you have a mint. You have my word."

Sighing, Mrs. Ashley snatched a candy from his hand. It was in a twist wrap and the shape of a gumdrop. "Thanks," she muttered.

"Take some for everyone on the bus," Dr. Chocker said. "It'll help everyone relax."

Mrs. Ashley shook her head. "No rewards for the boys. Mr. Harris included."

"Right." Dr. Chocker pursed his lips in disappointment but stuffed the remaining mints in his pocket. "Okay, then. I'll send you on your way as soon as you pop it in your mouth."

"Yes, doctor," Mrs. Ashley said, rolling her eyes. She quickly unwrapped the candy and stuck it between her teeth. "Happy now?"

"Well, no. Not really. I was hoping this day would've gone better." He patted Mrs. Ashley on the arm. "Go ahead on the bus and try to get some rest on the way to school. I'll be along shortly. I'll just explain to the farm staff and give our apologies."

Mrs. Ashley sucked on her mint and worked hard to relax. "In my opinion," she said, "the farm needs to apologize to us. By the way, where is Erma? I wanted to speak to her. You know, the lady that came in hot from the pickup."

Dr. Chocker nearly gagged, and he stumbled back. "Oh, ah, that Erma… she left."

"Funny. Her pickup is still here."

"No, I mean, she left, er, to the house. She's, uh, catering lunch for the farmworkers."

Mrs. Ashley gave her principal a careful look. "Frank, are you okay? You're looking awfully pale."

"Oh, it's just… it's been a long day. I'll tell her that you said goodbye."

"Right…" Mrs. Ashley put a hand on her temple and shook her head. She was feeling a bit tired. "Well, we'll be off," she said.

The other two buses were now pulling out and heading off the farm. She wanted to be right behind them.

"Wait!" Morgan Raycroft rushed off the porch of the brick house and hurried to the fence where they stood. "We, I, really need to see that boy. I believe he, well, took something from the farm."

Mrs. Ashley looked at the taller woman and shook her head. "Whatever he did, we'll deal with at school," she said. She sucked on the mint hard in her mouth. "Whatever he saw scared him, and he is not leaving the bus."

Morgan blinked and looked at her coolly. Fingering a pendant on her neck, she nodded. "Fair enough. Then, tell him we apologize for his bad experience at Sunnybrook Farm, but what he *thought* he saw was just a show for future visits. Tell him we hope he comes back real soon."

Mrs. Ashley frowned. It sounded like a threat. She'd come with the intention of asking this woman to help her husband with a job. Now, she felt nothing but revulsion. "I will tell him no such thing. Frank, we're leaving now."

"Safe travels," Dr. Chocker mumbled.

Ryan Raycroft waited for Dr. Chocker and Morgan at the steps of the brick house.

"Well?" Ryan Raycroft asked, frowning. "I'm assuming you didn't get the kid."

The principal shook his head miserably. "It's like I told you. Mrs. Ashley is like a mother hen with her students."

"We eat mother hens here," Morgan said. She turned to watch the small bus start its motor. "Did you at least make sure she took a mint?"

The principal nodded. "Yes, but only her. She wouldn't share with the others."

"Too bad," Ryan Raycroft said. "It would make things easier, but no matter. I'll have Stan and Moe after them in a few minutes. In the meantime, Morgan, we have Kenton and Banor on standby, right?"

"They're just finishing up lunch," Morgan said, grinning at Dr. Chocker. "But they'll be ready. They're always hungry for more."

Chapter 26

On the bus, Mrs. Ashley collapsed back in her seat, utterly exhausted. The large mint tasted amazing in her mouth and, as Dr. Chocker said, worked wonders to calm her nerves. Biting down, she released its full minty sweetness and let it slide down her throat. She felt bad for not grabbing one for Elliot… but she was so tired.

"Let's get out of here," she told the driver, closing her eyes. She yawned. "Oh, my… what a day."

"Alright-y, we're on our way," the driver said with a grunt. "You just relax, little miss. We'll take the scenic route home. I grew up on this island and want to show you some of the sights."

Mrs. Ashley blinked her eyes. "No, no. Take the shortest way possible. These kids don't deserve… and I need to get back…."

She found herself nodding off as the bus rumbled from the parking area and onto the side road heading away from the farm. Maybe a short little nap would help her…

She struggled to sit up. "Mr. Harris," she called back. "I'm exhausted… If I fall asleep … you watch… kids…okay?" She lay her head against the window and let her eyes shut. Sleep never felt so good…

Elliot relaxed his glare and sat back in his seat. He glanced over when his mom started to snore. He'd hoped she would've sat next to him and ask what was wrong and why he'd been late. It was hard to be mad at Tucker and his mom at the same time. He wished Skylar was there. Taking off his cap, he dropped it on his backpack and stared out the window. All at once, he sat up with a start.

"Hey, where are we going?" he asked.

They'd reached the end of the side road but had taken a right onto the island's main road. They were heading away from the bridge.

"Hey," he said louder. "This is, like, the wrong way."

"Scenic route," the driver said. "Relax, kid. It's a shortcut."

Elliot was not convinced but relaxed a little when they reached another road going left. The bus turned on this road, entering a stretch of grassy fields and sparse woods. They continued down it for several minutes when Elliot stood up from his seat.

"This isn't the way to the bridge," he said.

The driver ignored him.

Elliot looked over at his mom and saw her mouth open and eyes shut. She was fast asleep.

Sitting back down, he pulled his phone out of his backpack. It was a little past noon, and the sun stood high above the bus. Amazingly, his phone got a faint signal. Using his phone tracker, he found his current location. Zooming in on the map with his fingers, he gasped. "Hey, we're going totally the wrong way. We're heading north, not west."

"You're wrong, kid," the driver said. "The road circles back. You'll see."

"Then where's the bridge? We should've crossed it, like, twenty minutes ago!" Elliot threw another look at his mom, but she remained snoring. "My phone shows us going north!"

"Okay, maybe I'm lost. Hey, kid. Come over my left shoulder and let me see your phone."

"There aren't any road maps of the island," Elliot told him. "I just know we're moving the wrong way. My phone has us in the northern part of the island."

The driver snorted. "No way. Let me see that. Come by your window and lean over my shoulder. It's all right. The bus is going straight, and there's no traffic."

Elliot checked on his mom and then got to his feet. Putting his side against the window, he hopped up so his waist rested on the barrier separating his seat from the driver. Leaning over, he held out his phone. "See?"

The driver's name was Billy Roft. His family was one of the originals of Blue Island. As Elliot leaned over, Mr. Roft grabbed his metal coffee canister with his right hand. Ahead of him was an entrance to a dirt road heading into the forest. It was pocked with potholes.

"Look at my phone," Elliot started to say, "it—"

In one motion, Mr. Roft brought up his metal canister hard, its base slamming into the boy's right eye. Elliot's phone tumbled on the driver's lap as his small body flew back. The side of the boy's head cracked into the thick glass. Collapsing back into his seat, Elliot slumped against the window.

As he swung the canister, Mr. Roft turned the wheel and swerved the bus into the pitted dirt road. The bus's tires bounced and banged across it, sending the entire bus bucking like a wild bronco.

"What the heck!" screamed Gary as he lost grip of his phone and it went flying behind him. His entire body lifted from his seat several inches before crashing down.

Marcus and Bobby were both startled awake. Bobby banged his face on the window and bit his lip. He tasted blood.

"Sorry about that!" the driver yelled. "Poor section of the road."

Nobody had noticed the sudden attack on Elliot. Grumbling painfully, they settled as Mr. Roft veered back onto the main road. He hit the brakes and slowed to a stop, parking the bus in the middle of the road.

"Everyone all right back there?" he hollered, switching off the engine.

"Where'd you learn how to drive?" Gary asked rudely. He stood, rubbing his sore backside. "The school for the blind?"

The driver paid him no mind. Pulling off his seat belt, he snatched up the boy's phone that had landed between his knees. He got up to check on his passengers in the first seats. As he did, he glanced out the windows in all directions, wondering and waiting... what was taking them so long? This was the perfect time for the ambush. He saw nothing but grass and trees. Maybe they were sneaking in… He stopped between the first seats.

Elliot had tilted over and lay on his side with his legs bent under the seat. A dark bruise was forming under his right eye.

"You good, kid?" Mr. Roft asked gruffly. Bending, he smacked the boy's shoulder, ensuring he was out cold. The boy never stirred.

Satisfied, he glanced at the mother. She still snored and hadn't budged. Morgan's drugged mint had done its work. Mr. Roft grinned. "Never take candy from a stranger," he muttered. He straightened and moved toward the back. "Everyone alive back there?"

"No thanks to you," Bobby said, touching his mouth. "I got a bloody lip!"

Mr. Roft snorted. "I've had worse. Just suck on the blood, and it'll be okay."

Mr. Harris groaned as he handed Gary back his phone. It had smacked the teacher in the forehead. "Where are we, anyway? Are we almost back yet?"

"We haven't even crossed the bridge," Gary said. He stood and glared at the driver. "Where are we going?"

"Sorry about that." Mr. Roft shrugged. "Took a wrong turn." He winked. "Besides, I thought you boys wouldn't mind being a little late for school."

Bobby grunted. "That's true. What about you, Marcus?"

Marcus just stared out the window. His eyes were wide with fear. "I just want to go home," he finally said softly.

Moving back to the driver's seat, Mr. Roft paused once more by the kid he'd just knocked out. "Sorry about that, kid," he muttered. "Orders are orders." He leaned over and slid the kid's phone in the left back pocket of his green nylon pants. The boy remained breathing softly.

Reaching his seat, the driver sat down and soon started the engine. As it idled loudly, he reached under his seat and pulled out a long-range walkie-talkie. Ducking his head, he spoke softly into it. "This is Hound Dog to Base. I don't know the plan, but I got a situation here. If you got a plan, best do it quick."

A response crackled back moments later. *"Copy that, Hound Dog. This is Base. We see your location and a plan is in action. Proceed and do not stop."*

"Hound Dog here. What is the plan exactly?"

"Base here. It has to look like an accident. Do your job, Hound Dog."

Mr. Roft put down the walkie-talkie and glanced in the mirror over his head. The kids and teacher in the back didn't know what was coming. He didn't know either, but he had a bad feeling about it. The unconscious ones, he decided, were the lucky ones. Throwing the engine into drive, he got the bus moving again. Soon after, he heard the motorcycles.

Mrs. Ashley blinked groggily as her head bounced against the hard window. She'd been dreaming of her neighbors, the Goodalls. They were taking a chainsaw to their trees and making them fall on her house.

All at once, her eyes opened, and she sat up with a start.

"Wh-whoa," she said with a groan. "What's going on?"

"We're being chased by two motorcycles!" Bobby cried, sounding panicked. "We've been trying to get you to wake up!"

"Huh?" Mrs. Ashley rubbed her eyes and realized the buzzing chainsaw wasn't in her head but actually coming from outside the bus.

She stood in alarm and looked out the back. Two black motorcycles zoomed right behind them. The helmeted riders were dressed in black from head to toe. They were side by side and inches from the back bumper.

"Where are we?" she demanded.

"We're still on the island," Mr. Harris said, sounding scared. "We got lost."

"How did we get lost?" Mrs. Ashley demanded. "We were following two buses, and there's only one road to the bridge!"

Marcus sobbed out. "We're going to die! They're after me!"

"Hey!" Mrs. Ashley shouted. "We're not going die. Calm down!"

Gulping in deep breaths, she tried to shake off the pounding headache. How long had she been asleep? She checked on her son and saw his blond hair splayed out on the seat across from her. He lay on his side, fast asleep. Elliot, she knew, could sleep through anything.

"Can't we pull over?" she said to the driver. "Let these guys pass us?"

"No can do, miss," Mr. Roft said, gasping for air. "I think the brakes are busted or something."

One of the motorcycles roared closer, nearly touching the back of the bus.

"What about going faster then?"

"This is a school bus," the driver said. "I can't go past forty-five!"

"Use your radio and call for help!" Mrs. Ashley screamed at him.

Mr. Roft just shook his head. Sweat dripped down his head and face. "Sorry, but—"

He swung the wheel to the right, and suddenly, the bus was off-road, bouncing down a grassy incline.

Marcus and Bobby screamed. Gary just grabbed the front of his seat and held on for dear life. Mr. Harris whimpered and crouched in a ball on his seat.

"Stop it!" Mrs. Ashley yelled, leaning back against the window and propping herself up between the seat cushions. "Are you crazy?"

The driver just stomped on the gas. The bus nearly went airborne as it bounced over the uneven ground.

Mrs. Ashley saw Elliot start sliding into the aisle. "Elliot!" she screamed.

Seeing his face dangling over the seat, she saw a dark, ugly bruise around his right eye. Flinging herself from her window, she stumbled across the bus aisle to her son. She grabbed his loose arm, yanking him up. He flopped like a fish on a hook. Her other hand snagged him under the opposite armpit. Lifting him bodily, she collapsed into the seat and sat him across her lap. As she leaned back against the seat, feeling every bounce of the wild bus, Elliot sagged against her. She hugged him tight, wrapping her arms around his stomach and chest like a seatbelt. She was relieved to feel his chest rise and fall. Unconscious but alive.

"What is happening!" she cried. Looking up, she screamed.

The bus headed straight for a fallen oak.

At the last moment, the driver swung the wheel and ran the right side of the bus into the twisted roots of the fallen tree. In jarring impact, the bus leaped up over the roots, and in a deafening crunching bang, it struck the tree before grinding to a halt. The seat across from Mrs. Ashley, where she'd been sleeping minutes before, buckled and tore as a great branch punctured the bus wall, stabbing through the cushion.

Mrs. Ashley barely saw it as her head bashed against the window behind her. Seeing stars, she tried cradling her son but felt him slipping from her grasp as darkness closed in. Everything went black.

"What's the status?" Morgan Raycroft asked, walking casually into the headquarters room.

She flicked back her hair as she crossed the room to a worn easy chair. Across from her—looking like a quivering bundle of nerves and sweat—Dr. Chocker sat on a sagging couch, wringing his hands in his lap.

He'd found a signal for his phone and had sent a text to Mr. Charles, letting him know the small bus had been delayed but would meet them at school. Oh, and its radio was not functioning, so they did not have to worry if they didn't hear from the driver. To really make the teacher angry, he'd added that the small bus would be stopping for lunch on its own at a pizza place on the island. It would likely be late to school. Mr. Harris, Dr. Chocker had texted, would be treating.

Mr. Charles had not sent a text back in reply, but maybe his phone wasn't getting a signal yet. More likely, he was gnashing his teeth.

"The status?" Her brother Ryan Raycroft glared at her from where he stood behind the giant oak desk at the head of the room. He slammed down his walkie-talkie. "Let's see," he growled. "My sister, the so-called leader of The Pack, has opened our island to outsiders. Not just any outsiders, mind you, but to kids! And, so, for the first time in over fifty years, an outsider had spotted a member of The Pack. Committing murder. How is that for a status report?"

Morgan sniffed as she stretched out her legs. "That is not what I meant, and you know it. I brought those kids here to find the one I need."

"All I know is that I have to clean up your mess! Again!" Her brother leaned over the desk and snarled. His eyes flashed yellow, and his nails seemed to lengthen into claws. "You are pushing it, sister."

"The only thing I am pushing is for the cure, brother. And you are at my side because you know you want it!"

Dr. Chocker lowered his head and stared miserably at the floor. "Do you two have to fight at a time like this?"

"We're not fighting," Ryan Raycroft said bitterly. "I'm merely stating facts. Morgan, you messed up. Now I have to stage an accident and kill a kid. How does that sound?"

Dr. Chocker just made a whimper and squeezed his eyes tight.

The three were in the top corner of the brick house overlooking the farm's parking area. It was a large room with hardwood floors and sparse furniture. Besides the desk, chair, and couch, there was only a small table holding glasses and a bottle of wine. Framed pictures and photos of women since dead lined the long inner wall without windows. Each frame served as a memorial to a leader of The Pack. Morgan meant to have her photo up there one day... as the last leader ever.

Outside, the last of the visitors were still being ushered to their cars. As soon as the last bus pulled out, the farm had abruptly closed. The homeschooled brats were told to leave immediately but were dragging their heels. Unless told otherwise, the teenage volunteers were also being told to go.

Yet, Morgan somehow seemed pleased by the day's events. She leaned back in her chair.

"As I recall," she said, "I promised to find a child. Well, I delivered." Her right hand reached to her red pendant and squeezed. She looked across the room at her brother. "The boy witness? Don't kill him. He's the one. I can feel it. Bring him back alive. And then we'll finish this."

Ryan Raycroft stared back and then slowly nodded. He grabbed his walkie-talkie. "I trust your feelings, Morgan. I'll make the call in a minute. Moe and Stan are stopping the bus right now to take the kid. They'll be checking in at any time."

Dr. Chocker licked his dry lips and stared up at her with watery eyes. "What about the others?" he asked. "You know, my two teachers and the children?"

Morgan looked at him in disdain. "*Your* teachers and the children? Don't make me laugh. We gave you what you wanted. You have the money, and you now belong to us. Don't you worry about the others. Worry about yourself."

"The others will be fine," Ryan Raycroft said, straightening behind the desk. "Hopefully, they'll never know what happens."

"As if I care," Morgan said, stroking her pendant. "All I need is the boy."

"You should care," her brother said. He put his hands behind his back, holding the walkie-talkie. He stared at the wall where the latest frame had recently been hung. Sylvia Raycroft, his mother, stared back at him.

He missed Sylvia's quiet leadership. Ever since Morgan took over, things had been growing out of control. He knew Morgan had secretly sent members of The Pack to the mainland to watch and harass the Ashley family… his family. Morgan had always been jealous of their oldest sister, Minnie, Sylvia's favorite. Did Morgan's jealousy live on after Minnie's death?

"Blood of The Pack is on that bus," he said softly.

"Ha," Morgan said snidely. "You mean that teacher woman? She just married our nephew. She's no Raycroft."

"As I recall," Ryan said mildly. "That is how most of our past leaders came into the family, by marrying into it. Besides, I was talking about her boy."

Morgan rose and walked over to the table with the wine. "He's nothing but a runt. I looked him over already. I had hoped he could join The Pack as an alpha. He's barely baby food. There is no Raycroft blood in him. When Minnie left the family, she gave it up."

"He's still part of my family," her brother stated. "He's Minnie's grandson."

Pulling the cork from the wine bottle, Morgan sniffed. "Whatever you say, brother. Just get the boy to me."

That was when the walkie-talkie squawked.

Listening to it, Morgan dropped the cork and nearly smashed the wine bottle.

The bus had just wrecked, and Stan and Moe were moving in. The boy could be injured or worse.

"Copy that. This is Base. There's been a change of plan. Don't harm the kid or anybody else. We need him alive." Ryan Raycroft took a deep breath. "Morgan says he's the one. I repeat. *Morgan* says we need him alive, so bring him here unharmed. Do you copy?"

The two men acknowledged it but admitted it may be too late. The bus had wrecked pretty hard.

Dr. Chocker groaned, and Morgan's knuckles went white as she gripped the wine bottle hard. She didn't pour a glass.

Skylar waited impatiently at the bottom of the porch in front of the brick house. She held her cell phone in front of her and checked it every few seconds. Her forehead creased with worry. She'd tried three times to enter the house only to be rebuffed each instance. She tried explaining that she needed Teddy—he was the one who'd given her a ride to the island.

"Get another of your lot to take you back," growled the grizzled farmworker who'd answered the door the last time. He filled the frame with his meaty figure, and she vaguely remembered seeing him at the funeral. "You all go to the same school, don't ya? Better yet, get one of the homeschool psychos to drive you. Just don't come back here!" He then shut the door in her face.

Shaken, Skylar would've been fine with a ride from somebody else, but she had a huge problem. She tried calling her mom to check in and explain why Elliot had been late but couldn't get through. Elliot's phone also wasn't working. By now, the two should be off the island and in easy cell phone range. Something had happened.

Frustrated and scared, she remained standing at the bottom step of the porch.

Finally, the door cracked open, and Teddy stuck his head out. Seeing Skylar, he stumbled out and stood on the porch looking ready to collapse. The handsome teen looked worn and to have just finished losing a boxing match. He wore loose gray sweatpants and a matching T-shirt. Dark circles sagged under his bloodshot eyes, and he cradled his stomach with both hands.

"Sky?" he said, sounding surprised. "What are you doing here? You should be gone."

"Teddy, what's wrong?" Skylar asked. "You look terrible."

"You should see the other guy," he said, grinning sideways. "But seriously. Why are you still here?"

"Teddy, I don't know what's going on. But I can't reach my mom and brother on their phones."

"You can get a signal here?" Teddy asked dubiously.

"Not very well," she admitted. "But by the parking lot, it's decent enough. That's not the point. My mom *always* has her phone on when she's working. And my brother would definitely try to have it on for the trip. I'm telling you, Teddy. Something happened. I can feel it."

Teddy looked into her eyes and then grimaced. "Maybe they're just not near a signal."

"They should be by now! It doesn't take that long to get off the island. Besides, I have a bad feeling. Teddy, what do you know about 'Morgan breaking a curse'?"

Teddy's face went pale, and he gagged. "Wh-What did you say?"

"I heard some men talking about looking for a kid to end some sort of curse. What's going on around here?"

Teddy's eyes darted around, making sure nobody was watching. "Keep your voice low," he hissed. He took a deep breath. "Meet me at my car. I'll be there in five minutes. We'll go see if we can find that bus with your mom and brother."

Without waiting for a reply, he went back into the house. As the door started closing behind him, he doubled over and stifled a cry of pain.

Worried, Skylar hurried for the parking lot. She saw Teddy's navy blue sedan parked next to the minivan being loaded with the homeschoolers. The mom of the twins was the only parent there, and she was trying to convince the other homeschoolers to ride with her. The other parents were supposed to come an hour later to pick up their kids. It was a disaster.

"I can't ride with strangers," the girl was repeating over and over. "I can only ride with my mom or dad."

"I'll go if I can drive," a boy no more than twelve said. "I drive my mom's car all the time." He had a stack of Pokémon cards in one hand but eyed the van hungrily.

Standing in front of the open side door of the van, the poor mom had one twin climbing on her back and the other clinging to her leg. The girl sat on the gravel next to them, refusing to budge. The boy with the cards was at the driver's door trying to open it.

Skylar averted her eyes as she crossed to Teddy's car. She had no time to help. Her family needed her.

"Hey, Skylar," a boy called. She turned to see Tucker sticking his head out from the back of the van. "Tell, um, Elliot, that I'm sorry. Okay?"

Skylar's eyes widened. "Tucker!" she called. "I can't get in touch with Elliot. Has he texted or called you?"

"No," Tucker said. Then he frowned. "But it is hard to get a signal here."

"I can't reach him or my mom," Skylar said, fighting back tears. She bit back her panic. "I don't know where they can be."

Tucker's eyes widened. "Wait. I know how to find him!" He held up his phone. "Hold on!"

He disappeared into the van and emerged a moment later. Jumping out, dodging the struggling mom and kids, he ran to Skylar. He carried his backpack over his shoulder and phone in his hand. The twins and the girl were still screaming, and the mom never noticed him leaving.

Chapter 27

When Teddy arrived at his car minutes later, he found Skylar sitting in the front seat with a stocky kid with a head full of dark curls in the back.

"Relax," Skylar said quickly as Teddy opened the driver's door and gave her a quizzical look. "This is Tucker, Elliot's best friend."

"Hiya," Tucker said, wincing at hearing the best friend part.

"What's he doing in my car?" Teddy demanded. Still wearing his gray sweats, he carried a metal canister that he hid behind his back.

"He has an app that tracks Elliot's phone." Skylar took a deep breath. Her voice started to shake. "You're not going to believe this, but Elliot is still on the island. The last location has him like miles from here, completely away from the bridge." Her eyes filled with tears. "Teddy, what's going on?"

Teddy wrinkled his nose, and his nostrils started to flare, but then he blew out his breath. "I'll explain in the car," he muttered, climbing in the driver's seat. Jamming the key in the ignition, he started the car but did not put it into drive.

"What are we waiting for," Skylar said impatiently. "Let's go!"

"Not yet," Teddy said, avoiding eye contact with her. "There's somebody else coming. She knows the woods better than me."

Skylar frowned and looked out the window at the farm. She inwardly groaned.

Paige trotted towards them, carrying a camouflage backpack and a bitter smile.

"Hello, everyone," she said coolly when she opened the back door behind Skylar. "Sorry to keep you waiting."

"Just get in," growled Teddy through gritted teeth. He sounded menacing.

Feeling the tension take a new level, Tucker scooted away from the new arrival, squeezing behind Teddy's seat. The teen had adjusted his seat as far back as possible to accommodate his long legs, which seemed to have just grown. Tucker had to bend his knees near his chest to fit.

Once everyone settled in an awkward silence, the sedan lurched forward. As it left the farm, the mom finally stuffed the last child in the back of the van and hurried to the driver's seat before anyone could escape. She would never chaperone a homeschool field trip alone again.

Mrs. Ashley moaned as she climbed her way back to consciousness. Her head ached, and her left shoulder shot with pain when she tried to move it.

"Mom! Mom, wake up!"

Opening her eyes, she saw Elliot's worried face right above her. Tears streaked his cheeks, and his hair was a wild tangle as he grabbed her right shoulder, shaking it. But he was alive and awake.

"Elliot!" she said with a gasp. "Argh!" she cried out with pain as she forced herself to sit up. She'd been pressed against the window from the accident.

"Are you okay, Mom?" Elliot asked fearfully. He knelt on the seat next to her and watched her with frightened eyes, his brow creased with concern. He was the most beautiful sight she'd ever seen.

"Yes, of course! Come here, sweetheart. Let me look at you. Are you hurt?"

"I'm fine," Elliot said. He crawled onto her lap and sat on her knees, facing her, his own knees bent on the seat to either side.

Ignoring her painful shoulder, Mrs. Ashley grabbed his shoulders and surveyed him for damage. His eyes sported dark bruises, and his right eye had a much larger one. Another bruise marked his left cheek. Otherwise, he seemed okay. She ran her hands down his arms and thighs. Patting his back, she felt his phone in the back of his pants, but nothing broken. "Nothing hurts?"

"I'm okay. Really. What happened?"

"Well, sweetheart, we had an accident."

Mrs. Ashley suddenly went still. She wrapped her arms around Elliot's back and pulled him to her chest. Doing so, she whispered in her ear. "Look, sweetheart. I need to check on the others and… and make sure it's okay. But first, I need you to do something. You need to be brave."

Elliot gripped her shoulders and squeezed his understanding.

Patting his lower back, she moved her right arm around the back of the waist. "I'm going to stand up. I need you to look in the back of the bus and tell me what you see. Make sure the others are okay. Got it?"

There were a few whimpers in the back, but mostly, a heavy silence hung. The smells of burnt oil and exhaust fumes permeated the air.

Elliot put his chin on her sore shoulder and tensed. His hands gripped the back of the seat. "I see Mr. Harris," he whispered. "He looks like he's crying."

"Okay… good job, kiddo." Mrs. Ashley tightened her grip on his waist. Her hand of her sore arm grabbed the seat barrier in front of her. Biting her lower lip, she forced her aching body up, pulling Elliot into her arms as she stood. Upright, she quickly moved her left arm to support the back of his pants, ignoring the burning pain in her shoulder. Elliot may have been small for his age, but he was not easy to hold anymore. "Make a head count," she said. Her own eyes busily searched for the driver.

She remembered clearly. It had been no accident. The driver had wrecked the bus on purpose. And the two motorcycle goons had been right behind them.

"Glad to see you're awake," the driver said, standing by his seat. His back leaned against the front of the bus. The entire windshield was marred with white spiderweb cracks. He looked to be guarding the door.

Mrs. Ashley clutched her son tighter. Across the bus aisle, she saw a thick branch stabbing through the wall where she'd once sat. Her old seat was ripped and torn, white stuffing and dark springs spilled like guts. She shuddered. If she hadn't moved to grab Elliot, she would now be dead. Her gaze shifted back to the driver. He held a two-foot-long tire iron and leered at her. With only a red mark on his neck from his seatbelt, he looked otherwise unharmed.

"Nobody worry or panic," the driver said. Held in his right hand, he repeatedly slapped the iron into his left palm. "Just stay put and wait. Help is on its way."

"Elliot," Mrs. Ashley said. "Is everyone good back there?" She didn't want him to see the danger. The driver obviously meant them harm.

Elliot hugged her neck. "Yeah, I think so. Like, I see everyone now."

Mrs. Ashley wavered as she felt relief wash over her. "Good. Okay, I'm putting you down. I want you to walk ahead of me and sit in the back."

"You sit right back down, lady," the driver said with a snarl.

"I have to check on the students," Mrs. Ashley said, glaring at him. "Give me your First Aid kit."

The driver held up the iron threateningly. "Don't tell me what to do! Go check on the kids if you want, but they're fine. It wasn't even that bad of an accident."

"It was no accident." Mrs. Ashley nodded at the punctured seat with the branch sticking out. "And I consider that pretty bad."

The driver dropped his gaze but kept his iron raised. "Just go check on the brats," he muttered.

Elliot slid down from her arms. Mrs. Ashley moved to let him by and then crouched on the floor. Her bag had fallen and lay under the punctured seat.

"What are you doing?" the driver demanded.

"Getting my own First Aid kit," Mrs. Ashley said, grabbing her bag.

Breathing hard, she opened the small top zipper in front, pulling out a tube the size and shape of a marker. She slipped it in her pocket before quickly rising back to her feet. A gift from her husband, she now had a tube of pepper spray. She then followed Elliot up the aisle without looking back.

"Everyone okay?" she called, trying to keep her voice calm. Elliot walked with a slight limp. She put a firm hand on his shoulder, squeezing it tight.

In the middle of the bus, Marcus watched her with fearful eyes. He'd seen and heard how she'd checked on her son. She went to him immediately. Forgetting to be jealous, he just felt sick with dread. He knew the accident was because of him. They were coming for him. Mrs. Ashley was not his mom. She wouldn't protect him. No, she would do anything to save her son. That meant Marcus was like the old woman, dead meat.

His empty stomach lurched, and bile went up his throat. Swallowing the burning acid down, he pressed against the seat behind him and closed his eyes. When the bus left the road, he'd crouched on the floor and buried his head in the seat. The jarring impact of the crash had shaken him up, leaving him briefly stunned but otherwise unharmed.

Across from him, Mr. Harris stood against his window, rubbing his left wrist and blinking away tears. "Anything yet?" he asked, his voice tight with fear.

Gary stood in the next seat. He held his head in one hand and his phone in the other. "No signal," he said miserably. "We're totally messed up."

"I'm sure help will come soon," Mrs. Ashley said as she reached Gary's seat. "You okay?" She pushed Elliot into the seat across from Gary. She wanted to check his injured foot.

"This is not part of my contract," Mr. Harris said, biting his lower lip. "My wrist is swelling, and my nose feels like I just ran into a wall. How are you doing?"

"I was asking Gary," Mrs. Ashley said, bending in the aisle.

"Oh, I'm just great," Gary said sarcastically. "I'm stuck on a crazy island with a crazy bus driver who just tried to kill me. But at least I'm with my favorite teacher."

"He means me," Mr. Harris grumbled.

Mrs. Ashley decided to ignore them. Taking Elliot's left sneaker in her hands, she examined it closely. "Does this hurt?"

"I think I just twisted it," Elliot said. "It'll be okay." He winced when she turned his foot but didn't cry out. "It's not too bad."

"If it gets worse, let me know."

Bobby groaned from over the head of Marcus. "Dude, I think I passed out."

"Bobby," Marcus hissed. "They're going to kill me. I need to get out of here."

"Huh?" His eyes, still unfocused, peered over the seat at Marcus. "Who's going to kill you? Mr. Harris and Mrs. Ashley? Dude, you weren't driving the bus. This one isn't your fault."

Marcus just shut his eyes. Tears dropped down his cheeks. It was his fault. He knew it.

"Uh, Mom?" Elliot said. He sat on the edge of the seat, his feet in the aisle. Gripping the back of the seat in front of Marcus, he looked out the back of the bus. "Two guys are coming." He sounded scared. "It's the scarecrow guy and egghead from the funeral."

Standing, Mrs. Ashley stared out the back window. "Oh, no."

Eyes popping open, Marcus whirled to kneel on the seat and look out the back. "They're going to kill me."

Bobby also looked and groaned. "The motorcycle goons," he said.

Mrs. Ashley kept her gaze on the two men dressed in black. They'd left their helmets, and she recognized them immediately. The taller, scrawny man grinned toward the bus while the shorter, chubby man kept a hand in his leather jacket. They did not look like they'd arrived to help.

Chapter 28

"Everyone shut up!" the bus driver yelled. "Nobody moves, and nobody gets hurt!"

"What do they want?" Mrs. Ashley said. She kept her gaze trained on the men walking down the grassy field toward the bus.

"You'll just have to see, won't you," the driver said. He rested the iron on his shoulder while his left hand smoothed back his greasy hair. It was hot and stuffy on the bus. Sweat dripped from his face.

Keeping an eye on the back of the bus, he moved down the steps and kicked the doors open manually. The right front of the bus had ridden up the roots of the fallen tree, and the side of the bus had absorbed most of the crash. The front doors opened just beyond the tangled roots.

"Stan! Moe!" he yelled. "In here! We're all set and waiting!" Climbing up the stairs, he wore a smirk. "This will all end soon. Don't worry. They're not here to hurt you."

"We just want the kid!" the shorter of the men yelled as he started moving around the bus and tree. "Send out Marcus, and we'll be on our way!"

Marcus ducked down in his seat. "See?" he whimpered.

Bobby's eyes went wide, and his gaze darted to Mrs. Ashley.

Mrs. Ashley grimly watched the two men from the window. Then she turned to the driver. "Are you insane?" she asked.

"Shut up and bring up Marcus," the driver said, dropping his gaze. "He's the only one they want. Then we'll be on our way."

"In your smashed bus?" Gary asked sarcastically.

The driver's mouth tightened. "Just shut up and send Marcus up. Trust me. You don't want those two coming up here to get him."

Marcus crawled to the floor and was about to slide under the seat when Mrs. Ashley was at his side. She bent down and grabbed his arm.

"Marcus," she hissed. "Stay still."

Marcus drooped, hanging his head. He knew it. He was dead. Tears filled his eyes. His teacher was giving him up.

"Where's the boy?" yelled the taller of the men. They were now in front of the bus and approaching the door. "Once we have him, we'll send for help. You have our word."

"You touch one of my kids, and you'll have me to deal with!" Mrs. Ashley yelled. "You have *my* word." She remained crouched over Marcus and yelled over her shoulder. "Now, get away from this bus!" Turning to Marcus, she gave him a tight smile. "Nobody is going to lay a finger on you," she whispered. "That's a promise."

Marcus looked up at her in surprise and gave a slight nod.

"Billy Roft, you a-hole!" the shorter of the two men shouted. "That woman is supposed to be knocked out!"

Mrs. Ashley glanced toward the back of the bus and kept her voice low. "When I get up, move to the back. The others will join you. Bobby, you know how to operate the emergency door?"

"You bet," Bobby said, nodding.

"Good. When I give the signal, you open it and get everyone out. Run to the trees and wait for me."

Bobby licked the sweat off his upper lip. "Right." His voice had started to deepen that month but now went high and shrill. "What's the signal?"

"You'll know." Smiling, Mrs. Ashley rose. Her smile fell as she faced the front. Moving forward, she tousled Elliot's tangled hair as she went by. "Stay close to Bobby and Marcus," she whispered. She glanced over at Mr. Harris. "You're in charge until I get back."

The male teacher had his mouth open but made no sound. He managed a nod.

Mrs. Ashley stopped in the aisle in front of Gary's seat. "Okay, boys," she hissed over her shoulder. "Grab all your bags with food and water. Get to the back."

Outside the bus, the two men had paused and were discussing something.

The taller man glared up at the driver's back through the cracked windshield. "Why did you have to wreck the bus?" he asked. "Don't you know Morgan wants the kid unharmed?"

His partner started pushing his way through the tall grass, stepping over fallen branches and avoiding the roots. "If any of them kids are hurt, you're gonna regret it," he said. He reached the front door of the bus.

Billy Roft's eyes went wide with fright. The iron shook in his hand as he stared hatefully at Mrs. Ashley. "I caused an accident! Like I was told."

"You weren't told nothing." The shorter man shoved his way onto the bus, running up the steps. His taller partner was not far behind him. "Welcome, kiddies!" he crowed, smiling to reveal yellow teeth. "We're here to rescue you!"

Mrs. Ashley stepped forward, her hand in her pocket. "You get off this bus this instant!" she yelled.

Marcus watched in amazement as his teacher fearlessly went at the man. He couldn't believe she was putting her life on the line for him.

Bobby grabbed his shoulder. "I think the signal is about to come. Get ready."

"Give us the kid, and we will!" the taller man shouted from the second step. "Moe, get back there and grab Marcus. He's the one with the dark skin. Leave the rest alone."

"You will do no such thing!" Mrs. Ashley said. She seethed with rage. "He's my boy, and you're not laying a finger on him."

"Hold on, lady," Moe said, grinning crookedly. "Your boy is standing behind him. You don't understand. We ain't asking permission like we're your students. We're taking him."

The taller man, who had to be Stan, nodded. "That's right. Nobody is supposed to get hurt, but if you want to fight, I imagine that will change. You have your son to worry about."

"Right now," Mrs. Ashley said through clenched lips, "all those boys are my sons. Now get off this bus!"

She pulled out her pepper spray and lunged at Moe. Flipping the cap to arm the spray, she pressed hard, sending a stream into the surprised fleshy face.

The man shrieked and collapsed to his knees, clutching at his eyes.

"That's our signal," Bobby yelled above the screams of pain. "Let's go!"

He threw open the latch and kicked the door open.

"No!" screamed Stan from the front. He jumped up the last stair, shoving past Billy Roft. "Don't go out that way! It's—"

Mrs. Ashley cut him off with a stream of paper spray in his eyes.

Screaming, Stan stumbled and tripped over Moe, crashing into the aisle. Stan lay on top of Moe, and both men clawed at their faces, writhing in pain.

Tossing down his iron, Mr. Roft jumped into the driver's seat. He covered his face with both hands and wailed for mercy.

Satisfied the three would be out of commission for a few minutes, Mrs. Ashley pocketed the spray. She ran to the back of the bus, where Bobby helped Mr. Harris exit. The teacher had his sore wrist close to his stomach as he sat on the floor and hopped to the ground. She was relieved to see Elliot, Marcus, and Gary already out and standing behind Bobby.

"Get to the woods!" she cried. "Hurry!"

"You get out first," Bobby told her, reaching up his hand.

Bending low, Mrs. Ashley took it and jumped from the bus. She nearly fell to her knees, but Marcus grabbed her other arm and held her up.

"No!" she heard Moe yell from the bus. "The woods ain't safe!"

Gary responded by slamming the back door of the bus shut.

"We can't protect you in there!" Stan's voice was now muffled but clearly heard.

"Okay," Mrs. Ashley said, patting the shoulders of Bobby and Marcus. "Well done, boys. Now, let's move!"

"Where are we going?" Gary asked, eyeing the dense woods ahead of them. It was eerily quiet and still.

"Away from the creeps behind us," Mrs. Ashley said firmly. "Stay together, but move quickly!"

She pushed Bobby and Marcus ahead of her and stepped back to Elliot. "How's your ankle?" she asked him.

"It's, like, totally healed now, Mom," he said. He brushed the hair from his face. "Amazing how thinking you're going to die makes you feel better."

"Nobody is going to die," Mrs. Ashley told him. Putting an arm around his shoulder, she guided him in front of her. "That's a mom's promise."

Bobby grinned. "You mean, that's a *loco* mom's promise." He elbowed Marcus. "See, Mrs. Ashley wasn't kidding when she said she'd take care of us."

Marcus grunted and ducked his head. "Let's just go," he muttered.

Mr. Harris and Gary stayed right behind the mother and son while Marcus and Bobby led the way. Everyone besides Mrs. Ashley and Elliot carried their backpacks with water and food. The sun beat down over the trees, and the shade did little to cool the panicked group.

Dodging thick trees and avoiding fallen limbs, the group moved deeper into the dense forest. Soon, the brush thinned out, and the trees weren't so close together. Dead leaves crunched under their feet as they ran up and down small ridges, not knowing where they would end up.

As they went down a particularly steep hill, Mrs. Ashley moved to the lead. The kids, she saw, were exhausted and fueled only by adrenaline that was quickly sapping. At the bottom, they came to a flat area where a dead tree had tumbled from above. Another hill faced them. The trunk lay like a long bench in the valley. Stripped of bark, it resembled a long, naked bone.

"Let's stop here for a break," Mrs. Ashley said, breathing hard. "We'll get some water and figure out what to do."

"Sounds good to me," Mr. Harris said. "I don't think anybody followed us." He grunted. "We should be good."

Gary eyed the trees above them warily. "I doubt that," he muttered. "Do you realize there hasn't been one bird or animal since we got to this island and been in these woods?"

"So what?" Marcus said, trudging tiredly to the trunk. Setting down his backpack, he took a seat. "I just need water."

"Animals tend to avoid danger," Gary said. "This place isn't safe."

"Safe enough," Bobby said. He had his water bottle out and took a big gulp. "Thanks to Mrs. A, of course." Looking at his teacher, he held out his water. "You were awesome," he said.

Mrs. Ashley just took the water bottle and pursed her lips. "Gary is right. Something isn't right about this place." Without drinking, she passed the water to Elliot. "Let's keep our voices down and rest up. If you haven't eaten your lunch, have something now. We don't know when we'll get to eat again."

The air was still, but something tingled down her spine. There was a danger in the air, and she kept thinking about what Stan had yelled. The man had seemed scared of the woods. She watched her son sip down water. She had to protect him. Then she looked at where Gary now sat by Marcus. The boys were pulling out their lunches but paused to look up at her. Their eyes were filled with gratitude and trust.

Turning away, Mrs. Ashley saw Bobby take back his water from Elliot and give him half a sandwich. Her heart went out to these boys. She had to protect them all.

Mr. Harris tapped her back with his good hand. "They really don't pay us enough for this," he muttered. "You want some of my lunch? I have ham and Swiss."

"No, but thanks. Maybe I'll have a sip of water." Her headache had vanished during the stress on the bus but now returned in full force. She fingered her scalp just above her left temple and found a painful bump. At least her left shoulder had worked itself out. She knew it would be sore the next day, but for now, it felt fine.

Mr. Harris leaned his head close to her ear. "What are we going to do?" he whispered. "I mean, really."

"I don't know," Mrs. Ashley admitted. She glanced and saw Elliot and Bobby had joined the others to sit on the tree. The four boys looked wilted. "We need to find a way off this island."

"I was wondering. What did Marcus see? I mean, why do they want him so bad?"

Mrs. Ashley drew back and stared at Mr. Harris hard. "That is the least of my concerns right now."

"Yeah, sorry," he mumbled. Then he took a deep breath. "I was, uh, wondering. Should I try running for help? I mean, I can go off on my own…"

"And go where?" Mrs. Ashley said. "Tell me, where would you go?"

Mr. Harris had no answer. He ducked his head miserably.

Over at the fallen tree, Gary nudged Marcus on the arm. "So, are you going to tell us what's going on and why those guys are after you?"

"None of your business," Bobby said from his other side. "Leave him alone."

"It is my business if those guys are after me, too," Gary said.

Marcus took a bite of his peanut butter sandwich and refused to answer.

"Knock it off, boys," Mrs. Ashley said. "We're staying together and not fighting." She turned to Mr. Harris and crossed her arms over her chest. "Right now, the kids need us. I'm not going to abandon them, and neither are you."

"Right," Mr. Harris muttered. "Here." He pulled an unopened bottle of water from his backpack and thrust it into her hands. "When you're hungry, I'll be sitting with the kids." He shuffled away unhappily.

Mrs. Ashley turned her back on him and stared up at the hill they'd come down. She couldn't shake the feeling of danger. Unscrewing the cap, she soon took long gulps of water, realizing how thirsty she was. In moments, the water was gone. Her stomach growled as she wiped her mouth, letting her know she'd also skipped lunch.

She was about to take Mr. Harris up on his sandwich offer when a lone, mournful howl rose from the trees behind them. The first sign of a wild animal on the island did nothing to ease her fear. Though it sounded far away, the howl sent terror through her veins.

As soon as the wail died, Mrs. Ashley leaped to action.

"Let's go, pack up!" she said. "Time to move!"

She carried the empty water bottle to the log and tossed it to Mr. Harris. "Put all your trash in your bags, leave nothing behind. We don't want to make it any easier to follow."

"Yo, Mrs. A," Bobby said, looking apologetic. "I got to pee."

"Yeah, so do I," Marcus said.

Mrs. Ashley nodded tiredly. "Let's everyone take a pee break. Just don't go too far and keep in sight of each other. Mr. Harris, keep an eye out. I'm going to find a bush."

While Teddy drove, he held one hand on the wheel while the other rested over his belly. His eyes kept straying to the metal canister sitting on the console between him and Skylar.

Skylar had both hands gripping the top of her knees as she fought to stay relaxed. Her mom and Elliot were somewhere on this island. Something was happening, and she didn't know what it was, but she knew it was bad.

Tucker's phone had Elliot's last location somewhere in the middle of the island north of the farm. No roads were marked on the phone map, but Teddy said he knew how to get there. That had been ten minutes ago, and now Elliot's phone was out of range or not on. Tucker sat in the back, monitoring the tracking app. Doing so, he kept glancing at Paige. The farm girl had a smile on her lips as she watched Teddy drive. She started humming.

"Shut up," Teddy snapped. "Oh, man... this is not happening," he whispered. "This is not happening."

They were now zooming up an empty road, flying by grassy fields and a copse of trees.

"What is not happening?" Skylar asked. "Teddy, what is going on?"

"Go ahead and tell her," Paige said, not hiding the smirk in her voice.

Teddy glared in the mirror and then turned to look at Skylar. He rubbed his belly right over his navel.

Skylar noticed what seemed to be a slight bulge under his hand.

"Do you believe in werewolves?" Teddy asked.

Skylar stiffened and stared at his face, seeing if he was serious. "No, I mean, only in stories."

"Good, because they're not real." Teddy took a deep breath. "But there's something else. Listen, you got to believe me. On this island... Sometimes kids grow up to be wolf-men... part of The Pack."

"What?" Skylar asked, creasing her brow. "What do you mean?"

"It starts just after puberty," Paige said from the back. "Not every boy is lucky enough to go through the transformation. But if they do, it's called The Turning."

"Shut up, Paige," Teddy snarled, gripping the wheel tighter. "Look," he said to Skylar. "I'm not making this up.

There's some weird disease or... or a curse on this island. When a boy starts to Turn, he starts growing fur."

Paige grabbed the back of Skylar's seat. She stuck her head between the front seats. "It sprouts from the belly button," she said, smiling viciously. "Then it spreads downward and finally up the arms and head."

"Is she serious?" Skylar asked. Her face wore an expression of horrified disbelief.

Teddy only gripped the steering wheel with both hands. Then he nodded. "She's not wrong. But the transformation happens at varying levels. I mean, you can fight it. Stop it from happening. Plenty of men on the island have started turning and still keep their human selves. Others, though, have turned into full wolf-men. It's all about resisting or giving in."

"That was years ago," Paige scoffed. "The Turning is more powerful than ever now. It used to take months and years. Now it can be in days or even hours. It's all about the blood."

Skylar knew Paige was baiting her, but she couldn't help herself. A shiver ran down her spine. "What do you mean, blood?"

"Even before a boy turns, he is attracted to blood." Paige spoke with obvious glee. "When he does start The Turning, drinking blood increases its effectiveness. Once a wolf-man has a taste for blood, he craves more. He becomes less human and more powerful. Here on the island, we have a saying. Drink the blood to join The Pack."

"Just shut up!" Teddy yelled, his eyes bulging. "Shut up, okay?"

Paige shrugged her shoulders and sat back. "Just trying to help," she said, not sounding helpful at all.

Skylar started taking deep breaths as she felt her controlled panic start to well up. "What-What does this have to do with my mom and Elliot?"

Teddy's chest heaved as he fought to calm down. "One of the kids saw a wolf-man on the farm," he muttered. He looked over at her. His rich brown eyes were now bloodshot with a yellow tinge. "Once you start The Turning, you immediately become a member of The Pack. It's the island's job to protect The Pack, no matter what."

Skylar closed her eyes. "Please tell me it wasn't Elliot," she said. "He didn't see the... wolf-man, right?"

"No worries, there," Paige said cheerfully. "It was some other kid on his bus. We tried to get him off, but your mom had to play hero. It's her own fault she's in trouble."

Teddy didn't contradict her. "Look, Skylar," he said. His voice carried a deep hunger. "Morgan Raycroft is the leader of the island and Protector of The Pack. She, she thinks she has a way." He swallowed and kept his eyes on the road. "She wants to use the kid to reverse the curse, to turn the wolf-men back to full human forms."

Paige kicked the back of Skylar's seat. "She's a fool to think that way," she growled. "There are some on the island who don't want that. It's a blessing to Turn, not a curse. Wolf-men are stronger, faster, and much more powerful than puny humans." She looked at Teddy as she spoke.

The teen behind the wheel just shook his head. "Once you're a full wolf-man, or even partial, you're stuck on this island. Forced to live in the forest like a wild animal. Your life is ruined."

Tucker spoke up behind him. "Okay, um, so is that why no animals are here? The wolf guys ate them all?"

Paige laughed harshly. "That's right, kid. Even the birds are too scared to come here. Now you know why we have that farm. Those animals are the main food supply for The Pack." Her eyes glinted at him wickedly. "But be warned. The Pack will still eat you if they find you in the woods. They love human meat."

"That's enough!" Teddy shouted. "Everyone, just shut up and let me drive! We should be almost there."

"Uh, hey, I don't want to alarm anybody," Tucker said slowly, "but I hear motors. I think it's coming from the trees over there." He pointed past Paige to the right of the road.

"That would be the hunting party," Paige said with a grim smile. "When I left the house, they were getting their ATVs packed. You better hurry, Teddy. They're taking the shortcut through the woods. We don't want to be late."

Chapter 29

Elliot stood behind a wide oak and started lowering his pants' front. That's when he heard the low growl from the other side of the tree.

His hands started to shake, and he quickly pulled his pants back up. Taking a slow step back, he eyed the tree fearfully.

He'd moved up the hill above the clearing for privacy. Bobby stood with his back to him about twenty yards on the slope below him. Gary and Marcus stayed in the clearing to do their business near Mr. Harris.

A snuffling from just behind the trunk let him know he wasn't completely alone. Something was there.

Elliot tried to work saliva in his mouth, but none came. He didn't dare cry out.

"I'm not going to pee myself," he whispered. "I'm not going pee myself."

Then, from his left, he heard heavy breathing like a dog.

Slowly, he turned to face a clump of bushes just a few feet from him. He could feel unfriendly eyes watching him but couldn't make out anything there.

His stomach rose and fell rapidly as he sucked in breaths. His heart started to pound.

"H-Hello?" he said hesitantly.

A voice answered immediately. "Your kind don't belong here, little boy," growled a deep voice from the bushes.

Shocked, Elliot stepped back and tripped on a root. He fell on his backside, landing on his phone. Scrambling backward on his bottom with his arms and legs, he stared in horror at the bushes and then toward the tree.

Nothing jumped out. Leaning on his left elbow, he reached behind to pull his phone from his back pocket. He meant to throw it at any attacker and then run. Nothing came. He scrambled back a few feet more and then tentatively rose to his feet.

He knew he'd heard the voice.

Elliot looked around. He found himself alone… Bobby had finished and was gone.

He slowly backed from the bushes and the tree. Sweat trickled down his back and chest.

After retreating several more feet, he turned and ran. Ducking under branches and skirting brambles, he distanced himself from the terrifying voice. He stopped when reaching a small patch of bright green grass surrounded by trees. He relaxed slightly as the feeling of panic slowly drained. Nothing seemed to have followed him. Still, he couldn't be sure.

Looking down at his phone, he saw there was no signal. He returned it to his back pocket and hurried to find the others, searching for the hill leading to the clearing. After several yards of walking, he drew up short. The hill should be there by now. He'd left the grassy area and returned to dead leaves, but suddenly, every tree looked the same.

Elliot drew in a deep breath and slowly turned in a circle. The trees above were thick, with green branches blocking the sun. He had no idea of which way to go. He was lost.

From behind a thick pine to the right, he heard the low growl again.

His knees began to shake, and he suddenly remembered why he'd left the others. He grabbed the front of his pants and tried to keep from wetting himself.

"You better run, kid," hissed an unfriendly voice from a clump of bushes behind the tree. It was different from the first voice, even more guttural. "I like fast food."

Elliot stared in horror, his knees bent inward as the bushes seemed to grow and walk toward him. Then, a large paw swept around and grabbed the trunk of the tree. Sharp claws dug into the flaky pine bark. The bushes were actually a single monster.

Elliot moaned and felt his bladder give way. Wetness flooded down his legs, soaking his pants.

Tears sprang from his eyes as the raspy laugh sounded behind the tree.

"Wrong move, little boy." The creature's head slowly swung around the trunk, revealing a hideous wolf snout. Red eyes gleamed as the sharp teeth bared in an evil smile. It had to be nearly seven feet tall.

Elliot stood hunched with his soaked pants clinging to his trembling legs. Paralyzed with shame and fear, he stared up at the monster, waiting for the attack to come.

Just then, a shape dropped from a tree behind him. "Run!" roared a savage voice.

He felt a strong hand grab the side of his waist and shove him to the left. Elliot stumbled but kept his feet.

"Don't look back!" the savage voice commanded. "Go!"

Elliot needed no urging. Eyes opened wide, he bent forward and started pumping his arms and legs.

"You dare fight The Pack!" roared the beast from behind the tree. "You will pay!"

Ferocious snarls and barks erupted from behind him. It sounded like a dog brawl. Elliot didn't look back. These weren't the monster figures in his room. These were real and would eat him in an instant.

Thinking at any moment something would jump on him, Elliot ran faster. His sore ankle started to throb, but he didn't slow. Not knowing which way to go, he ducked under limbs, slapped away saplings, and jumped over roots.

He didn't know how long he ran. Finally, exhausted, he collapsed to his knees. Sinking down to sit on them, he knelt in a small clearing with bright yellow flowers. Thick brush lay at the edge of the clearing, where the flowers gave way to a blanket of lush forest grass.

After several gulps of air, Elliot threw himself forward and crawled to the brush. He pulled his phone from his back pocket before sitting cross-legged to catch his breath. Of course, it had no signal. He saw the time to be just after three in the afternoon. If he'd stayed home, he would be nearly finished with school.

Dropping his phone to the ground next to him, he put his head in his hands, resting his elbows on his thighs. His wet pants clung to his legs, and the acrid smell of urine filled his nostrils. He didn't care. His bruised face ached, and his ankle throbbed. Wet pants just completed his misery. He wanted his mom.

He bit down his sobs and ignored the buzz of flies around his face and pants. He'd just wanted to see Tucker… but now his friend was gone, and he was lost... and being hunted by monsters. After a while, he pulled his knees up to his chest and hugged them tight. Resting his chin between them, he wished all his might that his mom would find him.

"Where's Elliot?" Mrs. Ashley asked, returning to the clearing.

Mr. Harris and the three boys were pulling on their backpacks at the fallen tree. They all stopped to stare at her.

"I thought he was with you," Mr. Harris said, blushing when she gave him an incredulous look.

"He was just next to me," Bobby confessed. "I thought he'd finished before me. I mean, I didn't see him when I came back." He looked down, embarrassed. "I wanted to give him privacy, you know."

Mrs. Ashley felt a pressure build between her temples, and her head was ready to explode. Panic pumped from her chest with every heartbeat.

"No," she muttered. "No, this is not happening."

"Oh, but it is, sweetie," a harsh voice said.

A giant, horrible figure stood above them on top of the hill, around where Elliot had gone. He resembled a man injected with wolf serum straight from the comic books. He had to be nearly seven feet tall and was covered in grayish-brown fur and skin. A breechcloth covered his middle, and he wore nothing else. His thick chest heaved with ropy muscle. With pointy ears, a squashed nose, and sharp teeth, his face resembled a human skull smashed with wolf features. Sharp claws extended from his giant hands.

"Guys," Marcus said with his voice hoarse. "That's what I saw at the farm."

"Give me the child," the figure said, baring dark-black gums in a sneer. "And I will let you live. You have the honor of The Pack!"

Marcus groaned and inwardly crouched as if trying to disappear.

"Ohno, ohno…" Mr. Harris dropped his backpack and backed away. Then, breaking into a high scream, he turned and ran.

Marcus and Bobby watched him go with shocked faces.

Gary couldn't take his eyes off the beastly figure. "Im-impossible," he whispered.

"Boys, follow after Mr. Harris," Mrs. Ashley said, pulling out the remains of her pepper spray. "Let's go, move!"

Marcus moved first. He shouldered his pack and broke into a run. Gary and Bobby quickly followed suit. Mrs. Ashley went last.

Roaring, the beast leaped down the hill. "I will feast on your bones!" he cried. "The child belongs to me!"

Marcus found a trail cutting through the two ridges before veering down a gully to a narrow stream. He didn't see any sign of Mr. Harris and didn't look for him. He just ran. Bobby dropped back to let Gary pass him.

"Follow the stream!" Gary yelled to Marcus. "It might lead us to the river to get off his island!"

Bobby glanced over his shoulder and was alarmed not to see his teacher. Instead, he saw the beast coming. He ran faster.

He couldn't believe it. First, Mr. Harris and now Mrs. Ashley. Their teachers had abandoned them. Now, they were monster food.

Behind him, Mrs. Ashley had ducked behind the broken stump of an old tree felled by high winds. She held the pepper spray tightly and took a deep breath. Hearing the panting of the beast-man, she jumped out in front of him, hand holding the spray before her.

"Eat this, dirt-brain!" she shouted, unleashing the last of the spray.

Running on all fours, the beast-man, Banor, took it full in the face. Screeching, he staggered to the left before tumbling in a wild fall. His eyes and nose exploded in tremendous pain. In a tangle of limbs, he crashed into the rotting trunk of the broken tree. Flipping over, he rolled twice before ending up in a clump of brambles. Roaring in agony and fury, he grabbed at his stinging eyes and nose.

Mrs. Ashley stuffed the empty can in her pocket and raced after the boys. Reaching the stream, she saw a muddy footprint going to the right that she followed. She'd always enjoyed running when younger and tried to get her miles in as much as possible. Breathing hard, she caught up to Gary and saw Bobby and Marcus not far ahead. The boys were starting to stagger.

"Let's stop, boys," she called. "We need to find a place to hide before others come."

Hearing her, the boys slowed to a halt and gathered at the stream's edge.

Drenched with sweat, Bobby nearly sank to his knees in relief at seeing her.

"Wh-where's the... monster?" Marcus asked, wheezing.

Mrs. Ashley pulled the empty can from her pocket. "I fed him the last of the pepper spray. He'll leave us alone for a while."

The boys stared at their teacher in amazement. It was one thing to take down two men, but to face a seven-foot monster with just a little can of pepper spray? They eyed her with new respect.

"What's this about others?" Gary asked, breathing in deeply.

"That howl we heard was too far to be from that... that beast-man," Mrs. Ashley told him.

On cue, a howl rose from the forest, and others joined.

Gary's face went pale. "We are so dead."

"You should've turned me in," Marcus said miserably. "I... It's all my fault."

Bobby just wiped the sweat from his short hair. "I thought you left us," he said, bent over at his waist. "I mean, I turned around, and you were gone."

Mrs. Ashley just surveyed the area around her with a hard look. "Remember. I'm your parent right now." Her voice caught. "I know Elliot is out there, but right now, I have you three to take care of. I'm not leaving you."

The boys said nothing as they ducked their heads. Through their fear, they felt some relief. With their teacher with them, they had a chance.

The land on either side of the stream rose steeply. On top of the hill across the stream from them, Mrs. Ashley spotted a stone structure. Nearly hidden in the leaves, it looked to be an abandoned house. Half of its roof had collapsed, but it still stood.

"Come on, boys," she said gruffly. "Let's go up there and rest up."

"What if that… that beast comes back?" Gary said.

"Then we'll have to be ready for it," Mrs. Ashley said, her voice almost a snarl. She knew they would never be able to outrun the beasts. They would have to make a stand and hope for a miracle. "Look for strong sticks we can use as clubs, or better, spears. Just look for anything we can use as a weapon. Come on, let's move!"

Teddy pulled his car off to the side of the road and shut off its engine.

"What?" Skylar asked, alarmed. "Why did we stop? Is this the place?"

They were on a road cutting north through a field, with thick woods on both sides about a hundred yards from the road. Tall brown grass waved lazily in a breeze between the road and woods. Despite the tranquil scene, fear lay heavy in the air. The ATV motors had faded, but that could mean they were already there… wherever and whatever that meant.

"My phone has Elliot's last signal pretty close to here," Tucker said. He sat slumped with his knees propped against the back of Teddy's seat. Staring at his phone, he avoided eye contact with Paige. The girl kept grinning at him and licking her lips like he was her next meal. She was creepy.

"Relax," Teddy said, opening the driver's door. "I just need to take a leak. You three stay in the car."

He grabbed the metal canister and abruptly left the car, slamming the door behind him. Without looking back, he trotted toward the trees east of the road.

Skylar watched him go with a mixture of fear and anger. The story of the wolf-men still needed processing, but it felt true. Teddy was obviously a wreck when telling her. One part of her wanted to go after him to give him a hug. Another part wanted to yell at him for not going straight to her mom and brother. They had to be in grave danger.

"He's turning, you know," Paige said from behind her. "That's where he's going."

"He's using the bathroom," Skylar said through tight lips. "I know you don't like me, Paige. But this isn't about me and Teddy or you. I just want to find my mom and little brother."

Paige snorted. "You don't get it. Teddy is in The Turning. He's becoming a wolf-man."

"He's taking a leak, Paige. Just drop it!"

"Oh, yeah?" Paige laughed humorlessly. "Then why did he take his drink?"

"I don't know," Skylar said sarcastically. "To drink it?"

"Yeah, but drink what?" Paige leaned over the center console. "You see, Skylar. When you are in The Turning, you have two choices. You can fight it and try to stay more human or… you can embrace it. The quickest way to embrace it is by drinking blood. There's blood from a pig in that canister. I filled it up myself."

"You're a psycho," Skylar muttered. But her heart skipped a beat. She stared where Teddy had vanished through the tall grass and into the tree line.

"Wolf-men crave blood; they find it delicious." Paige smacked her lips. "And once they taste blood, they can't go back. They want more. They start running with The Pack."

"Just shut up!" Skylar yelled. She yanked off her seat belt and threw her door open. "Tucker, stay in the car! I'll be right back!" She then climbed out and ran toward where Teddy disappeared.

Tucker just ducked his head and tried to pretend to be invisible.

"Oh, no," Paige said with false sympathy. "You're left all alone with me. What are you going to do? What's your name again?"

"It's Tucker," the boy said without looking up.

"Great name, kid. Why don't you and I go and start searching for your little friend?"

Tucker glanced up at her. "Uh, do you mean we leave the car alone? I don't think that's a good idea. Teddy and Skylar both told us to wait here."

"Yes, but they also both left us. And..." Paige nodded toward the front of the car. "There's some serious smoke rising up from those trees. I'm guessing it's close to where you last saw the signal. Right?"

"No way..." Tucker's mouth dropped open. Out the windshield, he saw clouds of thick black smoke pouring upwards from behind the trees up the road, just around a bend.

Paige kicked her door open. "Come on, kid. Your friend needs you. Don't worry. I don't bite."

Chapter 30

"You really messed up, Billy Roft," Stan purred. "Didn't you?"

"I did everything I was told to do!" the bus driver said, almost pleading. He clutched his ample belly as if he felt terribly sick. "I made it look like an accident. It's you guys who messed up! You came too late! If that teacher woman were still asleep, none of this would've happened!"

"You wrecked the bus," Moe pointed out. "You could've hurt the kid we needed."

"And you let the witch woman have pepper spray!" Stan snarled, rubbing at his puffy, red eyes.

The three men stood in front of the wrecked bus waiting. Using Mr. Roft's walkie-talkie, they'd reported what had happened. Ryan Raycroft was on his way to assess the situation. Two ATVs were already en route and would start searching the woods. Some members of The Pack had begun hunting for the children and teachers—thankfully, they were told in time not to kill any yet, just to find them.

Mr. Roft stared back at his ruined bus and made no comment. He wished he'd never agreed to drive the bus to

Blue Island. He'd hoped to be rewarded for his work. Now, it may just be the opposite.

Moe lifted the walkie-talkie to his mouth and pressed the button. "This is Robin and Batman here calling base. What do we do with Billy Roft?"

Morgan's voice crackled through. "Make it look like an accident."

Billy's eyes bulged out, and he shook his head. "No!" He turned from the men and lumbered past the front of the bus toward the trees. "No!"

Stan and Moe only watched him go. The two men had red-rimmed eyes and dry mucus on their cheeks and leather coats. Despite it all, they cracked smiles. Didn't Billy smell what waited for him?

Just as Billy Roft made it to the trees, a member of The Pack stepped out to meet him. Hiding in the brush, he'd heard everything on the walkie-talkie. He just didn't understand the concept of "accident."

Billy's screams were cut short with a sickening sound of ripping flesh.

The wolf-man made short work of the bus driver. Swiping down his powerful claws, he ripped the driver's chest open while his wolfish snout bit into his neck. Blood sprayed, and the man twisted and fell to his side.

The wolf-man licked his black lips with a long tongue. Snarling at Stan and Moe, he turned and trotted back into the trees.

"Well, all right," Moe said, suddenly looking glum. He nodded at Billy Roft's bleeding body. "How do we make *that* look like an accident?"

The men ended up dragging the corpse up into the bus and sticking it in the driver's seat. Stan had a bottle of liquor in his coat pocket he'd been saving to celebrate the successful mission. Instead, he used it to start a fire in the bus that eventually spread to leaking diesel fuel. Massive flames and heavy smoke engulfed the bus, consuming everything on it. Smelling burnt human flesh, a wolf-man howled nearby in the trees. Others answered. The hunt was definitely on.

There were currently twenty-one members of The Pack living wild in the forest, the largest number ever recorded. Usually, the numbers stayed in the single digits, but recently, more teens were completing The Turning at an alarming rate. The process usually took days, if not resisted, and sometimes even months. Lately, though, it was happening in a single day, or in some cases, merely hours. Most were becoming full, or close to full, wolf-men.

To many on the island, it was a major concern. The youth were angry and wild, becoming uncontrollable. Something had to be done to stop it. But others on the island saw it as a blessing. The Turning was something to be embraced, not shunned and resisted. Becoming strong and powerful was the goal of life, after all.

Skylar cautiously pushed aside the low branch of the holly tree to enter the woods. "Teddy?" she called softly. "Are you there?"

She didn't see the teen and walked deeper into the woods. Seeing a faint trail in the green grass sprouting among the trees, she followed it.

"Teddy?" she called.

"Over here," his voice called in front of her. He sounded miserable.

She headed toward the sound of his voice, following the path.

"Careful," warned a woman's voice behind her. It was the same older lady's voice from before.

Immediately, she stopped and whirled around. Like before, there was nobody there.

Her heart pounding, she searched for signs of danger and then cautiously continued.

Eventually, the trail led her to a shallow pool at the bottom of a short incline. More like a giant puddle, the pool was only a few inches deep. Teddy knelt on one knee over it, staring at his reflection. He held the opened canister in one hand and clutched his stomach with the other. His back to her, he still sensed her presence.

"Why are you here?" he asked.

"To check on you," Skylar said. "Teddy, I'm worried. Not just about my mom and Elliot, but also about you. What's going on?"

"Did you believe me about the wolf-men?" he asked. He stood from his knee and turned to face her. His eyes were sunken, deep with pain and sadness.

Skylar stared into his eyes. "Teddy, I believe you. I mean, a few times at my house, I think maybe a wolf-man was there. Like the night I called you."

Teddy broke his gaze first and stared down at the grass. "There was," he said flatly. "That's why I came over. Remember how I looked around your backyard, kicking the leaves and stuff? I was hiding the tracks."

Skylar blinked. "Wait. You mean you didn't come to protect me? You just came to protect one of the wolf-men? Teddy, he was in my house! He scared my little brother!"

Teddy shook his head. "You don't understand, Skylar. I did go to protect you! I care about you and never want to see you hurt. But at the same time..."

"At the same time, what?" Skylar asked. "Your wolf-men come first? Are you really here to help my mom and Elliot? Or are you just protecting your precious wolf friends?"

"You don't get it, Sky! When you're from this island, you're always a part of it. You can't escape. Did you know you're only allowed to move off the island if it's first approved by a council? You must prove you can return something useful to the island." He glared at her. "Your father and grandmother were the first ever to truly escape. Some of the wolf-men were curious about that and were checking on you. Others were jealous."

"And is that why you were nice to me?" Skylar's face flushed. "You were checking on me? You were a spy for your island?"

"Shut up!" Teddy snapped. His eyes suddenly blazed with hate. Immediately, they softened. "No, I'm sorry. I didn't mean that."

Skylar stepped back, suddenly frightened. A breeze blew out from the trees, and she caught the foul scent of rot and rust. "Teddy, what is in that canister?" she asked. "Are you drinking…"

"Paige told you, huh?" Teddy said. His shoulders slumped. "I'm turning, Sky. I try to fight it, but it just feels so good… so right. I, I crave blood… I want it, okay?"

Skylar felt tears prick her eyes. "Oh, Teddy. You have to fight it."

"Why?" he barked. "So I won't look different? So I can conform to your ideals?"

"No! So you won't eat people and animals!" Skylar said. She took a breath. "Look. My mom has this corny saying. Everyone has challenges, but everyone can change."

Teddy laughed caustically. "Yeah, well, I guess I'm changing."

"Yes," Skylar said. "You are, but that's the point. Challenges can make you change for the better or the worse. Which changes are you making?"

Teddy smiled sadly at her. "When I turned thirteen I checked every inch of me for fur. I had none, and I was free. I wouldn't turn. Then I met you just a few weeks ago. Do you know I sprouted fur overnight? This is your fault, Skylar."

"What?" Skylar took another step back. "Teddy, you're scaring me." She glanced down at his belly. "And your stomach... it's moving!"

Grinning toothily, Teddy pulled up his shirt with the hand clutching his belly.

Skylar gasped in horror.

A thick wad of fur spilled out. Starting at the navel, the fur completely covered his lower stomach and disappeared into his baggy pants.

"You know, Skylar," Teddy said, his eyes narrowing and glinting with a yellow gleam. "Paige is right. There are other girls out there. You're not that special."

"Get away from me, Teddy," Skylar said, retreating back up the path. "You're not thinking right!"

"It's the bloodlust," Teddy said. "Once you drink blood, you want to go on your first kill. You usually kill the first animal you see."

"Then close your eyes!" Skylar yelled at him. "I'm not even an animal! I'm your friend!"

Teddy coughed, and his face contracted. Drops of blood shot from his mouth as, all at once, his canine teeth grew and sharpened. "Sorry, Skylar," he said hoarsely. "I'm hungry."

In the top corner room of the brick house, Dr. Chocker paced the area behind the desk. His suitcase of money waited downstairs, but he had little thought of grabbing it now. The day was becoming a complete disaster, even with the money. His bus lay burning in a field, totally off the grid. Two teachers and three of his students were lost in the woods. And he was in the middle of some crazed cult of wolf-men bent on taking one of his students to use as some human sacrifice.

To make matters worse, the school day was just about finished, and all buses should be back at the school. What was he going to tell the parents of Marcus, Bobby, and Gary? And what would he tell Mr. Charles about Mrs. Ashley and Mr. Harris? He stopped pacing and covered his face with both hands. He'd forgotten about Elliot.

"Pull yourself together, man," Morgan said with disdain. She sat on the sofa with her legs crossed and walkie-talkie in one hand. Her other hand held the red pendant. "Everything will turn out fine."

"Fine?" Dr. Chocker dropped his hands. "How do I explain the missing bus, teachers, and students? They should be back at school getting ready to go home about now!"

"Think of something," Morgan said. She narrowed her eyes at the principal. "Remember. You're part of this, too."

Dr. Chocker thought of something. Grabbing his phone from his pocket, he moved to the corner window and found a signal to make a call.

Reaching the front office of Leewood Elementary, he hurriedly explained there was a delay with the special education bus returning from the field trip. It would be arriving late—so late, in fact, it would be dropping the students off at their homes instead of returning to school. Oh, and the bus driver, Billy Roft, would then be taking the bus to his house for the night, so not to worry about it returning to school. He said he had already cleared it with transportation. Oh, and if any parents called, the office should give them his number, and he would personally explain the situation. He ended the call by telling the front office to go home early that day.

Finished, he walked in a daze from the window and collapsed beside Morgan. "I'll never get away with this," he said. "It'll never hold up."

"You still have hope." Morgan ran a tongue around her lips and smiled. "In a few hours, I will break the curse on this island. When I do, there's going to be a great storm. You can use the storm as an excuse."

"Excuse for what?"

"Terrible accidents happen in storms," Morgan said viciously.

Mr. Chocker stared out the window where the bright afternoon sun still shone through. He shuddered. Then, a slow realization crept across his face. His mouth sagged, and his body seemed to cave inward. "You're... you're going to kill me, aren't you?"

Morgan looked at him in disdain. "Kill you? No, Dr. Chocker, you know me better than that. I'll never kill you. My husband? He's the one to do that."

Dr. Chocker let off a low whimper that sounded like a sick puppy. He felt tears prick his eyes. "I... I'm a fool."

"Perhaps," agreed Morgan. "But my job is to protect The Pack. You helped with that greatly. You'll only die if you stop being useful." Her eyes flashed with determination. "If I get that boy... I can end everything tonight. Then we'll put things back together. You'll see."

Dr. Chocker looked over at her in horrified wonder. "You really do believe that, don't you? *Who are you?* And what's that thing on your neck you're always holding?"

She fingered the red pendant. "This island has ways to make things right." She sat up and uncrossed her legs. "Let me tell you a story, Dr. Chocker. Then perhaps you'll understand that you're part of something truly glorious. This is a story we tell all our kids on the island... sort of like how your school tells students about the nation's birth." She grinned at him. "This is the birth of the curse."

Breathing deeply, Dr. Chocker sat back on the worn sofa and listened. As he did, a great fear welled up in his heart. He was stuck in a crazed cult and was about to be responsible for the murder of one of his students. All because of his want of money…

Morgan told her story.

Chapter 31

When our people first came to Blue Island, it was wild and empty. Wolves roamed the forests, and even the natives stayed away. Some warned the first families, saying the island was cursed. They said evil spirits walked the blue fog that so mysteriously shrouded the island on many mornings. The first families were tobacco farmers from England, not heathen fools. They knew the land would make them rich.

Only when they started clearing the land did they realize they were not alone. Others were already living on the island.

An old woman and her grown son had a small hut deep in the forest. Nobody knew where she came from or why she remained. Years before, pirates from Chesapeake Bay used the river to hide out, and legend has it that Blue Island was one of their bases. Many believed the woman had been abandoned by the pirates. No matter, she was there, and she had a son.

She would appear through the fog when our people started clearing the land. *Leave this place* she would tell them. *This place is not for you.*

Our people ignored her. They had a charter to settle on the island and sacrificed much wealth to get it. They built a small community and continued clearing land.

Her son started visiting, sometimes at night but often in the mornings, hidden by fog. He wore nothing but animal furs and had hair on his body like a beast. Livestock started dying, their throats ripped out, and their flesh eaten. Tools were broken. People started hearing wolves and began to grow afraid.

Then, one night, my ancestor, Benjamin Raycroft, put a stop to this. He was a young man, newly married, and set on protecting his new home. He waited at the edge of the woods. When the wild man came through the fog as morning broke, my ancestor met him with an ax. The story says he hid behind a tree and waited for the wild man to sneak by. Then he cut him down from behind. He left the body at the edge of the woods for the old lady to find.

The old woman did find him. That evening, she walked into the clearing. She wore a black robe and... a red pendant around her neck. She spoke in gibberish and warned the families they would pay for the crime.

My ancestor met her and laughed at her. He told her to take her son and bury him deep. If she ever came back, she would meet the same fate.

No, the old woman told him. *It is you who shall meet the same fate. You shall take what my son had and live to regret it.*

It was the very next day that it began. Ben Raycroft woke up to find thick hair growing from his belly, right from his belly button. At first, he thought nothing of it. His wife even found it endearing. As the days went by, the hair thickened and spread. A wild gleam entered his eyes, and his teeth began to sharpen. He started spending more time in the forests hunting... one day, men came upon him crouching over a wild pig. He'd killed the pig with his bare hands and was eating it raw.

His wife grew alarmed and traveled deep in the forest to find the old woman. Finding her, she went on her knees and begged for mercy.

The old woman shook her head. It was too late. The power was not hers to give and take. Her husband brought it upon himself. *Soon,* the old woman said, *it will spread to the others.* The blood of her son would live on in the island community.

My ancestor's wife pleaded for a way to stop it. The old woman told her to bring her son back from the dead, only then would it stop.

Frightened, the woman returned home and pleaded with her husband to visit the woman and beg for forgiveness.

Ben only laughed at her. At first, he thought he'd been cursed, too, but then he began to see it as a blessing. He grew increasingly bigger, faster, and much stronger. He'd become part man and part wolf and loved the feeling. Then, one night, he returned from another hunt. He saw his wife waiting at the door with the family Bible. She said they had to pray for the curse to leave. A terrible rage filled his heart. How dare the woman accuse him of evil? Fog covered his mind, and in a fit, he attacked her. When he came to his senses the next morning, he found her body ripped and torn. He had killed his wife.

Filled with remorse, disgust, and utter sorrow, he vowed never to hunt again. Gathering and wrapping her body, he carried the remains to the old woman's hut. Laying it down, he fell to his knees.

Your woman has already come here, so why bring her back? the old woman asked him.

My ancestor pleaded with her to end it. For her to take the curse away.

I cannot, the old woman told him. She held up the red pendant. *What is done is done. It will never end. You have brought this on yourself. Now, you must live with it.*

Furious, my ancestor made to attack the old woman but then saw the body of the woman he'd loved. Again, he fell to his knees and begged her to tell him what to do.

If you wish to keep the curse at bay, you must fight the desire to become a beast, the old woman told him. *Your mind must crave to live the life of a human. The more you follow your beastly urges, the faster you shall turn. It shall become harder to come back until it is impossible. Then you will be a wolf-man and no longer a man.*

Is there no other way? he begged.

There is one other. The old woman told him she had recorded a ritual to end the curse for his wife, but she had refused it. The old woman held up a rolled-up manuscript. The man could take it if he wished.

My ancestor returned home heartbroken but determined. He had the manuscript. As he read it, he grew horrified. He discovered why his wife had refused it.

The manuscript carried the directions of a ritual to release the curse. He would have to trade the life of a son—sacrifice a young boy and then eat his flesh. The boy must be fully human and not have any signs of Turning. Eating the boy's flesh would purify the blood, and he would return to being fully human. Not doing so, the manuscript warned, would spread the curse to generations.

The man grew frightened. He believed the old woman held pure evil. Vowing to do away with the beastly curse himself, he fought against all animal urges. He cut off his furry hair as much as possible. In time, his beastly nature tamed, and his appearance softened. Yet, it still lurked and never left. It was a daily struggle.

Years went by. He found a new wife and settled on Blue Island, becoming a successful planter. Yet, the curse spread. Others in the community woke to find hair growing from their bellies. They were always young men. Some embraced it, others were horrified. Most followed my ancestor's ways of resistance and fought to tamp down the curse. Together, both groups forged a tight alliance that became known as The Pack. Staying on the island, isolated from the mainland, they raised families and forged a new way of life. Women, being immune to the curse, became caretakers of The Pack. Eventually, one woman rose to the rank of Protector of The Pack, the leader who ensured The Pack remained safe. The first Protector was the second wife of Ben, my ancestor Mathilda Raycroft. She wore a red pendant on a silver chain to mark her as the leader. Nobody knew where she'd gotten it from, but the old woman was never seen again.

The manuscript was hidden away and forgotten by many. Generations passed. The Pack grew and shrank but never went away. The Protector of The Pack, always a woman and always with the red pendant, became the island's leader. The entire island remained devoted to serving The Pack. For centuries, this has worked.

Not many years ago, The Pack suddenly increased. Those who cannot control the curse and appear more beast than man are called wolf-men. Right now, there are more wolf-men than ever before. The Turning, what we call the changing to a wolf-man, is happening much faster now and much more often. Nobody knows why this is the case.

The Protector of The Pack before me, Sylvia, my poor mother, claimed it was because the last church on the island had closed. She was a superstitious fool. Myself? I see it as part of the island's evolution.

You see, it is not easy hiding a pack of wolf-men on a small island in modern times. Our island needed money and protection. So they started The Business, which began shortly before the last church closed.

What is The Business? I imagine you can guess. I wasn't born when it started. My grandmother led The Pack then. She and her husband found a way to make good money.

It was back in the 1950s. A slicked-up northerner had come to Grantham stirring up trouble. It was during the Civil Rights movement, and back then, we had segregation. It worked fine, and many wanted to keep it that way. They didn't like any outsiders telling them how to live. My grandfather had tamped down the curse and worked off the island as a janitor at Grantham High School. When he heard of grumblings from the school administrators about this northern troublemaker, he told his wife about it. The island was struggling back then. My grandmother came up with an idea. She sent my grandfather back to school with a proposition. For a price, he promised to do away with the northerner. No questions were asked, but money exchanged hands. Then my grandfather took that northern upstart hunting out on the island.

You can imagine what happened next. The northerner disappeared, never to be seen again. That was the first kill. More would come. And just so you know, my family is not racist in the least. It was pure business.

Over the years, we've gotten rid of people of all colors for all types of clients with no discrimination. You see, once the first kill went so well, my grandfather found others willing to pay for a person to vanish. Mobs, gangs, and even government officials, I'm sure of it, would visit my grandfather.

Money poured in, and the last preacher on the island grew ashamed. He turned tail and left. After some investigators started poking around in the 1980s, The Business shut down. By then, our island was loaded. With good investments and our starting our own businesses, we're doing quite well with money. It's just that The Pack continues to grow in size and grows wilder. The woods are now hunted out, and the wolf-men are forced to survive only on farm animals. They hunger for more.

Chapter 32

All at once, Morgan blew out her breath and rose to her feet.

Dr. Chocker watched her walk to the window overlooking the farm with horrified fascination. The story she just told was ridiculous. Yet, his own eyes told him it had to be at least partly true. Wolf-men did exist.

"This leads us to today," Morgan said. She clenched the walkie-talkie tightly and stared out where the afternoon sun had started to sink beyond the barn. "You see, we can't sustain this way of life. The Pack wants to hunt and wants to kill. Most members, though, wish nothing more than to become human again. They want to do away with their beastly way of life."

"Th-That is something I can, uh, understand," Dr. Chocker said.

His gray suit had dried from the sweat in the morning but now felt hot and clammy again. If he hadn't seen it with his own eyes, he would never have believed such a wild tale… but watching Banor kill that woman… he shuddered.

"No, you don't understand." Morgan's face hardened. "My son… my son completed The Turning. He is now one of them. I'll do anything to save him. *Anything*."

She reached into her leather jacket and pulled out a thumb drive. "This is the family book. It has everything I just told you and all the notes about The Pack and the curse that my family has gathered over the years. Included is the ritual to reverse the curse. This is why I need that boy, Dr. Chocker. I'm going to stop the curse forever."

Dr. Chocker wet his dry lips. "But… but doesn't the boy have to be your own son?"

"That's just a theory, but this isn't some supernatural curse. Any boy would do. His blood just has to be pure and free of the curse." Her eyes gleamed. "One thing is for sure. Nobody is going to touch my son. If this Marcus boy doesn't work, I'll find another that will. You'll see." She returned the thumb drive to her jacket pocket and lifted her hand to the red pendant. "I always get what I want. Nothing is going to stop me, Dr. Chocker. Nothing."

The principal felt his knees shake. This woman, he knew, was insane. And he had exposed his entire fifth-grade class to her mad scheme. And now he was helping her kill one of his students. Having skipped lunch, he had nothing to throw up. He moaned instead, fighting back tears.

Tucker put a hand on his backpack but did not open his door.

"You know, I don't think so," he said, shaking his head. "I'm staying. I'll, um, wait for Skylar and Teddy. I mean, I'm sure they'll see the smoke, right?"

Paige stared in through the open door on the other side of the car. Her face twisted into a scowl. "Wrong answer, Tucker." She leaned into the door, crawling over the seat. "You're coming."

"Hey, now," Tucker said, pulling his backpack to him and hugging it to his chest with his phone. "What are you doing?"

Paige grinned at him. She crawled on her hands and knees in the backseat of the car toward him. She stopped inches from his face. "Teaching you to grow up. Get out of the car."

"So, this is not my idea of a first date," Tucker said nervously. "And, um, no offense, but you smell like poop."

"Shut up, you brat!" Paige reached out her hand and grabbed his curls, shoving his head into the door window. "Get out!"

"Ow! Get off!"

Paige let go and dropped a hand to his neck. "Get out of the car, Tucker!"

Fighting back tears, Tucker found the handle and pushed the door open. He stumbled out, holding his backpack and phone. Paige quickly followed, sliding out smoothly. On her feet, she kicked Tucker in the backside, sending him tumbling to his hands and knees.

"You should've stayed away, kid," she said, grinning. "Your kind never survives on this island. You made a big mistake coming here, kid. Trying to be a hero, huh?" She kicked him again in the back of his pants.

Tucker cried out. He'd fallen just next to the road. Landing on mostly gravel lining the pavement, his knees flared with pain.

"You just going to kneel there, bowing to the road?" Paige asked mockingly. "You should be bowing to me. Do you know what a Maiden of The Pack is? It's a girl who devotes her entire life to serving The Pack. She gives up everything to make sure it grows stronger. And that's what I plan to be."

Stepping next to him, she lifted a foot and placed it on his lower back. "And right now, I think I'm giving The Pack you. I control your life, kid. What do you say to that? Wish you'd stayed in that van, you stupid boy? I hope your friend was worth it. Too bad he's Pack food, too."

Tucker bit his lower lip. He could be sitting in the back of the van with Phileo right now. His phone under him still showed Elliot's last known location. Maybe Tucker didn't need Elliot as a friend, but he knew Elliot needed him right then. He switched his phone to the hand holding the strap of his backpack. Then he grabbed a handful of dirt and pebbles on the side of the road.

"Next time you pick on little kids," he said, "make sure you leave Elliot and me alone." He then rolled to his right, releasing his backpack and phone.

Caught off balance, Paige lurched backward. Furious, she went to face Tucker, finding the boy on his knees with his arm poised behind him.

"Bam!" he cried. "Let's add a little spice to that ugly face!" He threw dirt and pebbles, aiming for the eyes.

Screeching, Paige shied away. She wiped at her eyes and kicked blindly with her foot.

Tucker leaned his body to the side, easily dodging it. He then shoved her foot back.

The girl fell against the car and went to her knees.

"You're so going to die!" she screamed. She wiped furiously at her eyes with the back of her hands.

Tucker had grabbed up this phone and backpack. Scrambling up, he ran into the tall grass, heading for the trees where he'd last seen Skylar. He heard a ferocious snarl ahead of him.

Swerving to the left, he sprinted through the field parallel to the trees. The thick smoke still rose before him. Paige remained behind him at the car. He had nowhere to go.

"This way!" a young voice called from the trees on his right. "Hurry this way!"

Not seeing the source, Tucker just followed the voice. Slipping into the trees, he found himself on a narrow path.

"Over here!" the voice called in the distance. It sounded like a boy a few years older than him.

Tucker continued running toward the voice. He was never a fast runner but had decent endurance. His scraped knees rubbed against his pants and burned with pain. After a few minutes, he came to a stop.

"Okay, okay," he said, breathing hard. "I don't know who you are, but, um, who are you? And where are we going?"

The voice was silent. From up ahead he heard leaves rustling and the sound of a branch shaking.

"Oh, so now you want to be like that?" Tucker grumbled. "You want me to go that way?"

The branch shook again.

Behind him, he heard a loud howl in the distance.

"Yeah, okay," Tucker said. "Good idea. I'll go that way. Um, lead on."

He shouldered his pack and put his phone in his pocket. His phone had no signal, but he knew he was close to where Elliot had last been. And he was close to a fire, murdering wolf-men, and a crazy teenage girl. He hoped Skylar would be okay but knew she at least had Teddy to protect her. The ten-year-old boy knew Teddy liked Skylar.

Skylar ran from Teddy.

"Go ahead and run!" laughed Teddy, giving chase. "You'll never get away! I can smell you so much better now!"

Skylar didn't look back. The trees became menacing towers with long arms intent on grabbing her and guarding any escape. Everywhere she went, there were more of them. She lost her way to the field and the car.

A branch slapped into her face, scratching her cheek. Thorns tore at her jeans. She climbed a hill and leaped over a small ditch.

Suddenly, a shape leapt from her left, unleashing a loud roar. She had no time to dodge. Teddy smashed into her side, bringing her to the ground with him on top.

"Sky is falling, little chick," Teddy said into her ear. Grinning, he rose to a sitting position. Astride her waist, his knees squeezed tight, trapping her body.

Skylar couldn't get up anyway. Her breath had been knocked out of her in the fall, and her head had slammed against the earth hard.

Teddy eased the grip with his knees as she rolled to her back woozily, struggling for a breath. Looking up, her eyes went wide. Teddy leered over her, his mouth opening to show off his sharpened teeth. Rusty, sour breath blasted in her face. Skylar fought for air... dark spots formed in her vision.

"You know, Sky, you are a—"

Whatever Teddy meant to say was lost in a violent howl. Something huge came up behind him, and suddenly Teddy was pulled from Skylar and left dangling in the air.

"Leave her!" bellowed a thunderous voice.

Teddy went flying, tossed like a rag doll by an angry child. Only it was no child. An enormous wolf-man stood over Skylar, teeth bared from his wolfish snout.

Skylar went to scream but instead fled into unconsciousness. As her body went limp, Teddy bawled in pain somewhere above her.

She was blissfully unaware of the wolf-man bending over her and never felt the furry arms sliding under her legs and back, lifting her up.

Cradling the unconscious girl, the wolf-man hurried into the trees.

Teddy whimpered out her name as they left.

Elliot eventually rolled to his side and fell asleep. He woke up with a start with something poking his back, sniffing the back of his pants.

"Skylar," he groaned. "Lay off…"

Something poked his backside. His eyes snapped open. Seeing the grass before him, he jerked his body and kicked out his legs. Rolling to his knees, he faced the brush behind him. Nothing was there.

Then he heard hoarse breathing in the brush.

"O…Okay," he said, rising unsteadily to his feet. Seeing his phone lying on the grass, he reached out a hand and snatched it. "I don't know who you are… but I'll be going now…"

Putting the phone in his back pocket, he slowly walked across the clearing backward, facing the brush. Then he whirled around to break into a stumbling run. His sore body had gone stiff, and his bad ankle didn't want to work. He ended up gasping in pain. Throwing frequent glances back, he limped from the clearing. The sun hadn't begun to set, and he guessed he'd been asleep for around thirty minutes. That meant in a few hours, it would be dark.

Coming to a steady incline, he paused beneath it to lean against a thin pine. From below him, on the other side of the slope, he heard a faint voice.

He crouched instantly and wrapped a hand around the trunk, squeezing hard. After a moment, the voice spoke again, closer. It had a high-pitched tone, like a child's.

Instantly, his eyes widened. It could be his mom and her students. Then his brow furrowed in confusion. "Tucker?" he said.

Tucker felt like he'd been walking in circles for hours. Whenever he stopped or didn't know where to go, a rustle of leaves or branches sounded ahead of him. He dutifully followed without complaint. But now he'd had enough. He needed answers.

As he walked, he held his water bottle and munched on one of his cookies. His chef shirt was soaked with sweat.

"You know," he said. "If you tell me who you are, I'll share my cookies. They're pretty good. And I bet you're thirsty."

Rustling ahead of him told him to keep moving.

"Fine. At least tell me where we're going. Because I don't think I can go much farther."

They were walking beneath a hill when suddenly the rustling increased. Something large scampered into the brush to the right, running up the hill and away from Tucker. He barely saw a shadow, and then it was gone.

"Hey! You can't leave me now! Where'd you go? Come back!"

Silence answered him. His invisible guide had left him.

Tucker swallowed the last of his cookie and put his water bottle back into his backpack. The trees around him moved silently in a breeze and seemed to laugh at him. He suddenly felt very alone. Taking deep breaths, he held his belly and squatted low, trying hard to keep the panic from taking over his body. He waited for a few minutes, which felt like hours.

"Okay, fine," he said aloud. "Leave me. I'll just walk out here... all alone..." Tucker rose and walked in a slow circle. "Hello? Are you back?" There was no answer. "I'm just walking here..." He continued to go in a circle under the hill, hoping his mysterious guide would return. "Come on, I'm still here!"

Then he heard the greatest thing his ears had ever heard.

"Tucker? What are you doing?"

His eyes and mouth went wide as he spun to face the voice. Looking worn and filthy, Elliot stood staring at him from the hill.

"Elliot!" Tucker shouted. "I found you!" Forgetting his fatigue, he dropped his backpack and bounded up the hill to his friend.

"No, wait," Elliot said, backing up a little. He hunched and tried to hide his pants. Dark circles marked under his eyes, and above his right eye and left cheek, he sported dark bruises, but he was there. He was okay.

Tucker grabbed him in a fierce hug and lifted him up off the ground. "You have no idea how happy I am to see you!"

Elliot wiggled in his grasp. "Get off," he said.

Quickly, Tucker put his friend down and stepped back. He couldn't wipe the silly grin from his face. "This is amazing! I've been, like, wandering these woods forever looking for you."

Elliot dropped his gaze. "I thought we weren't friends," he muttered. He twisted his body to the side and wiped his hands on his shirt.

Tucker's grin faltered, and then he shook his head. "Okay, okay, man, I said some stupid things back there. I get it. But, come on, man. You did some stupid things, too. We always say and do stupid things. That's why we were best friends." He took a deep breath. "And, yeah, I guess I thought I didn't need you as a friend. But when I heard you were lost on this stupid island, I knew I was wrong. Elliot, I didn't know how to say it, but I missed you, okay? I didn't want to see you for only a minute and then never see you again. That would've totally stunk."

Elliot blinked and then eyed him carefully. "So we're friends?"

"Of course! Best friends."

"Good," Elliot mumbled miserably. "I, um, sort of, like, wet my pants earlier."

"Bruh," Tucker said. "Who cares? Remember when I wet the bed at your sleepover?"

"We were six, Tucker."

Tucker shrugged. "Yeah, well, after what I saw and heard today, I don't blame you, man. I nearly peed myself twice. And seeing your face, I'm guessing you've seen a lot worse than me."

Elliot relaxed and nodded. "In that case, it's awesome to see you, dude."

The two friends cautiously moved back down the hill.

"Do you have anything to eat?" Elliot asked when they reached the bottom. "I'm starving."

Tucker shrugged. "Well, I do have some of my famous homemade chocolate chip cookies. I guess I can share one."

"Really? Are you, like, kidding me? Tucker, you're an angel to me. Come on, give the cookies!"

The boys knelt in the leaves at Tucker's backpack to share their stories the best they could while snacking on cookies. As Tucker took out the food and water, Elliot told his story. Then Tucker told Elliot about his phone tracking him and about Skylar, Teddy, and Paige. Listening, Elliot chomped down six cookies and drank half the water.

"So Skylar is out here, too?" Elliot asked, wiping crumbs from his chin. He took another long sip from the water bottle.

"Yeah. I got separated from her and Teddy, though. That Paige girl, man, she went psycho, and I had to run."

"How did you, like, even find me in the woods?" Elliot asked. He'd already told Tucker about how he got lost from his mom and then been chased by beasts.

Tucker could only shrug and try to explain about the invisible guide.

Elliot nodded. "Yeah, I think something helped me, too."

Tucker looked around the woods and shuddered. "This is a crazy place, man. The sooner we get off the island, the better."

"Where should we go?"

Tucker licked crumbs off his lips and put the bag of remaining cookies, mostly crumbs, into his backpack. He added the water bottle, now nearly empty. "Let's just start going up all the hills we find. The town is on a hill, right? I bet if we get close to it, we can get phone reception. If not, we'll at least reach the river at some point."

Elliot groaned. "Okay, that sounds really smart, but do you, like, know how hard that's going to be? There are like a bajillion hills here."

Tucker pushed him in the shoulder. "Don't worry, man. I can carry your butt when you get too tired."

Elliot shoved him back. "I was thinking of you. Dude, you could never climb hills when exploring before."

"Remember? I'm bigger and stronger right now. Let's go!"

The boys got to their feet and started up the hill. With food and water in his belly and the joy of having Tucker at his side, Elliot's foot felt much better, and he walked with only a slight limp. Tucker still led the way, telling Elliot that since he was taller, he could see farther.

"Yeah, barely!" Elliot said. "Only by, like, six inches!"

The two never noticed the danger closing in.

On top of the hill, the boys glanced down the incline on the other side and then the steeper hill rising before them. There was no path, and thick brambles and brush awaited them on the next hill.

"You know," Tucker said, ducking his head and wheezing. "I think we need another break." Then he straightened and looked up at the trees. "Uh, Elliot?"

Elliot bent over his waist with his hands on his knees. Hair hung in his eyes, so he couldn't see his friend. "Yeah?"

"I don't think we're alone right now… Do you see anything in the trees?"

Slowly standing straight, Elliot brushed the hair from his face and stared up. "Was it a bird?"

"I don't think so, man. There's been, like, no birds on this island. I think I saw a person climbing or something. It was just flash."

Suddenly nervous, Elliot wiped dirt from his nose. "Yeah, I think I saw something like that back on the farm."

The boys searched above them and never saw the two figures move in behind them.

Elliot suddenly felt an arm wrap around his chest. Before he could struggle, something struck the back of his head. Stars exploded. He instantly went limp. The arm fell away, and everything went dark as his body crashed to the ground.

Tucker gave a start and saw a man dressed in camouflage staring at him with a crazed grin. He held a heavy leather strap in his hand. Elliot lay at his feet motionless.

Before Tucker could react, a crushing blow landed on the top of his curls. All at once, he lay in a heap next to his friend. The last thing he saw before consciousness left him was a pair of black motorcycle boots.

"I got him!" crowed the man in the camouflage. The beefy, grizzled farmworker from the pigpen slapped the thick leather blackjack on the side of his pants. "I got the boy!"

"That ain't him, Kenton," Moe muttered, putting a similar weapon in his pants pocket. "And neither is this one. Where'd he come from?" He nudged Tucker's side with his boot.

"Let me see," Ryan Raycroft demanded. Wearing camouflage like his younger brother Kenton, he moved from the bushes where he and Stan had hidden.

The men had heard the boys' voices and had slowly closed in, surrounding them on the hill. They'd hoped to have found Mrs. Ashley and Marcus.

Standing between Kenton and Moe, Ryan Raycroft stared down at the unconscious boys. He took off his camo cap and scratched the back of his head.

"You goof," he said to Kenton. "You just knocked out our great-nephew."

"Oh… well, he didn't tell me that!" Kenton said defensively. He wiped the corner of his mouth where dry, crusty blood remained. While he remained human, he sometimes would snack on a raw chicken. When this happened, his brain got addled.

"Remember, you have his picture on your phone," Ryan told him.

"Oh, yeah… it's just been a bad day with all those rotten kids on the farm. I didn't recognize him."

"No matter." His elder brother knelt at Elliot's side. "He'll be okay."

The boy lay on his stomach with his arms by his sides. Ryan brushed the hair from the boy's face and touched his shoulder. Morgan was right. The boy was scrawny. But he had Minnie's facial features. She'd been the eldest in the family and easily the best looking. He'd missed her greatly when she had left the island. Ryan patted the boy's back, feeling his bones. Minnie had done something right. She'd been determined to start a family free of the curse.

"Uh, boss?" Moe asked.

Ryan blinked and patted the boy's back, thinking of his eldest sister but also thinking about his current situation. "This can work in our favor." He looked up at Moe. "You and Stan reach Morgan on the walkie-talkie. Tell her we have Mrs. Ashley's son." He grinned. "I'm betting that teacher would love to exchange her troublemaking student for him. Until then, it's about time he got to hang out with his daddy's family."

Moe grunted. "What about the other kid? I think he's from that homeschool bunch."

"Let's eat him," Kenton said, licking his lips. "If I ever see those brats—"

"Shut up," Ryan told him. "He's going with us. How'd he get out here and find this kid?"

Moe gestured at the cell phone bulging from Elliot's back pocket. "Cell phone, maybe?"

"Right." Ryan jammed his cap back on his head. "Technology will be the ruin of us." Hiding The Pack in the modern world was getting increasingly more difficult. He really hoped Morgan's plan to reverse the curse worked.

He reached over and slid the phone from his great-nephew's pocket. Leaning over him, he patted the other boy's side and found his phone. Pulling it out, he held both phones out to Moe. "Destroy these and bury them. Then, keep up the search. I'm sure The Pack already has the scent of the others. Just make sure they don't eat any of them. Got it?"

"Got it." Moe headed off with Stan.

Kenton stood nervously by while Ryan remained crouching by the unconscious boys. The elder Raycroft seemed lost in thought. Then his eyes snapped open. "We'll take them to The Motel. You got the pickup parked at the fire road?"

"Uh, yeah. I think," Kenton said, scratching the back of his bald head.

"You get the other kid. I'll take Minnie's grandson."

"Of course I get the bigger one," Kenton muttered. He grabbed Tucker by the shoulders and yanked him to a standing position. Turning the limp body, he threw him up over his massive shoulders.

Ryan picked up Elliot more gently. He first rolled him to his back and cradled his neck and arms before lifting him.

"Got you, kid," he muttered. "Welcome to the family."

The two men carried their burdens down the hill toward the fire road. After a while, Ryan put Elliot's body up to his shoulder, throwing him over. "I just had a thought, brother," he said.

Kenton snorted. "Those are always dangerous."

"The ritual says the boy to be eaten must be a son of the island, correct?"

Kenton only shrugged, clearly not sure.

"Well, this boy…" He patted Elliot's thighs. "He has Raycroft blood in him. He's directly related to Benjamin Raycroft, the ancestor who started this all."

"Are you sure about that?" Kenton said, making a face. "Our sister left our family, remember? Besides, right now, that kid only smells like pee, not a Raycroft."

"Yeah," Ryan muttered. He eyed his brother with mild disgust. "He doesn't smell *that* bad." Then he brightened. "We can test it. The kid is pretty banged up. Once we get into cell phone range, call The Motel. Have a Pack Maiden waiting. Let's see if our little great-nephew has the healing blood."

He boosted the boy higher up his shoulder and squeezed the back of his legs tightly. "You will become a member of The Pack, kid, or you just might save it."

Chapter 33

The lone motel on Blue Island had never actually been open for business. The island got very few tourists and the rare visitor usually only stayed long enough for a single meal…with them being the main course. Called simply The Motel, it had been built for a single purpose.

Constructed at the edge of the forest three miles north of the community, the motel served as a gathering place for The Pack and their human families. Since it would be difficult to explain wolf-men wandering around the community to outsiders, such as delivery people, The Pack had to reside in the woods.

The Motel was one place where they could meet loved ones in a civilized setting. A single L-shaped building, it housed eight small units of typical motel rooms—each with a double bed, nightstand, dresser with television, a couple of easy chairs, and a bathroom with an oversized shower. These were all set up in one long row. At the end of the row, where the bottom part of the L extended, four larger units were built in an apartment-style for larger families. These held two bedrooms and a kitchen, with everything else being the same as the smaller units.

Everything about it operated as a standard motel except for the few rooms with an additional humongous mattress on the floor, like an oversized doggie bed. Otherwise, it had an office between the smaller rooms and the apartment units and even a swimming pool in the back.

When the 1997 maroon Ford pickup drove into the back of the motel from the woods, the pool was occupied by little Brie Carson and her older sister Fiona.

Ryan Raycroft hit the brakes to stop by the black metal rail fence bordering the pool. He lowered the driver's window and stuck his head out. "Hey, girls! Is your momma here?"

"Oh!" Brie squealed. She hopped off the pink float she'd been lying on, splashing in the water. "Are the boys here? Let me see!"

"She's got everything and is waiting in room four," Fiona called. She got up from the padded pool chair and stretched. "If it's all right, she said me and Brie could be there."

Kenton snorted from next to Ryan. "There's no place for little girls," he said.

Ryan elbowed him in his fleshy arm. "Their momma's the Maiden here, you idiot. She runs this place. We're the guests." He looked out back the window. "Sure, Fiona."

"Just keep your brat sister out of the way," Kenton growled.

Brie pulled herself out of the water to kneel on the pool's edge. She stuck out her tongue at the pickup. "I'm never in the way," she shouted.

Fiona rolled her eyes as she wrapped a towel around her red bathing suit. She carried another towel that she threw on her little sister's head. Brie wore a matching suit, and both girls sported the same short haircut. They looked like the same person, only at different ages. They were expected to follow in their mother's footsteps to become Pack Maidens.

Moments later, the pickup parked in front of room number four, its back end facing the door. The boys had been laid on their sides in the back, facing each other. Despite the bumpy fire road, they'd remained unconscious and didn't stir when Ryan slammed down the tailgate.

Helga, the girls' mother, exited the motel room and stared at the boys without expression. She wore a drab gray robe and had her graying black hair swept back from her pinched, wrinkled face. She didn't seem happy to see the pickup, but she rarely showed any emotion except irritation. As a Pack Maiden, she served as The Motel's manager and lived there year-round. The rest of the parking lot was empty. Helga's husband, who worked as the handyman for The Motel, had their jeep in town to pick up supplies. There were no families scheduled to visit until that weekend.

"Where do you want the boy?" Ryan asked. Leaning over the tailgate, he snagged Elliot's sneaker and dragged the unconscious boy toward him.

Helga walked up behind him and stared at the kid with distaste. Sniffing, she wrinkled her nose. "The shower," she said. "He's putrid."

Ryan dropped the sneaker and turned on the woman. A glare crossed his face. "I know you run this place, Helga, but I also know that you answer to Morgan. You don't understand. This boy is important, and I need to know if he can be healed. Now. I'm not worried about him being clean or smelling nice. It's for The Pack's sake. We have to know if he carries the blood of the island!"

Helga flinched and shifted her dark gray eyes back to the boy. Like her daughters, she was thin and had a wiry frame. Next to Ryan Raycroft, she appeared tiny and delicate. Still, she didn't want to give in so easily.

"Now I see where Morgan gets it from," she said. "The healing works best on clean skin."

Kenton climbed out of the passenger seat. He kept his distance. Despite his enormous size, he was afraid of the much smaller woman.

"The boy only has a few bruises, Helga," Ryan Raycroft said, refusing to back down.

"I'll be the judge of that." Lifting her right hand so her sleeve slid back, the woman stepped beside Ryan and grabbed the boy's leg. Taking a deep breath, she closed her eyes.

Ryan and Kenton watched in silent awe. They never understood the power Pack Maidens held.

Helga's eyes snapped open. She jerked her head to the open door behind her. "Take him to the bed and lay him on his back. His foot has a mild sprain, and his head needs some tending. Otherwise, he's fine. It's a waste of fusia," she muttered.

"Not if I'm right," Ryan said with a grunt. He pulled Elliot to the edge of the tailgate and soon had him up over his shoulder.

"What about the other?" Kenton asked. He wanted to finish his job and return to the woods, away from the spooky Maiden. What he really wanted was to resume the hunt.

"Put him in the next room," Ryan told him. "I want to know his connection to the island and why he was with our boy here." He slapped the back of Elliot's thigh. "Something about this, I don't like." He grimaced. "Then, once we don't need him, you can dump him in the holding pen."

"Good," Kenton said as he reached in to grab Tucker's foot. "That means we'll eat him soon."

Elliot woke up in a strange room with a lady pulling his shirt off.

Cracking his eyes, he saw a mud-colored quilt under him and a snot-green carpet covering the floor. His shoes and socks had been removed, but he was relieved that he still wore his green pants, which smelled heavily of urine. His eyes slid shut as the woman moved in front of him. He sat on the bed's edge, propped up by a firm hand on his back. The woman smelled of rotten meat. She grabbed the bottom of his T-shirt and yanked up, pulling it hard over his arms and head without care.

Too groggy to resist, Elliot let his arms flop to his sides. The hand on his back laid him back on the mattress. The back of his head ached, and his face felt like it'd been lit on fire.

He remembered being in the woods with Tucker and something hitting him... he had a bad feeling he was not being helped. As the woman examined him, the rotten meat smell grew stronger. He became aware of others watching.

The woman's hand pressed down on his stomach, and she moved it around his navel.

"I see no signs of fur," she said.

"He's still young," a man's voice said behind him. "That means nothing."

"There still should be signs," the woman said. "Usually those who will start The Turn have a tenderness at a young age."

"Just do the healing," the man muttered, not sounding overly pleased.

"Hush, and let me finish." The woman's hand moved up to his chest and covered his heart. "He beats strong. This one is not as weak as he looks."

"Does that mean—"

The man was cut off by the woman. "It means nothing. Let's see if he heals."

Elliot moved his head, trying to wake up from this strange dream. A rough hand brushed his forehead. "Relax, buddy," the man said. "We're helping you."

"For now," said a young girl's voice. She broke into a giggle.

"Hush, Brie," an older girl admonished.

Elliot lay still, too hurt and confused to know what to do. His eyes cracked open a sliver.

The woman wore a shapeless robe and held a small wooden bowl. His nose twitched. The bowl carried something putrid, smelling worse than rotten meat. Using her hand, she scooped something from the bowl and bent over Elliot.

He tried to flinch but felt something smack against his cheek. The woman began rubbing gooey paste all over his face.

Elliot tried to shake it away.

"Easy, fella," the man said soothingly behind him. Strong hands gripped his shoulders and held him still. "This is for your own good."

"Maybe," giggled the little girl.

The paste felt cool against his skin but carried a thick, rancid smell, like rotten butter mixed with rusty iron. Then it started to warm and burn. Stiffening, he started writhing, and the man pinned down his arms. Then, all at once, it cooled again, and Elliot relaxed. All the pain melted away. Slowly, his head cleared, and he began to fully awaken. Turning his neck, he looked down at his body and saw his injured ankle had already been slathered in the paste.

"It's working!" the man yelled, sounding elated. He released Elliot's arms, smacking his hands together in satisfaction.

"Yes!" said the little girl.

All at once, Elliot shot to a sitting position, gasping for a breath. He sat facing a wall with a flat-screen television and a mirror. In the mirror, he saw the woman, a man dressed in camouflage, and two young girls in bathing suits with towels around their waists. The man stood by the bed right behind him while the girls were a few feet in front of a plain white door. He stared at his own reflection. His hair had been tied in a loose knot above his head, exposing his face. Smeared with a greenish-brown paste, only his wide blue eyes were visible. His bare chest heaved up and down as his body raced with a burst of energy. All his aches had vanished, and he felt amazingly good.

"Welcome to the family, kid," the man said, slapping his bare back. "You're one of us!"

Elliot stared at the man's reflection in the mirror.

"Who are you?" he demanded. "Where's Tucker?"

"I'm Ryan Raycroft, your great-uncle." The man clapped a rough hand on his shoulder. "We share blood, kid." He seemed very pleased with himself. "We found you in the woods, you and your, er, friend. He's in the next room resting."

Elliot wanted to lick his dry lips, but the rank odor of the paste kept his tongue in his mouth. "What did you do to my face?"

The woman had backed toward the door and stood with the two girls. They were obviously related. The youngest looked about his age. He recognized the older girl as Fiona, the teen guide for his mom's class at the farm.

"We fixed it," the littlest girl said, grinning. "You're all better now."

"Nothing really wrong with him in the first place," the woman grumbled. Streaked with silver, her short dark hair curved wildly from her thin face. It looked like she stuck her face in a fan after smearing her hair with superglue. She looked down her nose at the boy.

Ignoring her, Elliot flexed his left ankle, amazed to find it pain-free and loose. Under the paste, his face felt fine, too. He lifted his hand and touched his cheek, feeling no discomfort.

"Go to the bathroom and wash it off," Ryan said, grinning.

Elliot slid off the bed and walked without limping to the open bathroom in the back of the room.

It was a large, spacious room, but it only contained a sink, a toilet in the far left corner, and an extraordinarily huge shower inside the door. A single small window was above the toilet near the ceiling.

"Where am I?" he asked.

Ryan had followed him in. "Go wash your face, and I'll tell you."

Turning to the sink across from the gigantic shower, Elliot soon bent over running water, scrubbing away the smelly paste. It melted away like hot butter, leaving his skin feeling moist and fresh. Amazingly, all his bruises were totally gone. Looking up to stare in the small mirror above the sink, he saw perfectly smooth skin. Dark circles were marked under his eyes, but his black eye had faded entirely, as had the bruise on his cheek.

"You just need some rest," Ryan said, standing behind him. "You're exhausted, buddy."

"How is this, like, possible?" Elliot said, awed. He traced his eye with a finger, feeling nothing. "I mean, how long have I been here?"

"When we found you and your friend, you were both unconscious, and we brought you straight here to a, uh, motel. That was about thirty minutes ago." Ryan smiled wide and put an arm around Elliot's shoulder. "You see, this island has a secret. Any person with the blood of The Pack can be healed by the saliva and blood of The Pack. It's mixed with herbs and animal fat to make the paste. The woman in there, Helga, is the magic worker. She's the one who put it together for you, kid."

"I helped!" the little girl shouted from the bed.

"Quiet and let them be," her older sister muttered. "Go help Mom clean up the paste on the bed."

"That's Brie and Fiona, Helga's daughters," Ryan explained. "They're training to be Maidens of The Pack."

Elliot nodded, totally confused. He stared at the big man in the mirror. "And Tucker is okay, too, right? Does he, like, get the paste?"

Ryan Raycroft lifted his hand to scratch his grizzled jaw. "Yeah, uh, your friend. Well, he's not from here. He has the wrong blood. You see, your father is my sister's boy. That gives you the blood of the island, meaning you're related to The Pack. The paste won't work for anybody not connected to The Pack, like your friend. So he's sleeping off... whatever knocked you kids out. Good thing we found you, huh?" Lowering his hand to Elliot's shoulder, he gave the boy a goofy grin through the mirror. "Those woods can be wild and dangerous."

Elliot slowly nodded but still looked confused.

Ryan Raycroft's hand pulled Elliot back into him, squeezing his shoulder. His face grew serious as he stared at Elliot's reflection. "Your grandmother was my sister. You have her eyes, you know." He suddenly wrinkled his nose. "Why don't I let you, uh, take a shower and get cleaned up, hey? Then you can get some rest."

Elliot pursed his lips and looked down at the sink, embarrassed. With the fusia smell mostly gone, his pants stunk of stale urine. He could feel them sticking to his legs. "Yeah, um, thanks."

"Hey, buddy, it's okay." Ryan wrapped both his arms around Elliot's shoulders, hugging his chest. It was something his mom and dad did, but Elliot did not feel comfortable with the man calling himself his great-uncle. The man leaned over him, pressing his hands against his upper stomach. He then smacked a hand over his belly button. "Does that hurt?" he asked.

Elliot shook his head, fighting the urge to shake free.

"Ah, you're still young," the man muttered, straightening. "It's not too late to Turn."

He released Elliot and gave him a pat on the head. "You can keep your warrior's knot if you want. Fiona tied your hair like that. It makes you more wolfish. Brie should be bringing you something to change into when you're washed up. Leave your dirty clothes in a pile, and Helga will clean them. Okay?"

"Uh, yeah. Can I see Tucker when I'm done?"

"Of course, bud." Ryan grinned down at him. "You're no prisoner, you know. You're family! While you shower, I'll be back in the woods searching for your mom. I understand she's still lost in there. I should be back tonight."

Elliot felt his heart surge with hope. "You're going to find my mom?" he asked. "Really?"

"You bet, buddy." Ryan smacked his arm. "After all, she's family too. And I'm sure she's worried sick about you."

"Here you go," Brie announced, marching boldly into the bathroom. She tossed a pair of black swimming trunks to Ryan. "It's all I could find to fit his puny body." She turned to Elliot and smiled wide. "You're Elliot. The healing paste is called fusia. Just so you know, I added the blood."

"Okay, Brie," Ryan said, his smile tightening. "That's enough. Let the boy clean up."

Elliot remained at the sink, staring down in shame.

"Oh, yeah," Brie said. "You wet yourself, didn't you?"

Ryan's smile turned into a glare. "Goodbye, Brie," he growled.

"Brie!" her mom shouted from the other room. "Come and change the sheet with me."

Brie rolled her eyes and spun on her heel. "Well, hurry up, Elliot," she said over her shoulder. "It's really boring here. You're the first excitement here in, like, forever."

When the girl left, Ryan stuffed the shorts in Elliot's middle and clapped him on the side. "Okay, bud. I'm off.

Watch out for Brie. She means well but is a handful!" Giving Elliot a wink, he left, firmly closing the door behind him.

Alone, Elliot looked in the mirror and stared at his unmarked face, wrinkling his brow. His day was getting stranger... and it was still not over. Daylight still peeked in through the window. He wasn't sure what to think about his great-uncle, but he knew he wanted to see Tucker. The two of them could figure things out. Leaving the sink, he went to the shower to find knobs nearly the size of steering wheels. Struggling with the large knobs, he got the water going with impressive water pressure. Waiting for it to warm, he used the toilet. Finished, he washed his hands and then shrugged off his filth-encrusted pants and boxers, putting them in a pile by the door. As he did so, he heard voices in the next room. Helga and Brie were right outside the door. Elliot made sure to quietly press the lock, securing the door. Then he put his ear to the door to listen.

It was a trick his mom taught him. Whenever she wanted to know what was happening in her class, she would pretend to go on an errand and then hide in the hall, listening through the door. That's how she discovered the bullies and leaders. When people thought they could speak freely, the truth came out.

"I hope he can be part of The Pack," Brie was saying. "He's pretty cute."

"So is the other boy," Helga said with a grunt. "You don't care about him?"

"Yeah, but he can never be part of The Pack. Besides, he doesn't get a name, so he doesn't count."

"Well, from what I hear, Elliot would do more good if he doesn't turn. The Pack needs his blood. Now finish with the pillowcases and get out of here."

"Okay, Mother. Know what? I'm going to find some pig's blood and do some experiments myself!"

"Before you do, check on the other one! The nameless one!"

Elliot slowly backed away from the door, more confused and frightened than ever. He stepped into the shower and immediately yelped. The hot water slapped against his skin like fire hoses. Still, as his body adjusted to it and the hot water drenched his skin, he shivered.

Chapter 34

Tucker heard Maria calling his name. She then smacked him with a hair brush. "Boy, hey boy… Wake up!"

His eyes fluttered his eyes open, and he groaned heavily. "Oh, my gosh…"

"Finally, boy!"

His bleary eyes cleared as his skull felt like somebody had used his brain like a punching bag inside it. It ached terribly. He looked up and saw a young girl kneeling on the bed, staring down at him. Not Maria… She reminded him of an elf from a fairytale with her thin face and crazed grin.

"Who… are you?" he asked groggily. "And where am I?"

The last thing he remembered was seeing some crazy guy knock out Elliot, and then… somebody had knocked him out. Reaching a hand up to his head, he patted his curls gingerly, finding the sore spot just behind his right ear.

"I'm Brie," the girl said brightly. "I've been trying to make you wake up."

"Oh, you're so kind." Tucker closed his eyes. "You're like the kindest person in the whole world."

"Thank you," Brie said. "I'm checking on you."

"Really? Great. You checked on me. Now go away." Tucker's eyes snapped open. "Wait. Where's Elliot?"

"He's in the next room, still in the shower," Brie said, rolling her eyes. "You're the only one I can talk to. My mom is busy, and my sister is super annoying."

"Oh, so it runs in the family," Tucker said. Groaning, he sat up and fought down nausea. "You remind me of Maria, you know."

"Who's that?"

"My super annoying eight-year-old sister."

"I'm ten," Brie said, sounding offended. "I just don't get out very much and don't see many my age. You know, this is where the visitors used to go for The Business. But that was before I was born."

"That's great." Tucker still wore his grimy chef shirt and black pants. "You said Elliot is in the shower? Well, you know, I think I'm going to take a shower too. Okay?"

"Sure," Brie said, not moving. "The bathroom is right there. Go help yourself."

"I sort of mean, you leave, and then I get privacy, and then I take a shower."

"That's okay," Brie said. "I'm fine."

"Right…" Tucker collapsed his head back onto the pillow and immediately winced as his aching head flared with more pain. "So, um, Brie… is this like a hotel room or something?"

"No, it's The Motel," Brie told him.

"And there're are locks on the door?"

"Of course."

"And Elliot is just next door?"

"In room number four," Brie told him. "I was there when he woke up, too."

"I bet." Tucker rolled to his side, away from the girl.

Brie just bounced happily next to him. "I helped put fusia on him. Do you know what fusia is?"

"Something great, I'm sure," Tucker said. With effort, he got himself out of bed and stood unsteadily. Once the room stopped moving, he stumbled to the end of the bed.

"Where are you going?" Brie asked.

"Oh, to turn on the television… In Elliot's room!" All at once, Tucker raced for the door. Throwing it open, he lunged outside into an empty parking lot. For a brief moment, he blinked at his surroundings. The motel looked stuck in a clearing right next to a thick forest. The afternoon sun began to set, and dark clouds were on the horizon.

"Come back!" Brie called. "Where're you going?"

Tucker didn't bother to look around too much. He threw himself at the next door, relieved to find it unlocked. Pushing it open, he tumbled inside before slamming it behind him. He jammed down the lock. His cheek pressed against the door as his body relaxed.

"Dude!" Elliot hollered from the bathroom. "Don't you knock?"

"Elliot!" Tucker cried. He straightened and threw back his head in relief. "Thank goodness! You're here!"

Elliot popped his head out of the bathroom door, steam coming out behind him. "Tucker! It's you! I thought you were that girl." He exited wearing black swim trunks and drying his long hair with a towel. "Thank you so much for not being her."

"That girl is the reason why I'm here. I'm trying to escape from her!" He stared at his dripping friend with sudden concern. "Elliot, where are we?"

"Um, well, I'll, like, try to explain…"

The boys moved to sit on the bed. Elliot moved to sit on his knees while Tucker sat next to him cross-legged.

Elliot explained what Ryan Raycroft said about rescuing them from the forest and bringing them to the motel place.

Then he told Tucker about the strange healing paste and what his great-uncle said about the blood and saliva.

"That's pretty gross," Tucker said. "But I'm glad you're okay, man."

"Yeah, tell me about it," Elliot agreed. "The stinky goo was all over my face." He took a deep breath. "Tucker, I don't trust anybody here. I think we still might be in trouble."

"You think? I kind of totally agree, Elliot," Tucker said. "There's something seriously wrong here, especially with that girl Brie."

"I don't just mean her. I mean that Ryan Raycroft guy. He said he's my great-uncle, and I have his blood, but he kept talking about The Pack. I think he's with the wolf-men."

Tucker shuddered. "So, do you think we're prisoners? I mean, they let us lock the doors from the inside."

"Um, about that..." Elliot knelt facing the door with Tucker on his right. Elliot's eyes went wide.

Tucker turned to see and froze with fright.

The door knob jiggled, and the lock popped. Something scraped against the door as it slowly started to open.

The boys drew close, both ready to shriek at the same time.

"Hi, guys," Brie cheerfully announced, leaning her head through. "Don't you know I have a key to all the rooms? Let's go sit by the pool. I want to talk to you two."

Elliot still clutched Tucker's arm, and Tucker still held a pillow in front of him like a shield.

"I kind of wish it was a monster rather than her," Tucker said, his breath returning to normal.

"Yeah," agreed Elliot, "like, totally."

While Tucker and Elliot cautiously followed Brie to the motel pool, Skylar opened her eyes to see a giant dog head looming over her face. A huge pink tongue hung just inches from her nose. Her eyes bugged when the head and tongue lowered. Just missing her face, the pink appendage went toward her right arm, lying bent beside her cheek.

Just like that, she was wide awake.

"Ew!" she cried, jerking her arm away. Her left arm shot up and pushed the slobbery snout from her face. "Stop that!" she screeched.

Amazingly, the dog jumped back and stood on his two feet. "Sorry," he said. "I, I was, trying to heal you. You see—"

"You were trying to lick me!" Skylar cried. "That's gross!"

Then she went very still. It wasn't a dream. Looking up, she saw a great wolf-man standing over her. Well over six feet, the wolf-man had broad shoulders and black fur. He wore only a breechcloth, but fur covered him head to toe.

Her lower lip trembled, and she lay back down. "Who… who are you?" she managed to ask. "You, you talk."

The wolf-man slowly raised his paws and took another step back. "I'm, I'm Bernard," he said gently. "I'm not going to hurt you. You're Skylar, aren't you?"

Skylar nodded. "Ohmygosh… You're a wolf-man."

"Yes," Bernard said bitterly, lowering his arms. "That's what they call us."

Skylar slowly sat up. "You saved me, didn't you? Teddy was after me…" Skylar looked at the wolf-man in amazement. "You threw him off me."

"Not all of us are monsters," Bernard rumbled. His voice sounded rough but also young, like somebody around her age. "Teddy should've never hurt you."

Skylar shook her head, trying to clear it. "So you know Teddy, and you know my name. Have you… have you been to my house?"

Bernard nodded his shaggy head. "A few times. My younger brother and I… We've been trying to help your family.

Members of The Pack don't like you very much. A few of my kin mean you harm." The wolf-man lowered his head as if ashamed. "It was Martin, my younger brother, who turned off the hot water that one night. He was close to your great-grandmother and was a little jealous."

"Jealous? Jealous of what?"

The great furry shoulders shrugged. "Of you and your brother... your life. Your dad's mom left the island and escaped the curse. Sylvia helped make this happen. She didn't help any others, just your family." Bernard sighed. "Sylvia was a great person but never did that for anybody else."

Skylar shook her head. "What do you mean we're free of the curse?"

The wolf-man looked down at her. "None of you are like me, are you?"

"No, I guess not. Oh, man, my head really hurts now."

"Relax. I am on your side. Right now, Martin is watching over Elliot. We caught his scent at the farm when we were… watching you." The wolf-man again looked ashamed. "Just for your own protection," he said quickly.

"You mean, you guys were at the farm?"

Bernard shook his head. "We were in the trees outside the fence. We were always pretty good climbers, and having this body only made us better."

Skylar looked around and saw she lay on the earthen floor of a small rectangular log hut. The size of her family room, the hut had two piles of thick blankets and a stump in the middle serving as a table. A single blanket had been put in the back corner that she lay on. A stack of books sat on the stump and more books were scattered on the dirt-packed floor. A small round window had been cut into the wall over her and a small doorway faced her across from her feet.

"Where are we?" she asked.

"After Teddy, uh, decided to leave, you were, well, unconscious. I carried you to a place where my brother and I like to hang out. It's near the main road, but far enough away nobody will find you. You're safe here, Skylar."

Skylar gave him a long look and finally nodded. She didn't like being in the arms of a wolf-man, but he'd saved her life. "Okay, but before I trust you, I need to know two things. First, how old are you?"

"I'm sixteen, and my brother is thirteen." His yellow eyes hardened. "He's the youngest of The Pack and should not be like this. What else do you want to know?"

"Why were you trying to lick me?"

Bernard blinked. "Saliva from The Pack cures injuries. I mean, if you're of the right blood. Your family is one of the original families of the island." He sounded embarrassed and a little awed at the same time.

"You were putting your saliva on me?" Skylar asked. She sounded grossed out.

"I was only trying to help you, you know, heal your arms."

Skylar looked at him and then at the scratches and welts that marked her arms. A few had scabbed over, but none were deep.

"Bernard, that's super gross."

"I was only healing you."

"They're scratches, not gaping wounds! Leave your saliva to yourself from now on, okay?"

Bernard bowed his head low and waved his right hand. "Very well, for you, I will let you suffer."

"Thank you. No, I mean it. Thank you for saving me from Teddy…" Then she gasped. "What about Tucker? He's Elliot's friend and—"

"The last I saw, my brother was helping him escape Paige." Bernard bared his teeth. "Paige is the one you need to worry about. She is obsessed with wolf-men. Since she can't become one, she wants to control them all."

"Okay, that does it. If you're against Paige, then I'm with you." Skylar brushed back her hair and rose to a knee. "So what's the plan?"

"To get you, your family, and the others off the island," Bernard growled. "We need to do it fast. Morgan Raycroft has some crazy idea that puts all of you in great danger. She is the leader of the island and is trying to turn all wolf-men back into humans."

"That's good, though, right?"

"Evil is evil," Bernard said flatly. "When evil does good, it's a lie. It only pretends to do good to do more evil." He looked down at Skylar. "Your grandmother taught me that."

"I never met her," Skylar confessed. Feeling her head spin, she moved back down to sit cross-legged.

"Sylvia was good to me. Everything changed when she died and Morgan took her place as Protector of The Pack. Morgan is not thinking right. Ever since her son Burton turned to a wolf-man, she's been obsessed with bringing him back to human, no matter the cost."

"And you?" Skylar asked, lifting her eyebrows. "You don't mind being a…wolf-man?"

Bernard growled. "I was born a human and will always act like one. That's something else Sylvia taught me. I will never become a monster, no matter what I look like."

Nodding, Skylar got stiffly to her feet and wiped her dirty hands on her thighs. "I believe you, Bernard. Thank you." She wobbled slightly as she wiped her hands and stumbled forward. Tripping, she fell onto the stump, knocking over the books, mostly crime novels.

"Are you okay?" Bernard asked, moving to assist her.

"Wait!" Skylar held up her hand. She knelt against the stump and allowed the dizziness to pass. "Before you even think about licking again, I'm fine. Let's just come up with a plan to make your plan of rescuing us work."

Bernard found a way to make a wolf look sheepish. Then he nodded. "Actually," he said, "I was hoping to start with rescuing a few others from this island first. There's this place called The Motel…"

Chapter 35

It took hours of hard work, but as the sun began setting, the decrepit, abandoned house became a fort. It had been Gary's idea.

When the boys and Mrs. Ashley made the trek up the hill earlier that afternoon, they each carried a bundle of long, sturdy sticks. Dumping them in front of the house, the group did a quick tour while keeping an eye and ear out for any pursuit.

They found the stone structure to be a small two-room house that hadn't been used for decades. Moss and vines covered the roughly stacked greenstone that formed the outer walls. There were two windows and a doorway in front and three windows in the back. All the glass in the windows had been broken. The front roof on the left side had collapsed, filling the space with rotting beams and disintegrating shingles. The floor was made of hardwood and surprisingly held up quite well. It was damp and soft in some areas, but it was durable. The best and worst feature of the house was it being on a hill and being built against a clump of thick vegetation with young trees pressing against the back walls. The front yard was clear of trees for several feet, allowing a good view of anybody approaching. The back allowed a quick escape route with lots of hiding places. Or, the front made it easy for them to be spotted and the back gave easy access for a monster or person to sneak up on them.

After looking around, they gathered in the front room by the doorway, next to the collapsed roof. Besides dirt and bugs, the house was empty, and they sat on the floor. Their backpacks with the remaining food and water were piled in the corner near the door.

"So, what do you think, guys?" Mrs. Ashley asked tiredly. "Should we stay here for a while?"

"Oh, yeah," Bobby said, stretching his legs before him and leaning back on his arms. "If monsters come now, I'm a buffet. I'm too tired to move."

Gary nodded, and Marcus gave a grunt. They were despondent and needed time to process the day and rest their bodies.

Mrs. Ashley forced a smile. "Okay, then. I'm going to step out and check around the area. I'll try to hide some of our tracks. Hopefully, they'll think we followed the stream."

Gary clicked his tongue. "I don't think so," he said. "They have wolf noses and can probably smell us a mile away."

"Thanks for that, Gary," Mrs. Ashley said. "I'll keep that in mind. You boys stay here and rest." She got to her feet and nearly broke in a run to leave.

"Think she's coming back?" Marcus mumbled. "Maybe she'll run after Mr. Harris."

"More likely, she'll search for Elliot," Bobby said. "She's nothing like Mr. Harris. She'll come back."

Marcus nodded. "Yeah… but then what? We can't stay in this dump."

Gary rubbed a hand over his sweaty hair, and he bit his lower lip. "You know, I think it has potential."

"I don't think we're moving in, dummy," Marcus said.

"Why? Is it better than your house?" Gary asked caustically.

Marcus instantly got to his feet, ready to fight. "Take that back, bubble-butt."

"Guys!" Bobby said, quickly standing between them. "Quit it!" He nodded at where Mrs. Ashley had left. "In case you forgot, Mrs. A's son is missing, and monsters are trying to kill us."

"Or just one of us," Gary muttered, dropping his gaze.

Marcus flinched as if slapped and abruptly sat down. "Don't forget about Mr. Harris," he said. "He's probably run to China by now. Wish I joined him."

Bobby glared at Gary before the boy could make another rude crack. "We need to work together and help Mrs. A."

Gary huffed and got slowly to his feet. "Okay, Marcus. I'm sorry," he said. "You know, I wasn't kidding about this place having potential."

Bobby looked at him. He knew Gary had a twisted mind but was pretty shrewd. His ideas couldn't be ignored. "What do you mean?"

"I think we can make this place into a pretty good fortress. You know, maybe make it someplace we can defend if attacked."

"Yeah, and throw our wooden sticks at the werewolves?" Marcus asked. "Great."

Gary crouched down, his voice growing in excitement. "Listen, man. Look around. There's plenty we can do. See all the broken windows? The glass is all over the ground and floor. We can use it to make spear points or knives or something. And we can barricade the door with sticks."

"Um, that sounds good," Bobby said doubtfully. "But barricading the door will trap us inside, right?"

"Maybe." Gary grinned. "Or, it'll trap the wolf monsters inside. Come on, I want to show you guys something. I didn't want Mrs. Ashley to see this."

With Marcus grumbling and Bobby curious, the two boys followed Gary to the back of the house.

Gary had discovered a root cellar in the second room. He led the boys to the back corner and showed them the floor cracks. He then opened a two-foot by one-foot trapdoor to reveal a rotting carton stuffed with several clear glass jugs, each full of clear liquid.

"Bottles of water?" Bobby asked, confused.

Gary chuckled. "No, son. This here is genuine moonshine. It can kill you if you drink it. But… if we can start a fire, it happens to be super flammable."

"And how would we start a fire?" Bobby asked doubtfully.

"Yeah, about that. Guys?" Marcus reached into his pocket and pulled out a small red lighter. "I sort of found this on the farm. Would this work?"

When Mrs. Ashley returned to the house, she found the boys waiting for her excitedly. They told her the plan to fortify the house and make weapons using broken glass and stones.

"I'll be like one of your STEM projects in science," Gary told her.

"You mean the ones you never did until the last minute?" Mrs. Ashley asked. But a spark glinted in her eye. She needed something to do to keep her mind off of worrying about Elliot. And the boys needed something to build their hope. "Let's do it!"

Bobby shuddered. "You know, most science projects don't end up with you being eaten if you fail."

"Then we'd better not fail," Mrs. Ashley told him. "But we need to do this as fast and quietly as possible. We're still being hunted."

The next hour was busy as heavy logs, brush, and sticks were moved up to the house. Mrs. Ashley and Marcus did most of the heavy lifting. Gary had them make a pile in front of the house and started using the sticks and brush to cover the front window and create a barrier in front of the door, allowing a narrow path to enter and exit the house.

Bobby spent time collecting shards of broken window glass and sat down with the sticks they'd collected. Finding the longest and strongest sticks, he went about trying to add sharp-tipped points. Sitting in front of the house near the brush pile, he struggled to make it work. After dropping the glass repeatedly, he finally managed to wedge a glass shard into the end of a stick, only to slice his left palm when his hand slipped. The glass tumbled free.

"Ah!" he cried, watching blood run down his hand.

Gary stopped by to offer advice. "Use your shoelaces, man. Wedge the glass in and tie it as tight as you can."

"Okay, but what about my hand?" Bobby asked. He gripped his cut with his other hand, and blood ran through his fingers.

"Amateur," Gary said. Taking off his shoes and socks, he covered a hand with his sock and grabbed a piece of glass. "I'll need your shirt sleeve, man."

Bobby sighed. "Just take it, man. I think it's already ruined." Blood splattered the front of it as he cradled his hands in front of his shirt.

Gary used the glass to carefully poke a hole at the hem of Bobby's left sleeve and then ripped it right off. He used it to bandage Bobby's hand.

"Hold it," he said, bending down.

Bobby squeezed his injured hand and watched Gary pull a shoelace from his shoe. Gary soon used the lace to tie the torn sleeve tightly over the cut.

"Man, that's tight," Bobby said, flexing his wrapped hand when it was finished. "Thanks."

Gary stood with his socks and threw them on Bobby's lap. "Wear these when handling glass, and don't cut yourself again. I'm too busy to be your nursemaid."

Bobby nodded sheepishly as he put on the socks like gloves.

"Oh, and I want them back," Gary told him as he returned to the brush pile. "They're going to be the wicks for the moonshine!"

Down the hill below, Marcus helped Mrs. Ashley pull up a heavy branch still covered in green leaves.

Marcus had mostly worked in silence, not daring to complain. He saw his teacher's tortured look as she went at the heaviest and most stubborn branches and brush. Marcus knew her thoughts had to be on her real son… not her dumb students. If only he hadn't snuck away and gone into the barn… if only he had listened more. He didn't know why he got in trouble so much… sometimes his body acted before his mind caught up.

"Marcus," Mrs. Ashley said suddenly. "It's okay. I'm sure Mr. Harris will find help, and… and Elliot will be fine. We just have to survive until help comes."

"What if the monsters come right now? I mean, we're not exactly hiding."

Mrs. Ashley blew out her breath. "I know I'm the grownup and should have all the answers, but that's not how life works, Marcus. Grownups make mistakes, too. The answer is I don't know. I just know I need to do something. Now, let's get this log up there!"

Several yards away, a young wolf-man lay low in the brush watching. His nose twitched as he smelled the scent of blood. Burton slowly got to his rear legs and backed away. He felt sick to his stomach. Turning into a monster had ruined his life. He allowed himself to grow angry, resentful, and selfish. Look at where it led him... Under his breechcloth, his tail slunk between his legs. He couldn't go after a teacher and a bunch of kids. The call had gone out to The Pack that one of the kids could be used to erase the curse. Just the thought of that made him want to cough up his lunch of cow meat. Having Morgan for a mom, he knew what it meant to erase the curse. He would have to eat a child. As he retreated from the ruined house and doomed children, his steps grew firmer and confident. He'd been tasked to find the kids and report back. Instead, he lifted back his hairy head and howled an "all clear" sign. He didn't know a hundred yards from him, one of his comrade wolf-men had already caught the scent of blood.

Hearing the howl so close, Mrs. Ashley and Marcus abandoned the branch and rushed back up to the old house. Bobby and Gary waited for them, each holding a crudely made spear.

"Are they coming?" Bobby asked. He squeezed so tightly against his stick that blood oozed out of his wrapped hand.

"I don't know," Mrs. Ashley gasped. "Nothing chased us. Are you guys okay?"

Gary nodded grimly. "But we have one last thing to do. Mrs. Ashley, I need to show you something."

Marcus and Bobby exchanged glances. What would their teacher think of Gary's moonshine plan?

Mrs. Ashley wasn't upset when seeing the moonshine bottles and hearing Gary's idea. "Sounds good," she said grimly.

"Really?" Gary said, surprised. "We're going to do it?"

Mrs. Ashley nodded. "Get it ready now, just in case anything comes. But give *me* the lighter. If we go down, I'll be the judge of when to use it. If we get attacked, I want you boys to focus on getting to safety."

Hours had passed since.

Mrs. Ashley now sat numbly on a fallen log just by the front door and stared into the woods. The three boys were inside the hut finishing a snack and getting rest. Gary had enclosed her spot with walls of thick brush and branches on three sides, so she should be pretty well hidden. He had also stuck a broken stick into the ground next to her, serving as a spear if she got attacked. It was a sweet gesture, but she doubted the stick would do much against the monsters they were up against. Bobby's glass-tipped spears were all in the house as a last line of defense.

Mrs. Ashley felt good about the hut but absolutely terrible about everything else. Elliot remained missing. He could be lying hurt somewhere… or be lost in the woods with no food or water… or could be… she couldn't think of it. She bit back a sob. Her boy needed help, and she could do nothing about it. If she hadn't had her three students, she would've left ages ago, searching the woods for her son, shouting his name, not caring who or what heard her. But she had to be there for Marcus, Gary, and Bobby. The three boys relied on her and needed her as much as Elliot did.

Somewhere deep in her mind, she felt a hint of resentment toward the boys. Of all her students, these were the three to cause her the most trouble. They gave her so much pain and could easily be blamed for putting her in this situation. She immediately squashed such thoughts. She was a teacher, and this was her job. She had a tremendous responsibility. Parents were trusting her with their kids. She would want the same treatment for Skylar and Elliot. She closed her eyes, thinking of her children. Was Skylar at home safe or frantically trying to call her? And Elliot… she clutched her stomach. She hadn't eaten since that afternoon and felt no hunger. The only hole in her stomach was from missing her kids.

"Hello up there!" called a man's voice. "Hey, there!"

Mrs. Ashley jumped to her feet and grabbed the stick next to her. "Boys," she hissed toward the house. "Stay inside and grab the spears. Be ready to move to the back!"

"If we have to jump out the windows, don't go out the left one," Bobby whispered to her. "That's the one I, uh, used as the bathroom."

"Not important right now," Mrs. Ashley growled back. "Just stay hidden!"

Clouds had moved in, darkening the dusky sky. Humidity hung thick in the air.

Mrs. Ashley gripped the stick with sweaty hands as she worked hard to control her breathing. Peering down, she saw movement from the stream.

Then, two men stepped into view. Stan and Moe looked up at her and raised their hands.

"We come in peace!" Stan yelled. "Our boss has a proposition for you!"

Moe nodded and spread out his arms. "We got no weapons and know you're up there."

"If we want, we can come up and take the kid by force," Stan warned.

"You just try it!" Mrs. Ashley yelled. "You touch one of those kids, so help me, I'll take you apart!"

Stan nodded. "Yeah, I'll bet you would." He grinned. "You took down Banor pretty good earlier… he still can't smell or see straight."

"Just tell me what you want and keep back!" Mrs. Ashley said.

The men had continued walking up, surveying the brush defenses and stone house closely. They were scouting it out, Mrs. Ashley knew. Now, they stopped.

"Well, actually," Stan said. "We were hoping to help you."

Moe nodded. "Yep, that's right. We figured you had more time to think about our earlier proposition. Give us the kid, Marcus, and go free."

"Only this time, we mean to throw in something extra." Even from the dusky light and distance, Mrs. Ashley could see Stan's stained teeth as he smiled. "We have your son, lady. You give us Marcus, and we give you Elliot."

An invisible dagger stabbed her heart. Mrs. Ashley stopped breathing. It was nearly beyond her worst fear. "N-no," she choked. "Oh, no, no."

"It's true, Mrs. Ashley," boomed a new voice. Ryan Raycroft strode to stand over the narrow stream. "Your son has a white scar, about three centimeters long, on his right shoulder. Hard see unless you're real close to it."

Mrs. Ashley abruptly sat down on the log behind her. Three years ago, Elliot had a fishing hook accident with Tucker and had needed a few stitches.

"Your son is okay," Ryan continued. "In fact, it's nice catching up with my great-nephew. He's a good kid." His voice hardened. "But my sister has a wild idea... If you don't give us Marcus, we might just use Elliot in his place. He's a better fit for what we have in mind."

All blood left her face as Mrs. Ashley tried to process what she just heard. Her son's life had just been threatened. She had the means to stop it... by giving away another mother's child.

She was about to stand up and tell Ryan she had to think about it when she heard movement from the house behind her. Glancing back, she saw Marcus staring at her with wide, fearful eyes. He looked so young and vulnerable. All his trust had been replaced with fear and a resigned sense of hopelessness.

"You can't do this!" Mrs. Ashley yelled, moving back to her feet. "They're children!"

"Sorry, Mrs. Ashley," Ryan Raycroft said gravely. "Your family is part of Blue Island. Everybody here serves The Pack, and all families are faced with drinking the blood sooner or later." His voice hardened. "Now, make your choice. Which boy do you want to save?"

"Both of them!" Mrs. Ashley shouted. "You can't hurt a child!"

"Wrong answer, lady," Stan said, shaking his head. "You can only choose one."

"You have until dawn tomorrow morning," Ryan said, sounding resolute. "When you decide to make the trade, just call down to Stan and Moe. They'll be waiting right here at the stream with a walkie-talkie. They'll call me, and I'll get your son back to you in less than ten minutes. Until then, he's ours."

Stan grinned and held up his walkie-talkie, waving it at Mrs. Ashley.

Moe gave her two thumbs-up. "If you want," he shouted, "we can make the trade now. Then, you can walk out of these woods and follow the road to North Community. Somebody will drive you back to the mainland there."

"It can all be over in a few minutes," Stan said. "Your call."

Ryan waited. "Come on, woman! What will it be? A troublesome brat with no family who'll miss him, or your own flesh and blood?"

Marcus remained in the doorway. He stood frozen like a statue, ready to crumble into dust.

"Just bring back my son and let us all go!" Mrs. Ashley finally yelled. "Don't do this!"

"You have until dawn," Ryan Raycroft yelled back. "I'm going back to check on your kid right now. I'll tell him how much you miss him!" Before he left, he crossed his arms in front of his chest and stared up. "Just remember this. If he dies, his blood is on your hands. You had a chance to save him but didn't!"

Mrs. Ashley could only fight back tears. Looking down, she saw she'd clawed her left wrist with her nails, drawing blood.

Chapter 36

Morgan slowly lowered the walkie-talkie and positioned her arms out from her, pointing them to the floor. She lifted her face to the ceiling and closed her eyes.

"Yes," she whispered. "Yes… This is it."

Not having moved from the couch, Dr. Chocker watched her with fascination and utter horror.

Morgan had just spoken with her brother Ryan. Mrs. Ashley and the children had been discovered in old stone ruins. They could get Marcus anytime they wanted… but her brother had other news. They'd found Mrs. Ashley's son in the woods. His blood fit the blood of The Pack. "Just maybe," her brother had suggested, "you're after the wrong boy."

Morgan had gripped the walkie-talkie tightly as her other hand had clutched the red pendant. "Raycroft blood started the curse," she'd said in the walkie-talkie. "Raycroft blood will now end it. Forget the others. Prepare the boy. The ritual will be done tonight."

"Hold on," Ryan had protested. "I gave that woman my word. She has until dawn tomorrow to make the trade. Let's make sure the Marcus boy doesn't fix everything before we start getting rid of family. I mean, we still have the other kids in reserve."

Morgan would not hear of it. She'd kept the pendant grasped firmly in her fingers. "We have the right boy, Ryan. Marcus was just the messenger who led us to the chosen one. Besides, that woman had her chance. Make sure you finish her and those brats tonight before the ritual. No witnesses can be left."

Ryan had sighed heavily in the walkie-talkie. "If the boy shows any signs of Turning to be in The Pack, he's one of us. If not... the ritual will be done."

"Fair enough," Morgan had conceded. "But you know, and I know, he is not Pack material. His only use to us is his blood."

Ryan had never answered.

Now, Morgan basked in her glory. In a few hours, she would have her son back to her. She would soon leave and prepare for the ritual.

Dr. Chocker wilted against the cushions. He wondered if he counted as a witness or an accomplice. Either way, he knew he was doomed.

Inside the pool fence, Elliot sat back in a cushioned lounge chair. Tucker lay on his side in his own chair next to him, fighting to stay awake. Between them, a small metal table held the remains of a microwaved pizza dinner. Tucker's backpack had been left in the woods, and Elliot missed his cookies. Brie, though, had promised to bring them back dessert. She'd run back to the motel to get something she promised that Elliot would absolutely love.

Elliot relaxed as a cool breeze blew in from the forest. Clouds had covered the sinking sun, and the temperature dropped to the comfortable seventies. Feeling the day's weariness wash over him, he'd just started to drift off when he heard Brie returning.

"Oh, great, Elliot," Tucker said, propping himself on an elbow. "There goes my rest." His brow wrinkled. "She's carrying a bowl of soup or something."

"You can totally have it," Elliot said, his eyes closed. "I think I'm going to, like, sleep the next one hundred years."

"Take a sniff of this, Elliot," Brie called loudly. "You're going to love it!"

Rubbing the front of his chef's shirt, Tucker struggled to sit, curious. "What is it?" he asked.

"Something just for Elliot, not for you," Brie said rudely. She walked carefully from the walkway leading to the pool, holding the bowl in front of her with both hands. Kicking open the gate, she marched straight to Elliot.

The boy sniffed, and his nose wrinkled in disgust. "Ew!" he said, opening his eyes. "What is that?"

"Don't you like it?" Brie said. She lowered the bowl to his chest, right under his nose.

Elliot scooted up and away from it. His lips puckered as he gagged. "Like, what is that stuff?"

Brie stared down at him in disappointment. "It's blood from a pig. You're supposed to go crazy over it."

"Ew!" Elliot said, turning his face away. "That's gross!"

"You're the crazy one," Tucker said to Brie. "You really think we like pig's blood?"

"Not you, just Elliot," Brie said. "He's supposed to slobber all over it and slurp it down."

Elliot just looked at her, horrified. "More like I would barf it all up!"

Brie shook her head sadly. "I guess my mom is right. You'll never be a wolf-man."

Tucker stared at her in disbelief. "And that's supposed to be a bad thing?"

"For him, it is," Brie said sadly. "If he's not part of The Pack, then he only has one use." She stood up, taking her bowl of blood with her. "Sorry, Elliot," she muttered. Then she turned and ran back out the gate, breaking into a sprint when on the sidewalk to the motel. Red blood sloshed over the bowl, splattering the concrete in her wake.

"Okay, dude," Elliot said when she'd vanished behind the building. "Like, we need to seriously escape."

Tucker nodded. "Yeah, but how?"

The boys still had no answer when, minutes later, lights from a vehicle lit them up from the forest. The pickup pulled beside the pool's fence, parking. Ryan Raycroft hopped out of the cab. Kenton slowly removed his bulk from the other side, shaking the truck when he exited.

"Hey, boys!" Ryan yelled. "You should be in your rooms getting some rest."

Elliot quickly got to his feet and trotted over to the gate. "Did you find my mom?" he called.

"Almost, buddy," Ryan said. "By morning time, we should have her… found."

Kenton belched loudly and headed past Ryan to the motel. As he did so, Ryan Raycroft nudged the big man's shoulder. He turned back to the truck's cab, leaning in the driver's window to grab something.

Tucker moved to stand behind Elliot. He put an arm on his friend's shoulder. "Sorry about your mom," he mumbled. "Hey, maybe we can steal the truck."

"Yeah, but, like, the only thing I know how to drive is in video games."

"Me too," Tucker said miserably. "Come on, best friend again. Let's go get our rest."

He wanted to cheer Elliot up, but could only keep his arm over his friend's shoulder as they left the pool.

As they passed by the office, Helga called to them that there were toothbrushes and toothpaste in the bathroom. "Help yourself, but do not make a mess!" she hollered.

Tucker nudged Elliot. "Let's use your bathroom. I'm sort of afraid Brie will be in mine."

Elliot managed a smile. "It'll be like our first sleepover, right?"

"Yo, not that bad!" Tucker grimaced.

He remembered dropping his brush in the toilet during their first sleepover. It had then turned into Elliot trying to flush it down while Tucker had tried using his hand to pull it out. Eventually, it took a plumber to get it sorted.

"The last one there gets hair on his toothbrush!" Tucker suddenly said, pulling Elliot's shoulder back.

"Hey, no fair! Cheater!" Elliot aimed a kick at the back of Tucker's pants.

For a moment, the two boys were best friends again, and their worries were put to the side.

Tucker managed to get inside the bathroom first by hip-checking Elliot at the last moment, sending the smaller boy tumbling onto the floor.

"Oops, did I do that?" Tucker yelled. "Too small, little boy!"

"Jerk-face!" Elliot yelled.

Tucker laughed as he pulled open the drawer under the sink. He looked at a pile of wrapped brushes and small tubes of paste. "What color do you want, Elliot? They're all green." He grabbed a brush and a tube.

"Let me pick it out," Elliot said, running to his side. "I want to make sure mine hasn't been used by a wolf thing."

"They're all the same, Elliot." Tucker opened his brush and squeezed toothpaste on it. "Yo, remember how we used to do the bodybuilding poses? You should see me now. I'm getting ripped."

"Only when you blow a stinker," Elliot said, opening his brush.

Tucker nudged him with his hip. "Take a load of this!"

Squatting, he bit down on his brush and flexed his arms. Foam leaked from his mouth.

"I'm the great wolf-man Tucker," he roared, nearly choking on his brush.

Elliot grinned and flexed a bicep. "I, like, totally have bigger biceps than you!"

The friends started making goofy faces and flexing in the mirror. Tucker pulled up his shirt, showing off his stomach, while Elliot kissed his right bicep.

And that was how Brie found them.

"What are you two doing?" the girl asked. She stood in the bathroom doorway with her mouth open. Her eyes looked teary.

Frozen and mid-pose, the boys looked at each other.

"Um…" Elliot said. "Brushing our teeth?"

Brie just shook her head. "I came to say good night and goodbye." Then she ran off. Before she left, the boys did see tears on her cheeks.

"What was that all about?" Tucker asked, pulling his shirt down and spitting in the sink.

"I don't think our manly bodies, like, impressed her too much," Elliot said, wiping toothpaste from his mouth.

Just then, Helga bellowed from the front of the motel. "You boy!" Brie had left the room door open so she was clearly heard. "Your mom's on the phone! Come in here and talk to her!"

Elliot's heart jumped in his chest. "My mom called here?" he asked incredulously. He dropped his brush in the sink and grinned in the mirror.

Tucker threw his brush in right after.

The boys exchanged happy looks.

"What are you waiting for?" Tucker cried. "Let's go!"

The boys were barefoot but still sprinted across the room onto the paved sidewalk without slowing. They turned to see Helga standing in front of the office with her arms folded in front of her.

Seeing Elliot, her mouth twisted in a cruel smile. "Sorry, but not your mom. It's for your friend."

Elliot came to a sudden stop.

Tucker bumped into his back and moved around him. "My mom?" he asked, stunned. "How did she even get this number?" Earlier, he'd tried the phone in Elliot's room, but there had been no tone.

"She's been calling around the island looking for you," Helga snapped. "Now hurry up in there. I need the phone."

Elliot followed Tucker, but the woman put a hand on his chest when he tried to enter the office.

"Sorry, boy," she said. "It's a personal call from *his* mom. Why don't you wait in your room." It wasn't a question. It was an order.

"Don't worry, Elliot," Tucker said. "I'll get my mom to pick us both up. I'll be in there in, like, two minutes."

The friends exchanged glances again. Nodding, Elliot finally turned and walked to his room with his head bowed. He moved a strand of hair from his eye, pushing it over his nose. He tugged it hard in frustration. Would Tucker's mom *want* to pick him up? Or would she blame him for getting Tucker into this mess? Then a terrible feeling creeped into his gut. Did Tucker's mom even call, or was this a plot to separate the boys?

Opening the door to his room, he tried to leave it cracked open and peek out. Then he saw Ryan watching him. Elliot quickly closed the door and ran to the bed. Leaping onto the mattress, he bounced on his belly and lay still. Then he waited.

Tucker never spoke to his mom. As soon as he walked into the office, he knew it was a trap. An old landline phone sat on the front desk off of its cradle. In front of the desk, Kenton stood holding a paper cup with blue liquid.

"Before you take the phone, drink this," Helga said, nodding at the cup. "It's medicine for your head."

"Actually, my head feels fine," Tucker said nervously. "I mean, it's like nobody ever hit it."

Kenton curled his lip at him. He held out the cup. "Drink. Now."

"No, thanks, I—" Tucker tried to back away, but Helga slammed the door. She then grabbed the back of his curls and pushed him toward Kenton.

"You will drink it, or I will shove it through your belly button," she hissed.

"Get off me!" Tucker yelled.

Kenton had him then. The beefy man moved with sudden speed, grabbing the front of the boy's shirt with one hand, twisting it tightly against Tucker's throat, prying up his chin. He then shoved the cup at his mouth, pouring the drink in.

With Helga holding onto his hair in the back, Tucker had little chance. Every time he opened his mouth to scream, blue liquid poured in. Sickly sweet and chalky, enough made it down his throat to cause him to feel dizzy. Then, the cup was empty.

Kenton dropped it to the floor, crushing it with his boot. He then flung Tucker against the front desk. Hitting hard, the boy fell to his backside and huddled in a heap of tears.

Helga glared at him as she went to the phone, picking it up. "Morgan? It's done. We'll prepare the sacrifice. The boy will be ready when you get here. Tell The Pack to gather at the table at the witching hour."

Tucker tried to sit up, but his body slumped to the side. Exhaustion crashed over his body, and he felt sleep taking over. He'd been drugged… was he to be the sacrifice? What would happen to Elliot? Tucker fought to stay awake, but it felt like his mind had fallen into a deep hole.

As he drifted away, a hard foot planted in his stomach and rolled him to his back.

"Get him on the sling, and we'll lower him down," he heard Helga say from high above him. "Wrap him tightly so he doesn't fall out."

"The Pack will feast on this one later," muttered Kenton. "Useless boy."

No! Tucker tried to cry out and kick. If he was useless, then Elliot…

The urge to sleep won. He only managed a slight murmur as he went under.

He never felt the hands grab his feet and start dragging his body across the floor to the corner of the office. A pool sling lay there, attached to two coiled-up ropes.

Tucker's journey down had only begun.

Elliot didn't move when the door opened behind him. He knew it wasn't Tucker. He'd dozed off for a while, and now darkness covered the windows. The room's lights had been switched on that afternoon, and now, the room was bathed in harsh light.

"You awake, buddy?" Ryan asked, stepping into the room. The door shut behind him.

"Go away," Elliot said.

"Come on, bud, I'm just checking on you."

Elliot rolled from his stomach and moved to sit on the edge of the bed. "Where's Tucker?" he demanded. "Where's my friend?"

Ryan lifted his cap and ran a hand through his thin hair. "Well, he should be off the island right now. His mom came and picked him up while you were sleeping."

Elliot glared at him. "You're lying! Tucker would've stopped here and said goodbye."

"Sorry, buddy." Ryan gave him a sympathetic look. "Your friend abandoned you."

"No, he didn't. That's what I did to him before. He'll never do it to me. Where is he?"

Ryan jammed his cap back on and ran a hand over his mouth, losing patience. "Look, buddy. I've been straight with you. I don't know how to say it, but you're part of this family. You're going to serve The Pack."

Elliot crossed his arms over his chest and just glared.

"I'm serious, kid." Ryan took deep breaths. "Look, I tried to reason with your mom, but she's more stubborn than a booger in molasses."

"You talked with my mom?"

"I offered to trade you for one of her students. She said no. I'm sorry."

Elliot's defense crumbled. That sounded just like her. Challenges and changes… his mom would never back down from a challenge and change from her way of thinking. She always did what was right in the moment. She wouldn't give up a student… but did that mean she would give him up?

Ryan reached into his camouflage jacket and pulled out a bundled leather belt and a folded cloth. He dropped his gaze. "This is for you. It's the uniform of The Pack. It makes you part of it. Put it on."

Elliot lifted his eyebrows in disbelief. "I don't think so," he said.

"You can put it on now, or somebody else can later. It's your choice, kid."

Behind Ryan, the door opened, and Kenton ducked his head in. He carried a paper cup with blue liquid. Helga followed and folded her arms in front of her, blocking the doorway.

"I have your medicine here, kid," the big man said, grinning. "Go get changed and drink it down."

"You know how to put on a breechcloth?" Ryan asked him, eyeing him with genuine sympathy. "It's what the Indians used to wear, you know. Each tribe had their own unique way. The Pack is like a tribe. You're part of it... it's actually a great honor for you."

Elliot slowly slid to stand from the bed. His knees trembled. His mouth went terribly dry. "Do I have to?"

Ryan Raycroft nodded. "The breechcloth is the uniform you wear when you officially step out of the world to become part of The Pack. You know, you're the youngest and first full human to be given such an honor." He avoided looking into the boy's eyes as he said this. "Do you need any help?"

Elliot shook his head slightly. "I can figure it out."

"I knew you were a smart boy." Ryan tossed the belt and cloth onto the bed. "Take these and go in the bathroom. Come out in five minutes. If you don't... Kenton is coming in to help."

The big man glared. "You better be out," he said.

Elliot nodded miserably. Taking the belt and cloth, he slowly walked to the bathroom. It felt like going to his funeral.

Shutting the door in the bathroom, he immediately dropped the belt and cloth and rushed to the toilet. His dirty clothes from before had been collected to be washed. He didn't bother locking the door. He knew they had a key.

Elliot had to escape fast. Stepping to the top of the toilet, he reached toward the small window. He was several feet short.

And it looked to be thick glass anyway. Desperate, he hopped down. Seeing the toilet paper, he grabbed the roll and rushed to the sink. Switching on the water, he soaked the paper good.

"Three minutes!" Ryan barked.

"Hold on!" Elliot yelled. "I needed the bathroom!"

He grabbed wet clumps of toilet paper and rushed into the shower. Working furiously, he slapped the soaked paper against the tile wall where it stuck. He then shaped it quickly.

"I'll give you two more minutes!" Ryan yelled. He sounded right outside the door.

Elliot felt sweat pour down his back. Nearly finished with his work, he pulled off his bathing suit and dashed from the shower. Snatching up the belt and cloth, he returned to the shower and closed the curtain. Then, he had to figure out the ways of a breechcloth.

The bathroom door crashed open a minute later.

"Where are you, you stinking brat?" Kenton roared, his bulk filling the doorway. His voice turned panicked. "I don't see him, Ryan." Stepping in, his eyes frantically swept the empty bathroom.

"Where could that little monster have gone?" Ryan said, moving to the doorway.

"I'm right here!" Elliot poked his head out of the shower curtain sheepishly. "I just needed to, like, adjust the cloth." He nervously stepped out and shut the curtain behind him. The cloth hung just above his knees and proved scratchy.

Ryan relaxed and threw Elliot a shirt. It was his skeleton shirt from before, cleaned and folded. "Wear this for now," he told him. "It'll be cool tonight."

Elliot took the shirt and quickly tugged it on, pulling it down over the scratchy breechcloth.

"Now for your medicine," Kenton said, turning on him. "Want to drink it like a man? Or fight back like a fool."

Elliot drank it like a scared little boy. When he'd finished the cup, he was told to sit on the bed while Helga took his hair and put it back in a warrior's knot.

"Tonight," she told him softly, "you will be a warrior for The Pack. Your name will go down in history. You will vanquish the curse. You will save The Pack. I thank you for this…"

Her words droned on, and Elliot's mind drooped as his head tilted forward. His eyes slid shut.

Finally, he collapsed into Helga's arms, and the woman laid him back on the bed.

"It is nearly finished," Ryan said, almost in disbelief. "Kenton, call Morgan and tell her the boy is prepared. His blood be upon us, and may it save our children!"

Kenton nodded and hurried out the door.

"Are you sure this is the best idea?" Helga asked, staring down at the sleeping boy. She brushed a stray hair from his face. "There is no turning back once Morgan has him."

"It's his mother's fault," Ryan said gruffly. He moistened his lips. "She had her choice."

"And we have our choice," Helga said. She sighed. "Very well. Go take care of that teacher woman. I'll wait with the boy. Be sure to thank her for her son."

Chapter 37

Skylar and Bernard settled by the stump in the hut to make their plans. Skylar had to take deep breaths to remind herself she was not dreaming. She'd been asleep for over an hour, and the sun had started to set. It was difficult to see, with no artificial lighting in the hut and clouds rolling in. For Skylar, this was a good thing.

She decided it was tough enough trying to focus on saving your family with a giant wolf-man sitting across from her, especially when he had rotten meat breath.

Despite the clutter of books, the hut was surprisingly well kept. The dirt floor was swept, and she noticed a broom leaning in the corner. Next to it was a cardboard box full of canned dog food and water bottles. Bernard brought her some water but never offered her food. She didn't ask for any.

Bernard noticed her glancing at the box. Instead of being embarrassed, he lifted his head proudly. "My brother and I don't slaughter the farm animals they bring us. We prefer to eat from a can rather than kill those miserable creatures."

It was Skylar who ducked her head in shame. "I-I saw the animals on the farm… I'm, I'm glad you don't hurt them."

Bernard shrugged his massive shoulders. "The others take care of that," he said gravely. "We just make sure we don't drink any blood they spill." He gave a toothy grin. "Besides, the food is not that bad. Want to try some?"

He panted out a laugh when he saw her face. "I'm only kidding. Let's decide what we'll do to keep your family from becoming the next meal."

Instantly sobered, Skylar nodded.

Before their plans got very far, Bernard's snout jerked up. His tongue licked his nose. "Somebody is coming… It sounds like Martin." His lips curled back, baring sharp teeth. "Something is wrong," he muttered. In a flash, he was on his feet.

Skylar heard nothing, but after a few moments, several soft yips came from the woods. She got to her feet and hesitantly followed as Bernard exited the hut. She hesitated just inside the doorway.

A young wolf-man dashed into view from the trees. He was thinner than Bernard and smaller, only a few inches taller than her. Otherwise, he had the same coloring and similar facial features, only softer.

"Bernard," the new arrival said, sounding panicked. "They have them. They took Elliot and his friend!"

Skylar felt her knees buckle. "No," she whispered.

"What else, Martin?" Bernard growled. "I smell fear on you. Are you being chased?"

Shaking his head, Martin looked behind him as if frightened. "I saw Burton. The Pack found the others. He said Ryan Raycroft is trying to trade Elliot to sacrifice one of the kids!"

Immediately, plans changed. Skylar made a fist.

"Get inside," Bernard said to Martin.

"We have to get Elliot!" Skylar said, stepping in the doorway to meet them. She was suddenly face-to-face with Martin.

Seeing her, the young wolf-man drew up short. His ears flattened, and his mouth opened in surprise.

"It's okay," Bernard said. "Skylar, this is Martin, my brother."

"I know you," Martin muttered, averting his eyes.

"Forget about introductions," Skylar said. She gripped a strand of her hair tightly with her fingers. "What are we going to do? *My* brother is in danger!"

Bernard opened his mouth but made no words.

"Her mom is stuck in the stone ruins by the stream with the kids," Martin told him. "Mr. Raycroft has men watching it. Some of The Pack are there, too, but something else is going on. Something big is being planned tonight. There's supposed to be a gathering of The Pack later."

"Where did they take Elliot?" Bernard asked.

Martin only shook his head miserably. He crouched to all fours inside the hut and looked ashamed. "Mr. Raycroft had a lot of men with him. They would've seen me, so I hid in the trees. I saw them drive off in a pickup... I just know they have Elliot and the other boy."

Skylar's shoulders sagged. "Tucker," she said. "Elliot and Tucker are captured."

Bernard looked down at her. "I... I think we wait," he said.

"What?" Skylar put her hands on top of her head. "Didn't you hear? Elliot is in trouble! And my mom—"

"Is going to be fine," Bernard told her gently. Over a foot taller than her, he had to duck to stand in the small hut. "From what I know, Morgan wants a boy alive. She's using your brother to try and trade for him."

"My mother would never do that," Skylar said. Her eyes brimmed with tears. "What's going to happen?"

"We'll wait for the gathering of The Pack," Bernard said. "Until then, we rest up. Once we know the plans, we can act. Trust me. They won't do anything until the meeting. The Pack must make decisions as one."

Skylar had no choice. She eventually settled back on the blanket and tried to keep her nerves in check. The brothers settled in the corner across from her by the door. They grabbed cans of dog food and water bottles and started a hasty meal. Somehow, she managed to fall asleep.

As darkness fell, Teddy's car drove into The Motel's parking lot and skidded to a stop in front of the office.

"Helga!" Teddy wailed as he carefully climbed from the passenger seat. "I need some fusia! Now!"

His right arm hung loosely out of its socket, and he sported a massive bruise on his forehead. He hobbled toward the office, gasping in pain with every step.

Paige exited the driver's seat and grinned. "I don't know, Teddy. I kind of like driving your car. Maybe you should stay that way for a while."

Teddy halted at the curb. He glared over at her with pain-filled eyes. "This is mostly your fault," he hissed. "Give me back my keys!"

"Go get healed first," Paige said. "I'll wait out here for you."

Helga stepped out of room number four and surveyed the teens with undisguised displeasure. Her daughters were down for the night in one of the apartments. She wanted to spend the last hour with the sleeping boy before he went on his journey to change the island forever. The last thing she needed now was dealing with two whiny teenagers. "I'm over here. What happened to you, Teddy? Get in a catfight?"

"It was Bernard," Teddy said sullenly. "He went psycho and attacked me for no reason."

Paige leaned against the car door and smirked with her hands in her hip pockets. "Teddy tried to do his first kill… Bernard got a little jealous."

Teddy ducked his head in shame. "Shut up, Paige. I wasn't going to hurt her."

"No matter," Helga said. She sighed. "Lucky for you, I made fusia earlier today. Room five is open. Go and lie on the bed."

Paige's eyes narrowed. "What about room four?" she asked. "What were you doing in there?"

"There's a guest in there right now," Helga said evenly.

"Who?" Paige asked. "There're no other cars here."

"It's not your business," Helga told her. "It's just one of the kids who escaped the farm. Morgan will be collecting him shortly."

Paige stood from the car. "Is his name Tucker? If so, he's a gift from me to The Pack. I get the credit. I'm the one who brought him here."

Helga surveyed Paige with distaste. "That boy is in the meat room. I'll be sure to let The Pack know of your generosity when he's eaten. Don't worry, Paige. You're well on your way to being elevated to Pack Maiden. Now go help Teddy to the bed while I get the fusia." She winced as she watched Teddy's painful movement. "Teddy, you'll need bed rest tonight. Once settled, let Paige take your car to her aunt's place. She can call your parents and let them know you're staying here tonight."

Fusia worked like magic, but it took more time with serious injuries. It was why the island never needed doctors and hospitals to care for The Pack. She didn't like wasting it on teen squabbles, but that was what happened when the teens were two hundred-pound-plus brutes with claws and teeth.

Paige smiled. "Don't worry, Teddy. I'll leave some gas for you."

"J-Just shut up," Teddy said miserably. "You sure… you didn't see where Sky went?"

"Hopefully she got eaten by Bernard or somebody else," Paige said sweetly. "Let's go."

She grabbed his injured shoulder, causing him to cry out in pain.

"Oh, sorry," Paige said, not meaning it.

Skylar woke to a long howl echoing over the forest, answered by another and then another.

Sitting up, she looked around, panicked. It was nearly pitch-black in the hut as night had fallen. She saw the brother wolf-men moving like shadows. They stood outside the hut and threw back their heads. Long, mournful cries sailed from their throats, joining the chorus of howls. Other howls continued to join until the wails covered the entire forest. Finally, they faded into silence.

"Oh, my… goodness," Skylar said, hushed. "What was that?"

"The call of The Pack to gather," Bernard said from the doorway. He had to bend at the waist to fit his massive head through. "Skyler, Martin and I must go. We'll find out the plan and return if we can."

Skylar got up from her blanket and walked across the darkened hut to Bernard. A fierce wind ripped the branches outside, and thunder rumbled in the distance.

"Bernard," Skylar said. "Don't worry about me. Just bring back my brother. Please."

Bernard grunted. "I will do everything and anything to protect him, Skylar. And your mom. Wait here and be ready for anything. Help yourself to the water. If you're hungry, there's canned—" he caught himself and grinned. "We'll be back soon."

Skylar nodded and watched Bernard slip out the door as silent as a shadow. Both wolf-men vanished in the night. Skylar sat cross-legged in the doorway and looked up at the black sky. Lightning flashed in the distance.

Back in Grantham, Mr. Ashley had just finished a productive day. In the morning, he'd applied for two jobs and then had a terrific interview with a financial company in Whitney for a project manager position. He felt good for the first time in weeks. After a hard workout with rock music, he showered and changed into comfy sweatpants and a T-shirt. It was a great time to relax.

He lay on his couch, waiting for his family to return to tell them the good news. With the television turned to a sports show, he started scrolling through his phone, looking for a good dinner recipe. Eventually, he lay back and relaxed his eyes...

The doorbell rang, snapping him awake. Looking at his phone in his lap, he saw it was after four.

Mr. Ashley frowned. "Sky?" he called. "El? Anybody back yet?"

Moving to a sitting position, he checked his phone and found no messages or texts about his wife running late. He imagined it must've been a busy day with the field trip, and she was now stuck at work. Poor Elliot would be miserable.

Mr. Ashley knew he would have to make something good for dinner. He guessed Skylar was off with her friends. One day, he would meet this guy friend of hers.

Yawning, he walked to the front door and stifled a groan. Through the window by the door, he saw Mr. and Mrs. Goodall standing on the stoop.

At least both of them wore fake smiles plastered on their tight faces.

Cracking the door open, he poked his head out. "What can I do for you?" he asked in a neutral tone.

Mrs. Goodall laughed loudly and held up a plate of cookies. "I made you cookies, my husband's favorite!"

Her husband, a short, potbellied man with an iron-gray crewcut, poured lemonade from a thermos into a paper cup. "Howdy, neighbor," Mr. Goodall said, smiling. "We just thought we should, you know, apologize for getting off on the wrong foot! I'm Jim, by the way."

Mr. Ashley lifted his eyebrows and stared. The Goodalls looked desperate to be friendly. "Ah, well," he said, "this is kind of a bad time. My wife is coming any minute, and I'm getting stuff ready—"

"Just try a cookie and wash it down with cool lemonade," Mr. Goodall said, smiling. "Then we'll be on our way."

"It's Be-Kind-to-Your-Neighbors Week at our church," Mrs. Goodall said. "So, you know, you're doing us a huge favor!"

"Yep," her husband added, presenting the filled cup. "It's all good from the Goodalls!"

Mr. Ashley fought hard not to roll his eyes. He dutifully took a cookie and the offered cup of lemonade. "Uh, thanks."

"Eat up!" Mr. Goodall encouraged. "We want to see how you like it."

"It's a new recipe," Mrs. Goodall said nervously.

Taking a bite, Mr. Ashley eyed his neighbors suspiciously. "A new recipe of your husband's favorite cookie?" he asked through the mouthful of dry cookie. It tasted chalky.

Flustered, Mrs. Goodall drew back the plate of cookies. "Oh, er, well, you know, he eats too many cookies, so I made these ones extra healthy. Good, right?"

Shrugging, Mr. Ashley downed the tepid lemonade in one gulp. He just wanted his neighbors gone. He would then call his wife to find out when she planned on being home with Elliot. "Thank you," he said. "But I need to get going. Goodbye."

He returned Mr. Goodall the empty cup and absently tossed the unfinished cookie into the grass. Mr. Goodall, he decided, had terrible taste. The cookie tasted like sweetened cardboard mixed with chalk.

Not waiting for a reply, he closed the door on the Goodalls and started for the kitchen. He had barely reached the couch when he thought a short rest would help him...

"Oooh... what was in that lemonade?" he muttered. Feeling dizzy and suddenly tired, he took a seat to clear his head...

At the end of the driveway, Mrs. Goodall took out her cell phone and texted Morgan Raycroft. She let her know Mr. Ashley would not be a bother that night. She had a cousin from Blue Island... a member of The Pack.

Chapter 38

The Pack gathering did not go as planned. Instead of uniting as one to support the sacrifice, there had been a split. Many did not believe the ritual was possible. Some members did not even want to change back into humans. Others wanted to kill and eat the outsiders without any ritual...

A couple, like Bernard, spoke against harming any child. He was instantly shouted down. He slipped to the back as many wolf-men eyed him with hatred. Word of him defending Elliot in the woods had reached their ears.

Razor, brother to Morgan, was the wolf-man who'd separated the boys and tried taking him down before Bernard had dropped in. He'd spent much of the afternoon licking his wounds and planning revenge. Seeing Bernard, he ran a black tongue over his sharp teeth and glared. Now healed, he would love a rematch.

Morgan solved the issue by sending the bloodthirsty members to her brother Ryan and announcing the ritual would be delayed. Those who did not want to kill the outsiders returned to their dens. She kept her family at her side and told them her plans. Her husband Banor and brother Razor listened attentively. Her son ducked his head but also had his ears perked.

They would secretly go ahead with the ritual and show the others it was possible. Then the rest of The Pack would want in. By that time, the Ashley woman and her wearisome students would be dead, and her boy sacrificed. Morgan would have her son restored. It was a trade she had no qualms making.

She meant for Banor and Razor to remain with her, but the two had unfinished business. Banor wanted to meet Mrs. Ashley again and then go after Marcus. Razor hoped to find Bernard. He had noticed the large wolf-man and his younger brother slipping away…

Morgan watched as the two wolf-men left the clearing by the dens to race to the stone hut. Kenton was waiting for her at the road with his truck. She couldn't wait for the full family reunion with her great-nephew.

Burton remained with his mother, too afraid to speak his mind. He wanted no part of the ritual… but at the same time… he desperately wanted to be human again.

Deep in the stone ruins, Mrs. Ashley sat in the dark corner above the root cellar with her head slumped to her chest. She'd been in that position since shortly after Ryan Raycroft left, probably to see her son… telling him the news that she would not trade her student for his safety.

Her mind was as dark as the night outside. When the thunder started to rumble, she thought it was the anguish deep in her soul.

Outside the ruins, her three students gathered around a small fire. Now that their position was known, they didn't care about hiding. Down below, near the stream, Stan and Moe had built a similar fire. They could be seen sitting behind it, roasting hot dogs.

The boys had no food left and held very little hope. When the howls had unleashed into the night sky several minutes before, they thought they were being attacked. Then the howls faded into the distance and went away. They could be back at any time.

Gary had built the fire soon after, ensuring it was several feet from the ruins. He'd made a hole in the dirt and piled small, dry wood scraps before lighting it with the borrowed lighter. Mrs. Ashley had handed it over without comment when he asked her for it. When he returned it, Gary had found her mumbling in a restless sleep. He'd laid the lighter on her knee before meekly returning to the fire.

Once the small fire started, Bobby added some of the leftover wood gathered earlier for the fort. Soon, bright flames were crackling against the night. Strong gusts blew from the north, but the trees protected the flames from going out as they danced wildly. It was a big accomplishment for the boys, but it rang hollow.

"This is the worst night ever," Bobby said glumly, as he sat back down from throwing another log on the fire. He avoided looking at Marcus.

Marcus sat on the ground, staring into the flames. He had his knees up and face hidden behind them. Gary stood between them, watching Stan and Moe down below them.

"What should we do?" Gary asked, keeping his eyes on the other fire. "I mean, we should do something."

"If you're going to say it, say it," Marcus said bitterly. "You want to turn me in for her son? Is that it?"

"No!" Bobby said quickly. "You know Mrs. A would never do that!"

"Yeah," Gary said. "Remember, she's your 'loco parent,' right?"

Marcus ducked his face into his knees, hugging his shins tightly. "Man, my own mom don't even care about me as much as her," he admitted.

"Yeah, sorry," Gary muttered. He wiped his hands on the front of his pants and looked down at Marcus. "Mrs. Ashley is the best teacher I ever had."

"That's why we need to do something!" Bobby said.

"Do what?" Marcus said, nearly shouting. He kept his eyes wide. Every time he closed them, he saw the poor old lady being stabbed in the back by the monster, the same one that had chased them earlier. "It's already too late, man. I messed up! I shouldn't have gone to that barn. I shouldn't even have gone on the field trip! Maybe I shouldn't even be born!"

"Hey, it's okay," Gary said, surprisingly gently. He squatted to be level with Marcus. "Look, I know I can be a jerk, especially to you."

"Yeah, and to Mrs. Ashley," Bobby added.

Gary nodded. "Yeah, and to her, too. But I do know that none of this is your fault. Marcus, you didn't choose to be hunted by these monster guys. That was them. It's like with bullies, man. The victim doesn't choose to be picked on. It's the bully who makes the choice."

"Gary is right," Bobby said. "Those guys down there, they're the jerks doing this." He glumly tossed a stick into the flames, watching it burst into flames. "Not you and not us. We just have to do something about it."

"It'll be a challenge," Gary said.

Marcus wiped tears from his eyes. "Yeah, yeah. Challenges turn to changes, right?"

"Right," Gary said. He exhaled in frustration. "We need to find a way to get Elliot back. I just don't know how."

Just then, something moved in the brush behind the stone structure. A twig snapped, and bushes rustled.

The boys froze.

A loud snuffling sound came from the darkness down the hill in front of the structure. The light from the fire didn't reach far, and the boys could only imagine what was out there.

Gary slowly stood from his crouch. "Um, I would say that was just an animal, but those wolf monsters ate them all, which means…"

"Uh, guys?" Bobby said, his voice rising. "Remember those two dudes down at the stream? They're kind of gone."

"Get to the spears," Gary said, kicking dirt on the fire. "Inside, hurry!"

The three boys were soon on their feet and turning for the hut. As they did so, the attack began.

"Surprise, kids!" Stan roared, shining a bright flashlight from only a few yards below.

"Change of plans," Moe said from beside him. "We're here not just for Marcus, but all of you!"

A dark shape leaped from the brush behind the ruin. Running across the roof, it jumped down to face the three boys. A giant wolf-man with thick brown fur and a full wolf head rose before them, baring claws and sharp teeth.

Another beast charged up the hill and easily hurtled the brush pile around the tree stump. He landed on all fours and slowly stood behind the boys.

"Remember me?" he roared. Fully recovered from the pepper spray, Banor blocked their retreat. The boys were caught between two wolf-men.

Marcus tried to swallow but nearly choked on his spit. He would never forget the monster who'd murdered the old lady. Backing away slowly, he bumped into Bobby's back. The taller boy had his eyes fearfully locked on the first beast. Gary stood next to them, his gaze going back and forth between the wolf-men. His eyes were huge, and his mouth was wide open. Unable to draw a breath, he looked ready to run and faint all at once.

Watching, Moe and Stan cackled with delight as they moved up the hill at a much slower pace. Carrying leather blackjacks, they slapped them against their thighs, acting more as cheerleaders than attackers.

"You guys know Banor, right?" Moe said.

"And now meet Razor!" said Stan. "He likes to 'meat' you!" He cackled at his pun.

"Get them, boys," Moe cried gleefully.

"Leave them alone!" Mrs. Ashley charged from the ruins, dodging around the brush pile blocking the doorway. She carried one of the handmade spears that suddenly looked flimsy compared to the gigantic wolf-man. She never slowed.

Razor, the brown furry beast, turned on the teacher. He easily knocked the spear aside, batting it with a huge paw.

Mrs. Ashley kept her grip on the spear but staggered. She fell to her knees.

Grinning, Razor raised his left paw with claws out. He went to swipe across her face.

Before he could, Bobby acted. Standing the nearest, the boy pulled a sock from his black shorts. His feet were bare in his sneakers as he charged the beast. Inside his sock was a hunk of sharp window glass. Unleashing a yell, he plunged the glass in the haunch of the wolf monster, just below the creature's breechcloth on the left.

The beast's face contorted in pain as he roared in surprise. His swipe missed Mrs. Ashley. His right arm swung toward the threat behind. Bobby tried to jump back, but had no chance. The beast's claws tore across the boy's right arm. Spinning away, Bobby fell to his knees, gasping in pain.

"No!" Mrs. Ashley screeched. Bringing her spear back up, she stabbed at the wolf-man. The tip merely bounced off the thick hide.

Razor turned back to her and grinned. "You look tasty," he said. He lowered his head and poised to pounce.

"Bring it!" Mrs. Ashley said with a snarl. She wanted to keep the monster focused on her and not Bobby. The boy appeared shocked as he clutched his bloody arm.

Meanwhile, Banor snorted as he moved toward Gary and Marcus. "You'll feel my wrath," he hissed.

Marcus didn't have to close his eyes to imagine the beast ripping claws into his back. He found his feet stuck in the ground, too scared to move.

"How about you feel more pepper spray," Gary said. Seeing Mrs. Ashley's brave charge had snapped him out of fear. Now, his mind turned cold and calculating. He stuck his hand in his pocket and pulled something out.

Banor immediately flinched, putting a paw to his nose. He remembered the terrible sting that had nearly ruined his eyes and smell.

This gave Gary and Marcus a chance.

"Get inside!" Gary yelled to Marcus. He moved in that direction, keeping an eye on Banor. "Hurry!"

Startled, Marcus broke from his trance.

Razor loomed over Mrs. Ashley and ignored the boys.

Marcus ran to Bobby, helping him up.

Bobby clutched his right shoulder with his wrapped hand. The claws had only nicked him but had ripped his remaining sleeve to ribbons. Blood streamed down his arm.

"Ohmygosh," he gasped. "I feel sick."

"Just get moving!" Marcus yelled at him, his eyes wild with fear.

Banor roared with fury and went to give chase.

Gary threw his object at his face. "Pepper bomb!" he cried, immediately turning to run.

Once again, Banor flinched. A stone bounced harmlessly off his arm.

At the same time, Razor unleashed his attack on the teacher with a thunderous roar.

As Razor leaped at her, Mrs. Ashley knelt and jammed the end of her stick into the ground, its point facing up. The wolf-man saw it late. He twisted his body in midair, landing on top of the spear so it grazed his torso and shoulder. At the same time, he tried to rip his claws down into Mrs. Ashley.

As soon as she felt the hot breath descend, Mrs. Ashley's survival instincts kicked in. She rolled to her right. Something sharp ripped across the left side of her back, right below her shoulder. It left a trail of hot pain. She ended up crouching near the brush barrier in front of the doorway.

Rising from her knees, she faced her tormentor. "Hurry, kids!" she yelled. "Get inside!"

Bobby staggered after Marcus. The two boys stared at Razor in front of them and then at Banor behind them. The door seemed awfully far away.

Gary never slowed his run.

"Not so fast!" Banor screamed. Infuriated by Gary's tricks, the beast jumped after the boy, landing near Mrs. Ashley. Gary veered away at the last instant. He put his hands to his face, expecting claws to rip down at any moment. Instead, a shape dropped from a tree above him.

"Cowabunga!" screamed a voice. The shape landed right on top of Banor's head, knocking the large wolf-man to his stomach.

"What's this?" Razor roared, turning from Mrs. Ashley.

"Not your best day, Razor," barked a deep voice from above. Another shape dropped from a tree, this one much bigger than the first. "You just got beat by a girl. Now you're going to be stomped by me."

The brown-fur wolf-man whirled to face the new threat. Seeing a larger black-fur wolf-man bearing down on him, he bent his ears back and hissed. "Bernard!" he cried. "I was hoping you would turn up, you traitor! You can't turn on The Pack!"

"I can when they attack women and children!" Bernard roared.

With ferocious howls, the wolf-men flew at each other, each going for the other's throat.

In front of the ruins, Banor shook his body angrily, knocking the smaller wolf-man free.

Rolling to his feet, this wolf-man was younger and much faster. "Get out of here!" he yelled at the human children staring at him. "I can only take this one for, like, seconds!"

"Come on, kids!" Mrs. Ashley yelled, getting to her feet. "Move inside!"

"Oh, no, you don't!" yelled Stan.

He and Moe charged the last distance up the hill. On either side of them, two pairs of wolf-men were locked in fierce combat. It was an all-out dog fight. By the dying fire, Banor stood over his smaller attacker, trying to use his strength and power to beat him down. Dodging his blows, the smaller wolf-man looked for opportunities to jump in to bite or scratch his larger opponent. Razor and his adversary were rolling on the ground to the right of the hut's entrance, biting and snapping. Blood and clumps of fur fell in their wake.

"Bring the rest of the wolf-men up here!" Moe yelled down the hill. "We have Pack traitors!"

Stan aimed his flashlight at Mrs. Ashley. "You stupid woman," he bellowed. "You caused this!"

Roars from below announced the impending arrival of more wolf-men.

Mrs. Ashley ignored the two men. She helped Marcus and Bobby move past her. "Get inside and to the back!"

Gary stared at the fighting wolf-men in terror. Then he saw Moe coming at him.

"Gary!" Mrs. Ashley yelled. "Move your butt!"

His teacher's words snapped him into action. Turning from Moe, he raced full speed past the fighting wolf-men. The stone ruins were a few feet in front of him. Not slowing, he leaped into the brush barrier he built to block the doorway.

Pretty stupid of me, he thought as sticks and thorns stabbed and scratched his arms and side.

Still, he managed to roll onto the other side and dive into the doorway. Marcus followed right after. Bobby paused in the doorway. His wrapped left palm leaned against the stone as his right arm dangled at his side, dripping blood.

"Mrs. A!" he cried. "What about you?"

"I'll be right behind you!" Mrs. Ashley yelled. "Get in the back!"

"No, you won't," Stan said with a leer. He brandished his blackjack and moved in where the teacher stood between the brush barrier and the entrance. "You're dog meat, lady."

"Leave her alone!" Bobby yelled. Dropping his hand from the stone, he reached into the doorway to grab another of his spears.

"Get back, Bobby!" Mrs. Ashley cried as the boy ran to stand by her side.

"Sorry, Mrs. A," he muttered. "But there're two of them this time."

"And more coming," Moe said, grinning as he joined Stan. Both with blackjacks, they moved in on the teacher and student.

Mrs. Ashley panted hard and crouched in a defensive position. Her back stung like it was on fire. "When I say run, you better run," she commanded.

"As long as you run too," Bobby said. He also crouched and pointed the spear out. He held it tucked under his left armpit while his torn right arm lay across his stomach.

Stan moved in first. Feinting toward Bobby, he went after the teacher. If she went down, he knew the boy would fall apart. Reaching his arm out, he grabbed at her hair while drawing his other arm back to strike with the blackjack.

Mrs. Ashley tried to dodge, but the pain in her back flared. Gasping, she fell to a knee. Stan's eyes lit up as he took a handful of her hair. Mrs. Ashley grunted in pain.

"No!" Bobby yelled, lunging forward with his spear. The glass tip ripped across Stan's shirt.

Surprised, the man jumped away, releasing the hair and dropping his weapon.

Moe stepped past his partner and grabbed the stick, yanking it from the injured boy's arm. Thrown off balance, Bobby staggered forward.

Dropping the makeshift spear at his feet, Moe swung the blackjack, landing a heavy blow to the back of the boy's neck.

Bobby crumpled to the ground without a sound. He lay sprawled on the dirt and didn't move.

"Bobby!" Mrs. Ashley yelled.

"Got you, you brat," Moe said, grinning.

Still on her knees, Mrs. Ashley snarled in fury. She grabbed the fallen spear. Yanking it up, she nailed Moe right between his legs. The man gasped in shock and dropped the blackjack. As he stood frozen in pain, Mrs. Ashley pushed the stick still between his legs. It swung like a gate right into Stan's knees.

Moe screamed shrilly and then fell to his side.

Stan jumped back and tripped over a root. He landed on his back in the tangle of brush built to hide the fallen log used as a guard post. His head cracked against the log, and he groaned in pain.

Shouts of men and the snarls of wolf-men surrounded the stone ruins. It sounded like it was being assaulted by an army.

The two pairs of wolf-men continued their brutal combat on either side of the ruins. Their growls mixed with grunts of pain as none of the beasts seemed to have an advantage. Banor's size was negated by his opponent's speed. Razor and his opponent were evenly matched.

Mrs. Ashley bent over Bobby and dragged his limp body up by his armpits. Tall and lean, he proved heavy and burdensome to lift. Snarling, she started dragging him back to the ruins.

Moe tried to kick to his feet at her but could only grimace in anguish. "We'll… tear you up!" he hissed.

Dark shadows were charging up.

Mrs. Ashley quickly took Bobby's non-bloody arm and turned him to face her. Squatting, she wrapped her other arm around his thighs, dumping him over her shoulder. Her back burned fiercely, and the weight nearly sent her crashing down. Maintaining her balance, she hurried to the stone entrance. She didn't look back.

"She's inside with the kids!" Stan yelled, sitting up and rubbing the back of his head. "Get her!"

"Rip her to shreds," Moe said, gasping. He lay on his back, grabbing the front of his pants. He looked ready to throw up.

Four members of The Pack raced into the clearing. Two leaped onto the roof and dropped into the hole. The other two jumped over the brush barrier, charging into the ruins. It was a death trap. There was no way out.

Inside the hut, Mrs. Ashley carried Bobby through the front room and into the back. Marcus and Gary waited for them by the middle window. They knew their teacher would come through. She always did.

"Bobby?" Marcus said, his voice tinged with fear.

"Just knocked out," Mrs. Ashley said with a gasp. "Get out of here and take him!"

Gary jumped up on the sill and hopped into the brush. Marcus quickly followed. Mrs. Ashley sat Bobby on the sill and dumped him into their arms. The boys dragged their friend into the bushes.

"It's on the floor just by your feet," Gary said as he vanished into the night.

The growls and roars in the next room let Mrs. Ashley know their defenses had been breached. A hard look went into her eyes.

"Never mess with my kids," she snarled. Reaching down, she picked up a glass bottle stuffed with a soaked sock. Taking the lighter from her pocket, she sparked a flame and held it to the sock. A red flame instantly ignited—it was dangerous moonshine. Without ceremony, she tossed the burning bottle into the next room. Then she dove out the window.

Behind her, the inside of the stone structure immediately erupted into a blistering explosion of liquid fire. A chain reaction of fiery blasts rocked the front room, sending a massive fireball blasting through the collapsed roof, arching several feet into the sky.

Gary had strategically placed moonshine bottles around the structure, pouring some out on the dry rot wood where the roof had collapsed. He'd then added his own water to the spot to mask the sharp smell of alcohol. His face had turned as red as his shirt when Mrs. Ashley had walked in to see his back as he'd finished peeing. His aim to create the most destruction possible seemed like a success. One bottle had been placed in the brush barricade before the door. As wolf-men rushed to help their comrades, the brush exploded in a fireball, shooting fire into their faces. Three went down, blinded and singed.

Moe screamed in terror as he rolled away as fire rained down on him.

At that moment, thunder crackled, and lightning lit up the sky.

Stan sat back with smoke coming from his hair and his eyebrows singed off. "My… my…" he stuttered.

"What happened?" Ryan Raycroft screamed, running up the hill. "What did you guys do?"

"It was that woman," Stan said, stunned.

"She blew herself up, and her kids," Moe said, sounding amazed. He beat at his charred pants. "She took out, like, half The Pack!"

Ryan Raycroft stared at the fiery ruins where the flames still licked out of the roof. An ugly look spread across his face. "She wouldn't do that. She had a plan. Where's your flashlight?"

Then, through the fire, a wolf-man jumped out. Screaming in terrible pain, he rolled on the ground. Flames burst from his fur. "Kill them!" he howled. "Kill them!"

Four other wolf-men were down, also writhing in pain. More screams of agony came from the burning hut.

Ryan Raycroft watched in horror as the great beasts were reduced to sniveling piles of burnt fur. The wolf-men rolling on the ground managed to extinguish the flames but were in no condition to rise anytime soon. Their fur was smoking, and they lay in the dirt, whimpering and moaning like sick puppies.

"It was one stupid lady and three brats!" he shouted. "How could you let this happen?"

Moe moaned and beat out the last spark on his camouflage pants. "It was Bernard and his brother. They attacked us…"

Ryan Raycroft gritted his teeth. "Where are those two moth—"

"Look!" cried a man coming up behind Ryan Raycroft. He held a powerful flashlight with the beam on the brush behind the house. "There they are!"

The light caught the wolf-men brothers. They were helping two kids flee with Mrs. Ashley right behind them. Bernard had another kid draped over his back.

"Tend to the wounded later!" Ryan Raycroft yelled. "We have fusia for them! Kill the traitors and get those kids and that lady!"

A platoon of men dressed in camouflage and carrying hunting rifles were coming up the hill. Paint blackened their faces, and they moved with a grim arrogance. Three more wolf-men were right behind them. The roar of ATVs filled the night as the reinforcements kept pouring in.

Chapter 39

Behind the burning ruins, Marcus flinched from the glaring light shining in his eyes. "What do we do?" he cried.

Mrs. Ashley fought the urge to scream and give up. When she joined the boys to crawl into the brush, they quickly found it impossible to move through in the dark. Trying to drag the unconscious Bobby through the brambles was not going to work. Then their mysterious wolf-men saviors called them over. They were just getting out when the light caught them. Now, they were sitting ducks.

"Martin," the larger wolf-man said. He held Bobby's limp form in his arms. "Lead them to the hut. Then, make for the road. I'll stay here and hold them off."

"There's no way, Bernie, and you know it," Martin said, helping Mrs. Ashley from the brush. Exhausted from his battle with Banor, he looked ready to curl up and sleep. He'd only escaped his larger opponent in the confusion of the exploding ruins. "There's too many for you, and we'll be caught in no time." His voice dropped. "We'll only lead them to Skylar... if we make it that far."

Mrs. Ashley's head jerked up. "Did you say Skylar?" she asked, her voice trembling. "Is Skylar here?"

"She's safe," the large wolf-man said. "But we're not. My brother is right. I can take one or two, but the rest will go right by me."

"And they have rifles," Martin muttered.

Marcus bit back a sob. He leaned against Gary and looked up at his teacher. "I—I can just go down. They—They want me."

"They want all of us, Marcus," Mrs. Ashley said. "Besides, I'll never let you go alone."

"We have to surrender," Gary said. "It's the only way."

Mrs. Ashley put her hand on his shoulder. "Gary, I don't think they'll accept our surrender after what I did to that hut."

"They wouldn't have accepted it before the hut," the large wolf-man growled. He sighed. "I'm Bernard, by the way. It was nice knowing you."

"Give up and get back down here!" Ryan Raycroft shouted. "Make it easier for yourselves, or I'll make sure your s—"

The roar of a fast-approaching ATV engine drowned him out.

As a spatter of raindrops started to fall, bright lights lit up the night. An out-of-control ATV raced toward the hill. It rocketed over the stream, blasting through the remains of the campfire Stan and Moe had left.

"What is that idiot doing?" Ryan Raycroft asked, moving to the hill's edge to watch the fast-approaching lights.

The advancing men stopped as well. The man holding the flashlight also lowered it to look.

Then, a muffled explosion occurred, and thick, dark smoke poured out behind the ATV. Another explosion came on the left.

"He's throwing bombs, boss," Moe said. He'd gotten to his feet and limped to Ryan Raycroft's side. "Who is he?"

"I don't know," Stan said from the other side of Ryan Raycroft. "But he's coming this way!"

"Look out!" Ryan Raycroft shouted. "Take cover! He has grenades!"

The men scattered, ducking for cover. They were not military and had learned their tactics from the internet. After what they'd witnessed with the stone ruins, they were not taking chances. The wolf-men ran the farthest, some jumping into trees. In moments, the ATV roared through the clearing with the smoldering ruins. A helmeted rider tossed another bomb from a crate behind him.

Another muffled blast sounded, and more dark smoke poured out.

"They're smoke bombs!" Stan yelled. "Somebody just shoot that guy!"

It was too late. Thick smoke smothered the entire area, glowing red from the burning fire in the hut. The ATV roared past.

"Hold your fire!" Ryan Raycroft bellowed. He covered his nose. "We're going to shoot ourselves!"

"Who is that?" Gary asked in amazement as the ATV lights found them. Emerging from the thick smoke, the vehicle jerked to a sudden stop right before them.

The two wolf-men bared their claws. The larger one, Bernard, put the unconscious Bobby over his shoulder away from the ATV.

The rider just looked at them and shrugged. "I guess you're on our side, right?" Then he pulled off his helmet.

"Mr. Harris!" Gary said with a gasp.

The special education teacher grinned back. "You guys ready to go home now? I told you I'd bring help."

Mr. Harris had never fully run away. Sure, maybe he *intended* to at first, but he'd been in a full panic then.

After nearly a full mile of running blindly through the woods, he stumbled to a walk. Completely lost, he miserably leaned an arm against a tree to catch his breath. Then it sank in.

He pressed his head against his arm as warm tears ran down his cheeks. He'd abandoned his students and had deserted Mrs. Ashley. She was among the few teachers who never spoke badly about him behind his back. And he'd left her to face a monster. What type of man was he?

A muffled groan escaped his throat. How could he ever face Mr. Charles again? Once Mr. Charles learned about what had just happened, every bad thing he said about him would not only be accurate, but it wouldn't be enough. Mr. Harris had forsaken his job, responsibility, students, and his colleague… to save his own skin.

Slowly, Mr. Harris stood from the tree. He couldn't let Mr. Charles ever know about his cowardice. He had to do something.

It was too late to turn back now. He was lost in the woods and had no idea where to find Mrs. Ashley. Much worse, there was a likely possibility there was nothing left to find.

No, that was not possible. He'd heard the screams when running, but they'd been screams of fear. In his heart, he knew they'd gotten away. They had Mrs. Ashley. She would never let anything horrible happen to her students, unlike Mr. Harris.

Feeling shamed and despondent, he started wandering through the woods. After a time, good fortune smiled down on him. He stumbled onto a dirt road cutting through the forest with fresh tire tracks. Keeping off the road, ducking behind trees and brush, he followed the tracks until hearing voices.

Falling to his hands and knees, he crawled over a rise and looked down at three sparkling red ATVs parked on the side of the dirt road. Three men stood several yards from the four-wheeled vehicles, discussing the best way to form a perimeter around the area to keep the teacher woman and the kids from escaping.

Mr. Harris felt relief flood down his entire body. Mrs. Ashley and the kids were not only alive, but they were also still free. And he'd managed to break through the perimeter guard. If he turned and kept going, he would be away from the monsters and crazy people of Blue Island. But that would mean deserting Mrs. Ashley and his kids again. And it would mean having to face Mr. Charles knowing that.

He ended up waiting behind the tree and watching. After a while, the men spread out and walked into the forest, totally abandoning the ATVs.

That was how Mr. Harris came to possess a powerful Renegade ATV with a crate full of smoke grenades. It also had a walkie-talkie that broadcasted all communications between Ryan Raycroft, the base of his operations, and most of his men. Mr. Harris heard directions on how to find Mrs. Ashley and the kids and then the plan to attack her that night. He just had to reach the stream, follow it, and wait for the right moment… Then it was showtime.

Mrs. Ashley ran to her colleague and threw her arms around him.

She instantly winced. "Ouch, my back!"

"Are you okay?" Mr. Harris asked, starting to get up.

"Stay there," Mrs. Ashley said quickly. "We need to move."

Bernard nodded. "The smoke won't stop them for long."

Mr. Harris settled in the seat. He dumped the nearly empty crate from the back. "This thing isn't meant for more than one person, but I can probably hold a couple more."

"I'll carry the injured one," Bernard said. "My fur should help clot the blood."

Mrs. Ashley looked worriedly at Bobby slumped against the massive wolf-man's shoulder and nodded. "I-I'm grateful."

"You can ride on my back," Martin said to Gary. "Just don't pull my fur or grab my ears."

Gary, stunned, just nodded.

Mrs. Ashley ended up sitting behind Mr. Harris with Marcus squeezing between them.

Somehow, while riding an ATV at night with no helmet and being chased by wolf monsters, Marcus never felt safer. Holding tightly to Mr. Harris's shirt, he relaxed as Mrs. Ashley wrapped her arms around his shoulders.

"How did you even know how to drive one of these?" Mrs. Ashley asked as the ATV rolled off, following Bernard.

"During the summer!" Mr. Harris shouted. "I race them with my cousins in North Carolina."

"Well, don't race anymore. We don't want any accidents!"

"You got it!" The ATV kept a steady pace, following the wolf-men through the night.

Thunder rumbled overhead. Rain began to pour out over the river. Strangely, after a brief spatter of drops, the island stayed dry. A thick fog started rolling in. In the flash of lightning, it appeared blue.

Mr. Ashley's blaring phone called him back to consciousness. It was completely dark, and a storm lashed outside. Heavy rain pelted the windows, and thunder boomed.

Wiping sleep from his eyes, he fumbled for his phone next to him. He was lying on the couch. How did he get there? He saw the time was near midnight.

"Ah, hello?" he asked, answering. He was so tired he forgot to check the number.

"Doug!" said a frantic woman's voice. "This is Tucker's mom. Sorry to call you so late, but one of Tucker's friends told me the craziest story."

"Ah, yeah, ah, hi." Mr. Ashley sat up and swung his feet to the floor. Tucker's mom had been close with his wife but never really got along with him. When Elliot had the trouble with the cooking contest, he knew Mrs. Romero mostly blamed him. "What's going on?"

"Well, one of Tucker's homeschool friends said Tucker never returned from his field trip to Blue Island today." Her voice started to break. "I thought… I thought he'd been at his friend's house, but he's gone!"

Mr. Ashley was suddenly awake. "Hold on! Bl-Blue Island, you say?"

Tucker's mom breathed deeply into the phone. "I don't know what's going on, but his friend said Tucker stayed behind to look for Elliot, that Elliot got lost on the island." She laughed nervously. "I'm just calling to see what you know about it. Elliot is at home, right?"

"Uh, yeah, of course." Mr. Ashley squeezed his eyes shut and then opened them. "Hold on, I mean, I think he's home…"

He suddenly panicked. He'd fallen asleep before supper. Why didn't his wife wake him? Unlike Elliot, he was usually a light sleeper. He muttered a bad word about the Goodalls.

"Mrs. Romero? I'm going to check right now."

"I mean, he wasn't even at Blue Island today, right?"

Mr. Ashley stopped at the stairs. His hand started to shake. "As a matter of fact, he was," he said. "My wife took him on a school trip there… and my daughter volunteered…"

"Oh, no," Mrs. Romero groaned in the phone. "I think they might be in trouble." She sounded scared.

Mr. Ashley took the stairs two at a time. "Elliot! Skylar!" he yelled. Running down the hall, he found Skylar's room empty. "No, no, no…" He dashed to the next room.

Sweat beaded on his forehead as lightning flashed outside, lighting Elliot's room. His unmade bed blinked before him, just as it was from that morning.

"I called the police already," he heard Mrs. Romero say. "They think it's some homeschool prank. I don't know what to do!"

Mr. Ashley didn't bother checking for his wife. He knew if the kids weren't there, then she wouldn't be there either. He stumbled to Elliot's bed and collapsed to sit on the edge. "What exactly did the police say?" he asked.

"Well, they called the island, and there was a school trip there, but all the buses had left without incident. There were no other missing people reported. Tucker's friend said an entire bus had been lost. I don't think the police took me seriously. Doug, I'm really worried."

"I'm taking you seriously. Let's call the police again and have them double-check about the school buses returning. Then I'm going to Blue Island myself."

Amazingly, none of the wolf-men died. The ones in the ruins caught in the fiery explosions were severely burned and now had no fur but had managed to jump to the ground and hug the earth at the last second. Most of the blast went over them, and their thick hide and fur shielded them from fatal injuries. Still, they were in a lot of pain and needed emergency help.

To make matters worse, the smoke bombs had set off several small fires all over the hill, and flames from the ruins had spread to brush and nearby trees. A forest fire could flare up at any moment.

Standing amid the carnage, as the last of the smoke finally cleared, Ryan Raycroft stared up at the blackened sky and shouted in fury. "Rain! Where's that rain when you need it!"

Strong gusts of wind blew instead, fanning the flames. All thoughts of hunting down the traitorous Bernard and Martin and catching that horrid teacher woman and the children were put on hold. The men and healthy members of The Pack were too busy saving the island from a disastrous fire.

"It's Morgan, boss!" Moe said, coming up to the angry Raycroft brother. Missing his eyebrows and wearing holey, singed camouflage, he meekly handed over a walkie-talkie.

"Morgan!" Ryan Raycroft spat into the device. "Cancel the ritual! We have problems."

"So I've heard," his sister said, crackling from the speaker. "Fix them. The ritual commences."

"Morgan, I got like six fires here! I need every man and wolf to be here!"

"I have only Kenton and Burton with me," Morgan said calmly. "I'm already at The Motel for the child. We will deal with the fire once I return Burton to being fully human. Then I will bring the rest of The Pack to feast."

"I want to be there," Ryan Raycroft's tone grew cold. "I want to see the ritual," he said.

"Do you?" His sister's voice sounded surprised. "I didn't think you had the guts to, you know, gut your own blood, especially Minnie's grandson."

Ryan Raycroft felt a growl escaping from deep in his throat. "After tonight, I do. That Ashley woman needs to see her child dead. I wish she could be there too."

"This is not a revenge game," Morgan said sharply. "This is fixing my son."

"I thought it was for The Pack."

Morgan's voice exploded from the walkie-talkie. "My son is The Pack!" Her voice calmed. "If it works on him, then the others can partake. Send me Banor and Razor. They can be witnesses and partake in the process as well. Then the others will know the ritual is true."

Ryan Raycroft snorted. "Just so you know, both are charred around the edges, but I'll send them. I wish you happy cutting."

"For The Pack."

"For The Pack," her brother returned.

He lowered the walkie-talkie and groaned as he saw thick smoke roll in… only it wasn't smoke. It was fog.

Mr. Ashley slammed on the brakes of the minivan and stared in disgust. Rain poured down, and the wipers fought to keep up. It was a wasted effort. He was stuck.

"This can't be happening," he muttered.

A large flashing sign blocked the road to Blue Island. It was closed due to flooding. The only way by land to the island was shut down.

Leaning back in his seat, he picked up his phone and called Tucker's mom.

"Sorry," he muttered when she answered. "You may want to stay put tonight and not bother coming down. The storm is flooding the road to the island. There's no way through."

"I called the police again," Mrs. Romero said. She sounded resigned. "They checked the school and said all buses came back… but one bus did go straight home and failed to check in. And there are some other parents from the school with missing kids… from the same bus. The police are at least taking me seriously now. I tried calling anybody on the island but can't get through."

"It's a bad storm," Mr. Ashley said. "But at the same time... I wouldn't trust a soul on that island."

Rain pounded on his van, sounding like a pack of wolves charging over concrete. He looked in the rearview mirror and, for a moment, thought he saw wolf shapes in the rain. He knew he was tired.

Mr. Ashley rubbed his bleary eyes. He'd tried calling his wife and kids repeatedly but could not reach any of them. Now, he could do nothing but sit and wait. And pray... "I'll stay here and let you know if anything changes."

"I'm coming to join you," Mrs. Romero said. "My husband will look after Maria. I have a feeling our boys need us."

Chapter 40

Tucker woke up on a hard floor in darkness. Much of the drugged drink had spilled on his shirt, and the effects hadn't lasted as long as they should. Still, prying his eyes open took great effort. His cheek pressed against cold tile, and he smelled something foul… like animal droppings mixed with rotting meat.

"Hey, he's awake!" a young voice said beside him.

"Hush, Woody," another kid said, sounding slightly older. "He might be a mean one."

"Nah, come on, Sticks!" a third kid said. "Nobody mean gets sent down here. The mean ones are the people who send the good ones here."

"Those two big guys were mean," little Woody said. "I mean, at first, they were."

Tucker sat up stiffly, and his eyes adjusted to the gloom. Looking around, he found himself sitting in a corner of a cavernous room full of crushed cardboard boxes. A faint greenish light flickered from across the room, providing the only light. Three small shapes formed a triangle with him in the middle. He saw they were two girls and one boy, all years younger than him. Wearing old pajamas and sneakers, they appeared filthy and starved but very curious.

"Um, hi?" he said. "Is this… the place you go, you know, when you die?"

"You think this is heaven?" the tallest girl said. Her long hair stuck out in every direction. "Kid, you're crazier than a cottonmouth with its tail in its mouth."

Tucker squeezed his eyes shut and opened them. He worked hard to grow into full alertness, but his body felt sore and tired. "I'm Tucker. Uh, who are you all?"

The kids introduced themselves as two cousins, Sticks and Woody, and their best friend, Salisbury. According to Woody, they'd been stuck in the room for a long time, like two hundred years. Then, some time ago, two big guys were lowered into the room. Finally, Tucker had just joined the little family.

"So, where are the two big guys?" Tucker asked.

"Doing what they do best," Sticks said.

"Sleeping," Woody and Salisbury said together.

Tucker nodded and shook out his curls. Dirt particles flew out. He looked across the room and saw a big patch of dirt and straw in the middle area, in front of the crushed boxes. This is where the foul smell came from. He was relieved to know it wasn't from him.

"So what is this place?" he asked.

"It's the holding pen," Salisbury said. She sat cross-legged and stuck a thumb in her mouth.

Woody crawled onto her lap and also started sucking his thumb. It held a dirty Band-Aid at its base.

Sticks sat with her knee up and watched them in disgust. "You two are going to get teeth so buck you can use them as stilts."

Salisbury just shrugged and wrapped her free arm around Woody's stomach.

"Holding pen?" Tucker said. He didn't like the sound of it.

"It's where we put animals to feed The Pack on big days, like celebrations," Sticks explained.

"Yeah," Salisbury added, pulling out her thumb. "Only now we're the animals." She ducked her head and hugged Woody tight. "We saw the good witch get kilt by the bad witch. Now we're being punished."

A chill went down Tucker's back. Was this what was meant by sacrifice? "So, um, are you sure no other kids like me are here? I mean, a smaller boy with darkish blond hair?"

"Nope," Sticks said. "It's just you. A bigger boy with curly hair."

Tucker hoped Elliot was in a better place. This place felt like a refrigerator and stunk of death.

Morgan carried the unconscious form of Elliot from the motel room. She'd wrapped him in a blanket and held him like a little child. Feeling the red pendant glow with approval, she marched to Kenton's ancient green Chevy pickup. Her middle brother waited behind the wheel, looking like a giant potato. She wondered, if he joined the feast, if it would give him better brains. It was worth a shot.

The rest of the parking lot was empty. Her son Burton had gone into the forest with Banor and Razor. The three wolf-men would be waiting at the sacrifice table.

Helga watched them go from where she stood in front of room five. She'd just finished using the fusia on Teddy and had gotten the call about the catastrophic events in the woods. More fusia would have to be made. It would be a long, busy night and a longer, busier day.

"If all goes well," she muttered, "this may be the last night I ever work here." She wasn't sure if this was something to rejoice over or cry about. No matter. For now, she had a job to do. The injured wolf-men were being transported in the backs of pickups to the main community of Blue Island—where an ample supply of fusia already waited. She would make her batch and join them in the morning. But there were still families expected at The Motel for the weekend in a few days.

"Brie!" she shouted. "Fiona! Get your keisters out here on the double! We have a room to clean! I won't be here tomorrow and want to see it clean before I leave!"

At the Chevy pickup, Kenton had the passenger door open for her. "You ready, little sister?" he asked. "Our boy looking good enough to eat?"

"Oh, shut your mouth," Morgan told him.

She ducked into the cab and plopped the sleeping boy in the middle seat. Then she climbed in, shutting the door. She wished she had her jeep but didn't want to get it dirty on the back roads of the forest. It was just another sacrifice she had to make. Over her black clothes, she now wore loose robes with a hood. She'd found them in Sylvia's closet and knew her mother had worn them on special occasions. What was more special than breaking a curse and getting her son back?

"Drive," she said to Kenton. From her pocket, she pulled out a printed copy of the ritual. In the back of the pickup, she already had the container of blood and the sheathed knife. Humming softly to herself, she put an arm around the unconscious boy and pulled him close. He was family, after all.

Skylar burst from behind the hut when the ATV pulled to a stop outside of it.

"Mom!" she shouted. "I thought you were somebody from the farm!"

She charged across the way, throwing herself in her mom's arms just as Mrs. Ashley climbed from the back of the vehicle.

"Careful," Mr. Harris warned. "Your mom hurt her back."

"Oh, it feels great right now." Mrs. Ashley squeezed her daughter around the neck and her shoulders. "I love you so much, Skylar."

"I love you too, Mom." Skylar hugged her back but then loosened her grip. "Mom, you're bleeding!"

Immediately, Mrs. Ashley let go and drew in a breath. "And Bobby! We need to take care of Bobby!"

Bernard had carried the boy to the front of the hut and laid him gently down on the soft ground. It was too dark inside the hut.

"We need bandages," he barked. "Now!"

"Are, are you going to, um, lick?" Skylar asked, following after her mom, who went straight to the boy's side.

"It won't work on him," Bernard said. "He's not the right blood. Don't worry. The cuts are ugly but nothing too bad. He has lost a lot of blood. Martin, get our First Aid kit."

Gary and Marcus stood near the ATV watching.

Marcus bumped shoulders with Gary. "Man, I don't know what to say… You were awesome back there."

Gary shrugged. "As soon as we get back, man, I'm inviting you and Bobby over to my house. But first, we have to get off this island. This isn't over yet. Look."

Gary pointed to the ground where a thick, dark cloud drifted in.

Marcus stared and felt his knees shake. "Oh, man. What is it?"

"It's not natural," Gary said. "This is creepy."

"Um, is there a place where I can use the bathroom?" Marcus called. "I feel sick…"

Skylar answered. "This is a true man's cave, kid. I already looked, and what you see is what you got."

Ignoring her, Bernard busily started ripping blankets into bandages as he stood above Mrs. Ashley.

The teacher knelt over Bobby and started cleaning his cuts with alcohol. "Good thing you're not awake," she muttered. "This has to hurt."

"Hey, you guys might want to hear this!" Mr. Harris called from the ATV. He held up a walkie-talkie with Ryan Raycroft's and Morgan Raycroft's conversation crackling through the speaker.

After listening, a hushed silence fell.

Bernard then handed over the torn blanket to his brother. "Finish this," he said to Martin. "I have something I need to do."

Skylar crouched next to her mother and held her close. "Don't worry, Mom," Skylar said. "Bernard will save Elliot. I know it."

Her mom just took in deep breaths. Then, she carefully focused on helping her injured student. She had Skylar help her wrap Bobby's torn arm and replace the dirty bandage on his left palm.

Bernard had already vanished into the forest.

The wolf-man didn't know where to go. He knew nothing about the ritual. He did know Elliot's scent. Sniffing the air, he hurried toward The Motel, racking his brain for where a sacrifice would take place. Then he knew.

In the northern area of Blue Island, high bluffs marked the coast of the river, going up to around thirty feet high. In the back of the bluffs was a rocky area leading into the thick woods. A small glade lay between the rocks and trees. Amidst this was a single cut stone in the shape of a block. It was said to be the only surviving section of the old woman's hut, the one who'd unleashed the curse on Benjamin Raycroft. Many believed the stone marked the burial spot for her son, killed by Benjamin Raycroft.

Thunder crackled, and lightning flashed over the river. On the island, the rain continued to stay away. The wind grew stronger as the fog rolled in thick and deep. By the time Kenton parked his truck near the trail to the glade, the fog covered his bumper.

"We can't go out in this," he complained to Morgan. "That fog is thicker than your gravy, and I eat that with a fork!"

Morgan ignored him. Throwing open her door, she stepped out. Elliot slumped to his side, still breathing evenly. As she stood to face him, a bolt sizzled behind her. Thunder exploded right after, almost on top of the truck.

Morgan's face beamed with a crazed look. "I hear you!" she screamed toward the sky. "You have been waiting for this! Now I'm coming!"

She pulled the boy from the blanket. Sitting him up in the truck with his back to her, she yanked off his shirt and tossed it on the floor.

More thunder roared its approval as she grabbed the boy by his waist and turned him to face her. "Your grandmother should see this day!" Then she got him over her shoulder. "Stay if you wish," she said back to her brother. "But if you want to drink the blood of power, this is your chance. Brother, you can be healed."

Muttering, Kenton stumbled from his seat and into nature's fury. The wind tore at his face, stinging his eyes and causing his clothes to whip behind him. He staggered to the back of the pickup. Reaching over, he picked up the jar of blood and the long knife.

The knife, wrapped in a waterproof container, had been passed down in the Raycroft family for generations, possibly from Benjamin Raycroft himself. Kenton clamped the blood jar under his arm and opened the container holding the knife. As soon as he took out the sheathed knife, the wind immediately died to a whisper.

Thunder and lightning continued dancing across the night sky, but now at a distance. Strangely, the island grew still. Around it, the river raged and the wind howled, but a tense quiet settled over Blue Island, particularly where Kenton stood.

Kenton's eyes bugged. He turned to follow after Morgan and saw the fog open up like a welcoming path guiding them through a cloud kingdom. Amazed, he followed after his sister. He never knew she had such powers… he thought Sylvia was the witch of the family.

Morgan carried the sleeping boy over her shoulder with one arm on his waist. The other arm reached up so she could hold the red pendant.

Back in the brick house corner room, Dr. Chocker stood facing the front window. Given the choice to accompany Morgan Raycroft or stay, he chose to stay… and now regretted it. Alone, he only had his memories to keep him company. He started to shiver and then ran back to the couch. Falling to his knees, he buried his head in the cushions. He hugged his middle tight. Haunted by unseen imaginings, he felt the blows and stings of a guilty conscience on his soul. He would not sleep that night or, perhaps, ever again.

Burton had not wanted to come. He'd met his mother at The Motel to tell her he was through listening to her. He would never hurt a child, even if it would turn him back. But then he'd seen her and had instantly felt cowed.

When Banor and Razor arrived, they took the young wolf-man and smoothly explained why they must go through the ritual. Sometimes, killing one to save many was the only way. They would be there with him. When it worked, Burton would go down as the greatest member of The Pack, the one to save them all. Best of all, he would be human again. He could return to his old life, finish high school, go to college… do anything he wanted!

He remained unsure but stood between the other two wolf-men when his mother arrived for the ritual.

A layer of fog covered the glade except for around the stone block. This is where the three wolf-men stood, as still as statues. Two had completed full Turnings, while Banor had completed only a partial. They were two separate generations representing The Pack.

Morgan, her dark robes flowing behind her, walked smoothly into the glade from the forest. A strange red glow from her neck lit her way. The boy remained slumped over her shoulder. Kenton followed in a stupor a few feet behind her.

Thunder quieted, and the eerie silence continued as Morgan reached the table. It was as if the island now held its breath. She gently laid the sleeping child from her shoulder onto his back. She then stepped back.

Lifting her hands over her head, she threw back her head and screamed.

The two elder wolf-men lifted their heads and joined her screams with howls. Burton hesitated and joined in.

Shaken, Kenton moved his huge bulk to the table, where he put down the knife and bottle as if they had suddenly burned him. He retreated to stand off to the side. Scared, he looked like he no longer wanted to be part of the ritual.

Morgan took the bottle and pulled out the cork. Saying words she knew by heart from the ritual, she poured the blood on the boy's chest and stomach, letting it cover his skin.

"Blood from an animal will mix with blood from a child…"

Lightning flashed.

Elliot's shoulders shifted. His waist twisted.

Morgan glared down and pressed a hand to his ribs as if trying to turn off his movements with a button. He should not be waking!

A roar sounded behind her.

Half asleep, Brie stumbled into room four with a bucket, sponges, and cleaning spray.

"Why do I always got to be the one to clean the bathrooms?" she mumbled tiredly.

Trudging to the back of the room, she entered the bathroom and set down her supplies. Flipping on the light, she sighed. It wasn't even that dirty. Poor Elliot had barely spent time in the room before… she couldn't think about it. She threw back the shower curtain and gasped. Elliot had definitely spent some time in the room.

Dried paper stuck to the back shower wall, spelling out a crude message.

SAVE TUCKER PLS

Brie suddenly had to vomit. Grabbing her throat, she ran to the toilet. After rinsing her mouth in the sink three minutes later, she ran from the room. The boy had a name, after all.

Chapter 41

Tucker sat with the three children, staring up at the tall teens before them. Donnie and Jake Brasco told him their story, ending with how they'd both been knocked out and woke up in some bizarre village of giant wolf dens. They were about to be eaten when one of the wolf people convinced the others to save them for later. Soon after, they'd had their heads covered in dirty sacks and led on a grueling hike. Somewhere along the way, they'd passed out and woke up in the room.

They'd been stuck there ever since, at least a week or so, they guessed. They also said they thought the room was originally built as an escape room, a last refuge from the wolf people if they ever went wild and attacked. Green-tinted emergency lights never went out along the side wall. There was a bathroom in the front corner and a huge closet on the far wall holding enough bottled water and canned food for at least a year—all people food, no dog food. The only thing missing was an escape route.

"And if I find one," Donnie said, "I'll get up there, get my truck back, and start taking names!" He smacked a fist into his meaty hand. "Those monsters will pay!"

Jake didn't share his bravado. He looked miserable and sick. "I don't want to see those wolf people again," he said, sounding like somebody much younger.

The three little children clapped when they'd finished.

"Their story is so better than ours," Woody said to Tucker. "They had guns and stuff."

"Yeah," Salisbury said, "but they never used them. And that's good. If you hurt The Pack, you die."

Tucker grinned tightly.

When the stories were finished, the cousins sat with them and passed around cans of cold beans they had to eat with their hands. Donnie and Jake started peppering Tucker with questions. They wanted to know all the crucial things happening in the outside world, such as who was winning the basketball playoffs and when high school graduation was.

Tucker finally told them to relax. "Guys, I'm like ten years old. I play basketball for fun, not watch it! And high school is not in, like, a million years for me."

Then, the ceiling started to open up. Twenty feet above the floor, a small square panel slowly lifted from the corner space over the bathroom.

"It's a wolf-man!" Woody said, covering his eyes with his food-smeared hands.

"Everyone, get quiet!" Donnie hissed. He carefully put down the empty can of beans he'd held. "If somebody comes down, we'll jump them!"

"They could be coming to eat one of us," Salisbury said seriously.

Instead, a young girl with short dark hair poked her head in. "Tucker?" she asked. "Are, are you down there? Are you awake?"

"Brie!" Tucker yelled. "I never thought I would ever say this, but, boy, am I glad to see you!"

"I, I've come to rescue you," the girl said. She looked over her shoulder. "But you have to hurry. My mom and sister are making fusia, but they could come here any second." She frowned when she saw the little kids and the cousins. "I've come for Tucker only. The rest of you need to stay and feed The Pack."

"Brie, you're not serious!" Tucker said. "Little kids are down here!"

"Don't forget us," Donnie said, elbowing his shoulder.

"Those kids are Pack food," Brie said, shaking her head. "I can only save you, Tucker. I know your name now."

"We all go," Tucker told her firmly. "Nobody is staying behind. Sticks, Salisbury, and Woody. And Donnie and Jake. We all have names, Brie. If you want to feed this pack so badly, you come down here and be their food."

Brie's eyes went large, and then her head vanished.

"Way to go, man," Donnie growled. "Now she won't free anybody! You could've gotten out and freed us later."

Suddenly, a rope ladder fell from the ceiling.

"Yes!" Donnie howled, smacking Tucker on the back. "Way to go!"

"Just hurry up and leave," Brie said miserably, peeking back in. "I hope never to see you again!" Then she was gone.

Donnie was already climbing the ladder. He would go first to make sure it was safe. Sticks soon followed, and Salisbury was at her heels. Jake went next with Woody wrapped around his neck. The little boy kept whimpering about falling.

"Won't happen," Jake said, huffing. "Because then I would have to fall too, and I won't like that. Just stay still. Okay, little guy?"

Woody squeezed his thin arms around the teenager's neck and nodded. He managed to get his thumb with the Band-Aid in his mouth as he leaned against Jake's shoulder.

Tucker went up last. Once again, hope surged in his heart. He now just had to find Elliot.

Elliot's eyes fluttered open in confusion. He lay on a rigid, bumpy surface that felt cool against his bare back and legs. Something wet dripped from his chest. A rank, rusty smell assaulted his nose. Lifting his head, he looked at his chest and gasped.

"Please tell me this isn't my blood," he said in a scared voice.

In the pale night, thick blackish blood covered his torso. He saw he wore a breechcloth, and he remembered. "Tucker?" he asked fearfully. "Mom?"

"Quiet, child!" commanded a harsh lady's voice.

Above him, a figure in black loomed. She wore a hooded robe and held a sharp knife. The blade was pointing at his chest. It slowly slid in the air until touching his skin. Starting just below his neck, the flat part of the blade traced a line to his navel.

A growl from his right let him know they weren't alone. He turned his head and saw three massive shapes watching. They stood in an eerie fog. Seeing their pointy ears and wolf features, his body started to tremble.

"Please…" he whimpered. "I want to go home…"

"You will, child," the woman promised. A red glow lit up her face and fell on Elliot. "Very soon."

Elliot drew back in fright. Turning his face, his cheek scraped bare rock. He knew he had to get out of there. But how?

He looked up again and saw the woman close her eyes, her hand reaching for the red pendant hanging from her neck on a chain…

"By the power I possess, I will take the h—"

Grab it, whispered a voice in his mind.

All at once, Elliot reached up and grabbed the necklace. Rolling to his right, his grip firm on the chain, he fell off the stone table. The necklace snapped and came with him. The red glow instantly vanished.

"Hey!" yelped the woman as if slapped. "No! Give it back!"

Elliot landed on his side, his arm clutching the necklace underneath his body. He scrambled to his feet and dangled the pendant in front of him. Amazingly, the wolf-men recoiled at the sight.

"Get back!" Elliot shouted. He felt a surge of power around him.

Then, a woman's voice in his mind called to him, loud this time. *No, Elliot! Throw it away!*

Shocked, Elliot dropped the pendant and hopped back. His back struck the stone table. A sharp blow to the back of his head hit next, sending him crashing to his hands and knees. He saw a bright flash and struggled to stay conscious.

"Get him!" howled the woman. "Get my pendant first!"

She'd struck him with the base of the knife. She gasped when the hilt suddenly cracked and broke in her hands. The old blade fell to the stone table, bouncing with a clang before falling into the dark grass, swallowed by the fog. The ritual was falling apart.

"No!" She dropped the broken fragments of bone and wood. "I'll rip that child's heart out with my hands!" She lunged for the fallen necklace.

Elliot struggled to his feet. His hand leaned back on the stone. Then he looked up. A tall wolf-man stood before him, baring his teeth.

"I'll finish him myself!" he hissed.

"Not until the ritual is complete!" the woman cried, bending down to find the pendant. "It's nearly done. Then he's yours."

Dizzy, Elliot flinched from the beast and covered his head with his hands. Doing so, he felt the warrior's knot in his hair. He couldn't go down without a fight. He made the best move he knew. He ran.

In the rocks above, Bernard stared down at Kenton's massive body. The Raycroft lay flat on his back with his arms extended to form a cross.

Morgan's brother had gone up to check out the roar. At finding Bernard, he smiled and relaxed. "You didn't come here to turn human, did you?" he asked.

"Actually," Bernard said. "I did. Only a monster will kill an innocent child. Morgan is the monster. The human thing is to stop her."

Kenton frowned and then slowly nodded. "Maybe... you have a point. These are strange times... The Pack is tearing itself apart, and we think killing children is the answer."

"Get out of my way, Kenton."

"Sorry, kid. But Morgan... Morgan is my... is sister... She is our... leader..."

The man started breathing hard, and sweat ran down his flabby cheeks. His eyes bulged. All of a sudden, he clawed at his chest. "Oh..." he moaned. Kenton's knees buckled, and he sank to his knees. "No..."

As the red pendant was ripped from Morgan's neck, Kenton's life was ripped from his chest. His eyes rolled back, and his massive body toppled back. He collapsed in a heap and didn't move.

Seeing Kenton Raycroft not breathing, Bernard leaped down to the glade below. His wolf eyes quickly found Elliot through the darkness. He saw the boy run as Razor pounced. The wolf-man batted the boy's shoulder, sending him crashing to the ground, where he rolled twice. He ended up on his stomach, stunned.

Morgan ran from the stone table and grabbed the boy's arm. Yanking him up, she used her other hand to snag the back of his leather belt. She dragged him back to the table. The glowing red pendant seemed to sharpen like a knife as it hung from her neck.

Bernard dropped to all fours and raced down the rest of the way. "No!" he roared.

Seeing him coming, Razor bared his teeth and charged to meet him.

Banor approached the stone table, dragging his son Burton with him.

"We will finish this," Banor growled. "You will get the first bite. You will be human."

Morgan released Elliot's arm and shoved him against the table. Grabbing the back of his neck, she pressed down. Barely conscious, the boy flopped over it with his back to the woman. His waist dug into the stone. The pain caused him to rouse, and he fought to shake free.

The hand squeezing his neck only tightened and pressed his cheek into the cool rock.

Morgan reached to her neck and grabbed the glowing pendant. As her fingers closed around it, a crack of thunder boomed. The red stone burned into a blade several inches long. It was like a tongue of fire searching for blood. "The heart of the child will rise to meet the tongue of the wolf!" she howled. "Blood will heal!" Morgan raised her hand over her head, holding the pendant like a knife.

A dark red light sprang from it like a blade.

Jagged lightning cut through the sky.

"No!" Burton cried. Running from his father, he jumped at his mother.

Sensing the attack, Morgan turned and struck blindly, yelling in triumph. The pendant flared a bright red, stabbing into the wolf-man's chest. It had found blood.

"M-Mother," Burton gasped. His eyes went wide, and his mouth sagged open.

"No!" Morgan screamed. "Burton! No!" She stared in horror as her son collapsed to the ground at her feet. Still clasped in her hand, the red pendant's light faded as blood dripped down from it.

Above her, Razor and Bernard locked arms in fierce combat. Using wrestling and wolf tactics, they each fought to pin the other and then rip out his throat. Hearing Morgan's wails, they rolled from each other and turned to see what had happened.

Suddenly released, Elliot staggered from the table and held his forehead, still slightly woozy. As it cleared, he turned to see the woman whirl from a fallen wolf-man and glare at him.

His eyes wide, he backed up, bumping into the stone table. He had nowhere to go.

"You will save my son, you wicked boy!" she cried. She raised the red pendant, and the red glow returned. It wanted more blood. "He will not die a monster!"

"No!" Bernard yelled. Launching himself from above, he landed on the stone table beside the boy and over Morgan.

"You!" Morgan spat. "You traitor! Get out of my way!"

"You will leave the boy alone." Bernard nodded his head at Banor, who knelt over Burton. "Go and save Burton."

Banor was already using his saliva to cover the gaping wound. The young wolf-man struggled to breathe.

Morgan sneered up at Bernard. "That boy you protect will not just save my son. He will save you, too! He will turn you back to human!"

Bernard reached down and scooped Elliot around the chest, lifting him up to him. The boy gasped but gave no resistance. He stood trembling on the stone table next to his rescuer.

"You think murdering a child makes you human?" Bernard growled. "You're the monster." Turning, he looked up at Razor. "If you want to be human, act like one."

Razor grinned wickedly. "In this world, getting what you want is very human, Bernie. Stand in our way, and you will join the boy. You'll both be dead."

Bernard could feel the boy's heartbeat thumping against his paw. He shook his head. "Humans can act like animals, but it doesn't mean they are animals."

Razor growled. "Suit yourself. I will kill you. Put down the kid, and let's finish this!"

"Another night." Bernard swung Elliot up and turned him to lie over his shoulder. He then jumped from the table, away from Morgan. Running across the glade, he made for the forest.

From across the beast's shoulder, Elliot glanced back at the woman. She watched him go with undisguised hatred.

Razor howled after them but did not give chase. The Protector of The Pack needed him. He jumped down and went to Banor and his injured nephew. Family always came first.

Burton breathed deep gasps of pain, but slowly, the healing properties of his father's and Razor's saliva worked. The saliva would keep him stable until they found fusia.

Morgan stood before the stone table, clenching the red pendant tightly. She watched her husband and Razor tend to her son, covering his wound with their saliva… it was a wound she had caused.

No! It was the boy's fault. Ryan was right. The Ashley woman needed to see her son die.

"Whatever happens next," Morgan said tightly. "They will *not* leave this island! Kenton! Kenton! Where are you?"

As the witching hour ended, howls of grief rose from the glade in the north. Morgan had found her brother. Then the sky opened up, sending sheets of torrential rain onto the island.

Bernard carried Elliot into the woods just as the deluge started. As the rain poured down, he kept the boy over his shoulder with a paw on his back. Elliot was stunned, exhausted, and scared. With his hands gripping fur tightly, he barely moved.

Bernard kept a quick pace. He dodged through trees and hopped over branches until he found a dense copse of trees and brush. Ducking under heavy branches, he settled down and placed the boy beside him.

"It's okay," he said gently. "You're safe now."

Wearing little, Elliot shivered. He immediately huddled against the beast.

Bernard put an arm around his shoulders, keeping him warm. The rain continued to hammer down, but the two were sheltered from the worst of it. Neither spoke.

After a while, Bernard saw Elliot had drifted off to sleep. He gently laid the boy down next to him.

He then licked at his own wounds from fighting with Razor. A cut on his left wrist started to close and heal. Feeling better, he relaxed and waited out the storm. He kept close to the sleeping boy, keeping him warm. As he stared into the soaking night, he saw the strangest thing.

A ghostly woman in a gleaming white robe walked toward him, cutting through the thick fog. She was like a bright light in the darkness, moving through the rain as if they were air bubbles. She never got wet. Reaching the copse of trees, she bent down, watched the sleeping boy, and then looked up at Bernard.

The wolf-man had seen many strange things in his young life, but nothing like this.

"If you eat him, you are human," the woman said. "Morgan has all but finished the ritual. Just go for the heart." She looked older and younger at the same time. With silver hair tied behind her, she had a lithe frame and a face with wisdom and youth. Her dark green eyes were vaguely familiar. It was something he could not describe and filled him with awe.

"If I hurt him, I am nothing but a monster," he said, surprising himself.

The woman laughed. "Look at you now! You are a monster!"

Bernard ducked his head. "I am what somebody else made me. But I choose to be what I will. I refuse to be a monster."

"Don't be a fool! At least let the others have their chance to return to human life."

Bernard put a paw on the sleeping boy's shoulder. He felt the boy's cold skin. He bared his teeth. "If any lay a hand on this boy or any other innocent, I will show you a monster."

The woman nodded. Then she smiled at him. "You answered wisely, Bernard. I may be seeing you again."

Bernard blinked and saw himself alone with a sleeping boy against his side. The woman had vanished. He thought he'd drifted off and had dreamed it, but it had been so vivid.

The fog had lifted around him, leaving a chill. With the boy curled close by his side, he stared into the night. He laid an arm over the boy's back to give him warmth. The rain continued to fall as morning slowly approached.

The storm finally passed through just before sunrise. As the dark clouds moved east toward the ocean, a blue sky with fluffy white clouds greeted the new day. The fog from the night before had completely vanished.

The sun had just started cracking when Donnie and Jake led a bedraggled group of children from The Motel into the forest. They'd spent the night hiding in an empty apartment room.

Once they'd escaped the holding pen, Brie had returned with the apartment key and an apology. "You know," she said to Tucker, "I'm awfully sorry about your friend. I didn't want him to get eaten, but he was too puny to be in The Pack." She sighed. "My mom said he would break the curse and turn all the wolf-men back to humans... but I wish he wasn't eaten. He was cute."

Tucker had to resist the urge to break her. He refused to believe Elliot was dead.

Once in the apartment, they had to be quiet so Brie's mom or sister wouldn't know they were there. Her dad, she explained, was spending the night in town due to the storm. This meant even though they were grubby and covered in grime, they couldn't shower.

Tucker did go to the bathroom for a rough sponge bath in the sink. As he stripped down to his boxers, he stared in the mirror. While he'd never seen one close up, the apartment was full of pictures of hulking wolf-men, bound with endless chiseled muscle. He knew he looked puny and soft in comparison. Yet, he was quite happy with his appearance. He didn't need to be stacked with muscle to be a better person. After what he went through, he was content with knowing muscles didn't make the man. Being himself was quite enough.

He just wanted his best friend back. Maybe he didn't *need* Elliot as a friend, but he had chosen him as his best friend. And best friends stuck together, no matter what.

"Hurry up," whined Woody through the door. "I gotta go!"

"You're taking too long," Salisbury chimed in. "What are you doing in there?"

"Okay, okay, just a minute!" Tucker quickly grabbed the clean sponge Brie had provided and started scrubbing his shoulders. Some things never changed.

After his rough bath, Tucker spent much of the night sitting on the floor, telling himself that Elliot was fine. As the storm raged outside, it became a prayer. The three younger children slept on one bed in a room while the cousins took the other bed. Even if Tucker had wanted to sleep, the snoring from Donnie would've made it impossible. It was a blessing when the heavy rain fell, drowning out the teen's loud snuffles.

Eventually, he nodded off and woke at the crack of dawn. The storm was gone, and Brie was kneeling in front of him.

Now used to such things, Tucker only stared at the girl.

"Hi, Tucker," she said, her face inches from his nose. "I hope Elliot isn't dead."

Tucker groaned and wiped his bleary eyes. "Thanks, Brie. When I see Elliot, I'll tell him you said that. Just so you know, you're like walking inspiration."

Still, he did thank her for saving them.

Hearing their voices, the others started to wake. Not long after morning broke, Tucker, the cousins, and the escaped children snuck away. They'd left the apartment after each had used the bathroom and had a cold breakfast of bagels and orange juice smuggled in by Brie.

"Don't let my mom or sister see you," she told them as they hurried around to the back of The Motel, past the pool and toward the forest. "My dad is coming to pick them up real soon and bring them into town. They're super mad about what happened in the woods. A lot of wolf-men got burned up."

Tucker raised his eyebrows. "You mean, the wolf-men didn't turn into humans? That means Elliot is okay, right?"

Brie brightened at that. "Hey, that's possible! But he could just not be eaten yet... or only a little eaten. Maybe only *some* wolf-men are back to human."

Tucker sighed. "Brie, I'm so not going to miss you."

Then, they reached the edge of the woods. Their only real plan was to escape The Motel, find the others, and somehow get off the island. The details to accomplish this would come later.

Brie said Mrs. Ashley had run off with two traitor wolf-men, so they had some hope. She told them to follow the fire road as much as possible since it led straight across the forest.

"Just don't be seen," she warned as the group hesitated to enter the trees.

"Or smelled," Donnie muttered, sniffing his armpits.

"Man, I wish we had our rifles," Jake said, nervously eyeing the woods.

The cousins stood in front, with the little kids in the middle and Tucker bringing up the rear. They'd paused right by the muddy dirt road Brie indicated.

"Don't you worry," Sticks boasted. "I know some of them wolf-men real well. I ain't afraid of any of them."

"Yeah, like when you peed your pants in the witch's house," Salisbury told her.

Sticks punched her arm and glared. "Let's just get moving!"

"I want to go home," Woody complained. He clutched the front of Tucker's shirt and pressed in tight. The little boy had decided Tucker would be his protector. He treated Tucker's shirt like his security blanket.

"We can't," Salisbury said. "It's way too far. The bad motel people will spot us, and then we'll be back in that black hole as wolf-men food."

Woody whimpered, and Tucker absently rubbed the top of the boy's grimy hair.

"We'll be okay," he said. "I think."

Brie stood watching them sadly. "Well, if all the wolf-men turn back to human, you'll be just fine. But if not, then—"

"Then Elliot is fine," Tucker said sharply, cutting her off. "Brie. Please. No more inspiration from you. Okay?"

Brie nodded and waved as the teen cousins finally led the group into the woods.

"No more talking," Donnie warned. "If anything comes at us, you kids run. Jake and I will fight it off. Right, cousin?"

Jake glanced at him in disbelief but then nodded. "Uh, yeah…"

The sun had still barely peeked over the horizon, and the air was cool with a faint breeze. After many days trapped in the dimmed, musty room, the little kids beat their chests and breathed deeply. The cousins also embraced the fresh air but kept low as they moved. Their eyes warily scanned the trees before them.

The ground and branches were soaked from the storm, and the group crept silently over the wet leaves. No animal sounds greeted them… It felt like walking through a graveyard.

Staying in the trees, they kept the fire road on their right. The road was marked with tire tracks filled with rainwater. They had been walking for several minutes when they heard an approaching engine.

"Quick!" Donnie hissed. "Hide!"

The group quickly scattered farther from the road. The teenagers lay in a clump of bushes. Unwashed, with dirty black shirts and camo pants, they blended right in.

Behind them, Tucker dove to his belly behind a fallen log. Woody instantly followed and cuddled against his side. He inserted his thumb into his mouth as Tucker put an arm around his side. Sticks and Salisbury ducked behind a thick maple tree next to them. Wet leaves soaked their clothes and skin. Tucker moved his arm to Woody's thin shoulders, squeezing tight. He silently prayed. What if Brie's mom or sister had discovered they were missing and called for help?

They all held their breath as the engine drew closer.

Then Jake jerked his head up. "Hey, Donnie," he said. "That sounds like your truck!"

Donnie abruptly stood up, clenching his fists. "That's because it is! I'd know that sound anywhere! Look, man!"

The familiar maroon Ford pickup soon came bouncing down the muddy earthen road toward The Motel.

Donnie didn't wait. He ran from the bushes, hopping down onto the road. Splashing through the mud, he stalked right into the truck's path.

"Oh, man," Jake said, rising in resignation. "Where family goes, you go." Taking a deep breath, he ran after his cousin.

Tucker lifted his head over the log and watched them go in horror. "What are you guys doing?" he hissed.

Woody pulled out his thumb and reached up to grip Tucker's collar. His arm trembled.

"Getting my truck back," Donnie called over his shoulder. His meaty arms ended in fists. "Nobody steals from a Brasco! Especially not my baby!"

Tucker just groaned and ducked back down. "Yep," he muttered. "Muscles definitely do not make the man."

Woody pressed against him and wiped snot on Tucker's shirt. His slobbery hand with the grimy Band-Aid remained attached to the older boy's collar.

Tucker hugged him tight and hoped wolf-men didn't drive stolen pickups.

Ryan Raycroft just had a horrible, no-good, sleepless night. He'd started it by fighting a crazy woman and three kids, only to end up on the losing side. Wolf-men burnt to a crisp needed to be treated. Then, he had to battle small forest fires for half the night. And, only after the fires were finally put out by hand, the sky opened up to dump buckets of water on him and the others—water they'd needed just moments before. To make it worse, during the deluge, he'd gotten a radio call from Morgan.

The ritual had been a disaster. His brother had a heart attack, and his nephew had been stabbed. Both were alive, but his brother hung by a thread. Only Razor's strong CPR had saved him. Hopefully, injections of fusia would do the rest. Young Burton had a hole in his chest but was on the mend. However, he refused to speak to his mother. And now his sister was on the warpath.

She had Ryan Raycroft spend the rest of the miserable night searching for any signs of the teacher and the kids, as well as Bernard and the kid Elliot. Apparently, the traitor wolf-man had stolen his great-nephew from being sacrificed.

Under different circumstances, Ryan Raycroft may have felt some inner relief knowing that, despite his best efforts, the innocent boy hadn't been killed… but after everything he'd gone through, he clutched the steering wheel in anger. The sacrifice was the whole reason the mess had started. Bernard and his twerp brother had ruined everything. And that blasted ATV driver… he had determined it had to be the other teacher from the bus. Apparently, some of his men left their ATVs unattended, and one had been swiped—the idiots.

So much for it not being about revenge. Morgan wanted them all dead—dead, dead, dead.

Unsurprisingly, the search did not go well in the raging storm. When it finally ended, and the sun mercifully pushed up to announce the new day, Ryan called for a pause. They all needed rest.

Completely exhausted, Ryan meant to crash at The Motel for the day. He would figure out a plan once he slept, showered, and ate something hot. At the moment, he just struggled to keep his eyes open.

Most of his men and uninjured wolf-men were sent to their homes to rest up. With the storm wiping out all scents and tracks, the wolf-men would have to start the hunt all over. A few remained behind to listen for the ATV motor and to try to catch scents of the two traitor wolf-men and the human outsiders. Ryan highly doubted this would work. He didn't worry too much about it. He would find his prey.

Bernard knew the forest but couldn't escape it, especially with a kid. He'd obviously left Mrs. Ashley and others. A single ATV couldn't carry all the adults and kids, so the teacher would be hiding, especially since at least one of the kids was injured. Just in case, the bridge was being watched. It was the only way off the island. The storm had left the river swollen, with high choppy water. Swift currents swept around the island. Swimming would be a death sentence. The teachers and kids could only escape if they miraculously found a car or something.

As he neared The Motel, two filthy teenage kids ran at him from the woods. One idiot stood right in his path.

"Now what?" Ryan Raycroft said with a groan.

He jammed on the brakes, skidding to a stop just a few yards from the idiot teen. Everyone on the island recognized him, but he barely knew faces, much less names. The teen in front of him looked vaguely familiar…

"Maybe they found the teacher," he muttered. He put the pickup in park. That would be great, but it would also mean he would have to go back…

Suddenly, his heart jumped. What if… what if the sacrifice had happened and this filthy teen was actually a former wolf-man?

Covering a yawn, he eagerly rolled down the window. Whatever it was, it had to be good news. The teen approached him with a big grin.

"What's the trouble, guys?" he asked.

"You have my truck," the taller teen said, reaching his door.

Ryan Raycroft barely had time to widen his eyes. Then he got punched in the face. It came fast, sudden, and super hard. His right eye blew up with pain. He saw stars as he jerked back in his seat.

"That's the trouble." The teen yanked open the door with his left hand and threw an uppercut with his right.

Chapter 42

Ryan Raycroft got punched in the face again. This one caught him on the chin. His head snapped back. Groaning, he sagged against the seat belt. Once it was unbuckled, he tumbled out onto the muddy road, landing in a puddle.

"Thanks for the gas, buddy," the teen said, climbing in the driver's seat. "Hop in the back, Jake, and tell those kids their trip just got upgraded to Brasco class!"

Ryan Raycroft struggled to a sitting position. His jaw ached, and his right eye throbbed. Both, he could tell, were starting to swell. Fog covered his brain. He sat in a cold, muddy puddle. Water leaked down the back of his pants, causing him to wake up. He watched in a daze as three little kids ran from the woods. They were dirty like the teens, but full of smiles. None of them gave him a glance as they were lifted up by the second teen into the back of the pickup.

Jake, Ryan's mind said dully. *That's Jake.*

"Where's Tucker?" Jake asked, putting a little boy in last.

"He said he needed to go back and get something," the tallest of the girls said. "He's running back to The Motel."

"I think it was his friend," the other girl added. "He said he had to go, and well… if you gotta go, you gotta go."

Jake stared into the woods and frowned. "Hope the dude knows what he's doing."

The driver grunted. "Jump in the back, cousin. We'll drop off these three tykes with their parents and come back for him." He turned to the back. "You know how to find your home, Sticks?"

The tallest girl stood just behind the cab and nodded with a smile. "Just head back to The Motel, and I'll tell ya where to go!" She giggled. "Brie said our parents thought we got swept away in a storm and drowned. Just wait until they see us!"

The little boy clapped and then looked toward the woods. "I wish Tucker came with us." He then moved close to Jake, who'd just jumped up. The little boy grabbed the front of Jake's shirt and held it tight.

"He'll be fine," the driver said, shifting the pickup into drive. He glared down at Ryan Raycroft. "Next time, give it a wash and wax."

He then stomped on the gas.

"Slow down!" Jake yelled, sitting down with the boy falling into his lap. The girls squealed but sounded more excited than scared.

As the pickup peeled off, it spat mud, water, and rocks behind it, right in Ryan Raycroft's face and lap.

Ryan groaned and flopped to his back. A rock had nailed him in the mouth, and now he had a bloody lip. It was going to be a miserable day. He thought about calling in sick… but his walkie-talkie was still in the truck. Sucking on his blood, he fought back tears.

Skylar barely slept that night. As the sun just started to rise, she got up from her blanket by the tree stump in the center of the hut.

Her mom slept restlessly in the corner closest to the door, with Mr. Harris in the corner across from her. The three boys slumbered in the back corner where she'd first wakened to meet Bernard. It seemed like that had happened ages ago… but it had been less than a day. Her brother was still missing. The ache in her heart would never stop until she had him safe.

She silently climbed from her blanket, listening to the steady breathing and snores. Mr. Harris sounded like a small buzz saw. All the sleepers were wrapped in blankets. The storm had brought a chill during the night. None of the blankets stirred as she snuck from the hut. She needed to find Martin.

Just outside the hut, the young wolf-man stood staring out into the forest. He snorted but did not turn when he sensed her presence.

The rain had left everything a soggy mess, but the sun was rising to a mostly blue sky.

"Hi, Martin," Skylar said. "What are you thinking?"

Martin now turned to her. "Nothing," he mumbled. "I mean, I think I know where Bernard might go if he finds your brother."

Skylar raised her eyebrows. "Let me guess. This motel place?"

Martin nodded. "He has a few kids and some guys stuck there as prisoners. He's been trying to find a way to free them before they're eaten… well, after last night, The Pack is going to be really mad. They're going to be looking for fresh meat."

Skylar stared at the wolf-man. "What are you waiting for? You lead, and I'll follow. Let's go."

Martin eyed her and then nodded at the hut. "We… leave them?"

"You were planning on leaving us already, right?"

Martin ducked his head. "I just… I want to find my brother."

"And I want to find my brother." Skylar took a deep breath. "Look, we can hurry, right? I mean, once we have Elliot and your brother back, we can get off this place. Until then, we're all in serious danger. Waiting around here won't help things. If Bernard and Elliot are in danger… we need to be there."

Martin nodded. "I… I guess."

Skylar reached a hand out to rest on the young wolf-man's shoulder. "I trust you, Martin. Let's go find our brothers, and we'll be back before anybody knows."

The young wolf-man needed no more convincing. "Stay close," he muttered.

The two slipped into the trees toward the unknown. The silent hut disappeared from view.

Elliot woke up that morning to find himself draped on the furry back of his new wolf-man friend.

"Oh, man," he croaked, nearly sliding off. "What are you doing?"

"Sniffing the trail," Bernard said. He'd been standing straight but now bent his back to let Elliot climb to a higher position.

With the sun just beginning to rise to their left, they were on a trail cutting through deep woods.

"Who are you?" Elliot asked. "I mean, thanks for saving me last night." He held the wolf-man's shoulders as his knees clung tight to the furry back. Thinking of the nightmare he'd lived through, he shuddered.

"My name is Bernard, and I'm a wolf-man, not a monster. I won't let anybody, or anything, harm you."

Elliot pulled himself up higher. "Seriously, like, thank you. I'm glad you're on my side." He gave a sideways look at the wolf-man's long snout. "You've helped me before. You were in the woods yesterday when I got lost."

Bernard grunted. "I, well, I've been watching you… My brother and I knew your great-grandmother. We'll do anything to help her." He ducked under a branch but avoided dropping to all fours. He was doing his best to be as human as he possibly could.

Elliot struggled to keep his grasp across Bernard's broad back. He pulled himself higher and then lunged to hold a single shoulder with both hands. His feet and body lay across the furry spine.

"I still, like, got caught," he muttered, thinking of Tucker.

"My brother lost you," Bernard said. "I had to leave when I, um, smelled your sister. She was in trouble, but I saved her."

Elliot's eyes went wide. "Really? You, like, know Sky?"

"Er, well, I just met her here. But I did see her in other places before. She's now staying at my… place. With your mom, of course."

Elliot climbed forward in excitement, his feet kicking into the fur. "Really? You have my mom *and* sister?"

"You're the last one, kid," Bernard said, unable to keep from grinning. "I rescued your sister first… She and I talked some, and she made sure I came and got you."

Elliot leaned over his hairy shoulder. He was small enough—and the wolf-man big enough—to put both elbows on the single shoulder. His body and legs dangled down the Wolf-man's back.

"So, wait. Are you, like, my sister's boyfriend?"

The giant wolf sniffed the air before answering. They were on a narrow trail now. "Just so you know, we're going to The Motel. I want to find a few friends there and hopefully get you some clothes."

"Yes! I have a friend there, too!"

Bernard seemed relieved to have switched subjects. At the same time... he couldn't resist.

"So, um, does your sister, Skylar. Does she have a lot of boyfriends?"

"No, not really. Like, she has this one guy, Teddy, she likes. But that's the only one."

Bernard cleared his throat loudly. "Okay, we can strike that one off the list... What does she like to do?"

Elliot lifted his eyebrows. "Um, no offense, but I don't think you're, like, her type."

"Forget I asked," Bernard growled, leaping forward.

Elliot slipped from his perch and barely hung on. The wolf-man quickened his pace. The boy clung to both shoulders now and did his best to keep from falling. He rested his cheek against the furry back and tried to calm his pounding heart. He couldn't believe he was actually getting a piggyback ride on a real monster... who had a crush on his sister.

Eventually, with the sun still climbing, the two reached The Motel just as the roar of a pickup faded in the distance, heading toward the center of the island.

Elliot hopped down from Bernard's back and ran ahead.

The wolf-man stayed just outside the tree line in the rear of The Motel, scanning for any danger. Satisfied, he followed the boy to the front, keeping his distance.

"Tucker!" Elliot cried. "Tucker!" He stood in the middle of the empty parking lot. The place looked abandoned.

"Elliot!" screeched a voice. Brie burst from her apartment and ran up to him in amazement. "I can't believe it! You're totally alive! Not even one bite mark is on you!"

"Oh, yeah, that's great." Elliot brushed back his hair and scratched his ribs. "Hi, Brie. Where's Tucker?" Suddenly remembering he was only in a breechcloth, he bent at the waist and backed from her. "And do you have, like, my clothes from yesterday?"

"Don't worry," Brie told him. "I saw your message in the shower." She drew herself up proudly. "I freed Tucker and the others. They left early this morning." She grinned. "My dad came and picked up my mom and sister, and none of them even know it yet. I'm going to be in total big trouble."

"What was that?" Bernard asked, trotting to join them. "Where did they go?"

Brie looked up at the great wolf-man and instantly moved to shield Elliot. "Whatever you do, don't eat Elliot! He has a name!"

Bernard just looked at her.

"Um, Brie?" Elliot asked. "My clothes?"

"Oh!" Brie cried. "You're the traitor wolf-man! You saved Elliot! Yes!" She turned to Elliot. "Let me go get your clothes!"

As Brie rushed to find his clean clothes, Bernard ran into the woods to search for any signs of the Brasco cousins and kids.

Elliot went to wait in room four. After using the toilet and washing his hands, he sat uncomfortably on the bed, shivering from the air-conditioning. He hoped Tucker was okay but was excited to see his mom and Skylar. Bernard told him he would take him there right after he dressed. He just had to find Tucker, and all would be well. Bernard hoped to find him on their way to his place.

Brie returned with his green pants, boxers, socks, and sneakers, but not his shirt. She brought him a plain blue shirt, which she promised was from her own personal collection.

"Just what I need," he muttered. But he thanked the girl. He couldn't wait to get out of the scratchy cloth around his waist.

Brie said she would go and find a hot breakfast for him and maybe a raw pig for Bernard. "You can be as loud as you want," she said before he shut the door in her face. "My parents won't be back until late. They're caring for all the hurt wolf-men in town."

Alone, thankful for the privacy, Elliot didn't go into the bathroom to change. He wanted to be away from this place as soon as possible. Earlier, when washing his hands, he'd used the mirror to smooth out his hair. The warrior knot had become undone in the rain, and his hair was a tangled mess. He didn't know why, but he wanted to look his best for Brie. Dumping his clothes and sneakers on the mattress, he moved behind the bed. He started pulling off the belt when he heard movement in the next room. He put his ear to the wall and listened.

"Tucker?" he said, scrunching his brow. He banged on the wall. "Tucker? Is that you, Tucker?"

A deep growl answered. Either Tucker had turned into the big bad wolf, or Elliot was in deep trouble. Stopping his knocking, he slowly turned. "Oh, boy…" Looking down, he saw he still wore the breechcloth. "Like, this is not happening."

He frantically got changed, throwing off the cloth and belt and pulling on his clothes. He'd just finished tugging on the blue shirt when a dark shadow passed over the front window covered in blinds.

Elliot froze in a crouch. He watched the shadow disappear behind the door.

The doorknob slowly turned. His eyes went wide with fright. He hadn't locked the door.

His breaths went sharp and short as he backed away. He thought about hiding in the bathroom but remembered it had no escape. As the door swung open, he dove to the floor and rolled under the bed.

"Hello in there," a familiar teen's voice said.

Elliot kept his mouth open as he breathed down his fear. It sounded like Teddy, but rougher—like he had knives stuck in his throat.

"Is that you in here, Elliot? You know, I can smell you…"

Heavy footsteps walked into the room. They moved to the bathroom and then turned back into the room.

Elliot lay on his belly facing the wall. His hands pressed against the floor, wishing he could somehow disappear inside it. He glanced to the left and sucked in his breath. His sneakers, socks, and breechcloth lay in a pile only feet from his head. Beyond the pile of clothes, two large feet faced him. Tufts of fur grew around the ankles, and the nails were long, yellow, and sharp. He dared not to breathe.

The feet slowly walked away from him and around the bed. Then they stopped.

Elliot squeezed his arms together tight. *Please don't see me… please don't eat me…*

Suddenly a thump sounded behind him and something snatched his ankle.

"Got you!" Teddy cried in triumph. He started pulling Elliot from under the bed as the boy screamed and tried kicking free.

Laughing, the teen grabbed his other ankle, too. Soon, Elliot was completely exposed. Releasing the ankles, Teddy put a knee on his backside, pinning him to the floor. A rough paw pressed against the boy's back.

"I never did have my first kill yet," Teddy said, his voice deepening.

Elliot tried desperately to crawl free, but his chest was pushed painfully against the floor. He could feel hot breath on the back of his neck and smelled sour breath.

The door burst open, causing the teen to look up with a start. Elliot turned his head and gasped.

"Leave my friend alone!" Tucker yelled. He stood in the doorway, his face a mask of fury.

Teddy laughed at seeing him. "Tucker, man, what are you doing? Do you want to die, too?

"You heard me!" Tucker said, walking into the room. "Get away from Elliot!"

"Or what?" Teddy asked. He wore his sweatpants and shirt. His shirt now bulged with muscle. Fur sprouted on his arms, but he appeared the same above his neck. Then he gave Tucker a dazzling smile, revealing rows of sharp teeth. "What are you going to do, kid? Spit on me?"

Tucker reached behind his back and pulled out a flare pistol.

When Tucker had watched in disbelief as Donnie got his pickup back, his mind was made up. If the cousins could act rashly to save something they loved, then so could he. Elliot had been his best friend and always would be. His parents, the miles between their houses, and even his new friends could never stop their friendship. If it did end, it would be between the boys and nobody else. And no hairy walking wolf was going to get in the way either. After telling the little kids that he needed to get his friend back, he hurried back toward the motel, leaving the safety of the pickup.

Tucker had just reached the parking lot when he'd heard Elliot's screams. As he'd raced without thinking towards them, Brie had come running from her apartment holding a flare gun.

"It's all I could find," she'd said breathlessly. "I forgot about that one in room five." She'd handed him the flare gun. "Careful, I already armed it."

Tucker had then run to the room where his friend screamed for help.

Chapter 43

"Eat this, sucker!" Tucker aimed at Teddy and pulled the trigger, shutting his eyes. A loud pop exploded from his hand as smoke and fire belched out.

Teddy screeched as the flare nailed him in the lower stomach. His sweatpants and shirt erupted in bright fiery sparks as the cloth ignited. The flare stuck to him like plasma as he stumbled back with the impact. Flames continued to spit out from his belly.

Elliot screamed in pain and fear as the sparks hissed onto the back of his pants. Free of Teddy, he crawled frantically away before stumbling to his feet. Hopping with pain, he ran to Tucker.

Tucker grabbed his arm, and they escaped the room together, slamming the door behind them.

Behind them, Teddy shrieked in agony as the fire only spread.

Outside, Elliot beat the back of his pants, his feet dancing in pain. "Man, Tucker," he yelped. "You shot me! You got my butt on fire!"

Tucker blew the smoking barrel of the flare gun. "Sorry, dude, but that guy had it coming. Too bad your butt had to get in the way."

Beating out the last sparks on his pants, Elliot shoved him in the arm. He cracked a grin. "That was, like, pretty awesome."

"Boys!" screamed a voice from the woods. "Elliot! What happened?"

The boys turned to see Skylar racing to them. Bernard and another wolf-man, smaller, were at her heels.

His pants were still smoking as Elliot smiled wider and ran to meet his sister.

Tucker stuck the pistol in his pocket and tried to put on a macho walk to follow. The barrel, still hot, burned his thigh.

"Ouch!" Leaping up, he pulled out the pistol and tossed it to the ground. Then he raced after Elliot.

Skylar caught her younger brother under the arms and threw him up to her shoulder, hugging him tight. "I finally found you, you stink-head! You had mom worried half to death!"

Elliot just hugged her back.

Tucker came up to her and gave a wave. "Boy, am I glad to see you," he said.

Skylar propped Elliot up in one arm and threw her other arm around Tucker. "Tucker, I love you! You're the best! Thanks for taking care of my butthead brother."

"Yeah, sure, anytime," Tucker said, blushing.

"Speaking of which," Skylar said, frowning, "Elliot, your pants are hot and have holes. And you smell like burnt toast."

"Just burnt butt," Tucker told her.

Brie joined them from where she'd been staring at room four.

"What did you do to that poor guy in there?" she asked, looking at Tucker in awe.

Bernard and the other wolf-man had moved away from the reunion and were looking at the room. Both had their claws bared.

The apartment door cracked open, and Teddy's pained face peered out. "Skylar!" he called. "Skylar, thank goodness! I thought I lost you! Oh, man, I've been so worried."

Skylar put down her brother and brushed his long hair from his face. "Wait here," she said pleasantly. "I'll handle this."

"Um," Elliot said, but his sister patted his head and smoothed wild tangles from his eyes. She kept walking.

Behind her, Bernard growled but made no move.

Tucker tugged on Elliot's shirt. "Your sister scares me when she's like this," he whispered.

"She's mad?" Bernard asked, sounding doubtful.

Elliot scratched his ribs and nodded. His other hand reached back and fingered a hole in the back of his pants. "She's, like, super mad."

The smaller wolf-man snorted. "Madly in love is more like it," he muttered.

As Skylar walked to the door, she fingered a strand of hair. "Hi, Teddy," she said neutrally. "You, um, look better."

Teddy kept most of his body hidden as smoke drifted from his shirt. The smell of charred hair and skin wafted from the room. "Skylar, I swear, I never meant to hurt you. I was just in so much pain!"

"It's okay, Teddy." Skylar smiled. "Really." She kept fingering her hair, pulling it tight.

"Really?" Teddy said. "I mean, we're cool?"

"Well, judging by your shirt, you're pretty hot." She leaned closer to him. "Just so you know. Lying and trying to eat me and my little brother are red flags. Do me a favor and never talk to me again." Releasing her hair, she stuck a hand in his face and shoved him back into the room.

Teddy stumbled back, and his scorched torso immediately flared in blistering pain. The flare had burned through layers of skin, leaving a large swatch of blackened blood and gore. He fell to his knees in shouts of pain and anger. Skylar slammed the door shut.

Brie ran to her, pulling a set of keys from her pocket. At the door, she took one of the keys. "This will lock him in from the outside," she said, sliding it into the slot. "We do it in an emergency if a wolf-man gets too wild."

Skylar nodded her thanks.

Finished, the two girls backed away. The others went quickly to join them. Howls of anguish erupted from behind the door.

Tucker slapped Skylar on the arm. "That was amazing," he said.

"Yeah," Elliot agreed. "I think you, like, got through to him. He won't visit us again, right?"

"Right," Skylar said, allowing a faint smile. She wrapped her arm around Elliot's shoulders, pulling him close. Her other hand formed a fist and rubbed the top of his head, giving him a light noogie. "Nobody messes with my butthead brother except me."

"Very nice," Bernard said, bowing. "I'll remember that."

"Uh, yeah," the young wolf-man said. "But we came to find the cousins and the little kids, right? We have a problem. They're still missing."

Tucker shook his head. "Don't worry. The crazy cousins went to bring the kids back to their parents. They'll be back. I'm sure of it."

Moments later, Tucker proved to be correct. They were still standing in the parking lot when they heard a vehicle approaching, its horn honking like mad.

"See?" Tucker cried before the others could react. "Here they come!"

Donnie soon pulled his pickup into the parking lot, sliding it to a stop.

"Tucker!" he cried. "We've returned, dude!" Then he saw Skylar, and his mouth dropped. "And… and who's this?"

"My friend," Bernard growled. He stepped toward the truck and looked down. "Remember me?"

Jake choked from the back. "That's the one… he saved us, remember? We thought we were dog food, and that one pulled the others off."

Donnie nodded and managed a sickly grin. "Well, we're headed off this island if you want a lift."

"Definitely," Skylar said. She still stood behind Elliot, gripping his shoulders. "But we need to make a stop and pick up a few others. Like my mom."

"Whatever you say," Donnie said. "Your wish is my command."

"Where're the little kids?" Bernard demanded. "Are they okay?"

"They wanted to see their parents, so we took them," Donnie said, shrugging. "Apparently, they never knew what happened to them." He shook his head. "Whoever this Morgan lady is, she's in a world of trouble, dude. The whole town was organizing a party to hunt her down when we left."

"You'd better go now," Bernard told Skylar. He ducked his snout into his shoulder as if pained. "This can get ugly."

Skylar pushed Elliot toward the pickup and turned to look up at the wolf-man. "What about you? Aren't you coming?"

Bernard looked down at his paws and then over at his younger brother. "I think Martin and I will stay." He stared into Skylar's eyes. "We'll go with you as far as the bridge. Then you'll never see us again."

Skylar rolled her eyes. "We'll see about that later. For now, let's go."

Mrs. Ashley groaned in her sleep. It felt like somebody had decided to comb her back with a metal rake. Shifting her body, she tried to turn away from the pain. Her eyes flew open, and she stifled a cry. Her entire back flared with agony. She immediately remembered everything. The smell of damp wool and earth filled her nose, as she lay on her side on a pile of blankets in the corner of the cramped hut. Breathing heavily, trying to control the pain, she pushed herself to a sitting position.

Mr. Harris had tried to look at her back before they'd gone to sleep but had been too nervous. Her shirt had been shredded, and bits of it mixed with the dry blood. At Mrs. Ashley's direction, he'd dumped disinfectant all over her torn shirt and injured back and did nothing else. She hoped the air would close the wounds for now. She would worry about fixing it once they got off the horrible island.

Blinking away sleep, she saw morning light leaking into the hut. Mr. Harris sat at the tree stump table with a pile of cans in front of him. He held one and was trying to read the label in the faint light.

The boys breathed steadily from the pile of blankets in the back corner.

"Good morning," Mrs. Ashley said softly.

Mr. Harris gave a start and nearly dropped the can. He glanced over at her and blew out his breath. "Oh, 'morning," he said. "Um, care for some breakfast? I have 'savory stew' dog food and 'choice cuts in beef gravy' dog food."

Mrs. Ashley crawled from her blanket and moved to join him at the stump. Her back was stiff and crusty, and she gingerly stayed on her hands and knees until she carefully sat cross-legged at the stump.

Mr. Harris put down the can and grabbed another. "Oh, here's some 'dog chili with vegetables,'" he said.

Mrs. Ashley eyed the cans and then the teacher with distaste. "Okay, please stop now," she said. "You're going to make me throw up. I think the boys and I will wait until we're off the island before eating. Now, if you find coffee, that's a different story."

Mr. Harris pursed his lips and nodded. He put the can down and looked up at Mrs. Ashley. "Do you think we'll really get off this place?" he said.

"You bet I do. Once I get Elliot back..." Mrs. Ashley blinked back tears. "We're all getting off it."

The two teachers sat in silence for a moment. They listened to their students' soft breathing, ignoring the morning chill.

Mr. Harris didn't ask how they planned to escape. The single ATV would never carry all of them. Once the engine started, it would give away their position. He didn't dare suggest or even think about taking it solo. He left the students and her once, but never again.

He glanced up at Mrs. Ashley. "You know, I've been a special education teacher for a long time... When I first started, the average career for my position was less than three years."

Mrs. Ashley tightened her lips and nodded. "Well, you've been doing your job longer than that."

He snorted. "Yeah... Want to know my secret?"

"What is it?" Mrs. Ashley asked, happy to keep her mind off her missing son.

"Special education. Most people see it as something bad. You know, they're embarrassed about it." Mr. Harris grinned. He picked up a can of dog food and examined the label. "Even some teachers at Leewood look down on me and my students. Like we're the dog food."

Mrs. Ashley frowned. "Come on, I don't think—"

"It's okay," Mr. Harris said, cutting her off. "Not you, just some. But know how I see it? I see special education as something like the Special Forces in the military. You know, the Navy Seals and stuff. When a school can't deal with a student, and it all seems hopeless, what do they do? They call in the special education teacher. I work with the students that nobody else can handle and the kids that teachers just don't have the time for." Mr. Harris ducked his head. "I view special education teachers as the secret weapon of schools… We sort of work on our own, but still with the teachers. I like to think of myself as some super commando in education."

Mrs. Ashley eyed Mr. Harris in surprise. "I guess I never thought of it in that way."

Mr. Harris shrugged. "Yeah, well… yesterday… Yesterday I actually got a chance to be the real tough guy. And, well… I ran." He glanced up at Mrs. Ashley. "You stayed with the kids while I panicked like a little kid. I ran off like a coward." He blinked away tears. "I left you… You're the real hero. I mean, the kids see me as this cool guy, but they look up to you. I turned my job into a game, but you live it for real life."

Mrs. Ashley shook her head. "No, don't think that way. Besides, you came back and saved us."

Mr. Harris snorted. "Only by accident. If I didn't run into the ATV just sitting there…"

Mrs. Ashley smiled. "I'll never forget seeing you charging up that hill, throwing those smoke bombs. At first, I thought you were one of them, but then I saw them scatter so fast. Whatever you did before, you *are* the hero now." She reached across the tree stump to grab his hands. "I'll never say anything about you running off. If you hadn't, we wouldn't be here."

Mr. Harris nodded his head gratefully. He glanced down at the cans again. "Um, you sure you're not hungry? I see a can of 'tender turkey dog bites for sensitive stomachs.'"

At first, Mrs. Ashley thought the moan had come from her, but then blankets twitched in the back corner.

Marcus threw an arm up in the air. "No," he muttered, twisting in his sleep.

Immediately, she lunged to her feet, ignoring the stinging pain from her back.

"Is he okay?" Mr. Harris asked, quickly rising to his feet. He glanced down at the can in his hand. "I didn't mean to upset him that bad."

"Bad dream," Mrs. Ashley said. She knelt before the boys and lightly put a hand on Marcus's ankle. "Marcus," she said gently. "Wake up."

Lying between Gary and Bobby, Marcus shot up to a sitting position, his eyes snapping open wide. His dirty shirt clung to his chest, damp with sweat. Seeing Mrs. Ashley, his face relaxed, but then he burst into tears.

"What is it?" Mrs. Ashley asked. "What's wrong?"

"I… I saw the old lady…" Between big gulps, Marcus tearfully started telling his teacher what he'd seen in the barn.

As she listened, Mrs. Ashley moved in and gave her student a hug, again ignoring her back. "It's okay, Marcus," she said. "It's okay… I won't let anything bad happen to you. I got you. The poor lady… is in a better place."

Mr. Harris backed awkwardly to the front of the hut. "If you're okay," he muttered, "I'm going to go out and, uh, water the bushes."

Mrs. Ashley just nodded, keeping her focus on her students.

Gary and Bobby were now awake. They listened as Marcus told about the terrible murder that had started it all.

"I still see her," Marcus said, finishing the story. He still hugged Mrs. Ashley and didn't loosen his grip. "And that monster… the one from last night… I know he wants to kill me."

Bobby winced as he sat up. His injured arm was in a sling and his left palm had a bandage wrapped tightly around it. He awkwardly nudged Marcus in the arm.

"Ah, man," he said. "I'm sorry."

Gary grunted. "You don't have to worry, Marcus. We have the nicest, toughest teacher watching out for us. That creep won't bother us again. If he does, just yell 'pepper spray.'" Shifting in his blanket, he moved to lean against Mrs. Ashley.

Mrs. Ashley reached an arm from Marcus and patted Gary on the shoulder. "Well, I won't forget your destructive STEM experiment anytime soon. Please tell me I didn't teach you that."

Gary shook his head. "I got that one on my own. My parents both work, so I've got a lot of time on my hands." He sounded a little sad.

Mrs. Ashley gave his shoulder a squeeze. "I know your mom and dad very well, Gary. I pretty much text them every weekday, you know. They both love you very much and worry about you. You know that, right?"

"Yeah, I guess." Gary wiped an eye. "I... I do hope to see them again."

"You will. We'll get off this island soon. Just as soon as..." Mrs. Ashley stopped. She glanced behind her and groaned. "Skylar... Skylar, where are you?"

"Uh, I think I heard her go off with that wolf guy," Gary admitted, lowering his eyes. "I thought I was dreaming..."

Mrs. Ashley closed her eyes and bit back a scream. Her son was missing. And now, so was her daughter.

Mrs. Ashley's first reaction was to go off and search for her kids, but she had three students huddled around her. It was like the confusing game of baseball... When the ball is hit to you and there are runners on the bases, where do you throw the ball? It all depended on the situation. Right now, the situation dictated that she do nothing.

She had her students to care about, and Bobby needed his bandages changed. Her own kids… she could only pray they were safe and hope her decision was the best. It was not easy being a parent and a teacher at the same time…

"I'm sorry," Marcus muttered.

Still in the back corner, Mrs. Ashley sat facing the hut entrance, staring out in hope and despair.

Marcus knelt behind her, leaning on her shoulder.

Gary pressed on her right side, and Bobby gingerly leaned against her left shoulder. All the boys seemed ashamed.

"It's okay, boys," Mrs. Ashley said tiredly. "I know Skylar can take care of herself."

"Yeah, but I never thought you cared about us so much," Marcus said. "I mean, like, all the times you yelled at us… I thought it was because you didn't like us."

Mrs. Ashley sighed. "Look, Marcus. Teachers aren't always perfect, either. We make mistakes, just like you do. I'm sorry if I ever hurt you… I just want you to be your best, and sometimes I do the wrong things to try to make it happen."

"Trust me," Gary told her. "Most of the time when you yelled at me, I deserved it… I just never wanted to admit it."

"Yeah," Marcus said. "And I always thought you liked the girls better."

"Because they don't get in trouble like us," Bobby said. He smiled. "Except maybe Cynthia."

Mrs. Ashley reached out her hand and ruffled Bobby's matted hair. She knew he liked Cynthia.

"Look, boys. I care about all my students. Just sometimes I expect them to understand me before I understand them. We have to work together to make a classroom work."

"Oh, yeah," Marcus said. "Challenges and changes, right?"

Mrs. Ashley chuckled. "Yeah, something like that. Teachers need to change a little for the students, and students need to change a little for the teacher."

"Or change a lot in our case," Gary muttered. "You have a tough job, Mrs. Ashley."

"But worth it." Mrs. Ashley glanced out the hut again. "Just as soon as my kids come back…"

That was when they heard the screaming.

Going to use the bathroom, Mr. Harris paused outside the hut. He eyed the parked ATV and then the noiseless woods. He'd been hiking in plenty of woods and always enjoyed the peace and quiet… only the silence now proved eerie and blared warnings of danger rather than tranquility. Before going off to find a tree, he hurried to the ATV. A single smoke bomb remained, jammed in the back of the seat. Taking it, he stuffed the bomb in his pocket.

"Just in case," he muttered. "A commando is always prepared."

He quickly moved into the trees, looking for one he could use as a bathroom. After only going several yards in, he drew to a halt.

The chilly air had started to warm but hung heavy and still. Yet, the hair on the back of his head rose from a warm breeze.

Mr. Harris slowly turned his head.

A tall, lean wolf-man stood right behind him, covered in thick brown fur. The beast had arms dangling to the ground near his feet. Both hands and feet ended in long, curved claws. Bulging black eyes stared down at the teacher as the wide mouth revealed rows of razor-sharp teeth.

"I remembered Bernard had a secret hut out here," the wolf-man said. Drool dripped from a long tongue that ran across the sharp teeth. A gob flew out and smacked Mr. Harris in the forehead. "Looks like I came just in time for breakfast."

Mr. Harris felt his knees shake. He suddenly didn't have to go to the bathroom anymore. His right hand slowly went to his pocket that held the smoke bomb. *Special Forces*, he told himself. *Don't panic.* He slowly pulled the bomb out and put it in front of him, out of view of the wolf-man.

"You, you know Bernard, huh?" Mr. Harris said. "He's... nearby."

The wolf-man shook his head and sniffed. "My nose tells me he's not, puny human." He opened his mouth again to blow hot breath on the human's neck. After the night before, the wolf-man enjoyed seeing the human's fear.

Mr. Harris ducked his head, still facing away from the beast. His free hand moved to the top of the smoke bomb, slowly twisting the key loose. "Funny... My nose tells me you guys don't brush your teeth. Maybe this will freshen your breath." Mr. Harris suddenly armed the bomb and turned on the monster.

Snarling, the wolf-man went to bite the man's head. Instead, he got a mouthful of pink smoke.

As the smoke burst, the wolf-man paused in surprise, his mouth still parted. Mr. Harris rammed the bomb into the open mouth.

The teacher then ran for the hut. "Get ready!" he screamed. "We're being attacked!"

The wolf-man behind him fell to his knees, clutching at his throat. Shocked at the teacher's actions, he'd swallowed while stumbling back. The bomb was now stuck in his throat. Thick pink smoke poured from his nose and mouth as he fought for a breath. Finally, after thunderous coughs, he spit out the smoking bomb. Gagging, he collapsed to the dead leaves, surrounded by heavy pink smoke.

"I will get you," he said hoarsely. Rising to his feet, he blindly went toward the hut. Reaching the clearing, he growled as the smoke cleared to reveal Bernard's hut. "You're mine, you—"

A metal can thudded into his chest. Another can smacked his ear, causing him to yelp in pain.

"Stay away!" cried Mr. Harris. "Try beef chunks, it's healthier!"

The teacher stood in front of the doorway with two more cans in his hands. Mrs. Ashley stood behind him, glaring. She held a can of her own, poised to throw.

The wolf-man's eyes went wide. Before he could move, another can flew at his face. He ducked just in time. When he stood, yet another can bounced off his shoulder.

"Here's more," Gary said, handing more cans out the door.

The Pack had never met such resistance. In the past, the outsiders had reacted in total fear and almost begged to be eaten. These ones were something else. Stunned, the wolf-man was slow to react as more cans were fired at him. One nailed him right in the snout.

Pain exploded, and the wolf-man found himself on his knees. More cans thudded against his shoulder and forehead. He stared down to see labels of dog food staring back at him. Fighting back tears, he turned and stumbled away. A final can caught him in the back of his skull.

Whimpering, he jumped back into the pink cloud. He'd had enough. Unable to see, he fell to his belly and crawled, choking on the thick smoke.

The wolf-man had been one of the scouts and had come alone. He had broken The Pack's code of always hunting together. Now, he slunk away with his tail between his legs.

The pickup pulled out of the parking lot. Skylar and Elliot sat up front with Donnie while Tucker and the wolf-men took the back with Jake. Sitting on top of the cab, Bernard served as a guide.

As they left The Motel, Brie's parents were just pulling in. Fiona gave them a dark look from the back of the jeep but then turned her gaze toward her little sister. Brie stood waving at the pickup with a broad smile on her face. Helga, watching in the jeep's front seat, decided right then she was done with being Maiden of The Pack. Let Paige have the job. She would get her husband to move back to town, or better yet, off the island.

Teddy pounded against the reinforced door of room four, still howling in anguish. He wanted fusia.

The pickup roared away.

Eventually, following Bernard's directions, they made it to the road near the wolf-man's shelter. They had just parked on the side of the road when pink smoke drifted up from near the edge of the woods.

"Oh, no," Skylar said with gasp. "Mom!"

"Stay here!" Bernard yelled. "Nobody leaves the truck!"

He hopped from the cab and raced for the woods. Martin was at his heels.

The rest immediately piled from the truck and watched them go worriedly.

Skylar stumbled into the field, with Elliot following.

"Shouldn't we, you know, be ready to go?" Jake asked nervously. "You know, stay in the truck, like, um, Bernard said?"

His cousin shook his head. "Man, we go when the others come back. Nobody is being left behind."

Tucker nodded in affirmation. He still stood close to the truck in case Donnie changed his mind.

It was still morning, but the sun was climbing high. Brother and sister stood beside each other, anxiously hoping all was well.

Bernard charged back to the hut to find Mr. Harris in the doorway. The teacher faced him with a can of 'beef stew chunks for puppies' held over his head like a grenade.

Bernard dropped to all fours and cocked his head. "Are you playing fetch, trying to feed me, or want me to open that for you?" he asked.

Mr. Harris dropped his arm and relaxed. "Oh, am I glad to see you. I thought you were one of the others."

"Where are my children?" Mrs. Ashley yelled, pushing behind the teacher. "Skylar is gone, too!"

Bernard immediately rose to his feet. "They're safe and waiting with the truck. We need to leave now. That smoke will bring others."

Moments later, Mrs. Ashley exited the woods to see her son. Elliot stood with his hands on his hips, searching the trees for her. Skylar stood behind him, pulling at her hair.

Mrs. Ashley immediately straightened and broke into a stumbling run.

Bernard followed her. He carried Bobby in one arm and pushed Marcus and Gary before him. After a final glance over his shoulder, he broke into a grin. His eyes went to Skylar.

Mr. Harris brought up the rear. He still carried the can of dog food, just in case.

Seeing his mom, Elliot dashed across the short field.

Hunched over with pain, Mrs. Ashley met him in the middle. She fell to her knees to give him a hug.

"Careful, Elliot," Skylar said, coming up behind them. "Mom got hurt. Her back is cut."

Elliot drew back. "Really?"

"I'm afraid so, kiddo." Mrs. Ashley put a hand on his cheek and looked at him. "But you look wonderful. Your face is all healed."

"Yeah, I know." He scrunched his brow. "Why don't you put the saliva stuff on it? It'll, like, go away in no time."

Skylar lifted up her eyebrows. "You mean… like licking it?"

Elliot gave her a weird look. "Huh?"

In the end, Bernard did have a little fusia in his First Aid kit. After dropping Bobby off at the pickup, he ran back to retrieve it. When he returned, he announced there were no scents or signs of pursuers. Still, they had to hurry.

With Skylar's help, Mrs. Ashley sat in the tall grass and had her back smeared with the fusia. The others waited by the pickup as the two Ashley females were hidden by the grass.

"What is this stuff?" Mrs. Ashley asked as Skylar started smearing paste on her injuries.

Her daughter drew in her breath at seeing the torn flesh from the claw marks on her mom's back. The cuts were deep. Remembering Bernard's instructions to fill the wounds with the paste and Elliot's confidence in it working, she barely hesitated.

"Mom, you don't want to know," she said, slathering the paste on the slashes. "Just tell me if it hurts."

"Oh, my… it actually feels good…"

The cooling and burning paste worked its magic. Skylar watched in shock as the paste started to bubble and hiss. Bits of bloody cloth and grit oozed out as the healing began. Right before her eyes, the torn flesh started to smooth over. Being married into the Raycroft blood was enough to receive the benefits of fusia.

"I still won't let him lick me," Skylar muttered, causing her mom to throw a look over her shoulder.

"What was that?"

"Nothing, Mom. Your back is pretty much healed!"

Skylar tugged down the back of her mom's shirt, covering the dark marks on her skin, the only remains of the injuries. Mother and daughter soon raced back to the others.

When Bobby, Gary, and Marcus reached the pickup, they immediately went to Elliot. Mrs. Ashley's son stood near the tailgate with Tucker as the three boys walked right up to him.

Gary threw his arms around the surprised boy, giving him a hug. "You made it!" he cried.

"Oh, man, are we glad to see you," Bobby said. He smacked Elliot's shoulder with his bandaged palm. "Your mom totally saved us."

"Bruh, man, your mom is the best," Marcus said. He shoved Gary in the back. "Lay off him, bruh. Now that he's safe, don't choke him!"

Elliot stared at the three boys in amazement as Gary backed off, but kept smiling.

"Seriously, man," Gary said. "We owe your mom, and she wanted more than anything to find you again."

Elliot brushed back some hair from his face, trying to wipe a tear without anybody noticing. "Yeah, and thanks for, like, making sure my mom got back, too. I'm glad to see you guys." He glanced to his right. "And this is, ah, Tucker. My best friend."

"We know Tucker, man," Marcus said. "He's the pumpkin pudding kid!"

Tucker shook his head, standing up straight. "Not anymore more, bruh," he said. "Now I'm the flare gun kid."

The five boys immediately fell into talking about their adventures until Mrs. Ashley and Skylar returned.

Shortly after, the pickup was loaded with kids and adults. Mr. Harris and Mrs. Ashley squeezed into the cab with Donnie. Instantly, his driving improved, and he didn't come close to breaking the speed limit. Bobby, his face pale, sat against the cab, cradling his injured arm and hand in his lap. Gary and Marcus sat on either side of him. The three were firm best friends and had no wish to be separated. Jake dozed in the corner against the tailgate. Tucker and Elliot sat at the other end of the tailgate, already planning summer sleepovers.

Skylar took a spot next to her brother and his best friend. She leaned against the side facing the woods where Bernard and Martin ran along the tree line, matching pace with the truck. A smile tugged at the corners of her mouth.

They were finally heading off the island.

Chapter 44

They'd reached the main road and approached the bridge when Donnie eased on the brakes.

"Keep going," Mrs. Ashley said grimly. "They can't stop us from leaving."

"They can certainly try," Donnie muttered. "And I'm not planning on hurting my truck."

Mr. Harris started taking deep breaths. He was seated in the middle, and there was nowhere to go. He closed his eyes.

Standing in the middle of the road in front of the bridge, Morgan Raycroft had her hands crossed in front of her. She was flanked by Razor and Banor. As the pickup neared, she reached a hand up to her necklace.

Looking miserable, Dr. Chocker stood behind them, leaning over the short railing of the bridge. Below him, high choppy water surged, left over from the storm.

"Stop right there!" Morgan cried. She held up her red pendant. "I command you!"

"Keep moving," Mrs. Ashley murmured to Donnie. "Not too fast, not too slow."

The teen nodded. Beads of sweat prickled his brow.

The wolf-men on either side of Morgan Raycroft growled and flashed their claws.

In the back, the children now huddled in a clump against the cab with Skylar and Jake standing behind them. Skylar made sure she had her arms around Elliot and Tucker. She was not going to lose her brother again.

"Leave them be!" Bernard yelled, charging across the field with Martin right on his heels.

The brothers were on four legs and quickly outpaced the slow-moving pickup.

"How nice of you to join us," Morgan spat. "The traitorous pack brothers."

"You're the traitor!" Martin yelled from behind his brother. "Sticks told us what you did to Sylvia! You murdered her!"

Morgan's face went red like the pendant in her hand. "Get them!" she screeched. "Kill the traitors!"

"No!" Skylar screamed.

She watched in horror as the wolf-men by Morgan moved to meet the charging brothers with raised claws.

Brutal combat broke out on the bridge as the beasts snarled, scratched, and bit at each other. Bernard locked arms with Razor, engaging in a violent wrestling match. Martin jumped on the bigger Banor and snapped at his throat. The two twirled in a deadly dance.

Morgan watched with a fierce glee, holding the pendant and pointing it toward the pickup. "I will have your boy when this is done!" she cried.

"This is too freaky," Donnie muttered behind the wheel. He'd stopped the pickup and now fumbled to throw it in reverse.

Suddenly, a strong gust of wind blew from seemingly out of nowhere.

The combating wolf-men were by the rail. Razor tried to drop his body and grab Bernard by the torso. As he did so, the sudden blast of air caused him to stumble. At the same time, Banor leaned over the rail, trying to shake Martin off his head. Suddenly, the four wolf-men tumbled over the railing, almost as if a giant hand had batted them off the bridge. The four fell with cries of fright before crashing into the foamy water.

"Banor!" Morgan cried. Releasing the pendant, she rushed to the rail to look over. "He can't swim!" She turned back to the pickup, her eyes livid. "You will pay!" She grabbed the pendant and closed her eyes. Power seemed to radiate around her.

Panicked, Donnie only managed to put the pickup in neutral. He stared in horror. Mr. Harris had his eyes squeezed shut. Mrs. Ashley kept her gaze on Morgan and refused to blink.

"Oh, for goodness' sakes!" Dr. Chocker had backed away when the fighting had started. Now, he strode to the woman and grabbed at the pendant. "Let it go, Morgan!"

"No!" screeched the woman.

She spun and tried to beat off the principal. Her foot caught the railing. Instead of reaching out to grab a support, she held tightly to the pendant. She was falling, bringing Dr. Chocker with her. The principal had lunged for the necklace and grabbed her shoulder. They both let off shrieks as they flew toward the water. Landing with splashes, they did not surface.

"Park the truck!" Mrs. Ashley yelled, throwing open her door.

Skylar had already hopped down and was running down the incline from the road to the edge of the swollen river. "Bernard!" she screamed. "Martin!"

Mrs. Ashley scanned the water for any sign of life. Strong waves crashed against the bridge, and a fast current was sweeping out to the deeper part of the river. She saw a branch zoom past, but there were no signs of life.

"I'm so sorry, honey," Mrs. Ashley said, moving to hug Skylar. "I don't see them."

Elliot and Tucker had left the truck and joined them. Tucker stood at his best friend's shoulder as Elliot took his sister's hand and squeezed it tightly. He pressed his cheek against her arm.

Several yards down the river, they heard a moan.

"Bernard!" Skylar cried. Pulling away from Elliot and her mom, she ran to the voice and stopped short.

The two brothers lay side by side on a sandy stretch of the shore.

A woman dressed in gleaming white robes stood between the wolf-men, watching Skylar. She wore a faint smile. "Hello," she said.

Skylar staggered back. "You're her," she said. "You're the woman who talks in my mind!" She breathed in deeply. "Are you, are you, like, my guardian angel?"

The woman chuckled. "No, but I do help him sometimes. You keep him busy." The woman drew herself up to her full height. "I'm your great-grandmother Sylvia Raycroft. Before she died, I promised my daughter that I would look after her family." She smiled. "I'm keeping that promise, even after my death."

Elliot stood beside his sister and grabbed her hand again. "You don't look like her," he said. He'd seen photos of his great-grandmother. This woman was thinner and looked much younger, even with her silver hair.

"Oh, do you not think so? This is my soul, not my body, Elliot."

Elliot clenched Skylar's hand tighter, and he pressed against her. "You know my name?"

"Of course I do." She smiled warmly. "I was given forty days after death to roam the earth. During that time, I watched over you and your family, Elliot... I knew Morgan would be causing trouble. This is my last day." She looked at Skylar. "Before I go, I owe a gift to some friends."

Skylar absently lay a hand on her brother's head as she stared in amazement. Even after all she'd seen, seeing her great-grandmother's ghost gave her goose bumps.

Her mom moved up behind her and put her arms around her and Elliot's shoulders. "Kiddos, what are you doing? Who are you talking to? We need to check on Ber--"

"Shh!" Skylar said, feeling her knees tremble. "Just a second, Mom."

Her great-grandmother crouched down next to the two motionless brothers. As she did so, a thick fog formed under her, drifting over the wolf-men and completely enveloping the woman.

Although she did not see or hear the woman, Mrs. Ashley knew something was happening as both her kids stiffened. She squeezed their shoulders tightly as she saw the mysterious fog cover the shore where the wolf-men lay.

Slowly, the fog lifted.

"She's gone," Elliot said, wrinkling his brow.

Skylar barely heard. She stepped forward, and her eyes went wide with wonder. The woman had vanished. So had the wolf-men. Instead, two human boys blinked groggily and looked up in confusion. They lay on their bellies and seemed amazed. One looked around sixteen, and the other a few years younger.

"Martin?" asked the older of the two. Tall with lean muscle, he had deep brown skin and short black hair. As he stood, his confused face turned to a wide smile. "I don't believe it! Martin! We're back!"

"Bernie?" the younger boy said. He crawled to his knees and stared up with a dazed expression. He looked like a younger version of the older boy. "Is this real?"

His brother smiled wide. "Sure looks like it, little brother!" He reached down and pulled his brother to his feet.

The teens laughed joyfully and then abruptly cut off as they noticed the family watching them. Suddenly, they were aware they were wearing only breechcloths... with loose belts.

"Oh, great," Martin groaned as he hastily tightened his belt. "Where's the fur when you need it?"

Just then, a fierce storm of honking erupted from the other side of the bridge.

"Karen!" yelled Mr. Ashley. "Kids? Where are you?" He parked the minivan on the bridge and now struggled to climb out.

"Dad!" cried Elliot.

Leaving the brothers, he led the charge up to the road. His mom quickly followed and soon passed him. Skylar paused long enough to smile back at Bernard before running after.

Tucker watched them go with slight envy. He'd seen the fog appear and heard Skylar and Elliot speaking to an invisible woman but had no idea what had happened... only that the wolf-men brothers had miraculously turned human. Now his best friend ran to his family, leaving him alone.

Elliot paused at the bridge and looked back, meeting his gaze. "Come on, Tucker!" he called. "You're part of this too!"

Tucker grinned and broke into a trot. Elliot reached out his hand and grabbed Tucker's wrist to pull him up the last step. "After what you did, man, you're, like, family."

"What?" Tucker asked. "Burning your butt?"

Elliot smiled sheepishly as the two walked toward the bridge. "Does that mean we're even?"

"You bet, dude. One burnt butt totally equals a sprained ankle and ruined pumpkin pudding."

"Don't forget your black eye and that stupid video," Elliot muttered, nudging his friend's arm.

"Oh, yeah." Tucker wrapped his arm around Elliot's neck and put him in a headlock. He delivered a light punch to his ribs. "Now we're even."

At the edge of the bridge, the two boys then linked their arms around each other's shoulders and watched the reunion. Elliot's parents met on the bridge in front of the minivan.

Skylar had also stopped to watch, hanging back a few feet and peeking glances down at the river, where the brothers were still staring at their arms and legs in amazement.

"I so thought I'd lost you!" Mr. Ashley said, squeezing his wife. "What happened?"

His wife gave him a long kiss. Then she said, "Doug, after what I've seen, we're no longer sleeping in on Sundays. We're finding a good church and going every week. End of discussion."

"Sounds good to me," Mr. Ashley said, dazed. "Just as long as the Goodalls don't go to the same one."

Then his kids joined the hug. Tucker stood just behind them, grinning. Elliot reached an arm out and grabbed his shirt, yanking him into the huddle.

Another minivan pulled up and parked behind the first. Both vans were covered in filth at the bottoms. As soon as the water started to recede, Mr. Ashley had driven through the roadblock, and Tucker's mom had followed soon after. Now, it was the first-ever traffic jam entering Blue Island.

"Tucker!" Mrs. Romero yelled, kicking open the driver's door. "You better be here, or else!"

"Mom!" Tucker shouted. He pulled from Elliot.

"Tucker!" his mom cried.

Tucker ran around Elliot's family, throwing himself in his mom's arms as she raced onto the bridge to meet him.

Leaning against the cab, the three boys stood in the back of the pickup, watching it all.

"Man, I got tears," Gary said at the end, wiping his eyes.

"Not a bad field trip, huh?" Bobby said from the middle. He nudged Marcus with his good arm. "Don't worry, man. Mrs. Ashley is still our loco mom."

Marcus stepped back and kneed him in the backside. He had tears in his eyes, too.

In front of them, Jake opened the passenger door and slid in next to Donnie.

Donnie glanced over at him. "Hey, cousin, how about you drive us home?"

Jake stared up at him. "Really?"

"No way, man!" Donnie cried. "Are you joking? This truck is my baby, man!"

As Jake called Donnie the biggest jerk on the planet, Mr. Harris sidled up and leaned an elbow against the pickup's side, just below where Gary stood.

He cleared his throat. "Hey, look, guys, um, I was wondering if you could, maybe, you know, tell Mr. Charles how I did on this trip. You know, at the fifth-grade graduation, tell him how I—"

"How you did what?" Bobby asked innocently, peering down from over Gary's shoulder. "Ran away and left us?"

"Yeah, I can tell him how fast you ran," Gary said seriously. "You're a good runner, Mr. Harris."

"I was running for help," Mr. Harris muttered. He pushed from the pickup in disgust.

"Hold up," Marcus said, pushing past Bobby to stand by Gary. He grinned down at the teacher. "If you show us how to ride a four-wheeler like you do, you got a deal, Mr. Harris. You'll be the hero!"

"And give us smoke bombs," Gary added. "That would do it."

"So you could let one off in the boys' bathroom?" Mr. Harris asked. "Forget I ever asked." As he stalked from the pickup, a small grin spread over his face as he caught sight of the river. "I'm going to go fish our principal out of the water. Maybe *he'll* appreciate my talents and give me a raise."

Waterlogged and miserable, Dr. Chocker had managed to fight the current. He now stood in shallow water by the bridge. His gray suit jacket had split at the shoulders and hung loose over his round belly. He spit a stream of water and looked ready to cry.

"Hey, boys!" Mr. Harris called back. "Maybe tomorrow we can finally find out if Dr. Chocker has more than one suit!"

Dr. Chocker was pretty sure that wouldn't happen. He would lay strong odds that he'd be arrested by then. While wallowing in misery on the farmhouse couch during the night, his phone had blown up with text messages and calls from frantic parents and school officials.

Something about a missing bus and missing students… He'd ended up turning off his phone and had spent the night by the window, hoping the lightning would strike him down.

Now, he stumbled for land too miserable to care. Ignoring Mr. Harris and his extended hand, he'd just reached the shore when his foot got stuck in the mud. Tripping, he fell with a splat right on his face. Everything was ruined.

Not long after, Morgan Raycroft washed ashore farther up the coast of Blue Island. Waterlogged and freezing, her leather clothes clung to her skin. She could barely crawl over the sand as she gasped for breath.

"Where is it?" she rasped. "Where?" She clutched at her bare neck.

A pair of feet walked across the sand toward her. The feet made no prints in the sand.

"Hello, Morgan," Sylvia Raycroft said. "Looking for something?"

"I need the pendant," Morgan muttered. "Where is it? What did you do with it?" Then, her eyes widened in fear. "No… who are you?"

"I think you know, Morgan. I'm here to offer you my motherly advice, something I failed to do enough of in my life."

"You're no mother! You're dead! I killed you!"

"I didn't do a good job with my children, did I?" Sylvia smiled sadly. "I let myself get caught up in the lust for power, just like you. Only, unlike you, I changed my ways. Tell me, Morgan. That pendant you covet so much, are you controlling it? Or is it controlling you?"

"It's mine!" Morgan said with a snarl. "You know nothing about it!" Feeling stronger, she got on her hands and knees and frantically searched around her for the red pendant necklace.

"I know enough to fear it, something you never learned. I had to control my urge to use its power and eventually stopped relying on it. When that happened, I was a useless vessel." Sylvia eyed her daughter with pity. "You should know, Morgan, what happens to empty vessels. They get replaced."

"Shut up!" Morgan snapped. She went to curse the apparition but suddenly saw only the empty sand. She desperately searched the sand. "Where did it go?"

"Looking for this?" A teen girl walked slowly onto the beach. She held up a red pendant dangling from a silver chain.

"Yes!" Morgan screeched, collapsing to her stomach in relief. "Thank you, Paige. Thank you!" She pushed herself up to her knees, not caring about the sand on her clothes and face.

"Thank me?" Paige asked, if confused. "Whatever for?"

Morgan went still. As she knelt in the sand, she eyed the young girl. "I'll give you power, Paige. You'll be the youngest Pack Maiden."

"Oh, you'll give me power?" Paige asked mockingly. "Sorry, but I already have it." She looked behind her. "Boys, I think you're ready for your first kill. And The Pack is in need of a new Protector."

Morgan's eyes widened with fear. The pendant sparked a red light above her, mocking her. "N—no," she said. "No! Where's Banor?"

"Gone," Paige said sweetly. "So is Razor. There's a new generation taking over. The old ways are gone. Goodbye, Morgan."

A young wolf-man, still in the midst of The Turning, strode toward her. Behind him was her son Burton.

"Wait!" Morgan cried. "You don't understand! You need the family book! The thumb drive!"

Shadows fell over her.

"Me need something from you, Morgan?" Paige said, looking down at the pendant in deep admiration. "I already have everything I need." She clutched the pendant and giggled. "Be sure to finish this time, Teddy. I don't want my number one wolf-man making a fool of himself again."

Wearing only a breechcloth, Teddy growled. Fur covered his shoulders and most of his legs. His burned stomach had fully healed. He had drunk the blood. Now, he wanted more. Teeth bared, he bore down on the woman in the sand.

"No!" Morgan's screams were drowned out by howls and roars. Her only grace was that Burton hung back. He did not drink her blood.

The first rule of the family book made one thing very clear. It was never the Protector *of* The Pack. Instead, it was the Protector *from* The Pack. The island and the Protector always worked together as one to keep The Pack safe… and from ever escaping and running wild.

The sand ran with blood as Paige started laughing.

Razor and Banor were still missing.

In the small bathroom of a quaint house on Blue Island, a little boy sat in the tub filled with warm water. The water quickly darkened with grime. Ignoring it, the boy held his right thumb to his face. Breathlessly, he started to pick at the dirty Band-Aid at its base. Soon the grubby bandage came free, falling to the water.

Woody's eyes went wide and he shot to his feet in excitement. He kept his eyes on his thumb.

"Sticks!" he howled. "It worked! It really worked! The wart is all gone!"

The door burst open and not his cousin, but his momma rushed in. "Get back in that water before I make your butt itch!" she said. "Your cousin is downstairs waiting for you to get cleaned up proper."

Woody instantly sat back down with a splash. "But Momma, look! My thumb is better!"

His momma blew out her breath, blinking away tears. Moving to the tub, she knelt and rubbed Woody's filthy hair. "Don't you ever run off and scare me again. If any member of The Pack even sniffs a hair on you, I'll jerk a knot in his tail so tight he'll be howling soprano."

Woody dropped his head guiltily and pressed his thumb to his chest. If anything scared him more than the wolf-men and witches, it was his momma. He knew he was safe with her.

Down below, Salisbury elbowed Sticks in the ribs. Freshly cleaned and wearing shorts and T-shirts, the girls sat shoulder to shoulder on the worn couch. Their parents and a host of neighbors were in the kitchen organizing the parade of casseroles and cakes that had flooded in soon after the children had miraculously returned. Through the bustle, they'd heard Woody's announcement about his wart.

"See?" Salisbury said. "Told you it would work."

Sticks grinned and elbowed her friend back. "So I guess it was all worth it, huh?"

Salisbury shuddered and hugged her ribs.

That Saturday in Whitney, Phileo's house became a very busy place. It hosted a fifth-grade party for Phileo and his friends and a tea party for young Lily and her new friend Maria. While the parents worked in the kitchen, the girls played downstairs. Upstairs, Elliot, Tucker, and Phileo played an online battle game against three other boys across town. Marcus and Bobby were over at Gary's house playing against them.

Marcus and Gary fought over the controller in Gary's living room while Bobby egged them on wearing a fresh sling and bandaged hand. It would be another week before he could think about playing baseball again, but it was okay. Marcus would take his spot until then. The boys had already arranged for Bobby's dad to drive them to the next game that Monday. Mr. Harris, after his display of throwing dog food cans, had agreed to be one of the assistant coaches... as long as Gary helped.

Later, at Phileo's house, when Maria went to get her brother and Elliot for the barbecue supper, she found them watching in awe as Phileo added a mod to the game, turning the characters into giant wolf-men. Boys were so weird, she decided, rolling her eyes. She was glad to have found Lily. The two girls had spent the day making edible slime.

Skylar was the only member of the Ashley family who was not present when dinner started. She was on a "sort-of" date with the new kid. Bernard and Martin had just moved into

Grantham that day, living with their aunt. She was showing the boys around town. The three would go to the house later for cake and ice cream. They didn't want to be late for that. Tucker had created the cake from scratch.

In the meantime, a letter sat in the Ashley mailbox from a lawyer on Blue Island. Sylvia Raycroft's will had been found. Mr. Ashley's great-grandmother had left an inheritance for him… he would never have to look for a job again if he so desired… he now owned his own company and had more money to his name than he would ever know what to do with.

On the same day, out on Blue Island, investigators probed the wild claims of "wolf-men" and murders… and found nothing substantial.

Apparently, Morgan Raycroft had created a wild plot to kidnap her great-nephew. She'd used her family as unknowing accomplices. This was after Billy Roft, a known drinker, had gotten drunk and crashed his school bus, dying in the process. A mix-up in communication led to the poor students and teachers on the bus being stranded on the island overnight… mainly the fault of the disgraced principal, Dr. Chocker, who'd been caught stealing funds from the school.

The principal sat in jail and had already agreed to a plea bargain supporting the investigation's findings in exchange for a much lighter sentence. The "wolf-men" were just people in costumes to scare off visitors…

Morgan Raycroft had vanished and was believed to have drowned with her husband during the intense storm. Ryan Raycroft was busy packing and would "disappear" before he could be caught by authorities. His brother Kenton, who'd miraculously recovered from his heart attack, would join him.

Erma Jenkins was being sought out for questioning. Without a body, she was assumed alive, just missing. Eventually, she would be considered another drowning victim.

The lead investigator happened to be a rather powerful government official… who had used Blue Island services in the past. She would let the outsiders spread their crazy stories… If the Ashley family or any other family wanted to pursue the matter, they would have zero support and almost no evidence. Nobody would believe them, and it would soon become another wild conspiracy theory.

Meanwhile, in the community of Blue Island, Mikey Evans turned fifteen that day. Earlier, angry and confused about life, he'd gotten out of bed with a sore belly. When going to the bathroom, he'd looked down to see a long tuft of hair sprouting from his navel.

He was offered a cup of blood that night … and wasn't sure. Should he drink it?

Acknowledgments

Working as a teacher is not easy, nor is being a student. Being a parent is also hard, and so is growing up. In short, life is tough. Everyone faces challenges and must overcome obstacles. It is unbearable to do it alone. Love, compassion, and teamwork make it possible. Thankfully, I had an abundance of all three when creating this book (and, more thankfully, no wolf-men trying to eat me).

To all those who made the dream a reality, I send a heartfelt huge thank you. I only ask for forgiveness from those I alienated during the process (when I write, I drop off the edge of the world). And to my friend who made the challenge of who could write the better monster book, this is my first attempt.

Thank you to my parents, family, and friends for all the support and feedback. A huge thank you to Ce-ce Cox of Outside Eyes Editing and Proofreading. As always, your fantastic work has brought my writing to life. Also, a thank you goes to Diana Cox of Novel Proofreading for all her expertise and wisdom. And not to forget, the terrific team at Word-2-Kindle, thank you for all your patience and services.

A final thank you goes to Blue Island and all its residents for living in my imagination and making this book possible. Please do not send any wolf-men after me at night. My dreams are scary enough. I am already afraid of the dark.

Gregory Saur is the author of *Drowning Hate, Best Shot Forward,* and many other novels for younger readers. He has a fear of the dark, blood, wolf-men, and pretty much anything that scares him… which makes perfect sense. He is not afraid of boldly going where nobody has ever gone before, just as long as he does it in his imagination. You can rarely find him on Facebook, but he will probably ignore you if you do. He is afraid of people, too.